The Best
AMERICAN
ESSAYS
2001

The Best
AMERICAN
ESSAYS
2001

Edited and with an Introduction
by KATHLEEN NORRIS

ROBERT ATWAN
Series Editor

HOUGHTON MIFFLIN COMPANY
BOSTON · NEW YORK 2001

ISSN 0888-3742
ISBN 0-618-15358-6
ISBN 0-618-04931-2 (pbk.)

Printed in the United States of America

DOC 10 9 8 7 6 5 4 3 2 1

Contents

Contents

Foreword

WHILE TEACHING college writing courses years ago, I remember hearing a syllogism that may, it strikes me now, help explain the enormous popularity of the personal memoir. It went something like this: "You write best when you write about what you know; what you know best is yourself; therefore, you write best when you write about yourself." As a syllogism, this seemed valid: the conclusion followed logically from its premises, no? So why didn't I then receive better essays when I assigned personal topics?

As anyone can see, the conclusion rests on dubious assumptions. The premises sound reasonable, but they raise some fundamental questions. Do people really write best about the subjects they know best? We see evidence all the time of experts not being able to communicate the basic concepts of their professions, which explains why so many technical books are written by both an expert and a writer. There are brilliant academics so committed to their vast research that they can't bear to part with any detail and thus clog up their sentences with an excess of information. If a little knowledge is a dangerous thing, too much can sometimes be an impediment to clear and robust expression. The Shakespeareans do not always write the best books on Shakespeare.

And can we also safely conclude that we know ourselves best of all? If so, then why do so many of us spend so much time in psychotherapy or counseling sessions? Surely, the pursuit of the self — especially the "hidden" self — has been a major twentieth-century industry. Self-knowledge, of course, confronts us with another logical problem: how can the self be at the same time the knower and the known? That's why biographies can be so much more revealing than autobiographies. As Dostoyevsky said in his *Notes from Underground:* "A true autobiography is almost an impossibility . . . man is bound to lie about himself."

Yet the illusion that we do know ourselves best must serve as both comfort and inspiration to the new wave of memoirists who seem to write with one finger glued to the shift key and another to the letter *I,* which on the keyboard looks nothing like it does on the page, thus appropriately symbolizing the relationship between that character and the "self" it presumes to represent. Today's writers' market is flooded with autobiography — now more likely to be labeled "memoir" in the singular, as though the more fashionable literary label promises something grander. Memoirs (the term was almost always used in the plural) were customarily written by public figures who recorded their participation in historical events and their encounters with other prominent individuals. General Ulysses S. Grant's two-volume *Personal Memoirs* (1885–86) were bestsellers. The old memoirs were penned by well-established individuals in the twilight of their careers; the new memoir is frequently the work of an emerging writer aspiring to be well established.

The memoir is easily abused by those who feel that the genre automatically confers upon the author some sort of importance. It's only natural, isn't it, to be the heroes or heroines of our own lives? And as the main protagonists how can we resist the impulse to occupy center stage and not consider ourselves gifted with greater sensitivity, finer values, higher moral authority, and especially keener powers of recollection than any member of our supporting cast of characters? The most interesting autobiography ever conceived, I think, must be Mark Twain's. Partially written, partially dictated, never published in its entirety, and never according to his intentions, in many ways a colossal failure of a book, Twain's autobiography grappled with every psychological and compositional difficulty characteristic of the genre. Twain knew how easy it was to exhibit ourselves in "creditable attitudes exclusively" and tried to display himself as honestly as he could. It was a noble experiment, but it proved impossible: "I have been dictating this autobiography of mine," he wrote, "for three months; I have thought of fifteen hundred or two thousand incidents in my life which I am ashamed of but I have not gotten one of them to consent to go on paper yet."

To say that memoir, autobiography, and the personal essay can be easily abused is not to disparage these vigorous genres. The democratization of the memoir has resulted in many wonderful books, not a few crafted by young or relatively young writers. I remember being in a Greenwich Village bookstore in 1976 with a friend who was struck by the arrogance of Paul Zweig's newly published *Three Journeys:* "Autobiography — hell, the guy's not even forty!" I remember chuckling at that remark and later agreeing that an autobiography composed in one's mid-thirties perhaps was, as Christopher Lasch argued shortly afterward, a prime example of what he memorably called *The Culture of Narcissism.* Yet I would feel terrible about my response only a few years later when I learned that Zweig had been diagnosed with a nasty form of lymphoma. He would die at forty-nine, struggling to complete a second series of memoirs, *Departures* (1986); its conclusion remains one of the most compelling and illuminating essays I've ever read about someone's final days.

What prevents personal writing from deteriorating into narcissism and self-absorption? This is a question anyone setting out to write personally must face sooner or later. I'd say it requires a healthy regimen of self-skepticism and a respect for uncertainty. Though the first-person singular may abound, it's a richly complex and mutable *I,* never one that designates a reliably known entity. One might ultimately discover, as does Diane Ackerman in the intricately textured essay that opens this collection, "a community of previous selves." In some of the best memoirs and personal essays, the writers are mysteries to themselves and the work evolves into an enactment of surprise and self-discovery. The "strange thing about knowledge," William T. Vollmann says in the essay that closes the collection, "is that the more one knows, the more one must qualify perceived certainties, until everything oozes back into unfamiliarity." Surprise is what keeps "life writing" *live* writing. And, finally, as Kathleen Norris aptly observes in her introduction, there must be what she calls *resonance* — a deep and vibrant connection with an audience. The mysterious *I* converses with an equally mysterious *I.*

The Best American Essays features a selection of the year's outstanding essays, essays of literary achievement that show an awareness of craft and forcefulness of thought. Hundreds of essays are gathered annually from a wide variety of national and regional publications. These essays are then screened, and approximately one hundred are turned over to a distinguished author, who may add a few personal discoveries and who makes the final selections.

To qualify for selection, the essays must be works of respectable literary quality, intended as fully developed, independent essays on subjects of general interest (not specialized scholarship), originally written in English (or translated by the author) for publication in an American periodical during the calendar year. Periodicals that want to be sure their contributors will be considered each year should include the series on their complimentary subscription list (Robert Atwan, Series Editor, *The Best American Essays*, P.O. Box 220, Readville, MA 02137).

I would like to dedicate this sixteenth volume in the series to the memory of Charles Frederick Main (1921–2000), a marvelous teacher, Renaissance scholar, and warm and generous man. As always, I appreciate the enormous help I receive from the people at Houghton Mifflin, especially Janet Silver, Eric Chinski, Larry Cooper, and Erin Edmison. It was a great pleasure this year to work with Kathleen Norris, whose prose and poetry I've admired ever since I began this series in 1985. In fact, hers was one of the first essays I encountered back then. It appeared in *The North Dakota Quarterly* and later grew into her wonderful book *Dakota: A Spiritual Geography*. In 1985 my publishers and I weren't sure we'd find enough genuine essays in a given year to issue an annual volume. Coming early on, her essay convinced us that the series was indeed possible. In subsequent essays and books, Kathleen Norris has subtly and patiently explored the dynamic relations between our participation in communities and (to borrow an outdated expression from the Dominican nuns who taught me as a child) our "inner resources." That theme and its variations can be discovered at play throughout her splendid collection.

R.A.

Introduction:
Stories Around a Fire

WRITING IS DONE in solitude, and without much hope of gaining worldly fortune. But the culture of celebrity that permeates American life on the cusp of the twenty-first century has in the last decade trickled down so that even lowly writers can indulge in the illusion that, at least while we are promoting a book, we are somebody. The first time I landed at an airport on a book tour, I assumed that the person greeting me at the gate was a volunteer or an employee of the store where I was to read that night. When I said it was kind of her to offer to carry my garment bag, she insisted, "But this is my *job*." I had encountered my first "author schlepper," known to the trade as a "media" or "literary" escort, to distinguish them from the other kind. As we made our way to her car, I stood a bit taller. I had a handler; I had arrived.

A few years later, I spent three days in San Francisco with an escort whose previous employment had been in public television, and during traffic jams we sang songs from *The Muppet Show*. She knew all the words; I did the best I could. The book I was promoting was about the two years that my husband had spent living on the grounds of a Benedictine monastery in Minnesota, and was full of stories about discoveries I had made: the fact that monks have a unique, home-grown sense of humor, that celibate people can make good friends, developing a remarkable capacity for listening, and that their wise understanding of human relations had helped me to better understand and appreciate my own marriage. I would not have thought this was bestseller material, but people were buying the book, and I was glad to read from it in stores. Sharing the stories made the people come alive for me again — the elderly monks in the monastery nursing home who were an inspiration, and the beleaguered young nuns who bravely struggled with the uncomfortable emotions raised by the cursing psalms.

On our last day together, my escort said to me, "I think I get it. You're a real writer." Surprised, I asked her what she meant. "I mean," she replied, "you didn't write a book in order to get a radio talk show." Her experience to date in the Book Biz had been with self-proclaimed counselors and spiritual gurus who regarded their books as steppingstones to greater things. And the escort quickly realized that she was merely one of the "little people" they would use and discard on their climb to the top. Authors screamed at her over trivial matters; one writer of a book on relationships banished her from a bookstore because she was "giving off negative energy," and then appeared a few minutes later preening and smiling before the audience, a model of calm assurance. A psychic phoned her at 3 A.M. to see how many copies of her book were in the stores they were to visit the next day. Because she wanted to keep her job, the woman did not respond by saying that if she were truly a psychic, she would already know.

It is safe to say that none of the writers in this book are struggling to put words on paper because they want a radio talk show or a syndicated column in the daily newspaper. They don't want anything at all other than to tell a story, to explore an idea or situation through the act of writing. Unable to escape the sense that *this story must be told,* the writer of literature more or less reluctantly concludes, *I am the person who must tell it.* Or try to tell it. An essay, after all, is merely an attempt. It has no presumption of success and no ulterior or utilitarian purpose, which makes it unique, a welcome open space in the crowded, busy landscape of American life. A place to relax and take a breather.

Human storytelling was once all breath, the sacred act of telling family stories and tribal histories around a fire. Now a writer must attempt to breathe life into the words on a page, in the hope that the reader will discover something that resonates with his or her own experience. A genuine essay feels less like a monologue than a dialogue between writer and reader. *This is a story I need,* we conclude after reading the opening paragraph. *It will tell me something about the world that I didn't know before, something I sensed but could not articulate.*

An essay that is doing its job feels right. And resonance is the key. To be resonant, the dictionary informs us, is to be "strong and deep in tone, resounding." And to resound means to be filled to the depth with a sound that is sent back to its source. An essay that works is similar; it gives back to the reader a thought, a memory, an emotion made richer by the experience of another. Such an essay may confirm the reader's sense of things, or it may contradict it. But always, and in glorious, mysterious ways that the author cannot control, it begins to belong to the reader.

And the reader finds that what might have been the author's self-absorption has been transformed into hospitality. Detail that could seem merely personal and trivial instead becomes essential and personal in the truest, deepest sense, as it inspires us to take in this story, recognizing in it something greater than the sum of its parts. It is our story too, the human story of work and rest, love and loneliness, grief and joy. In the essays in this book we are invited to take time to notice how the world goes on, and how often it is the simple things — a student's letter, the memory of a first job, the markings left in a library book, an old friend's recipe for yellow pepper soup, or a glimpse of night sky — that allow us to dwell on the issues of life and death that concern us all.

Kathleen Norris

The Best
AMERICAN
ESSAYS
2001

DIANE ACKERMAN

In the Memory Mines

FROM MICHIGAN QUARTERLY REVIEW

I DON'T REMEMBER being born, but opening my eyes for the first time, yes. Under hypnosis many years later, I wandered through knotted jungles of memory to the lost kingdoms of my childhood, which for some reason I had forgotten, the way one casually misplaces a hat or a glove. Suddenly I could remember waking in a white room, with white walls, and white sheets, and a round white basin on a square white table, and looking up into the face of my mother, whose brown hair, flushed complexion, and dark eyes were the only contrast to the white room and daylight that stung her with its brightness. Lying on my mother's chest, I watched the flesh-colored apparition change its features, as if triangles were being randomly shuffled. Then a row of white teeth flashed out of nowhere, dark eyes widened, and I, unaware there was such a thing as motion, or that I was powerless even to roll over, watched the barrage of colors and shapes, appearing, disappearing, like magic scarves out of hats, and was completely enthralled.

What I couldn't know was how yellow I had been, and covered with a film of silky black hair, which made me look even more monkey-like than newborns usually do, and sent my pediatrician into a well-concealed tizzy. He placed the cud-textured being on its mother's chest, smiled as he said, "You have a baby girl," and, forgetting to remove his gloves or even thank the anesthesiologist as was his habit, he left the hospital room to find a colleague fast. Once he had delivered a deformed baby, which came out rolled up like a volleyball, its organs outside its body, and its brain, mercifully, dead. Once he had delivered premature twins, only one of which survived the benign sham of an incubator, and now was a confused, growing teenager he sometimes saw concealing a cigarette outside the high school. Stillborns he had delivered so many times he no longer could remember how many there were, or whose. But never had he delivered a baby so near normal yet brutally different before. He knew that I was jaundiced (which he could treat easily enough), and presumed the hairy coat was due to a hormonal imbalance of some sort, though he understood neither its cause nor its degree. When he found the staff endocrinologist equally puzzled, he decided the best course was not to worry the mother, who was herself not much more than a young girl, and one with a volatile marriage, from what he'd heard from a mutual friend at the country club. He decided he would tell her that the condition was normal — something the baby would outgrow ("like life," he thought cynically) — and prescribed a drug for the jaundice, lifting the clipboard in the maternity office with one hand and writing the prescription carefully, in an unnecessarily ornate script, which was his only affectation. As he did so, New York State seemed to him suddenly shabby and outmoded, like the hospital on whose cracked linoleum he stood; like the poor practice he conducted on the first floor of his old, street-front, brick house, whose porch slats creaked at the footstep of each patient so that, at table or in his study, or even lying down on the sofa in the den wallpapered with small tea roses, he would hear that indelible creaking and be halfway across the room before his wife knew he hadn't merely taken a yen for a dish of ice cream or gone to fetch a magazine from the waiting room; like the apple-cheeked woman he had married almost twenty-five years ago, when she was slender and prankish and such a willing chum; like the best clothes of most of his patients, who had made it through the Depression by doing with less until less was all they wanted; like the shabby future of this hairy little baby, on whom fate had played an as yet unspecified trick. It was that compound malaise that my mother saw on Dr. Petersen's face as she glanced over the clean, well-used crib at her bedside and out of the hospital window just as Dr. Petersen was walking to his car to drive home for lunch and a short nap before his afternoon hours.

My mother let her eyes drowse over the crib, where her baby, a summoned life, was lying on its stomach, knees out like a tiny gymnast, still faintly yellow, and still covered with a delicate down. If anything, she found me more vulnerable, a plaintive little soul whose face looked rumpled as an unmade bed when it cried, and whose eyes could be more eloquent than a burst of sudden speech. She sang softly as she held my tiny life in her arms, my every whim and need encapsulated in a body small as a trinket, something she could carry in the crook of her arm. How could there be a grownup in so frail and pupal a creature, one so easily frightened, so easily animated, so utterly dependent on her for everything but breath? If only her husband could be there to see her, she thought as she watched my hand move like a wayward crab across the sheet, if only he could have gotten leave to be with her. There was no telling how long it would take the Red Cross to get word to him that he had a baby girl. And what would he make of such news, anyway, in a foxhole somewhere in the middle of France, with civilians and soldiers dying all around him, at his hands even, what would he make of bringing this new civilian into the world? Though nearly over, the war seemed endless. The radio had run out of see-you-when-the-war-is-over songs. His letters were infrequent and jaggedly expressed, not that they'd talked much or even politely before he'd left. Marrying him had been like walking into a typhoon. But once in it, her pride had prevented her from returning to her parents' house in Detroit. They had warned her about marrying a man as "difficult" as he was, and, anyway, they still had so many children at home to feed and clothe on her dad's poor salary. She had always been a trouble to them, wanting to go to the fairyland of "college" when there were six other children to give minimum schooling, then running off with him when life on the South Side became suffocating. If she couldn't be a good daughter, or a good wife it would seem (no matter how pliable she tried to be), she could at least be a good mother to this odd little being. When would he return? In shameful moments, she almost wished he wouldn't; it would mean a reprieve, a chance to start life over with someone who shared more of her interests and barked at her less over trivial matters like his fried potatoes not being as crisp as he wished when he walked in the door at 7 P.M. and wanted nothing from the world but a perfect, ready dinner. His mother had always managed it for the menfolk in her family, for whom she'd baked and cooked and tended all afternoon, until they walked in hungry and demanding at nightfall, and he demanded it from his wife, period. It was the least she could do while he was out working hard to earn money for the bread she ate, etc. etc. No, he would probably return from war, and life would go on, though perhaps the experience would mellow him. If not . . . well, she could always have another baby. She looked at me. Just imagine, the baby was alive and didn't even know that. What a helpless, lovable bundle she had created! She spent the rest of the afternoon watching me and fantasizing about my limitless future.

My infant years might have happened in an aquarium, so silent and full of mixing shapes were they. How strange that a time filled with my own endless wailings, gurglings, and the soothing coos and baby talk of my mother should remain in my memory as a thick, silent dream in which clearer than any sound was the blond varnish on my crib, whose pale streaky gloss I knew like a birthmark, as it was for so many months of my life. At one, six months is half of a lifetime, and for half my lifetime I'd lain in my crib watching how the blond wood bars seemed to stretch from floor to ceiling, my mother's hands coming over them, though it seemed nothing could be higher. My mother's hands always appeared with a smile on her face, which I knew only as a semicircle that amazed me with its calm delight which each day renewed. It would rise over my crib like one of those devastating moons you can't take your eyes off of. I would knit my forehead, perplexed for a moment, and then smile without thinking about it, and my mother's soft hand would stretch over the bars to touch me, though the touch I couldn't remember in later years, nor any sound. It was a time of shapes and colors, and the puzzling changes in the air as the day moved and I could see the sunlight on a thousand flecks of milling dust, watch the sky turn blue as a bead, then strange, vapory colors ghost through the dark and frighten me before night fell. It was a time of complete passivity and ignorance. Odd things happened to me which I could neither explain nor predict. Life was like that, full of caretakers appearing over my crib wall, sometimes carrying things with shapes and colors so vibrant they startled me, things that would ring or chatter or huff. Long, ribboned, shiny things I found especially monstrous, and sometimes a shocking blue or yellow would be so intense it made my ribs shiver and my eyes scrunch closed. When that happened, the caretaker's face would change like a Kabuki mask, and through my wet, twitching eyes I would see the moon-mask waiting, watching, filled with delight. The moon shone on me daily. Often, in the black ether I sometimes woke in, when the blond crib varnish was nowhere to be found, I could sense the moon's presence standing nearby and watching me, feel its warm breath and know it was close, transfixed by my every stirring. Sometimes the moon would vanish for long spells and my ribs would shake. Sometimes the moon would appear, all angles like a piece of broken glass, though usually that happened only when another face, shattery and florid, was there, too. To see their faces shuffle and twist scared me, though I didn't know what "scared" was exactly, only that my bones felt too large for my body, my eyes seemed to draw closer together, and I forgot everything but the grating noise, the awful, scraping barks. My thoughts, such as they were, were like a dog's or an ape's. Things happened, but what a thing was I didn't know, nor could I fathom the idea of happen. Not thoughts but images paraded through my days, and feelings I couldn't associate with anything special like a part of my body or a soft blanket. I was like a plastic doll, except that I was, and, if death had taken me, I would not have known it. There was no confusion, no thought, no sentiment, no want. But, for some reason, the blond crib wood pleased me. I touched it with my eyes, I drank it, I smelled its glossy shimmer. When I watched it, I was not with my body but with the wood. I explored its details for long, blond hours; then I explored the sunlight catching dust in the air. Each time I explored them, or a fluffy being put next to me, or a twirling color-flock above me, it was as if I had stepped onto another planet where nothing was but that sight, nothing mattered, nothing gave me deeper pleasure, nothing came to mind.

At two, most of my excess body hair had fallen off like scales, except for a triangular swath above my fanny, and a single silky stripe from my ribs to my pudendum. My skin softened to the buttery translucence of a two-year-old's, and my black hair made me look like an Inca. Things had names. All animals were "dog," all people were "mommy" or "daddy," but my voice could follow my pointing finger, and when it did it was almost like touching. I was enchanted equally by oddly shaped animals and kitchen utensils, and the maple jungle of recoiling legs below the dining room table. My world stopped at the shadowy heights of the closet, but some things were close to me that were lost to my mother — the clawed plastic brackets holding the bottom of the long mirror in my parents' bedroom, the heavy ruffles along the sofa that tickled my knees when I climbed up to straddle the armrest and play horsey, the sheet of glass on top of the low coffee table, into whose edge I would peer each day for long, dizzying spells, transfixed by the bright, rippling green waves I saw there.

Some parts of the house had no mystery, and consequently I never visited them. For example, the two closets facing each other in the tiny foyer. Long ago, I'd discovered nothing of any interest was in them, just overcoats, scarves, boots, and drab clothes in cellophane cleaning bags. Toys for Christmas or birthdays were hidden in the bathroom closet upstairs, the one I could just reach at three years old by standing on the toilet, leaning forward until I could brace one foot on the windowsill, and then leaping onto the lowest plywood shelf while grabbing hold of an upper bracket with one hand. I could swiftly explore with the other before I fell onto the bathmat. Only once had I actually touched a box, but I could see them up high, brightly colored and covered with unfamiliar words that soon enough I would know by heart. Games I had tired of were kept there as well, forgotten so completely I thought they were brand new. Sometimes, while I was banging down the long flight of carpeted stairs on my fanny, as I loved to do and always did when my mother wasn't around to scold me for it, it would occur to me that I had played with such and such a toy before, long ago, almost beyond remembering. Early one morning, I walked into my parents' bedroom and stood by my mother's side of the bed. Slowly my mother opened her eyes and, seeing me standing so close to her, smiled a spontaneous full-hearted smile. She held my tiny hand for a moment, enraptured by her child's presence. Then, reassured by the rightness of all things, I scampered out of the room, walked down the hallway whose boards creaked even when my slight weight strained them, jumped into the carpeted stairwell as if it were a lifeboat, and gleefully bumped down the stairs on my fanny.

It was a lonely world for me, my mother knew, what with my father on the road selling until late at night, and my mother herself making ends meet by canvassing for long hours on the telephone. Half the money she made she put in an account my father didn't know about, just in case she one day had the courage to bundle me up and leave him. I had turtles and fish and dolls to play with, but no children who lived close enough to be casual with. And, often, I would come to her mopey in the middle of the day, complaining pathetically that I was "bored." How could a three-year-old be bored, she wondered, and where could I even have learned such a word? Then she would feel sorry for me and devise some games with empty egg cartons or paper bags and crayons I could play at her feet while she continued telephoning anonymous users of unnecessary products to ask them intrusive questions about their laundry or eating habits or television viewing. Oddest of all was my father's response to me. Perhaps it was because he was away when I was born, or because he feared being vulnerable and weak, or because he had not been raised in a demonstrative home himself, but whatever tenderness I sought upset him. He recoiled at the thought of brushing my hair or bathing me. My lidless appetite for love and attention suffocated him. My zest made him nervous, perhaps because it seemed faintly erotic, and that aroused in him feelings that disgusted and frightened him. And whenever I ran to him, as I did mainly on Sundays, since I rarely saw him during the week, he would always find ways and reasons for not holding me, turning his head when I tried to kiss him, keeping me just out of reach when I wanted to snuggle. My mother wondered how such a revulsion could be, and, if she dared to broach the subject with him, he would yell and storm out of the room, muttering "Women! Always some nagging, pea-brained nonsense!" and other irate things, until, finally, she thought the scenes worse for me than the withheld affection.

At four, I had a tower of gaily colored plastic records, and I knew how to make them sing on the toy record player. But for long hours I would listen to a slow, plaintive song, "Farewell to the Mountains," which I played over and over as I sat on the living room rug and grew more and more withdrawn. What would a four-year-old dream about? My mother often wondered when she saw me like that, and wondered too if it was normal for a child to be so subdued. But to find out she would have had to have spoken to someone — a friend, a doctor, or, most horrifying of all, perhaps even a psychiatrist, which was a shame only whispered about in nice families. In fact, it was no longer possible for such a family to be "nice" at all if one of its members admitted to insanity by seeking a psychiatrist. My mother shuddered at the thought, as she fed stray wisps of hair back into her pageboy, and checked her list for the next household to call about their consumption of presweetened cereal. She could hear "Farewell to the Mountains" softly wailing in the next room, and knew I would be sitting inertly by the speaker, dreaming of whatever things a four-year-old dreamt of. A new doll, perhaps, or a dog . . . my experience was so limited, thank goodness; how could the daydreams hurt me? She lifted a pencil with which to dial the next number, so as not to callus her index finger. In less than a year, I would be going to kindergarten, with playmates and things to do, and life would be smoother.

In the living room, while my lugubrious record repeated, I dreamt of escape, of life beyond the windowpanes, of gigantic trees that led into magic kingdoms, of strange, cacophonous animals, and endless kisses and hugs, and a giant dollhouse in which I could live, and flowers so big and perfumed I could crawl into them to sleep, and, most of all, I dreamt of a sleek black horse which I had seen on television and had been utterly thrilled by. How it had reared and flailed when people tried to get near it. How it arched its tail and shone in the dazzling sunlight when it ran up the side of a mountain. How it lathered and whinnied and looked ready to explode. I dreamt of playing with the frantic black horse which would scare and excite me and, sometimes, if I were very good, let me get close enough to stroke and ride. Together we would run out to those flat, funny-bushed prairies that stretched forever and we would make the sound of rain falling as we galloped. On her way to bed, my mother would peek in on me, and most days she would find me wide awake at midnight, lying quietly in my bed like a tiny Prince of Darkness, my brain raw as henna, just pacing, pacing. If insomnia was unusual for a child, it was normal for me. There was a switch in my cells that wouldn't turn off at night, which is not to say that I was one of those rare few who could get by with little sleep and wake to conquer the world. If I slept badly, I was tired the next day, and, since most days I slept badly, I was mostly tired. Dark circles formed under my eyes, and I looked oddly debauched for a four-year-old girl. Once, my mother gave me a quarter of one of her sleeping pills, and out of that cruel prankishness of which children seem the liveliest masters, I had pretended not to be able to wake up the next morning, even though my mother shook and shook me. When I finally deigned to open my eyes and fake a spontaneous yawn, I found my mother in a cold sweat and the most attentive and adoring spirit, which lasted all day. After that, she just let me grope for sleep by myself, but insisted on a ritual "going to bed" at 8 P.M., since at the very least I would then get some rest from lying still.

It was hard to say who looked forward most to my going to school. Six times my mother practiced the route with me, holding my hand as we walked through the vest-pocket-sized plum orchard that separated my street from Victory Park Elementary School. There was a more conventional way of getting there, of course, full of sidewalks and rigid corners and car-infested streets, but it was twice as long and meant crossing three intersections. My mother preferred to lead me across the street my house sat on and watch me as I walked down the well-worn shortcut leading almost unswervingly through the orchard. Only one part of the path, twenty yards or so, dipped behind a stand of bushes and out of view. But at that point I would be able to see the crosswalk guard clearly, since she was always there, to-ing and fro-ing in her yellow jacket and bright red sash. Perhaps another mother in another city would have been frightened to let her five-year-old walk into an orchard alone each day, but in my hometown crime was not a problem. As I had discovered, boredom was. And the orchard was full of such extravagant smells and sights: low, scuffly hunchbacked things with long tails, Chaplinesque squirrels that looked like gray mittens when they climbed trees, mump-cheeked chipmunks, insects that looked like tiny buttons or tanks, feathered shudders in high nests, chattery seedpods, and tall, silky flowers with long red tongues hanging out. Best of all I liked to see the ripe plums, huddled like bats high above me. With my Roy Rogers tablet in one hand and a brown bag lunch in the other, I would go to school each day in a fine mood because I knew I had the orchard to look forward to. Then, too, I liked this new business of dressing up: purple corduroy pinafore, gray check with a lace collar, red and white jumper striped like a candy cane. White ankle socks, black patent leather shoes, matching ribbon. I would take my seat in the classroom and

do the lessons and play the games and sing the songs, and in the afternoon I would come home again, through the orchard alive with
buzzing and twittering, at the other side of which would be my
mother, dependable as sunlight, waiting in a pale shirtwaist dress,
her hair curled into a long pageboy roll.

The novelty of school lasted only a few months. The lessons were
dull, the games were always the same, the other children were so
distant and alien. They seemed to share a secret I alone didn't
know. What they said was different, what they laughed at was different, what they saw was different. When I drew the plum bats curled
high in the trees, or used six crayons to draw a rock, which
everybody knows is gray, *airhead*, they teased me mercilessly, or,
worse, ignored me for hours. Most of all, I liked running games in
which I ran until I dropped in an exhausted heap, or spun around
in circles until I got dizzy. Next to that, I liked looking at the butterfly and rock collections in the science locker, and sometimes I
would spend all of recess playing with the kaleidoscope. The other
children played jacks, or marbles, or house, or cowboys. I liked
cowboys, but wanted to be the horse, not a man shooting nonstop
and pretending to die. In time, I discovered the knack of talking
like the others, but it was hard to sustain, and though I dearly
wanted the friendship of the other children, nothing I could do
seemed to endear me to them. I was different; it was as if I had
spots or a tail. I hovered on the edge of elementary social life, making a friend here, a friend there, mainly among the boys, who
didn't mind including me in their running and jumping games,
where more bodies made little difference. At home, my father had
begun taking photographs with a Kodak box camera he had
bought at a flea market, snapshots of the family and neighbors on
special days like Fourth of July or Christmas. The first time I saw a
photograph it was as if a bucketful of light had been poured over
me. In the picture people were always smiling, frozen happy forever. I pestered my father to take more and more pictures, and
pleaded until he let me keep a few from each roll, to line up on my
pink, Humpty-Dumpty decaled dresser next to the bed. With my
dolls sitting rigid in a semicircle on the bed, and all the smiling
faces in the photographs, I had quite a large gathering for mock
tea parties and classrooms and cowboys and family fights, in one of
which a doll's pudgy plastic arm snapped off.

Though I knew the orchard well, and loved to play in its chin-high weeds, bopping the teasel heads with a bat, or hunting for "British soldiers," red-capped fungi, among the blankets of green moss, my sense of geography was very poor. Getting anywhere was a blur. The world seemed without boundary, unimaginable and infinite. Even though, on most days, I had no desire to go farther than my neighborhood, I sensed the world dropped off at a perilous angle just beyond it. I was frightened at the literal perimeter of what I knew. Had I been a grownup, I might have been reminded of the Duke Ellington song "There's Nothing on the Brink of What You Think." What did I fear? I didn't know. It was not a rational fear. Just as wailing for my mother if we became separated in a supermarket was not a rational act. I just feared. But the fear fled when I was with a gang of children strolling the neighborhood, as we did each Halloween when, often, we would go as far afield as three or four streets away, bags laden, ready to perform the simple acrobatics it took to con strangers out of sweet booty. Spreading my loot on the living room floor afterward, I would go through it with my mother, who adored sifting the haul and always got all of the Mary Janes, which I loathed the taste of.

One day, as if a typhoon had just ended, my father died of an ailment that sounded to me like "pullman throbs," and thus disappeared from my life the same stranger he had always been, a lodger who directed my life with his shouts, who had absolute control over my fate, and could not be appealed to by tears or reason. He had been an omnipotent, mysterious stranger who left the house before I got up each morning and came home after I went to sleep each night, and on weekends was sullen and tired. He only ever seemed to read the paper or watch television or sleep or yell at my mother or slam the door to their bedroom, after which I would sometimes hear my mother crying. For some reason he never had time for me. In my heart, I knew it must be my fault, that I must be somehow unworthy of his love, his attention even, the way the newspaper or television at least had his attention. I understood deep down in my soul that something serious must be wrong with me, that I lacked something — I wasn't pretty enough, or smart enough, or funny enough . . . I didn't know what quality exactly — whatever that alchemical thing was, I lacked it. Otherwise he would surely have loved me. I had tried in prismatically different ways to delight him, to please him, ultimately to win him. Some mornings I would spend fifteen minutes choosing the right ribbon — checked versus striped, plain edged or lace, flat cotton or broad glossy satin — and then tug on my embroidered ankle socks, and deliberate over the dresses in my closet as if I were a floozy primping for the man who brought my chocolates and cheap jewelry on Sundays. I was like a war bride with a shellshocked husband at home, attentive to his every whim, trying hard to reconstruct their tender armistices. After so many silent, private years, I seemed suddenly to be an extrovert, and my mother delighted in the long-awaited change toward what she saw as a normal, if hyperactive, childhood. Without understanding why exactly, I would play the clown whenever my father was around, dancing little jigs, doing impressions of TV characters, pretending to be a dog by fetching his slippers in my mouth and then sitting up in front of him as he read the newspaper in the enormous, rose-colored armchair by the picture window, my tiny hands lifted and loosely flapping like paws. Sometimes I would bake him ginger cookies, his favorite, which my mother would let me cut with bright red plastic cookie cutters shaped like men and women, clowns, and Christmas trees, into which I would press candy buttons and eyes. When he was around, I would follow him like a tropic flower the sun, needy, riveted, always open for warmth. Sometimes he would take me on his knees, or pat my head lightly, and, when he did, I would feel happy and even-hearted all day. But most days he simply ignored me, or yelled at me for pestering him, and, when he did, I would try extra hard to please him. I would eat my food without playing with it first, though I loved taking dollops of mashed potatoes in my hands and rolling them into balls for a snowman, which I would stand on the rim of my plate while I ate. Once, for Sunday lunch, mother and I concocted a "Happy Jack" out of a tomato, tunafish salad, and a hard-boiled egg, scooping out the tomato, filling it with tunafish, and toothpicking the egg upright in the middle. I painted paprika eyes and mouth onto the egg with a wet finger, stuck in a whole clove for a nose, and then attached the cutaway tomato lid with a toothpick to make a beret. Then I dressed up in my Halloween clown suit, and presented it to my father on a dinner plate. He laughed out loud, and hugged my shoulders by wrapping one of his enormous arms around them, and that pleased me so much I was contented for days. But nothing less extreme seemed to waylay his thoughts, which were always galloping away from me. Then he died, and it was as if a door had slammed shut. There was no warning, no reassurance; he just left. Though I had not gone to the funeral, I understood that dead meant being broken beyond repair, as my mother had explained it, and could see that, when it happened, grownups cried torrentially and then walked around gloomy and snuffling for days, as if they shared a secret cold. I understood that he was gone now on weekends, too, and that he had left without saying goodbye to me, though perhaps, surely, he had said goodbye to my mother. While he lived, he would at least wave when he left. Now there was not even that. Now I could no longer even try to please him. Without meaning to, I reverted to my sullen, dreamy ways. My mother shook her head and, without going into details, told friends that his death had come "at the worst possible time for everyone."

The last instruction I received as each hypnotic session came to a close was that I would remember only what I felt comfortable with. It was a relative fiat, and it worked, letting just enough of my subterranean past seep through to give me a sense of origin, of development, without reminding me of any war crimes that might alarm me. And so it was no surprise that in my waking life I remembered little of my recaptured childhood: its sensory delights, a few events, and its tense, poignant moods. Whether or not a crucial drama lay salted away in my memory, I never knew. Once, coming out of the well of a trance, I noticed my eyes were sore and my nose blocked from crying. Where had I gone? Toward a sexual event? A violent one? I didn't know. At first, the childhood I began discovering mystified me, its iceberg fragments were so high-focus and yet remote. And what was there between the fragments I didn't wish to remember? But gradually, as slants of my past surfaced, I felt as if I had adopted a child on the installment plan, a child that was myself, and it felt good suddenly to be part of a community, even if it was only a community of previous selves.

BEN BIRNBAUM

How to Pray: Reverence, Stories, and the Rebbe's Dream

FROM IMAGE

ABOUT A THIRD of the Babylonian Talmud is story — or "incidents" in the Talmud's unpretentious phrasing — and the death of Rav Eliezer on folio 28B of the tractate *Berachos* is one of the work's many formula incidents: familiar blossoms that brighten even the most severe juridical terrain. The narrative convention in this instance is this: a teacher is dying, and his students get to ask him one question before the curtain falls.

Rav Eliezer was no common teacher. Likely born early in the second half of the first century, he became one of the men who devised rabbinic Judaism following the destruction of the Jerusalem Temple in 70 C.E., and without whom Israel and its jealous god would long since have joined Egypt, Babylon, Assyria, and their jealous gods in the purgatory of museum blockbuster shows. And the men who stood by Eliezer's deathbed were clearly worthy of their master. For notwithstanding his condition, they ran one right up under his chin. "Teach us," they said, "the ways of this life so that we may be worthy of life in the World To Come" — which is to say they asked him how to gain eternal life. And Eliezer joined his final breaths to brace a suitably comprehensive answer: "Care for the honor of your colleagues; teach your children to shun rote memorization, and seat them on the knees of those who have studied with the sages. And when you pray," he concluded, "*da lifne me ata omdim*" — know before Whom you stand.

While it may seem uncharitable to criticize a dying man for not rounding on a tough pitch, respect for the Talmud's own relentless standards of discourse requires us to observe that Rav Eliezer's statement is a wobbly double down the line — prolix and not absolutely coherent (scholars still argue about the translation and import of the phrase here rendered as "rote memorization"). And as any moderately experienced student of Talmud would know, Rav Eliezer's final teaching does seem but a pallid echo of the bracing assertion found in the tractate *Avoth* that the world exists for the sake of three things and three things only: charity, study of Torah, and prayer.

Eliezer's last sentence taken alone, however — his declaration regarding prayer — is another matter, a blast so pure, long, and true that it has withstood the caviling of eighteen centuries' worth of rabbinic color commentators and stands today as the definition of a definition of Jewish prayer, linked to the subject the way "All Gaul is divided into three parts" is linked to Latin, or as Atlanta used to be linked to air travel in the South back when Delta was king of the regulated skies: "You can go to heaven or hell, but you gotta go through Atlanta," they said. Likewise, you can go anywhere you like in the consideration of Jewish prayer, but first you need to make your way through "Know before Whom you stand."

Know: prayer is neither delirium nor reflex; it calls for an attentive intellect, what the rabbis called *kavannah* — intentionality. There is no accidental prayer.

Know before Whom: Whom, not what. Prayer is personal. The God of the Habiru is not an abstraction, is not nature, fate, or time decked out in a white beard. "An 'I' does not pray to an 'It,'" Abraham Joshua Heschel wrote in a twentieth-century color commentary on Eliezer's final words.

Know before Whom you stand. Prayer does not take you into your self or out of our world. It is not a transcendental meditation. The relaxation response is not its goal. Nor is prayer oratory. Rather, prayer places you in proximal, eyes-front relationship with the Creator. And so the Hebrew word for liturgical prayer is *tefilah,* an invocation of God as judge.

But the Talmud is merely the glorious Talmud. It is not Judaism; it is not the lives of men and women, lived in the valleys and on the flats — holy ground that is nonetheless ground.

One day about sixteen hundred or so years after Rav Eliezer did his best to answer the last question he ever heard, a Russian Chassidic rabbi known as Shneur Zalman of Ladi was praying alongside his son and, turning to the boy, asked what bit of scripture he was using to focus his prayers. The child answered that he was meditating on the phrase "Whatsoever is lofty shall bow down before Thee." Then he asked his father the same question: "With what are you praying?" The rabbi answered, "With the floor and with the bench."

In Brooklyn, New York, in the early 1950s, I learned to pray as most of us learn to pray: with the floor and with the bench, or in my case with the sheet linoleum and the gunmetal folding chairs in the Young Israel Synagogue of New Lots and East New York, a brick shoebox with painted-glass casement windows that stood at the corner of Hegeman Street and Sheffield Avenue, shouldered by a dry cleaner's and by a long row of squat apartment buildings that we called brownstones when brownstone was not yet an evocation of a lost urban Elysium but simply a word that described a stone so modest and common that it had no real name.

The Young Israel of New Lots and East New York was a devoutly Orthodox congregation, and the world it supported was suffused with prayer: morning, afternoon, and evening worship; blessings before drinking Coke or eating cookies (and they were not the same blessing); blessings after each meal and when putting on new clothes and after burying the dead. There were prayers to be said prior to an airplane flight, prayers of thanksgiving to be said upon landing safely, and dense kabbalic prayers on newsprint certificates that had to be taped to the headboards of cribs to ward off the demons and imps who joyed at murdering infants in their sleep.

We recited prayers as we climbed into bed and prayers as we groped for the off switch on the alarm clock; prayers when catching sight of a Jewish sage or a gentile sage (as with Coke and cookies, different blessings). There was even an extraordinary requirement to offer a prayer of thanks for bad fortune as for good. And each Friday evening at the Sabbath eve meal in every house I knew, fathers placed hands upon the bowed heads of their children, and prayed aloud in Hebrew: "The Lord bless you and guard you. The Lord shine His face upon you and be gracious to you. The Lord turn His face toward you and give you peace" — a prayer and a gesture of benediction torn dripping from the pages of the Torah, as old as love and fear.

We families who were attached to the Young Israel of New Lots and East New York lived in a whirlwind of invocation, praise, thanks, blessing, petition, song, and Psalm. But we also lived in rows of attached houses in a clotted and crowded place, a place where the Rav Eliezer's injunction to "know before Whom you stand" in prayer had to compete for attention with the injunction of the baby's croup, the injunction of the worn clutch on the DeSoto, the injunction of the willful teenager, the injunction of the twenty sales you needed to make before dusk if you were to earn the commission you were already sorry you'd taken in advance. And so, while prayer was frequent, it was frequently words — words spoken with an eye on the clock, with an ear attuned to the telephone or the cough from the upstairs bedroom or the spear point of anxiety lodged in the heart.

And I was a boy educated to be pious and learned. I knew very early Rav Eliezer's instructions for gaining the World To Come. I knew Maimonides' extraordinary ruling a millennium later that a man who has returned from a journey may abstain from worship for as long as three days, until he regains the degree of concentration that prayer requires. I knew the story of the Chassidic master Levi Yitzchok of Berdichev, who refused to enter a certain synagogue, saying there was no room for him in the building, so cluttered was it with words spoken without love or fear that had not risen to the Upper World but lay strewn in heaps on the floor like common trash.

And I, knowing these things, knowing what God expected of us, how could I make sense of the mumbled words, the tossed-off readings, the careless petitions, the hurried mumblings that so often passed for prayer and worship in the Young Israel of New Lots and East New York and on the streets and in the houses nearby? How could I reconcile God's demands and the demands of Brooklyn? Was it possible that the World To Come was a domain set up only for saints or those who lived in Manhattan between 57th and 96th — people who had nothing to worry about and so could pray with proper *kavannah?* Was it possible that just about everyone I knew and even loved would never make it into God's eternal care?

And then I read the story of the Rebbe's dream. This happened when I was eleven or twelve years old, on a Sabbath afternoon in the Young Israel *shul*, in the parched hiatus between the late afternoon service and the evening service that concluded the Sabbath. Bored, waiting for the Sabbath to bleed away into the week so I could again listen to the radio or spend my allowance, I picked up a children's magazine that was lying on a folding chair in the sanctuary.

I don't remember what the magazine was called, but I remember it as the Orthodox Jewish analog to *My Weekly Reader.* Distributed to students in yeshiva elementary schools, it offered stories from scripture and Talmud, Torah puzzlers, photos of grinning boys in black yarmulkes who had memorized one hundred or five hundred *mishnaim,* and profiles of heroes from Abraham to Hank Greenberg. And the back cover was always a cartoon story, and that's where I turned first and where I found "The Rebbe's Dream." And here it is as I remember it.

Once, in a village in eastern Europe, there lived a rebbe known for the quality of his prayer. From every side people would come to hear, to be inspired, to watch this man climb the ladder of prayer from *kavannah* — intentionality — to *d'vekut* — the loving consciousness of God — to *hitpashtut ha-gashmiyut,* the highest rung of prayer, when the soul falls away from the body and enters the Upper World and God's immediate presence.

And one night the rebbe had a dream. In the dream an angel came to him and said, "If you would learn to pray properly, you must go study with Rav Naftali of Berzhitz." The rebbe was a pious and humble man, and so the very next morning he set out for Berzhitz, which turned out to be an isolated hamlet in the Carpathian Mountains in eastern Galicia. After a week of travel he found himself in the village synagogue, and there he waited until the local Jews assembled for evening prayer, and he asked who among them was Rav Naftali. They replied that there was no Rav Naftali in the village. He said that he'd been told on good authority that there was a Rav Naftali in Berzhitz and had in fact traveled a long way to speak with him. "Distinguished sage," one man then said, "someone's played a cruel joke on you for which God will surely take revenge. There is no Rav Naftali here, and the only Naftali at all is Naftali the woodsman, who lives up in the hills and is no rav for certain but a *proste Yid*" — a coarse Jew — "not the kind you would care to know." And all the other men nodded.

The rebbe was deeply disappointed, and decided to leave Berzhitz the next morning. But that night, asleep on a bench in the synagogue, he again dreamed that the angel came and said, "If you would learn to pray properly, you must go study with Rav Naftali of Berzhitz." When the rebbe awoke he decided that before he went home he would go to see this Naftali the woodsman. Perhaps the other villagers were mistaken about the man, he thought. Perhaps he was in fact a *lamed-vovnik*, one of the thirty-six hidden saints whose identity is known only to God, and for whose sake alone the world is each moment spared the destruction it deserves.

And so he walked most of the morning on a rutted road through the forest until he came to a clearing where there stood a log-walled cabin and a horse shed. And he knocked on the door and a woman admitted him. "I'm a traveler seeking a place to rest," the rebbe said. The day happened to be a Friday, and so the woman invited him to stay for the holy Sabbath, and the rebbe sat in a corner of the house and studied from a book of Torah he'd brought with him.

Shortly before sunset, the rebbe heard the sound of a horse and wagon. A few minutes later a short, big-bellied man with a dark tangled beard entered. He stood an ax in a corner of the room, washed his hands and face in a bucket of water, and immediately began to mumble the prayers of greeting for the Sabbath. The rebbe was not impressed with the looks of his host or with his hurried prayers, but he joined him in worship, and then the two men sat down at the table to eat the Sabbath eve meal.

Together they said the blessing over the wine, and the rebbe took a few sips from his cup while Naftali drained his cup and immediately filled it again. Then came the blessing over bread. The rebbe ate a slice of challah, and Naftali ate half a loaf. Then Naftali's wife brought out a baked carp and served the rebbe a slice. Naftali ate the rest of the fish to the bones. The woman brought a pot of chicken soup to the table, then a dish of boiled chicken and turnips, then a fruit compote of apples and berries. Naftali ate prodigiously of each course, all the while drinking glasses of wine and hot tea.

And then, after he had quickly recited the blessing after meals, Naftali stood up, wished his guest a good night, and went off to sleep. In a minute the small cabin echoed with the sound of his snoring.

The next day, at the Sabbath dinner and then later at the third Sabbath meal, Naftali's wife brought heaps of food to the table, and Naftali ate like a dozen men, devouring every heap that was placed before him.

Saturday night arrived, and the rebbe was ready to leave, to go home, convinced he had misunderstood his dream. And so he said farewell to his hosts and thanked them for their hospitality. "Learned rabbi," Naftali then said, "so you don't go away thinking the worst of me, allow me to tell you a story. All my life I've had a great appetite for food, and that has been a blessing, giving me the strength to earn my living. And then one day a few years ago, I was alone in the forest when bandits attacked me. They were going to take my wagon and tools and kill me. And so I prayed to our Creator, saying, 'I have no learning, I have no pious habits — all I have is an appetite. But if You give me the strength I need today, for the rest of my life when I eat on Your holy Sabbath, I will eat for You, only for You.'"

The rebbe returned to his own village. He lived many more years. And when people told him how impressive and uplifting his prayers were, he was sometimes heard to reply, "Whatever I know about prayer is as dust compared to the knowledge of my master, Rav Naftali of Berzhitz."

That is the story of the rebbe's dream that I read many years ago in cartoon form in the dull hour between *minchah* and *maariv* in the Young Israel of New Lots and East New York. And when I had finished reading, I knew that what I had read was as true as Rav Eliezer's deathbed instructions, or Maimonides' ruling, or Levi Yitzchok's judgment. I knew I had read a story that could change your life if you weren't careful, or maybe if you were careful.

My guess is that if Rav Eliezer had been hanging around the Young Israel Synagogue of New Lots and East New York that afternoon, reading over my shoulder, he would probably have reached a similar conclusion about the power of the story of the rebbe's dream, and been none too happy about it.

A member of the most unfortunate generation of Abraham's seed prior to 1939, Eliezer grew up at the edge of a chasm that split history. On the far side, the centuries-old order of ritual animal sacrifice by a caste of priests in a Temple on a particular hill in a particular kingdom in a particular land promised through God's covenant to the people of Israel. On the near side, silence and devastation. "From the day the Temple was destroyed, a wall of iron set itself between Israel and her father in heaven," Rav Elazar ben Pedat declared in one of the most frightening sentences in the Talmud.

Attempts to jump the chasm (or break through ben Pedat's iron wall) were plentiful, dramatic, desperate, and, in nearly all instances, doomed: a series of schisms, asceticisms, revolutions, and bloody martyrdoms. And in the midst of these convulsions came the response formed by Rav Eliezer and his colleagues (along with Christianity the only response to the Temple's destruction that has prevailed into our time). It was a response that through Mishnah and Talmud, through custom and law, rebuilt the faith of Judah on this side of the chasm as rabbinic Judaism: a faith made for a people in literal and figurative exile, "a pilgrim tribe," in the words of George Steiner, "housed not in place but in time," and worshiping a God also in exile, whose place was nowhere and everywhere, whose face was invisible and always manifest.

And the core of that rabbinic inspiration was the substitution of word for blood, of poetry for the knife, of the Young Israel Synagogue of New Lots and East New York for Jerusalem — of orderly, communal, regularized prayer for orderly, communal, regularized animal sacrifice. And so, these rabbis declared, just as sacrifice in the Temple had brought forgiveness of sin, so now did prayer. Just as sacrifice in the Temple had been a principal obligation on religious festivals, so now was prayer. As sacrifice had been the means by which one expressed gratitude for a harvest, for a child, for escape from danger, so now was prayer.

Berachos, the tractate of Talmud most concerned with prayer, not only contains hundreds of detailed instructions for liturgy and worship but is replete with signposts that direct people's attention to the Torah-endorsed link between the lost world of Temple and the new world of synagogue. Rav Hiyya bar Abba, for example, speaking on folio 14B–15A, in the name of his teacher Rav Yochanan, describes how a man should begin his day: "Scripture," he declares, "considers all who relieve themselves, wash their hands, put on phylacteries and recite the *keryat shema* and pray to be like those who build an altar and sacrifice upon it." Thus did Rav Eliezer and his fellow rabbis try to connect present and past.

But even the noblest bridge admits the chasm. With all due respect to Rav Yochanan, the Temple priest's ablutions are not Everyman's morning piss. In her erudite history of rabbinic prayer, *To Worship God Properly,* Rabbi Ruth Langer nails the radical implications of Rav Eliezer and company's invention this way: "When prayer became incumbent on all the people, not simply upon the priests in Jerusalem, then all the people became equally responsible for contact with God."

That's not a bridge; it's a new explosion. And like other theological explosions — the Reformation, for one good example — it could well have resulted in a shattered core and a score of diminished and localized shards, some perhaps dedicated to gluttony, or sexual ritual, or dismaying forms of sacrifice as the way to please or placate God.

Da lifne me ata omdim: "And when you pray, know before Whom you stand." If one listens with a particular kind of care, Rav Eliezer's final words can sound like a desperate cry for order.

By coincidence (a condition that, like tragedy, is ineluctably joined to Jewish history), Chassidism, the eighteenth-century revivalist movement that produced the story of the rebbe's dream, was also a theological explosion, another response to yet another discontinuity in Jewish history. The crack first appeared in 1648, when an unprecedentedly murderous pogrom destroyed three hundred Jewish settlements in the Ukraine. As in the first century, the unimagined tragedy led to millennial hysteria and a brace of messianic pretenders, two of whom failed dismally, publicly, and shamefully, in the aftermath of which an exhausted Judaism fell into a clinical depression, a stupor of sadness, anxiety, guilt, and obsessive regard for religious regulation.

Led by a set of charismatic rural religious leaders — not all of whom were rabbis — Chassidism took root in the backwater villages of western Galicia. Theologically, it placed heart above mind, man above text, loving-kindness above learning — seeking to reconnect Judaism with a God who had placed His people on Earth so they might rejoice in His blessings.

As regards prayer in particular, Chassidism became infamous for flouting rabbinic regulations: for praying too late and too early; for praying too loud and too fondly; for dancing and singing in the midst of liturgy; for concluding the morning prayer with a whiskey toast to the day's remembered martyrs. It was said of Rav Chayim of Tzanz, for example, that he would stand for hours in prayer — not speaking the liturgy, but ecstatically repeating: "I mean nothing but You, nothing but You alone; nothing but You, nothing but You alone."

And there was Rav Moshe of Kobrin, who in reciting the preamble to just about every Jewish blessing — "Blessed art thou, Lord our God"— cried out "blessed" with such fervor that he had to sit and rest before he could continue with "art thou"; and the Koznitzer Maggid, who would dance on a table during worship; and the dark-visioned Kotzker Rebbe who once chastised a man who complained that his heart ached when work kept him from praying at the prescribed hour: "How do you know that God doesn't prefer your heartache to your prayers?"

How, indeed, does one know what God prefers? Once when I was a boy in the Young Israel Synagogue of New Lots and East New York, late on a Sabbath morning, the men were preparing to return the Torah scroll to the ark after the reading so we could finish the service and go home to eat the Sabbath dinner. A man came forward from his seat and picked up the Torah from the reading table and would not let it go, would not let the service continue. A short, balding man in a navy blue suit, he put his arms around the Torah and his cheek against its silk covering, as one would hug a child in need of comforting. All activity stopped. The white cotton curtains that closed off the women's section of the *shul* parted, and the women and girls stared. Several men — leaders of the *shul* — went up to the man who had seized the Torah. They whispered to him and he whispered in reply without raising his eyes to look at them. From where I stood I could see sweat on the man's high pale brow. And then the word passed from row to row and chair to chair: the man who held the Torah had that week been diagnosed with terminal cancer. Nothing could be done. But he knew, as we did, that no harm could come to a person who held the Torah. Of course he knew, as did we, of the thousands of martyrs over the years who were killed while embracing the Torah — even, in some cases, while in the Torah's embrace, wrapped in the scroll by the murderers. But that was a mystery and old news. In the Young Israel of New Lots and East New York, Torah was life and this was today. And so the man held the Torah and would not let it go.

No one would take the sacred scroll from him under these circumstances, and besides, it was unseemly to wrestle over a Torah. And if it fell to the ground, a general fast would be required.

I don't remember how the episode ended, but I remember it did not last long. I imagine he grew tired: a Torah scroll — roll upon roll of parchment, line upon line of God's word — is heavy in several ways.

At the time, I saw what this man did as an extraordinary act of prayer and supplication — the most extraordinary I'd ever seen. But was it prayer, or was it the reverse of prayer, an act of irreverence, of selfishness?

From the perspective of those who must build and maintain the stage on which prayers of every sort can play themselves out, the question is not easily answered. As Rav Eliezer knew, and as the rabbis who denounced Chassidism and in some cases excommunicated its leaders knew, if each member of the congregation dances on the table, if each roars the first words of the liturgy and falls to the floor, or kidnaps the sacred scroll, or decides that heartache or a quart of pickled herring with onions will do as a substitute, it won't be long before prayer faces man and not God, before the stage collapses under the weight of self-indulgence. On the other hand, if there can be no daring or originality or creativity in prayer, then no human being will mount that stage except out of a sense of duty — and certainly no imaginative human being will want to see what happens there, which means that prayer and religious observance will attract none but the reverential — which is a very different crowd from the reverent.

I happen to be of that generation of Abraham's seed whose members carry the names of those who died in the Shoah. Binyahmin Rand was my murdered great-grandfather. Likewise, my brother Akiva is named for Binyahmin's son. But Jewish history being the aforementioned tangle of coincidence and tragedy, Akiva also happens to be the name of Rav Eliezer's most eminent student, who, as it happens, is also known for the words he spoke in answer to his own students' final question.

In this case, the teacher was being flayed alive by the Romans, his flesh torn from the bone with metal combs. The students' question: How can you stand in silence while undergoing this torture? And like Eliezer, Akiva replied well enough that his words are remembered. "All my life," he said, "I've wondered how I would be able to fulfill the commandment of loving God with all my heart and soul and life." Great-Uncle Akiva's end was not so efficacious. After witnessing the first murderous assault on his village's Jews, Akiva survived the war as a partisan, went to the new state of Israel as a refugee, married, fathered two children, and one day sat in a warm bath and cut open his wrists.

My brother Akiva was born only thirteen months after I came into the world, and as I was from the go raised to be learned and pious, he took the other available option and raised himself to be a lout — quick-tempered, quick-fisted, stubborn, angry, and un-learned. And then, when I was nineteen and he was eighteen, we changed places — or, more accurately, I determined to become a lout, which allowed him to become learned and pious.

Thirty years or so later, Akiva is the dean of a yeshiva in Yiddish Jerusalem, has thirteen children and a dozen grandchildren, and wears a long black beard and a black hat. I am an editor and writer at an American Jesuit university, have three children, no grandchildren, no beard, and own no hat that Akiva would consider worthy of a grown man's head.

For nearly two decades, Akiva and I had almost no contact, but now we meet every year or two when business brings him to the States, and we talk gingerly about the remaining things we have in common: family and Torah.

When Akiva visited Boston two years ago, I had begun to think about prayer and reverence, and so, over a breakfast of lox and eggs at a kosher deli, I asked how he understood 2 Samuel, chapters five and six, a text obsessed with reverence before God.

It's the story of David, newly made king, and how he goes with his army to bring the ark of the covenant to his new capital of Jerusalem. Relinquished by the Philistines after it caused them plague, the ark had since been stored in the home of Avinadav. And with the help of Uzuh and Achyo, two sons of Avinadav, David begins carting it home. (The English translation I use is from Judaica Press, tin-eared but simply accurate.) "And they came to Goren-Nachon, and Uzuh put forth [his hand] to the ark of God, and grasped hold of it, for the oxen swayed it. And the anger of the Lord was kindled against Uzuh, and God struck him down there" because only a Temple priest may touch his flesh to the ark.

Angry at God and fearful, David abandons the ark on the spot, returning to claim it three months later only after hearing that the man (a Gittite, no less) who had taken the ark into his house had since been blessed by God. And so David the brilliant opportunist brings the ark to Jerusalem "with joy. . . . And David danced with all his might before the Lord; and David was girded with a linen ephod" — which is to say, a short shift, which is to say that in the course of dancing with all his might before the Lord and all the people who lived in his city, the king of Israel exposed himself.

And Michal, David's first and much neglected wife and daughter of his old rival Saul, looks out at the procession and sees "the king David hopping and dancing before the Lord; and she loathed him in her heart." Later, after appropriate pomp and sacrifice, David heads home, where Michal greets him with: "How honored was today the king of Israel, who exposed himself today in the eyes of the handmaids of his servants, as would expose himself one of the idlers." This seems fair and sharp instruction from a born princess to her husband the randy former shepherd, but it is also an act against God's anointed, as David scornfully makes plain. "And David said unto Michal, 'Before the Lord who chose me above your father, and above all his house, to appoint me prince over the people of the Lord, over Israel; therefore I have made merry before the Lord. . . .' And Michal the daughter of Saul had no child until the day of her death." End of chapter and verse.

What makes the text difficult, I told Akiva, is that here we have Uzuh, who lays a hand on the ark so as to keep it from falling to the ground — he gets zapped for all his good intentions. We have Michal, the princess and queen, for pointing out correctly to her husband that leaping up and down in a short *ephod* in a public place was behavior ill suited to royalty — she is cursed with barrenness. And then we have David, who for exposing himself before the ark and before all the people — no consequences.

The centuries have of course left us with plenty of rabbinic exegesis, most of it overheated. Some commentators, for example, have tried to sacramentalize David's behavior by saying that his *ephod* was not really a common *ephod* but the jeweled *ephod* worn by the Temple priest. Others have tried to explain God's extraordinary anger against the well-meaning if dimwitted Uzuh by developing a midrash that discovers four serious sins in Uzuh's one act of touching the ark. The inventive details do not bear repeating. Regarding Michal, another midrash says that she wasn't really cursed but had angered David sufficiently that he never again went to bed with her. But Akiva didn't try to pass off any of this on me. Instead he offered the following.

It's easy, Akiva said (the words he has always used when explaining something he understands and I don't). Uzuh, he said, was struck down not simply because he reached out to steady the ark, but because he did so simply to steady the ark, like a clerk filing a folder, like a librarian shelving a book — without awe or love. And Michal was punished not because she chastised the king, but because she did so "loath[ing] him in her heart" and not out of concern for God or the kingdom or the people. And as for David, he was forgiven because what he did — while inappropriate, demeaning, embarrassing, and certainly unsuited to royalty — he did "with all his might before God," which is to say, with selfless devotion. That's what Akiva told me.

And so, while eating lox and eggs, did my learned brother elucidate the difficult text and, though he didn't know it, at the same time provide an answer to the question of how Rav Eliezer and Naftali the woodsman and King David and the men and women of the Young Israel of New Lots and East New York might all be worthy of eternal life. "With all your might before God" will do it every time — will make a prayer of eating, of dancing, of singing, of kidnapping the Torah, even of an offering of mumbled words.

And here I could stop, standing foursquare on the Torah and my learned brother's midrash. Unlike my brother, however, I'm a modern. I can't feel comfortable except if I rest on vexatious ambiguity, the rough mattress I'm used to. And so a final story that returns me to the Young Israel of New Lots and East New York — the place where I received the chilling intimation, while reading the story of the rebbe's dream, that law and midrash were insufficient, that creation was in the final analysis too spirited or opaque or enigmatic or obdurate to submit itself to any study except that conducted by a blind heart.

The story is about prayer and the Chassidic tradition of drinking a postworship *L'Chayim* each morning in memory of the day's listed martyrs. But more importantly, it is about the handful of men who made up the Young Israel's first minyan of the day, who

prayed earliest and fastest and got on with it, and who blessed me
for a time by taking me into their odd company, allowing a milky-
skinned boy of thirteen to be counted as a man each dawn at the
sacred corner of Hegeman and Sheffield.

Tradesmen and shopkeepers, widowers who smelled of the cam-
phor chips in their dresser drawers, men who were too angry or
restless to lie next to their wives all night, they rose before dawn
and made their way through the darkness to the corner of Hegeman and Sheffield, where they stood beside their gunmetal chairs
below the Eternal Fluorescent buzzing behind its shield of painted
glass, before the ark decorated with an emblem of guardian lions
yawning as if they'd been up all night arguing. And the moment
the clock showed sunrise and they could count ten men, they
began.

Never since have I heard such fast prayers, like a torrent sweeping the gutters, slaking the wilderness at the corner of Sheffield
and Hegeman, the *uhmeins* leaping like startled trout. Maybe it was
twenty minutes to the finish — thirty on Monday and Thursday
when we had to read Torah — and then we rushed to the long table below the bookshelves at the back of the sanctuary.

And one of the men took the Seagram's from the secret ark
behind Maimon's commentary on the Mishnah, while another
brought tray of shot glasses, heavy as bad news, from the caterer's
kitchen, and together we took into our bellies the first golden happiness of the day, crying out a "*L'Chayim*" — To life! — in memory
of some saint we did not know but whose death on this date was
somewhere recorded, we believed. "For," as I wrote in a poem published a few years ago:

> . . . the world was old
> and men died each hour,
> some of them saints or martyrs,
> while someone else, whose job it was,
> wrote names and dates
> (and what fuel was used to start the job,
> and the final words, if intelligible).
> And if we didn't have the details
> at Hegeman and Sheffield,
> that couldn't be our fault
> that we should have to suffer.

So *L'Chayim* and again *L'Chayim*.
The hoax of International Brotherhood. *L'Chayim*.
The stink in the air shaft. *L'Chayim*.
The boxcar of broken shoes. *L'Chayim*.
The traitor baseball team. *L'Chayim*.
The martyr behind the deli counter. *L'Chayim*.
The bone in the sea-root's grasp. *L'Chayim*.
The silent wife at the Sabbath meal. *L'Chayim*.
The girl in a summer dress
who passes as you sit in the steamy elevated car
and makes you remember what you once believed, *L'Chayim*.

And then each man went off to business or breakfast except for old Mr. Auslander, who stayed to wash the shot glasses and hum "Bali Hai" at the hallway sink generally reserved for the priests' Holy Day ablutions. While I, damp-eyed, happy apprentice to the saints, who had to be in eighth grade and cold sober in an hour, hurried home in the new light among gentile dog walkers, beneath muscled sycamores, in the perfume trail of girls from public high school, home to the dark-eyed mother in a frayed robe, home to the dying sun of butter in the galaxy of the oatmeal bowl.

CHARLES BOWDEN

The Bone Garden of Desire

FROM ESQUIRE

ROSSINI, the great opera composer, could recall only two moments of real grief in his life. One, when his mother died. And the second time was out on a boat when a chicken stuffed with truffles fell into the water and was lost.

Sometimes, when he was nearing death, I'd go over to help Art cook. I'm down on my knees on the patio, and Art is sitting in a chair with a beer. He has grilled steaks to a cinder and caught the juice. And now I pound the meat with a claw hammer until it's infused with cloves of garlic and peppercorns. Then I shred it with my fingers, put it all in a bowl with the saved juice and herbs, and then simmer. This is machaca according to his late wife's recipe and it takes hours, and this is life, or the best part, he believes as he sits in the chair while I bend and pound to spare his battered old joints. It is a deep taste of something within his bones.

We are outside in the old downtown barrio while I pound in the desert sun, and nearby are the justicia flaming-orange flowers and the chuparosa with the buzz of hummingbirds and the nicotiana reaching up twelve, fourteen feet, the pale green leaves, the spikes of yellow flowers, the costa hummingbirds with purple gorgets that seem to favor it, and Art beams and says, "My birds, my plants."

He takes another swig of beer, and beads of cold moisture fleck the can. Maybe it is the mouth, I think, as I sit down in the garden, swirling red wine in my mouth, dry wine, the kind that reaches back toward the throat and lasts for maybe half a minute on the tongue.

Anyway, when we made the machaca, Art was alive then, and being alive is gardening and cooking and birds and green and blue, at the very least. He was relaxed. I pounded the garlic and pepper, and grilled flesh hung in the air. He told me that during the Korean War, his navy ship made a run from Philadelphia to Europe, and during the Atlantic crossing five officers went over the side and nobody ever writes about stuff like that. But he knows, he was there and all fell overboard at night. They were all assholes, he said.

The beef was tender, the chiles hot, but not too hot, just enough to excite the tongue, and the seasonings bite, the garlic licks the taste buds, and I began to float on the sensations as Art drank his beer and the plants grew and stirred, the hummingbirds whizzed overhead and then hovered before my face, my tongue rubbed against the roof of my mouth, and it is all a swirl of sensation as I remember that summer day cooking.

I also remember Art (died February 11) sitting down in my garden in a chair on a Sunday in January, the last day he left home under his own power. He could barely walk then, his chunky body dwindling as the cancer snacked on various organs, and his skin was yellow from the jaundice. He held on to my arm as we crept through the garden, down from the upper bench, past the bed of trichocereus, under the thin arms of the selenicereus snaking through the tree overhead. He looked over by the notocactus, with their dark green columns, their tawny rows of bristles and small bubbles of white down on their crowns where the yellow flowers would finally emerge; he looked over there where I'd scattered Dick's bone and ash and he said brightly, Hi, Dick (died August 23).

We sat in plastic chairs surrounded by garden walls that were purple, yellow, and pink, colors to fight back all the nights. He knew he'd be dead in two or three weeks, and he was. He knew he'd never see this spring, just as Dick had never made it to the previous fall. And five months before Dick had been Paul (died March 9). And five months after Art would come Chris (died August 6).

The cooking had begun earlier, like the gardening, but both took hold of me around the time my friends started dying. I remember

walking to the market, coming home and flipping through books
for recipes, and then cooking. While the sauce simmered, I would
open a bottle of red wine and begin drinking. There was never
enough red wine, never. I was always cooking from Italian recipes
because they were simple and bold and I loved the colors, the red
of the tomatoes, the green skin of the zucchini, and because I like
peeling garlic and chopping onions and tearing basil. The oil mattered also, the thought of olives, and I preferred the stronger,
cheaper oils with their strong tastes. I used iron pans coated with
green enamel on the outside. There would be scent in the air.

The garden also went out of control. I put in five or six tons of
rock. Truckloads of soil. I built low terraces and planted cactus and
a few herbs. I had no plan and the thing grew from someplace in
my mind.

I must tell you about this flower, *Selenicereus plerantus*. It opens
only in the dark; it begins to unfold around 9 P.M. and it closes before dawn, slams shut at the very earliest probes of gray light.
When it blooms, no one can be alone at night, it is not possible,
nor can anyone fear the night, not in the slightest. This flower
touches your face, it kisses your ear, its tongue slides across your
crotch. The flower is shameless, absolutely shameless. When it
opens its white jaws, the petals span a foot and lust pours out into
the night, a lust as heavy as syrup, and everything is coated by the
carnality of this plant. It opens only on the hottest nights of the
year, black evenings when the air is warmer than your body and
you cannot tell where your flesh ends and the world begins.

A month, maybe a month and a half, before Chris died, he came
over in the evening. He could not control his hiccuping then —
the radiation, you know. And he found it better to stand in his
weakness than to sit. He wore a hat; his hair was falling out. So we
were out in the darkness, him hiccuping and not drinking — he
just did not want that beer anymore — and the flower opened and
flooded the yard with that lust, the petals gaping shamelessly, and
we watched it unfold and felt the lust caress us and he hiccuped
and took it all in.

He understood that flower, I'm sure of it.

Blind Old Homer wrote that no part of us is more like a dog than
the "brazen belly, crying to be remembered." By the twentieth century, there were fifty or sixty thousand codified recipes in Italian

cooking alone. By the mid-twentieth century, Italians were eating seven hundred different pasta shapes, and one sauce, Bolognese, had hundreds of variations.

What can death mean in the face of this drive? What can death say at this table? I tell you: Art called up when things had gotten pretty bad and said he had this craving for strawberry Jell-O.

There must be something about the mouth, about the sucking and the licking and the chewing and the sweet and the sour. The pepper also, and the saline. An English cookbook of 1660 suggests a cake recipe that consumes a half bushel of flour, three pounds of butter, fourteen pounds of currants, two pounds of sugar, and three quarts of cream. There is a leg of mutton smeared with almond paste and a pound of sugar and then garnished with chickens, pigeons, capons, cinnamon, and, naturally, more sugar.

The dark green flesh of the cactus glows with life from the ash and ground human bone. I've come to depend on the garden, and so I stare at the Madagascar palms, their thorny trunks bristling under the canopy of the mesquite tree. Red wine swirls against my tongue because this bone gardening, this wall of green flesh, has all become hopelessly oral with me. I eat, therefore I am. I appreciate nothing, devour everything.

Art found out about the cancer after Thanksgiving. He couldn't really eat. It wasn't the chemotherapy, since he'd passed on that after having a first bout with the colon cancer, and to be honest, the doctors didn't recommend chemo or any other therapy. They gave him prescriptions for opiates and advised him to take lots of them and not to worry. But he didn't like them, didn't like having his mind turn to mush, and besides, he was an old narc, and I think pill popping didn't quite sit right with him. But he couldn't eat, just had no appetite, and when he ate, he felt kind of sick. The cancer was everywhere, of course, with the liver just being the signature location.

So I took him over some marijuana brownies and that evening he took two and then spent half the night in the kitchen — frying steaks and potatoes, whipping up this and that, and gorging. And after that, he refused ever to take another brownie.

Art said they upset his stomach.

But, Lord, that one night, he came alive and tasted deeply.

*

She has the gift of writing exactly the way she speaks and speaking exactly the way she thinks. For years I have gotten letters from Barbara, and they are always fresh and clear and without any of the filters we generally use to guard our hearts. When she writes of her son's death, her words remain the same. Paul was not a surprise to her. She is an artist, her father was an artist, his father was an artist. And it has never been easy — art is not made by the easy, but it has been in the house for generations and felt like a part of life. She told me that's what she put on his tombstone: ARTIST.

At first she was very angry. Not at Paul, at least not in a way she was ready to say, but at the people around him who introduced him to heroin and then did nothing as the drug took over his soul. Shouldn't they have done something? Didn't they realize what they had unleashed? Aren't they responsible? And, of course, the questions were sound and the answers were deserved and Paul was still dead.

She works, she organizes his papers, letters, his art work. She revisits the studio, the pipe, the rope, a boy hanging there. She writes me, "Found out Paul hung for over 8–9 hours. That would not have happened had I been there. 8–9 hours *after* he was found. Fuck the criminal codes. My baby hung by his neck for as long as 14 hours. I didn't think there could be more pain."

They take away the mints because the case is metal. They scrutinize the carton of cigarettes also and then I'm allowed on the ward. Dick is puzzled by the shower, why the head is buried up some kind of funnel in the ceiling. It takes him weeks to figure out they are trying to prevent him from hanging himself. Of course, he cannot think clearly, what with the steady dose of electroshock treatments. He'd checked himself in after the suicide attempt failed. He had saved up his Valiums, taken what he figured to be a massive dose, and then, goddammit, still woke up Monday morning when by any decent standards he ought to have been dead. It was the depression, he told me, the endless blackness. He could handle the booze, and when he was rolling, that was a quart or two of vodka a night, plus coke, of course, to stay alert for the vodka. There was that time he'd checked into detox with blood oozing from his eyes and ears and ass. But he could handle that. He was working on the smoking, didn't light up in the house, you know.

But he couldn't take the depression, never tasted blackness like that. I'd go out in the evening to the ward and we'd sit outside in the walled yard, kind of like a prison, and for two days I tried to get him to pitch horseshoes. Finally, on the third night, he tried but couldn't make the distance between the two pits. The shoes, of course, were plastic, lest the patients hurt one another. But we worked on it, and he got to tossing okay.

We'd been friends for a good long time, business partners once, and we'd survived being in business together, so we must've really been friends, and he'd always been like me, riding a little rough-shod over the way life was supposed to be lived, but he'd kept his spirits up. Not now.

When he got out, I'd go over and take him to the store. He could not move. I'd walk him from the car into the market and then walk with him up and down the aisles. He could not connect with food. I'd buy him bananas because his potassium was low, and lots of green vegetables. He couldn't abide this; he told me he'd never eaten anything green since he was five. Then I'd take him through the checkout and home. The place was a wreck. One day I showed him how to clean off one square foot of the kitchen counter. He watched me do it. I said, Look, you do a foot a day and if you don't do a damn thing else, you'll feel like you did something. His face remained passive.

I'd bring him over and cook dinner and make him eat it. Then we'd sit in the yard, he'd stare out at the cactus and trees, and his eyes would glaze at the twisting paths and clouds of birds. He could hardly speak. The blackness, he'd say by way of explaining.

My huge Argentine mesquite arced over the yard. Nobody believed I'd planted it myself, dug the hole and everything, and that when I put it in the ground, it did not come up to my knee. I remember when I planted it, a woman was over and I told her what this little sapling would become and she said, Nope, it ain't gonna happen. But it did.

I kept trying to get Dick to plant trees. But it was like the horseshoes. It came hard.

In 1696, Mme. de Maintenon, Louis XIV's longtime mistress, writes, "Impatience to eat [peas], the pleasure of having eaten them, and the anticipation of eating them again are the three subjects I have heard very thoroughly dealt with. . . . Some women, having supped, and supped well, at the king's table, have peas waiting for them in their rooms before going to bed."

Peas are new to the French court and all those lascivious mouths and expert tongues are anxious for this new sensation. I applaud this pea frenzy. Who would want a stoic as a cook?

Mme. de Maintenon, sixty-one years old, now secretly wed to the king, stalwart of court etiquette, she likes her pea pods dipped in a sauce, and then she licks them. Yes, she does.

Going up the stairs, I instantly miss the sunlight. Outside, Brooklyn in January is brilliant and the sea is in the air. The stairs feel narrow and dim and cold and dank, and it is like leaving childhood behind for the grave. In my memory, Paul is a child, permanently around the age of, say, ten. I've seen his later photographs on driver's licenses, and the face seems gaunt, the eyes hollow. I'm afraid of finding the room those eyes came from, finding it upstairs at the end of these seemingly endless flights of stairs, with almost no light, a chill in the air, and that dampness that says no one cooks in the kitchen and the woman is never in the bed.

But the machinery standing in the gray light of the big room comforts me. I have stumbled into a surviving pocket of the nineteenth century, that time when people still believed that they could throw themselves at problems and wrestle with materials and fabricate solutions. The morning bleeds through the large windows and glows against the shrink-wrap machine. He had a thing about shrink-wrap — the more you stressed it, the stronger it became. I soak up the room and feel at peace. This is a proper shop for a craftsman and his craft. His craft was pretty simple: he was going to be the best fucking artist in the world and show that all the other stuff was shit. He was going to cut through the fakery and the fashion and get to the ground floor, the killing floor, the factory floor. He was not about tricks or frills or style. He was brutally simple and industrial-strength. I can feel him here, his mouth a firm line, his hair carelessly framing his totally absorbed face, his body bent over slightly as he tinkers with some project, oblivious to everything, including himself, pushing on relentlessly toward mastering a riddle that only he sees or feels or can solve. He's forgotten to eat for a day, his dog watches him silently from a corner of the big room, a stillness hangs over everything and is only slightly broken by the careful movements he makes.

Over in a corner of the shop is the apartment he carved out of the vast cavern of the old factory, and sketched on his door is an arrow pointing down to the floor and a message to slide the mail under here. It has the look of something a twelve-year-old would do. And enjoy doing. I half expect Orville and Wilbur Wright to tap me on the shoulder, or to hear old Henry Ford laconically announcing idiot-savant theses about the coming industrial age. I'm in the past, a place Paul picked to find the future. There is a feeling of grime everywhere, an oil-based grime that has come off machines as they inhaled and exhaled in the clangor of their work. I stand over a worktable and open a cigar box of crayons and carefully pluck two for myself, a blue and a red. I ask a friend of Paul's a question, and he visibly tightens and says suddenly that he can't stay in here anymore. He says he is still upset. So I go alone and look down the narrow hallway to the door to this loft/studio/factory floor and glance up at the stout pipe; it looks to be six or eight inches in diameter. Then I come back to the factory room and see a piece of a black doormat that Paul had nailed to the wall. It says quietly, GET HOME.

I think, Well, shit, so this is where he hung himself.

King Solomon's palace was probably one warm home. He lived with seven hundred wives and three hundred girlfriends and somehow everybody tore through ten oxen a day, plus chunks of gazelles and hartebeests. The Bible said the wise old king had twelve thousand horsemen charging around the countryside scaring up chow for the meals back home.

Money does not replace the lust for food. Or the flesh. Nothing replaces it, nothing. Sometimes it dies, this appetite, sometimes it just vanishes in people. But it is never replaced. By 1803, one restaurant in Paris had kept its stockpot bubbling twenty-four hours a day for eighty-five years. Three hundred thousand capons had gone into the pot over the decades. This is what we like to call a meaningless statistic. Until we open our mouths. Or catch the scent of a woman. Or lean over into a bloom raging in the night.

*

I'd come out to the ranch, a two-hundred-acre remaining frag-
ment of the fifty to eighty square miles that once wore his family's
brand, and we'd sit on the porch and have a beer. Chris worked as
a carpenter and enjoyed life. He knew every plant and rock for
miles around. He didn't seem to give a damn about being born
into money and now living without it. I never heard him say a word
about it. He cared about when one of his cows was going to calf.
And he liked not owning a horse — he prided himself on getting
along without one and in wearing sensible boots instead of narrow,
high-heeled cowboy boots like every other person in a western city.

He'd show me things. The foundations of a settler's cabin down
the hill. The little collapsed house he and his first wife lived in
along the arroyo. An old Indian village.

I remember the village clearly. We walked for an hour or two or
more and then hit a steep incline under the palisades. Chris
paused and pointed out the hawk and falcon nesting sites. Then
his legs went uphill at a steady pace, like pistons. At the top, we slid
through a narrow chute and were upon a small village on a mesa.
At the entrance was a low wall and piles of rocks for throwing at in-
vaders. This was clearly a fort people fled to in some time of trouble five hundred years or more ago.

Chris had been coming here since he was a boy. The place, like
almost everything else in the area, was his secret. We sat up there in
the sunshine, swallowing a couple hundred square miles of scen-
ery and saying little. He was like that. I hardly ever heard him complain. Things just are. And if you look around, they're pretty good.
Have a cold beer, a warm meal. And take in the countryside.

In the first century, Apicius put together a manuscript that lets us
visit the lust of the Roman palate. The empire made all things possible — Apicius once outfitted a ship because he'd heard some
good-sized shrimp were being caught off North Africa. The em-
peror Vitellius, said to be somewhat of a pig at table, favored a dish
of pike liver, pheasant brains, peacock brains, flamingo tongues,
and lamprey roe. Apicius is supposed to have killed himself when
he was down to his last couple of million bucks because he could
not bear to lower his standard of living. Before there was a language of words on paper, there must have been a language of food.
Speech begins with the fire and the kettle. I am sure of this.

*

When I was drinking at the grave, I didn't feel quite right. I'd been uneasy about leaving Dick, worried about two days away. I'd gone down and gotten him bailed out a few days before, done the shopping trips, talked to him about the importance of cleaning a counter. All of that. We had sat in the yard and watched the woodpecker eat insects in the throb of the August air. His speech was very slow and nothing seemed to ever lift, nothing. He'd been fired, the drinking had come back, the electroshock didn't seem to do much good, and the gambling dug in deep until he had about a hundred thousand on the credit cards. So we'd sit in the yard and I'd explain that you can't beat a slot machine, that you can't win. He'd say, That's it, that's it, you can't win.

So when I left for a memorial mass in a distant city for a murder victim named Bruno Jordan who'd crossed my path, I felt ill at ease. Out at the cemetery after the mass, we stood around the grave drinking beer and talking, and then we went back to the house in the barrio for dinner, one cousin looking down at the grave and saying, Hey, Bruno, see you back at the house.

The next day, when I came through the door, the phone was ringing. They'd found the body. Dick had been dead two days. He'd died clean, nothing in his body. He'd accidentally tripped on the rug, hit his head on the dining room table, that was it. He'd been working on a book about the drinking life.

Dick had always had one terror: that he would die drunk.

So God smiled on him.

I feel surprisingly at peace. Walking the few blocks from the subway, I took in the Brooklyn street, warming to its resemblance to the endless warrens of houses and factories I knew in Chicago. It looked just like the places Paul lived as a boy, and I thought, You cagey guy, you found the Midwest in New York. Behind the factory-now-loft stands a Russian church, thrown up in the 1920s by those determined to keep the lamp of faith lit on a distant shore. Across from that is a small park with beaten grass, the kind of sliver of light our urban planners have always tossed to the inmates of our great cities. It all felt very comfortable to me. When Paul was a small boy, I can remember walking across the tundra of Chicago to visit his parents' apartment and passing scenes just like these in this pocket of Brooklyn. And the workspace itself, with its patina of grime from machines, its workman's bench, its monastic sense of craft, hard work, and diligence, recalls the various places Paul toiled as a boy — his room, the cellar, the corner grabbed in some cottage in the country. That's part of the sense of peace I feel pervading me. I think to myself, Paul, you kept the faith.

I've gotten up before dawn and gone over his letters, which I've brought with me, and the bank statements, all the while sipping coffee in a mid-Manhattan hotel. The numbers on the statements blurred as I sat amid businessmen who were studying CNN on the lounge television, and then I'd look back down at the bank statements and feel as though I were watching the spinning dials of a slot machine, only this machine always comes up with the same result: a hundred dollars a day. December, January, February, the steady withdrawals are punctual and exact. I thought to myself, Paul, you create order even in your disorder. So later when I stand in the big room where he tore at the limits of what he called art and plunged into some place he hoped was behind that name, when I touch his row of tools on the workbench and admire his shrink-wrap machine in one corner, whirring in my head is this blur of numbers as he swallowed his earnings in a grim, orderly fashion. I look over at the wall, the one punctured by the hallway leading to the doorway and the stout pipe against the ceiling, and read once more the doormat still whispering, GET HOME. I reach up and rip the black message from the wall. This one I am taking home.

Paul was up to something here. I know this in my bones.

He kind of scowls and comes limping across the kitchen at me, saying, No, no. He takes the knife and says, Here, see, you gotta do this rocking motion, and with that he chops the hell out of the cilantro. Art will be dead in three weeks, and this is his last hurrah, teaching me how to make salsa cruda. He's real yellow now, wheezing all the time, and beneath the yellow is the color of ash.

He's got these papers to straighten out, and we go over them. He's going to do a bit of writing, and so I bring the office chair and computer. But then he can't sit up anymore, and we try to jury-rig something in the easy chair. And then that's too much and the damn fluid is building in his body, he's all bloated and distended, and, by God, he tells the nurse who comes to the house each day, he's gotta get the swelling drained at the hospital. And she says,

That won't do any good, you're not sick, you're dying. He listens without so much as a blink, I'm sitting right there, and then he pads down the hall to his bedroom, lies down, and sleeps. In twenty-four hours, he goes into a coma. The next day, he's dead after a night of family praying and shouting over him — ancient aunts hollering messages in his ear for other family members that have gone to the boneyard ahead of him. His cousin, the monsignor, says the funeral mass.

I can still taste the salsa and smell the cilantro and feel that rocking motion as he tries to show me the right way to wield the knife. And to make salsa, his salsa, as he learned it from his wife, Josie, who learned from her parents and back into the brown web of time. Like everything that matters to the tongue, it is simple.

- Put five or six sixteen-ounce cans of whole TOMATOES into a big pot, reserving the liquid. Coarse-grind the tomatoes in a food processor, a short pulse so they come out in chunks and not puree. Now add them to the reserved juice.
- Cut up two or three bunches of GREEN ONION, in very thin slices so that you end up with tiny circles. Now very finely cut up a bunch of CILANTRO.
- Add five cans of diced GREEN CHILES, a teaspoon of GARLIC POWDER, and the onion and cilantro to the tomatoes and their juice. Sprinkle a teaspoon or two of OREGANO. Taste it and adjust seasoning.
- Now start crushing CHILTEPINS (*Capsicum annuum* var. *aviculare*) and add to taste. Add salt. Taste again. Keep crushing chiltepins until it is right for your tongue.

That was the last time I really saw him move, when he was trying to teach me how to make salsa cruda. He knew some things can't be allowed to end.

The bottom line is always simple, and the way to this line is to get rid of things. I stand at a hot stove and make risotto, a rice dish of the Italian north:

- Melt some butter in oil, then sauté some CHOPPED ONION, toss in the RICE, and coat it with the oil; add the liquid (make the first ladle white wine, then go with broth) a half cup at a time, constantly stirring.

- In twenty minutes, the rice is ready, the center of each kernel a little resistant to the tooth, but ready. Each grain is saturated with the broth and onion and oil flavor.
- Then spread the rice on the plate to cool and eat from the edge inward. Pick a brilliant plate with rich color — I like intense blues and greens, you know — to play off the white. Some mix in A HALF OR FULL CUP OF GRATED PARMESAN to the rice to make it stickier. I just sprinkle some on top and usually favor Romano, because it has more bite. But that is your choice.

The rest is not. After all, we are in Paul's workshop, a thing to be kept clean and simple and direct. The difference between good art and good cooking is you can eat cooking. But the important part, the getting rid of things, it is always there and the kid knew it.

The kid worked. Like most products of the Midwest, I can't abide people who fuck off and don't do things. I can remember my father sitting at a kitchen table in Chicago with his quart of beer, telling me with a snarl that in Chicago we make things, but in New York they just sell things.

I look up at the torn drywall. When Paul didn't answer the phone, his uncle flew from Chicago to New York and took a cab over here to Brooklyn. Clawed his way through the drywall — I look up at the hole he made — and found Paul swinging from the big pipe. He'd left a note and neat accounts on the table, plus his checkbook, so everyone would be paid off proper.

I hum to myself as I look up at that pipe. Hum that song by John Prine about the hole in Daddy's arm where all the money goes.

It got so he couldn't do much. One day his ex-wife, Mary, stopped by the ranch to check on him, and he was sprawled in the doorway, half in the house and half out, surrounded by the dogs and cats.

So Mary took him into town. He'd been busy at the ranch despite his weakness as the cancer ate. He'd been building check dams to cure a century of erosion; he planted a garden, put the boots to the cattle, and let the hills come back. He said ranching was over and it was time for the earth to get some other kind of deal. I'd run into him a week or so before at the feed mill and he was chipper. His hair had just about all fallen out because of the radiation, but he said he felt good. He was in town to get a part for the pump.

He was real lean by then, and when I went down to see him at

Mary's place, he was stretched out in bed. He wanted to talk Mexico, the people, the plants, the cattle, the way the air felt at night. I brought down some pictures of Mexico and we hung them around the room. He was having some kind of magic tar shipped down from Colorado that was supposed to beat back the cancer, and he was tracking the pennant race also. People would drop by at all hours to see him, since the word was out that he was a goner. He'd smoke a joint with them, talk about this and that, especially Mexico, which he knew was color and sound and smell and taste and a wood fire with a kettle on the coals. Some of the time he lived down there in a shack with a campesino family. When he fell in the doorway at the ranch, half in and half out, he was pretty much set to go back to Mexico. That was on hold at the moment as he tackled dying.

He lasted about a week. I went over one day, and he was propped up in bed so that the tumor blocking his throat didn't pester him too much. He said, Chuck, I got some great news. We just got two inches of rain at the ranch.

Yes. I can smell the sweet grass as the clouds lift.

She is at war with herself, the life within her fighting the death without her. And she knows this. And she writes me this. She says, "So after I talked to you, I went out to the cemetery. The sun was out here and it was a beautiful day. Snow in patches hugging the earth in lovely patterns making me realize the earth has temperatures of variation, like a body. I had not realized that before. Then as I drove back, a rage overtook me and I raped and pillaged. I went to where I used to live along the beach and cut branches from bushes I know will bloom (not in obvious places or so they would hurt the bush or tree). Many, many branches that filled up the trunk of the car and the backseat. It took an hour and a half to get them all recut and into water all over my house and closed porch. I've been cutting forsythia and 'forcing' it, but haven't tried these others — redbud, cherry, baby's breath, flowering almond, weigela (probably too late a bloomer), lilac (doubt this one will work). . . ."

As she writes this to me, it is March, a month when boys hang themselves, a month when winter has stayed too long. A month when spring is near and force may be applied.

*

I don't trust the answers or the people who give me the answers. I believe in dirt and bone and flowers and fresh pasta and salsa cruda and red wine. I do not believe in white wine; I insist on color. I think death is a word and life is a fact, just as food is a fact and cactus is a fact.

There is apparently a conspiracy to try to choke me with words. There are these steps to death — is it seven or twelve or what? fuck, I can't remember — and then you arrive at acceptance. Go toward the light. Our Father who art in heaven. Whosoever shall believe in me shall not perish. Too many words choking me, clutching at my throat until they strangle any bad words I might say. Death isn't the problem. The words are, the lies are. I have sat now with something broken inside me for months, and the words — death, grief, fear — don't touch my wounds.

I have crawled back from someplace where it was difficult to taste food and where the flowers flashing their crotches in my face all but lacked scent. My wounds kept me alive; my wounds, I now realize, were life. I have drunk a strong drug and my body is ravaged by all the love and caring and the colors and forms and the body growing still in the new silence of the room as someone I knew and loved ceased breathing.

I remember standing in the room with Art's corpse, so warm, his heart had stopped beating maybe a hundred and twenty seconds earlier, and I stood there wondering, What has changed now, what is it that just took place? And I realized that I had advanced not an inch from where I stood as a boy when I held my dying dog and watched life wash off his furry face with a shudder. I do not regret this inability to grow into wisdom. I listen to Chris saying, Good news, two inches of rain at the ranch. Look up at the stout pipe Paul picked for the rope. Hear Dick slowly trying to explain — in words so soft I must lean forward to hear them — why he cannot pick up a plastic horseshoe in the evening light at the nuthouse. Then these pat words show up that people offer me and these pious words slink away like a cur flinching from this new stillness on the wind.

Almost every great dish in Italian cooking has fewer than eight ingredients. Get rid of things or food will be complex and false. In the garden, there is no subtlety. A flower is in your face and is never named Emily. Be careful of the words; go into the bone garden and then taste desire. So it has taken months and it is still a matter of the tongue and of lust. And if you go toward that light and find it, piss on it for me.

I would believe in the words of solace if they included fresh polenta with a thickened brown sauce with shiitake and porcini mushrooms. The corn must be coarse-ground and simmered and stirred for at least forty minutes, then spread flat on a board about an inch thick and cooled in a rich yellow sheet. The sauce, a brew of vegetable broth, white wine, pepper, salt, some olive oil, and minced garlic, is rich like fine old wood in a beloved and scarred table. When you are ready, grill a slab of the polenta, having first lightly brushed it with olive oil, then ladle on some sauce. And eat. The dish is brutally simple. But it skirts the lie of the words of solace; it does not deny desire.

Never deny desire. Not once. Always go to the garden and the kitchen. Whatever death means, the large white cactus flower still opens in the evening and floods the air with lust and hot wet loins. The mushroom sauce on the corn mush will calm no one, either.

That is why they are better than the words.

As I sit here, Chris is to the south, Art is to the west, Paul is back east, and Dick is in the backyard by the fierce green flesh of the cactus. These things I know. The answers I don't know, nor am I interested. That is why food is important and plants are important. Because they are not words and the answers people offer me are just things they fashion out of words. A simple veal ragú is scent and texture and color and soft on the tongue. It is important to cut onions by hand. The power of the flower at night is frightening, the lust floods the air and destroys all hope of virtue.

There will be more blooms this spring — the cactus grew at least ten feet last year. They will open around nine in the evening and then close at the first gray light of dawn. I'll sit out there with a glass of red wine and the lights out.

When I tell people about the blooms, about how they open around nine and close before sunrise and do this just for one night, they always ask, Is that all?

Yes. That's all.

JAMES CAMPBELL

Travels with R.L.S.

FROM THE NEW YORK TIMES BOOK REVIEW

ONE EVENING in the spring of 1880, Robert Louis Stevenson dropped into the bar of the Magnolia Hotel in Calistoga, at the head of the Napa Valley. There was little more to the town than the springs, the railway station, and the enticement of a fortune to be made from mining gold or silver. The West was still pretty wild. Inside, someone asked Stevenson if he would like to speak to Mr. Foss, a stagecoach driver; Stevenson, always alert to the suggestion of travel, said yes: "Next moment, I had one instrument at my ear, another at my mouth, and found myself, with nothing in the world to say, conversing with a man several miles off among desolate hills."

It was "an odd thing," Stevenson reflected, that here, "on the very skirts of civilization," he should find himself talking on the telephone for the first time. Later, he adapted the incident for use in a novel. "May I use your telephone?" asks Mr. Pinkerton in *The Wrecker* (1892), one of the earliest occurrences in literature of that polite request.

Stevenson and his wife, Fanny, were in the middle of their honeymoon, spent mostly in an abandoned California silver mine. Throughout his life, Stevenson preferred to circumnavigate civilization, with its increasing reliance on contraptions, and steer toward the rougher fringes. Wherever we catch sight of him — tramping in the Highlands of Scotland or shivering in the Adirondacks or sailing in the South Seas, where he feasted with kings and cannibals — Stevenson is self-consciously turning his back on the Victorian idol, progress. In similar spirit, he chose the past more often than the present as a setting for fiction. His most popular novels — *Treasure Island, Kidnapped, The Master of Ballantrae* — are set in a semimythical realm, where the fire of adventure catches on every page. Stevenson loved the sound of clashing swords; he didn't want them getting tangled up in telephone wires overhead.

Yet, though he might try to avoid it, Stevenson was destined to be a modern man. He was born 150 years ago in Edinburgh, into a family of civil engineers, esteemed for its technological genius. His grandfather, also Robert, was Britain's greatest builder of lighthouses, and his graceful towers continue to guide sailors today. Three of Robert Senior's sons followed him into the profession, including R.L.S.'s father, Thomas, who made his own mark in the field of optics. Among his various inventions are louvre-boarded screens for the protection of thermometers (these are still in use) and the marine dynamometer, which measures the force of waves.

It was expected that Louis would enter the family business in turn, and a great wringing of hands greeted his announcement to the contrary. He told his father that he wanted to be a writer, which Thomas Stevenson regarded as no profession at all. We can imagine the consternation in the solid bourgeois drawing room when Stevenson's letters arrived bearing pleas such as "Take me as I am . . . I *must* be a bit of a vagabond." This was written in his final year at Edinburgh University, and a vagabond was precisely what the graduate set out to be: longhaired, careless about food though never without tobacco, walking through France or planning an epic ocean voyage; a far cry from the offices of D. & T. Stevenson, Engineers. He was forging the template for generations of college-educated hobos to come. "I travel not to go anywhere, but to go," he wrote in *Travels with a Donkey* (1879). "I travel for travel's sake. The great affair is to move." Compare that with Jack Kerouac, as he climbed into a car with Neal Cassady three-quarters of a century later: "We were leaving confusion and nonsense behind and performing our one and noble function of the time, *move*."

Stevenson would not be an engineer, but he left his own lights, in Scotland and across the world, by which it is possible to trace his unceasing movement. No other writer, surely, is as much memorialized by the words "lived here" as he is. There are five houses with R.L.S. associations in Edinburgh alone, not to mention the little

schoolhouse he attended as a child and the lavish gardens opposite the family home in Heriot Row, where he played and, the fan-
ciful will have you believe, first acted out the quest for Treasure Island. I have shadowed Stevenson up to the northeast of Scotland,
where he tried his hand at being an apprentice engineer, back
down to the Hawes Inn at South Queensferry, where David Balfour
is tricked into going to sea in *Kidnapped*. It still serves rum and ale.
There are landmarks in Switzerland, on the French Riviera, and on
the Pacific islands where the adventure of his final years took place
among a peculiar clan of relatives and natives.

Recently, I stumbled across a place where Stevenson lived briefly
in London: Abernethy House. Now a private dwelling, it was once a
lodging house. It stands in a secluded corner of Hampstead, where
no cars and few pedestrians pass by, and which seems little
changed from Stevenson's day. He stayed here when he was twenty-
three. High up on a hill, and separated from foggy London by
farms and heath, Hampstead was kind to Stevenson's tubercular
lungs. It left a healthy impression on him, let's say; and Abernethy
House left its mark, too, for Stevenson wrote an essay, "Notes on
the Movements of Young Children," about a scene witnessed from
his bedroom window. His friend Sidney Colvin, who was also staying at Abernethy, called the essay "merely an exercise," but it is
among the first pieces in which we hear the mature, intelligent
voice of the writer he would become.

One day, Colvin found Stevenson entranced by the sight of some
girls skipping rope in the street below. The youngest was particularly appealing: "The funniest little girl, with a mottled complexion and a big, damaged nose, and looking for all the world like any
dirty, broken-nosed doll in a nursery lumber-room, came forward
to take her turn. While the others swung the rope for her as gently
as it could be done . . . and playfully taunted her timidity, she
passaged backwards and forwards in a pretty flutter of indecision,
putting up her shoulders and laughing."

The description is capped by a typical note: "Much as I had enjoyed the grace of the older girls . . . the clumsiness of the child
seemed to have a significance and a sort of beauty of its own." Ethereal traces of R.L.S. are to be found elsewhere in Hampstead. I cannot pass the old pub Jack Straw's Castle without seeing the dog that
Stevenson met there in 1874, "looking out of a gate so sympatheti-
cally that it has put me in good humor." And it was while standing

on Hampstead Hill one night that he gazed down on London and imagined a technological miracle of the future, "when in a moment, in the twinkling of an eye, the design of the monstrous city flashes into vision — a glittering hieroglyph." He is anticipating the effects of electricity and a time when the streetlamps would be lighted "not one by one" by the faithful old lamplighter, but all at once, by the touch of a button. Not for him improvements in optics, and his father's "azimuthal condensing system"; give him the flickering gas lamp and the "skirts of civilization" any day.

Lamps of one sort or another occur frequently in Stevenson's writing. In addition to this essay, "A Plea for Gas Lamps," there is another, "The Lantern Bearers," and his poem for children, "The Lamplighter," which celebrates an old custom: "For we are very lucky, with a lamp before the door, / And Leerie stops to light it as he lights so many more." Then there is the memoir he wrote in California, while waiting for Fanny to extract herself from her unhappy first marriage, in which he describes how, when a child and sick, his nurse would take him to the window, "whence I might look forth into the blue night starred with street lamps, and see where the gas still burned behind the windows of other sickrooms." And the lights shine again, with a subdued glow, in the obituary he wrote of his father in 1887. Thomas Stevenson's name may not have been widely known, yet "all the time, his lights were in every part of the world, guiding the mariner."

A year later, Stevenson chartered the schooner yacht *Casco* and became a mariner himself, sailing circuitously through the South Seas for Samoa. With his mother in tow, as well as his wife and stepchildren, he had, in a sense, entered the family business at last. By then, a very modern cult of celebrity had grown up around the author of *Treasure Island* and *Dr. Jekyll and Mr. Hyde,* and Stevenson found it difficult to evade admirers and the press. After his death in 1894, Fanny recalled how they set out from Tahiti, where they had been living in contented isolation, and set their sails for Hawaii. When they reached Honolulu, "the change from our simple, quiet life to the complications of civilization . . . proved confusing to a degree almost maddening." There were crowds of visitors at the door of their cottage, numerous letters to be answered and — there it goes again — "the almost constant calls to the telephone."

ANNE FADIMAN

Mail

FROM THE AMERICAN SCHOLAR

SOME YEARS AGO, my parents lived at the top of a steep hill. My father kept a pair of binoculars on his desk with which, like a pirate captain hoisting his spyglass to scan the horizon for treasure ships, he periodically inspected the mailbox to see if the flag had been raised. When it finally went up, he trudged down the driveway and opened the extra-large black metal box, purchased by my mother in the same accommodating spirit with which some wives buy their husbands extra-large trousers. The day's load — a mountain of letters and about twenty pounds of review books packed in Jiffy bags, a few of which had been pierced by their angular contents and were leaking what my father called "mouse dirt" — was always tightly wedged. But he was a persistent man, and after a brief show of resistance the mail would surrender, to be carried up the hill in a tight clinch and dumped onto a gigantic desk. Until that moment, my father's day had not truly begun.

His desk was made of steel, weighed more than a refrigerator, and bristled with bookshelves and secret drawers and sliding panels and a niche for a cedar-lined humidor. (He believed that cigar-smoking and mail-reading were natural partners, like oysters and Muscadet.) I think of it as less a writing surface than a mail-sorting table. He hated Sundays and holidays because there was nothing new to spread on it. Vacations were taxing, the equivalent of forced relocations to places without food. His homecomings were always followed by day-long orgies of mail-opening — feast after famine — at the end of which all the letters were answered; all the bills were paid; the outgoing envelopes were affixed with stamps from a brass dispenser heavy enough to break your toe; the books and manuscripts were neatly stacked; and the empty Jiffy bags were stuffed into an extra-large copper wastebasket, cheering confirmation that the process of postal digestion was complete.

"One of my unfailing minor pleasures may seem dull to more energetic souls: opening the mail," he once wrote.

> Living in an advanced industrial civilization is a kind of near-conquest over the unexpected. . . . Such efficiency is of course admirable. It does not, however, by its very nature afford scope to that perverse human trait, still not quite eliminated, which is pleased by the accidental. Thus to many tame citizens like me the morning mail functions as the voice of the unpredictable and keeps alive for a few minutes a day the keen sense of the unplanned and the unplannable. The letter opener is an instrument that has persisted from some antique land of chance and adventure into our ordered world of the perfectly calculated.

What chance and adventure might the day's haul contain? My brother asked him, when he was in his nineties, what kind of mail he liked best. "In my youth," he replied, "a love letter. In middle age, a job offer. Today, a check." (That was false cynicism, I think. His favorite letters were from his friends.) Whatever the accidental pleasure, it could not please until it arrived. Why were deliveries so few and so late (he frequently grumbled), when, had he lived in central London in the late seventeenth century, he could have received his mail between ten and twelve times a day?

We get what we need. In 1680, London had mail service nearly every hour because there were no telephones. If you wished to invite someone to tea in the afternoon, you could send him a letter in the morning and receive his reply before he showed up at your doorstep. Postage was one penny.

If you wished to send a letter to another town, however, delivery was less reliable and postage was gauged on a scale of staggering complexity. By the mid-1830s,

> the postage on a single letter delivered within eight miles of the office where it was posted was . . . twopence, the lowest rate beyond that limit being fourpence. Beyond fifteen miles it became fivepence; after which it rose a penny at a time, but by irregular augmentation, to one shilling, the charge for three hundred miles. There was as a general rule an ad-

ditional charge of a half penny on a letter crossing the Scotch border; while letters to or from Ireland had to bear, in addition, packet rates, and rates for crossing the bridges over the Conway and the Menai.

So wrote Rowland Hill, the greatest postal reformer in history, who in 1837 devised a scheme to reduce and standardize postal rates and to shift the burden of payment from the addressee to the sender.

Until a few years ago I had no idea that if you sent a letter out of town — and if you weren't a nobleman, a member of Parliament, or other VIP who had been granted the privilege of free postal franking — the postage was paid by the recipient. This dawned on me when I was reading a biography of Charles Lamb, whose employer, the East India House, allowed clerks to receive letters gratis until 1817: a substantial perk, sort of like being able to call your friends on your office's 800 number. (Lamb, who practiced stringent economies, also wrote much of his personal correspondence on company stationery. His most famous letter to Wordsworth, for instance — the one in which he refers to Coleridge as "an Archangel a little damaged" — is inscribed on a page whose heading reads "Please to state the Weights and Amounts of the following Lots.")

Sir Walter Scott liked to tell the story of how he had once had to pay "five pounds odd" in order to receive a package from a young New York lady he had never met: an atrocious play called *The Cherokee Lovers*, accompanied by a request to read it, correct it, write a prologue, and secure a producer. Two weeks later another large package arrived for which he was charged a similar amount. "Conceive my horror," he told his friend Lord Melville, "when out jumped the same identical tragedy of *The Cherokee Lovers*, with a second epistle from the authoress, stating that, as the winds had been boisterous, she feared the vessel entrusted with her former communication might have foundered, and therefore judged it prudent to forward a duplicate." Lord Melville doubtless found this tale hilarious, but Rowland Hill would have been appalled. He had grown up poor, and, as Christopher Browne notes in *Getting the Message*, his splendid history of the British postal system, "Hill had never forgotten his mother's anxiety when a letter with a high postal duty was delivered, nor the time when she sent him out to sell a bag of clothes to raise 3*s* for a batch of letters."

Hill was a born Utilitarian who, at the age of twelve, had been so frustrated by the irregularity of the bell at the school where his father was principal that he had instituted a precisely timed bell-ringing schedule. In 1837 he published a report called "Post Office Reform: Its Importance and Practicability." Why, he argued, should legions of accountants be employed to figure out the Byzantine postal charges? Why should Britain's extortionate postal rates persist when France's revenues had risen, thanks to higher mail volume, after its rates were lowered? Why should postmen waste precious time waiting for absent addressees to come home and pay up? A national Penny Post was the answer, with postage paid by the senders, "using a bit of paper . . . covered at the back with a glutinous wash, which the bringer might, by the application of a little moisture, attach to the back of the letter."

After much debate, Parliament passed a postal reform act in 1839. On January 10, 1840, Hill wrote in his diary, "Penny Postage extended to the whole kingdom this day! . . . I guess that the number despatched to-night will not be less than 100,000, or more than three times what it was this day twelve-months. If less I shall be disappointed." On January 11 he wrote, "The number of letters despatched exceeded all expectation. It was 112,000, of which all but 13,000 or 14,000 were prepaid." In May, after experimentation to produce a canceling ink that could not be surreptitiously removed, the Post Office introduced the Penny Black, bearing a profile of Queen Victoria: the first postage stamp. The press, pondering the process of cancellation, fretted about the "untoward disfiguration of the royal person," but Victoria became an enthusiastic philatelist, and renounced the royal franking privilege for the pleasure of walking to the local post office from Balmoral Castle to stock up on stamps and gossip with the postmaster. When Rowland Hill — by that time, *Sir* Rowland Hill — retired as Post Office Secretary in 1864, *Punch* asked, "SHOULD ROWLAND HILL have a Statue? Certainly, if OLIVER CROMWELL should. For one is celebrated for cutting off the head of a bad King, and the other for sticking on the head of a good Queen."

The Penny Post, wrote Harriet Martineau, "will do more for the circulation of ideas, for the fostering of domestic affections, for the humanizing of the mass generally, than any other single measure that our national wit can devise." It was incontrovertible proof, in an age that embraced progress on all fronts ("the means of loco-

motion and correspondence, every mechanical art, every manu-
facture, every thing that promotes the convenience of life," as
Macaulay put it in a typical gush of national pride), that the British
were the most civilized people on earth. Ancient Syrian runners,
Chinese carrier pigeons, Persian post riders, Egyptian papyrus
bearers, Greek *hemerodromes,* Hebrew dromedary riders, Roman
equestrian relays, medieval monk-messengers, Catalan *troters,* international couriers of the House of Thurn and Taxis, American
mail wagons — what could these all have been leading up to, like
an ever-ascending staircase, but the Victorian postal system?

And yet (to raise a subversive question), might it be possible
that, whatever the profit in efficiency, there may have been a literary cost associated with the conversion from payment by addressee
to payment by sender? If you knew that your recipient would have
to bear the cost of your letter, wouldn't courtesy motivate you to
write an extra-good one? On the other hand, if you paid for it yourself, wouldn't you be more likely to feel you could get away with
"Having a wonderful time, wish you were here"?

I used to think my father's attachment to the mail was strange. I
now feel exactly the way he did. I live in an apartment building
and, with or without binoculars, I cannot see my mailbox, one of
thirteen dinky aluminum cells bolted to the lobby wall. The mail
usually comes around four in the afternoon (proving that the
postal staircase that reached its highest point with Rowland Hill
has been descending ever since), which means that at around
three, *just in case,* I'm likely to visit the lobby for the first of several
reconnaissance missions. There's no flag, but over the years my
fingers have become postally sensitive, and I can tell if the box is
full by giving it the slightest of pats. If there's a hint of convexity —
it's very subtle, nothing as obvious, let us say, as the bulge of a can
that might harbor botulism — I whip out my key with the same excitement with which my father set forth down his driveway.

There the resemblance ends. The thrill of the treasure hunt is
followed all too quickly by the glum realization that the box contains only four kinds of mail: (1) junk, (2) bills, (3) work, and (4)
letters that I will read with enjoyment, place in a folder labeled "To
Answer," leave there for a geologic interval, and feel guilty about.
The longer they languish, the more I despair of my ability to live

up to the escalating challenge of their response. It is a truism of epistolary psychology that, for example, a Christmas thank-you note written on December 26 can say any old thing, but if you wait until February, you are convinced that nothing less than *Middlemarch* will do.

In October of 1998 I finally gave in and signed up for e-mail. I had resisted for a long time. My husband and I were proud of our retrograde status. Not only did we lack a modem, but we didn't have a car, a microwave, a Cuisinart, an electric can opener, a cellular phone, a CD player, or cable television. It's hard to give up that sort of backward image; I worried that our friends wouldn't have enough to make fun of. I also worried that learning how to use e-mail would be like learning how to program our VCR, an unsuccessful project that had confirmed what excellent judgment we had shown in not purchasing a car, etc.

As millions of people had discovered before me, e-mail was fast. Sixteenth-century correspondents used to write "Haste, haste, haste, for lyfe, for lyfe, haste!" on their most urgent letters; my "server," a word that conjured up a delicious sycophancy, treated *every* message as if someone's life depended on it. Not only did it get there instantly, caromed in a series of analog cyberpackets along the nodes of the Internet and reconverted to digital form via its recipient's modem. (I do not understand a word of what I just wrote, but that is immaterial. Could the average Victorian have diagrammed the mail coach route from Swansea to Tunbridge Wells?) More important, I *answered* e-mail fast — almost always on the day it arrived. No more guilt! I used to think I did not like to write letters. I now realize that what I didn't like was folding the paper, sealing the envelope, looking up the address, licking the stamp, getting in the elevator, crossing the street, and dropping the letter in the postbox.

At first I made plenty of mistakes. I clicked on the wrong icons, my attachments didn't stick, and, not having learned how to file addresses, I sent an X-rated message to my husband (I thought) at gcolt@aol.com instead of georgecolt@aol.com. I hope Gerald or Gertrude found it flattering. But the learning curve was as steep as my father's driveway, and pretty soon I was batting out fifteen or twenty e-mails a day in the time it had once taken me to avoid answering a single letter. My box was nearly always full — no waiting, no binoculars, no convexity checks, no tugging — and when it wasn't, the reason was not that the mail hadn't *arrived,* it was that it hadn't been *sent.* I began to look forward every morning to the festive green arrow with which AT&T WorldNet welcomed me into my father's "antique land of chance and adventure." Would I be invited to purchase Viagra, lose thirty pounds, regrow my thinning hair, obtain electronic spy software, get an EZ loan, retire in three years, or win a Pentium III 500 MHz computer (presumably in order to receive such messages even faster)? Or would I find a satisfying little clutch of friendly notes whose responses could occupy me until I awoke sufficiently to tackle something that required intelligence? As Hemingway wrote to Fitzgerald, describing the act of letter-writing: "Such a swell way to keep from working and yet feel you've done something."

My computer, without visible distension, managed to store a flood tide of mail that in nonvirtual form would have silted up my office to the ceiling. This was admirable. And when I wished to commune with my friend Charlie, who lives in Taipei, not only could I disregard the thirteen-hour time difference, but I was billed the same amount as if I had dialed his old telephone number on East 22nd Street. The German critic Bernhard Siegert has observed that the breakthrough concept behind Rowland Hill's Penny Post was "to think of all Great Britain as a single city, that is, no longer to give a moment's thought to what had been dear to Western discourse on the nature of the letter from the beginning: the idea of distance." E-mail is a modern Penny Post: the world is a single city with a single postal rate.

Alas, our Penny Post, like Hill's, comes at a price. If the transfer of postal charges from sender to recipient was the first great demotivator in the art of letter-writing, e-mail was the second. "It now seems a good bet," Adam Gopnik has written, "that in two hundred years people will be reading someone's collected e-mail the way we read Edmund Wilson's diaries or Pepys's letters." Maybe — but will what they read be any good? E-mails are brief. (One doesn't blather; an overlong message might induce carpal tunnel syndrome in the recipient from excessive pressure on the Down arrow.) They are also — at least the ones I receive — frequently devoid of capitalization, minimally punctuated, and creatively spelled. E-mail's greatest strength — speed — is also its Achilles' heel. In effect, it's always December 26; you are not expected to write *Middlemarch*, and therefore you don't.

In a letter to his friend William Unwin, written on August 6, 1780, William Cowper noted that "a Letter may be written upon any thing or Nothing." This observation is supported by the index of *The Faber Book of Letters, 1578–1939*. Let us examine some entries from the *d* section:

> damnation, 87
> dances and entertainments, 33, 48, 59, 97, 111, 275
> dentistry, 220
> depressive illness, 81, 87
> *Dictionary of the English Language,* Johnson's, 61
> Diggers, 22
> dolphins, methods of cooking, 37

I have never received an e-mail on any of these topics. Instead, I am informed that Your browser is not Y2K-compliant. Your son left his Pokémon turtle under our sofa. Your column is 23 lines too long. Important pieces of news, but, as Lytton Strachey (one of the all-time great letter writers) pointed out, "No good letter was ever written to convey information, or to please its recipient: it may achieve both these results incidentally; but its fundamental purpose is to express the personality of its writer." *But wait!* you pipe up. *Someone just e-mailed me a joke!* So she did, but wasn't the personality of the sender slightly muffled by the fact that she forwarded it from an e-mail *she* received, and sent it to seventeen additional addressees?

I also take a dim, or perhaps a buffaloed, view of electronic slang. Perhaps I should view it as a linguistic milestone, as historic as the evolution of Cockney rhyming slang in the 1840s. But will the future generations who reopen our hard drives be stirred by the eloquence of the e-acronyms recommended by a Web site on "netiquette"?

BTDT   been there done that
FC   fingers crossed
IITYWTMWYBMAD
         if I tell you what this means will you buy me a drink?
MTE   my thoughts exactly
ROTFL   rolling on the floor laughing

RTFM   read the f——— manual
TAH   take a hint
TTFN   ta-ta for now

Or by the "emoticons," otherwise known as "smileys" — punc-
tuational images, read sideways — that "help readers interpret the
e-mail writer's attitude and tone"?

    :-) ha ha
    :-(boo hoo
    (-: I am left-handed
   %-) I have been staring at a green screen for 15 hours straight
   :-& I am tongue-tied
   {:-) I wear a toupee
   :-[I am a vampire
   :-F I am a bucktoothed vampire with one tooth missing
=|:-)= I am Abraham Lincoln

"We are of a different race from the Greeks, to whom beauty was
everything," wrote Thomas Carlyle, a Victorian progress-booster.
"Our glory and our beauty arise out of our inward strength, which
makes us victorious over material resistance." We have achieved a
similar victory of efficiency over beauty. I wouldn't give up e-mail if
you paid me, but I'd feel a pang of regret if the epistolary novels of
the future were to revolve around such messages as

Subject: **R U Kidding?**
From: Clarissa Harlowe <claha@virtue.com>
To: Robert Lovelace <lovelaceandlovegirlz@vice.com
hi bob, TAH. if u think i'm gonna run off w/ u, :-F, do u really think i'm
that kind of girl?? if you're looking 4 a trollop, CLICK HERE NOW:
http://www.hotpix.html. TTFN

I own a letter written by Robert Falcon Scott, the polar explorer, to
G. T. Temple, Esq., who helped procure the footgear for Scott's
first Antarctic expedition. The date is February 26, 1901. The envelope and octavo stationery have black borders because Queen
Victoria had died in January. The paper is yellowed, the handwriting is messy, and the stamp bears the Queen's profile — and the
denomination ONE PENNY. I bought the letter many years ago because, unlike a Cuisinart, which would have cost about the same, it

was something I believed I could not live without. I could never feel that way about an e-mail.

I also own my father's old wastebasket, which now holds my own empty Jiffy bags. Several times a day I use his stamp dispenser; it is tarnished and dinged, but still capable of unspooling its contents with a singular smoothness. And my file cabinets hold hundreds of his letters, the earliest written in his sixties in small, crabbed handwriting, the last in his nineties, after he lost much of his sight, penned with a Magic Marker in huge capital letters. I hope my children will find them someday, as Hart Crane once found his grandmother's love letters in the attic,

> pressed so long
> Into a corner of the roof
> That they are brown and soft,
> And liable to melt as snow.

FRANCINE DU PLESSIX GRAY

The Work of Mourning

FROM THE AMERICAN SCHOLAR

I

MOURNING is my theme, and a stack of recently published volumes on "grief work," as the counseling industry now calls bereavement, accumulates on my desk. If books are any harbinger of the communal psyche, taboos against the theme of death — an issue more rigorously banned from public discourse, in our time, than the most explicit sexuality — might well be waning. Consider these literary highlights: the most enduring title on the current bestseller list, *Tuesdays with Morrie,* chronicles the author's conversations with his dying mentor; the 1999 Pulitzer Prize for drama was awarded to *Wit,* which concerns a woman living through the last months of terminal cancer; outstanding among the nonfiction books of 1998 was Leon Wieseltier's *Kaddish,* a record of his mourning for his dead father; the spring's most prominent novel was Saul Bellow's *Ravelstein,* which is arguably an AIDS-memoir-cloaked-as-fiction; and among First Books, the literary phenomenon of the year is Dave Eggers's *A Heartbreaking Work of Staggering Genius,* the saga of two brothers, aged twenty-one and eight, who bravely and often farcically grieve for the deaths, six weeks apart, of their mother and father.

But the bulk of this literature of bereavement, a subdivision of the "recovery" genre filled with such buzz phrases as "coping responses," "task-based grief," "tactics for healing," and "tools for recovery," is far more pragmatically inclined. Typical recent titles are *The Mourning Handbook* and *Living with the End in Mind: A Practical*

Checklist for Living Life to the Fullest by Embracing Your Mortality, which describes itself as "a comprehensive, well-thought-out plan for preparing for death." Some of Bereavement Lit's most popular offerings suggest "strategies" for coping with the death of mothers, such as *A Mother Loss Workbook: Healing Exercises for Daughters.* And within that category lies a specific subdivision that urges us to see mom's passing as "A Way to Grow," such as *Remembering Mother, Finding Myself* and *Losing Your Parents, Finding Your Self,* the latter of which, the publishers claim, is bound "to strike a chord with baby boomers everywhere."

The shift of consciousness might well be traced to the pioneering work of Elisabeth Kübler-Ross, who for the third consecutive decade is urging us to weave the expectation of death into our understanding of life, to look on it as an expected companion rather than a dreaded stranger. Baby boomers — that demanding generation which came of age in the 1960s — are indeed beginning to confront the anxieties of aging and mortality. And the AIDS epidemic, which makes us cohabit with death more poignantly than at any other time in recent memory, may also be playing a dominant role in loosening our traditional reserve. It is worth noting that men are increasingly taking over the role of public mourner traditionally assigned, in the West, to women. The most unspeakable of losses, for instance, the death of children, is now frequently chronicled by men, some of them prominent journalists — witness *Being Brett: Chronicle of a Daughter's Death,* by Douglas Hobbie; *Give Sorrow Words: A Father's Passage Through Grief,* by Tom Crider; and *In the Wake of Death: Surviving the Loss of a Child,* by Mark Cosman.

The literature of widowhood — still predominantly a female genre — is equally abundant and often bears startlingly upbeat titles, such as *From Grief to Gladness: Coming Back from Widowhood* and *Widow to Widow: Thoughtful, Practical Ideas for Rebuilding Your Life* (readers' comments on Amazon.com: "indispensable tool," "great resource," "add to my wish list"). These titles are indeed far less melancholy than those given to books that suggest "coping techniques" for the owners of dying pets — *Angel Pawprints: Reflections on Loving and Losing a Canine Companion* and *Cold Noses at the Pearly Gates.*

Seeing this is America, there has also been a proliferation, in the past two years, of consumer-oriented books on circumventing the funeral industry by doing your own embalming and coffin making, such as *What Happens When You Die: From Your Last Breath to the First Spadeful*. There is a spate of works that deliberately resort to humor as a healing alternative, such as *Cry Until You Laugh: Comforting Guidance for Coping with Grief* and *The Definitive Guide to Underground Humor: Quaint Quotes About Death, Funny Funeral Home Stories and Hilarious Headstone Epitaphs*. I might note that I found only one book in this cornucopia specifically dedicated to losing fathers (*Longing for Dad: Father Loss and Its Impact*), and that the title that takes the cake is a widow's tale called *I'm Grieving as Fast as I Can*.

Freud would have been particularly appalled by that last title. And after leafing through a few of the above texts, sitting down to his great essay "Mourning and Melancholia" is like hearing the Emerson String Quartet strike up Beethoven's *Grosse Fugue* after suffering through hours of Mantovani's Strings. "Mourning and Melancholia" (the original German title is *Traüer Arbeit*, "The Work of Mourning") is majestic, aloof, austere, uncompromising. It remains the great classic on the issue of bereavement, and if one were forced to sum it up in two words, they would be "Time Out." Mourning, Freud constantly reminds us, is hard, slow, patient *work*, a meticulous process that must be carried out "bit by bit" (that phrase is repeated a half-dozen times), over a far vaster amount of time than twentieth-century society has allotted to any ritual of grief. Crucial to this toil, he tells us, is our careful examination, "piecemeal," as he puts it, of each association, each place, each belonging once shared with the departed *(don't* sell the house the first year, *don't* hasten to put the clothes away, continue to polish his/her silver). Equally essential are those traditional gestures of ritualized grief (memorial services, visits to a grave or commemorative site) that confirm the absence of the dead one. In this slow, long-drawn-out, and gradual work of severance, Freud writes, "each single one of the memories and situations of expectancy which demonstrate the libido's attachment to the lost object is met by the verdict of reality that the object no longer exists. . . . When this work has been accomplished the ego will have succeeded in freeing its libido from the lost object."

What happens if the work of mourning does not proceed on this detailed and stately course, if the enormous energy available for the labor of grief does not find its proper tools or associations? It can become what Freud calls "pathological mourning." Like those spirits of the dead in Greek literature who, if improperly mourned, return to cause malevolent mischief — devastating crops, destroying whole towns — the psychic energies of mourning, if repressed, can wreak grievous harm. They can turn inward into a dangerous process of self-devouring (as when we "eat our hearts out"). They can metamorphose into what we now call depression, a condition for which Freud preferred the more resonant, tradition-laden term *melancholia*. And, most tragically, they can give rise to self-hatred and self-destruction. "The patient represents his ego to us as worthless, incapable of any achievement and morally despicable, he reproaches himself, vilifies himself and expects to be cast out and punished. . . . This . . . delusion of mainly moral inferiority is completed by sleeplessness and refusal to take nourishment, and . . . by an overcoming of the instinct which compels every living thing to cling to life."

It is not traditional, but very useful, to read Freud and Homer simultaneously. What is most striking in both texts is the sheer energy civilized folk have devoted to rituals of mourning. Here I am in books 5, 6, and 7 of *The Iliad*, looking in on the clamorous terror of Homeric battle. Lances are being driven clear through eye sockets, livers, and genitals, brains pour out of mouths and severed heads, limbless torsos spin like marbles about the black-blooded earth, men catch their gushing bowels in their hands, crashing "thunderously as towering oaks" onto the blood-soaked ground, and throughout this mayhem there remains on both sides one obsession, one concern: to call an occasional truce that will let each side bury its dead properly. So onto this field of carnage warriors ride, carrying the olive branch, announcing a respite that will enable each camp to carry out its funeral rites. By mutual consent, and for this purpose only, all fighting stops. And on both sides the night is spent in lamentations, in washing and anointing the treasured corpses, in adorning funeral pyres with flowers and drenching them with wine, in honoring with cleansing fire the bones that will eventually be carried back to the warriors' homes. Quite as high and treasurable as wealth and fame, Homer intimates throughout this epic, is the honor of a proper funeral, and life's principal terror is the disgrace of being insufficiently mourned and inadequately buried.

Juxtaposing Freud and Homer over the years, I've come to understand that rituals not only express feelings but mold them and tame them; that mourning rites serve in great part to protect survivors from the excesses of their pain; and that agnosticism does not excuse us from respecting these institutions. For the less a society believes in the existence of a "soul" or "spirit," the more it may need to seek reassurance in specific funeral rites. In the view of some extreme materialists, in fact, whatever "spirit" we possess might rely all the more on a proper handling of our only dead-sure reality — the body. Think of the care lavished for decades on Lenin's embalmed remains in the belief that his psyche would continue to guide the nation as long as his body avoided corruption! Communism may never recover from Vladimir Ilyich's prosaic, unceremonious interment.

Mind you, until recently my own family has never been much good at mourning. There is the case of my stepfather, who bade me get rid of my mother's clothes within a week of her death, sold the house they'd lived in for forty-nine years within the month, and promptly had his second, near-fatal heart attack. There is the case of my husband's aunt, eighty-six-year-old Rosalind, who, after the death of her second husband, committed suicide while staying at a summer hotel with her baby sister, my eighty-four-year-old mother-in-law. "Just send her ashes parcel post!" her sons bellowed on the telephone from New York when queried about funeral arrangements. And there is the case of my own father, the love of my early life, whose only daughter is as late a mourner as can be found.

II

When my father, an officer in the Free French Air Force, was shot down over the Mediterranean in the first summer of World War II — I was nine years old — the news of his death was hidden from me for well over a year. My parents' marriage had been an unhappy one. I had always been under my father's supervision, idolizing my distant mother, a seductive, formidably ambitious woman, alternating warmth and glacial narcissism, with whom I had seldom even shared a meal until I came into her charge. She continued to hide his death from me after we came to America, leading me to believe that he was still alive, "somewhere in the Resistance." The news would be broken to me only by a family acquaintance. I wept solidly for months, and for years to come would follow strangers down the streets for hours under the delusion that my father was still alive, carrying out secret missions. There were precise geographic obstacles to my performing any of those gestures of ritualized grief needed, as Freud puts it, "to confirm the absence of the dead one." The burial site — a vast military cemetery on Gibraltar — lay thousands of miles across the ocean, and was made further unreachable by war.

My mother had been in love for years with a friend of her youth, and remarried soon after my father's death. The suddenness of the wedding, to which I was not invited, may have made my bereavement all the more complex. "The funeral baked meats did coldly furnish forth the marriage tables," says the quintessentially melancholic griever, Hamlet, upon his mother's remarriage. As my new parents banqueted on their long-awaited happiness, I was shunted out of their lives for weeks at a time to stay with various friends, warmhearted exiles as impecunious as we, whose only guest facilities were a living room couch. On these makeshift beds I often woke throughout the night shaking with tears, and was barely able to stay awake during the school day that ensued. I remember weeping with particular violence every time one of my birthdays came around, terrified that I was *getting very old*. "I am *decaying* with time" — such was the anxiety that plagued me as I turned twelve, thirteen, fourteen — "I'm getting so old that I can die at any time now." (It's worth noting that it was the theme of "Suicide and Children" — leitmotiv of a psychoanalytic conference held in Vienna in 1912 — that first inspired Freud to write "Mourning and Melancholia.") There was no one to whom I could communicate my anxiety; such confessions would have singled me out as "weird" among my peers, and my relationship with my mother was dictated by one delicate strategy — my attempts to win her love by being the cheerfully successful, "attractive" teenager, while constantly reminding her, as an extra bargaining chip, that I could not forgive her earlier neglect.

So in the following American years, my blissfully remarried mother would continue to evade every mention of my father, wipe away every trace of the warrior lying in his military grave thousands of miles across the ocean. Like my stepfather, she geared all activity to goals of social advancement and career, worked prodigiously hard, gambled, laughed, dined and entertained the years away as she sought out the company of the powerful, talented, and wealthy. (The dead are none of these; snobs are seldom good at mourning.) And within a year or two, I began to play her game, I began to forget with her, for it was by far the easier and lazier path. Gorgeous, fabulously successful, renowned for her scathing wit, she had survived the upheavals and famines of the Russian Revolution, a serious case of tuberculosis, an unhappy first marriage, the turmoil of our exodus from occupied France. Throughout this she had avoided all soul-searching and conversation, all mention of and confrontations with the past, and I wanted a piece of her action — her might, her power over others. We were the newly minted family in the new country off to a phenomenal new start. I joined my new parents in their memory-destroying dance, I collaborated like a traitor, I soon transferred to my charming, generous stepfather the affection I had borne for the dead warrior. I came to know the euphoria of burying the ancestral past rather than burying the dead. As for the terrors of my nightly awakenings, by late adolescence they were efficiently repressed, waning apace with most memories of my father, with most conscious interest in his life or death.

III

It is 1948 and I am a freshman at Bryn Mawr, playing the role of Ismene in a college production of Jean Anouilh's *Antigone*. According to what I've just learned in Western Civ, Antigone, custodian of primeval ritual observances, preserver of tribal memory, confronts her uncle Creon, the archetypal male technocrat who, in his obsession with political expediency, is ready to violate any divine law that stands in his way. Against the advice of her accommodating sister, Ismene, she safeguards her dead brother, a rebel against Creon's state, from suffering the greatest dishonor in Greek society — being left "unburied, food for the wild dogs and wheeling vultures." Following the dictates of her conscience and of the Greek religion, she offers her brother the burial rites forbidden him by Creon and suffers the consequences, going to her grave "unsung, unwed." Male *polis* versus female hearth: I have quite grasped these essentials and here I am, a proto-Marxist and militantly secular eighteen-year-old, sympathizing totally with the docile, pragmatic, panicky Ismene, even enjoying moments of approval for the tyrant Creon. Prosperity and survival above all! The orderly society must continue! The forces of progress must prevail! Antigone, in my eyes, is an unintelligibly *archaic* creature, morbid and freakish in her addiction to rites that I find *antiquated, meaningless* (I remember thinking those very words). How I disdain Antigone when she tells me, "You've chosen to live, and I to die." How I relish the moments when I chide my sister for venturing on "hopeless quests," for being "much possessed by death."

Only decades later did I grasp the link between Ismene's limp obedience to Creon and my own cowardice about the rites and rights of a dead one lost in war. Only recently have I realized that the role of Ismene, "that beauteous measure of the ordinary," as Kierkegaard describes her, was the one my mother and I had played together for some years. And I would continue to play it for decades to come. A few months after my rendering of Ismene, I received an unsettling letter from a beloved aunt and uncle, my father's favorite cousins, whom I had revisited briefly since the war. They were informing me that my father's body was about to be repatriated, that his remains were due back at the ancestral vault in Brittany the following July, that our family was gathering for the final burial, that everyone, of course, expected me to come. It was a few years after the war's end; I was eighteen years old. I remember a sense of being assaulted, of being threatened in some very private space that I now realize was the site of an inchoate, deeply sunken grief: how dare they order me to cross the ocean and appear on such and such a day for an abstract and tedious family duty! I was my mother's child; I remember thinking those very words: *tedious, abstract*.

So even though I fully planned to be in France that summer, I wrote back to my aunt telling her not to expect me; I crassly lied and said I could not leave the States that year. "Thank you for letting me know, there's no way I can make it, I'm so glad you'll be there." By which I meant, thanks for minding my business, just take care of it without me. Don't bother me with Memory, I was also saying, echoing my mother. I, too, was burying a parent through the slothful route of a postal service.

IV

Unlike Freud, who assigns to the work of mourning an evenly calibrated, methodical, almost industrial pace, Elisabeth Kübler-Ross divides the process of accepting death, which can be applied as well to the course of grief, into five often tumultuous stages: (1) denial ("No, not me"), (2) rage and anger ("Why me?"), (3) bargaining ("Yes, me, but . . ."), (4) depression ("Yes, me"), (5) acceptance of death ("It's okay, my own time is close"). Kübler-Ross's schema is not that different from the Judaic view of the mourning process, which recognizes the following four phases: (1) three days of deep grief, often ritualized through the *kriyah* or rending of clothes, symbol of the rage and internal tearing asunder that survivors often feel upon their loss; (2) seven days of mourning — "sitting *shivah*" — during which relatives and acquaintances visit the mourners, who are thus able to retell and relive their memories of the deceased and share their emotions; (3) thirty days of gradual readjustment; (4) eleven months of remembrance and healing.

According to these approaches, I seem to have been one of those pathological Hamletian mourners who spend decades in a folly of stage 1. For a few years in my twenties I was settled in Paris, with a job as a journalist. I knew only too well the exact site of my father's tomb at his family's vault in Brittany, but did not once return to visit it. I saw my father's closest friend and confidant, Pierre F, one of the dearest persons of my childhood, and changed the subject whenever he began to speak of his dead comrade. I turned away from the charming, accomplished woman who I knew had been my father's lover for several prewar years, and I never called either one of his companions during the several visits I made to France in the following fifteen years. When visiting with my aunt and uncle, subtle, prescient beings who had grasped the nature of my reticence and knew never to press me on the issue of my father, I prattled on about politics, my Paris men and jobs, and later my marriage, my two children.

But many of us are thrust out of that first stage of rage and denial by the approach of middle age, that often cataclysmic time of reassessment which can readily unclench a flood of new emotions about memory and grief. In the spring of 1970, almost thirty years after my father's death, I suddenly felt an urgent, unprecedented need to learn all there was to know about him, craved every shred of information about his character, his idiosyncrasies, the nature of his fate. When I went to Paris that year, I asked my uncle to help me look up both of my father's only surviving friends. The beautiful woman had just died the previous year. Pierre F was suffering from terminal cancer, and a month after I'd returned to the United States I received a note from my uncle telling me that Pierre had died. I'd arrived at the treasures — the repositories of much of the information I was seeking — a few months too late.

In the following years, my regret and guilt, my long-repressed tenderness for these two links to my childhood, turned into a new wave of rage and self-hatred, as did every aspect of my long cowardice concerning my father's memory. If I followed Kübler-Ross, I would say that, like other grievers disadvantaged by history or circumstance, I jumbled the three middle stages of mourning — anger, bargaining, depression — into one dangerously turbulent phase. The plight of such survivors is described in a recently published volume of my Bereavement Lit collection, *Ambiguous Loss: Learning to Live with Unresolved Grief*, which deals with the perilous belated syndromes caused by the loss of loved ones "not known to be alive or dead," "missing in action, lost due to immigration or adoption." Such mourners can relive the self-reproaching depression they suffered in their youth, such as those fits of anxiety I knew as a child when I had woken, weeping, in near-strangers' living rooms. ("Ambiguous loss," I read in the book just cited, "is unique in that the trauma goes on and on . . . [and] alternates between hope and hopelessness.") Much of life's meaning can be threatened. There can be impulses to self-destruction. "My heart was utterly darkened," Saint Augustine wrote as he relived the death of a boyhood friend. "I became a great riddle to myself, and asked my soul, *why she was so sad, and why she disquieted me sorely;* but she knew not what to answer me."

I sought help. It was suggested that I should, at long last, visit my father's grave.

During an extended stay with my aunt, whom I finally encouraged, indeed constantly exhorted, to share every crucial and trivial

detail she remembered about our mutual lost love — be it his generosity, his expertise in tennis and Oriental art, or his heroism in
war — I finally acquired the courage to return to the ancestral
vault where he is buried. There is a passage in my novel *Lovers and
Tyrants* in which I describe the first visit of my protagonist, Stepha-
nie, to her (my) father's tomb:

> I kneel down on the sealing stone which stands between me and the
> dead, that separates his body from mine. . . . And then suddenly my lib-
> eration comes. I am free now, kneeling on the stone, suddenly free and
> shaking, my head resting against the rusty metal handle that could be
> lifted for our reunion. I weep, I shake, I pound at the floor with my
> head, I kick it, I beat it with my hands. . . . He is there, he is there, he is
> there. Above all else he is now allowed to live in my memory, totally re-
> stored and whole now, as if resurrected, the reality of his death ac-
> cepted, faced.

I may have been a bit optimistic in that passage. But I do know that
I've rejected Ismene and come close to embracing Antigone. I've
come to understand that Creon's refusal to accept an equipoise between the rights of the living and those of the dead — a balance essential to our psychic survival — is what brings on his own destruction.

I've also come to know that healthy mourning has to do with re-
learning reality; that we must cease to desire the loved ones' return
and must recreate a new psychic space in which we continue to
love them in absence and separation. Above all, I now realize that
we can only continue to propagate their values, their lives' meanings, by some dynamic interaction with the story of their lives, that
information is our most valuable treasure, that we may have to
learn those life narratives before we can begin the proper work of
grief.

So go for it! I say to my students when they inform me that they
want to tape the recollections of a grandmother, a great-granddun-
cle, their own guardians of tribal memory. Go for it now, or you
may get there too late, as I did. Do it for me.

V

It is June 2000, and there's so much to do at Mother's grave! I must
prune the rhododendrons, give them a particularly good feeding

after this arduous winter, perhaps put in some new evergreens on either side of the tombstone that surmounts her ashes and bears her name and dates — Tatiana Iakovleva du Plessix Liberman, 1906–1991. She lies half a mile from my house as the bird flies, less than a mile on foot. In the proper weather I can even walk a few hundred yards down my road and cut across a wide swath of fields, and there she is under a bed of myrtle, at the northwest end of my village cemetery. My husband and I chose this plot for our entire family a few decades ago. I have been easy, familiar with death ever since my near breakdown at my father's tomb. Mother had gone in first, waiting for us, and now, as of the past winter, my cherished stepfather's name and dates are engraved below hers. After I've pruned and fed the rhodies I must weed the myrtle, a hellish task to get at the lawn grass without breaking the delicate roots — I am possessive, tidy if not narcissistic about Mother's grave, as she was with her own appearance in life. I feel guilty, for instance, about the current sparseness of the foliage on the rhodies; I failed to wrap them in burlap last fall, as I had in previous years, to shelter them from our icy winters. It had been a hellish November, with my dearest friend, Ethel C, dying just four days before my stepfather, and as I moved from mourning to mourning I kept forgetting the burlap each time I went to visit Mother. . . . Beyond my frequent horticultural checks, and birthdays and Christmases, I come to see her on every important occasion of the year — before taking a trip abroad, for instance, as if to get her blessing, and when a new grandchild is born, to share the joy, and upon crises, to glean counsel. . . . I suppose that having her near me, visitable upon a moment's whim, is a way of taming her, of having her under my control. For by the time I reached adulthood she had tried to make up for the past with invasive possessiveness, generosity. I had fought back, guarding my frontiers at every step, deviously continuing to charm her while reminding her that I'd never quite forgiven her theft and botching of my father's memory. A decade ago, when she started shuttling back and forth to the hospital and I knew she had no great time left, I started visiting her obsessively, regretting — too late, of course, it is always too late — that I had not started earlier to give and to forgive. She was deeply pleased, but continued to take pleasure in plying her sarcasm. "You know, everyone loves me except you," she once announced, sitting up from her pillows as if she were serving for the match.

"You," she said, pointing her long clawed finger, "are merely *afraid* of me." She fell back on her bed. "Just teasing," she added with a grin of sadistic satisfaction. Take that. She died a few weeks later. I sat with her in the intensive care unit a few hours before her end, pressing my face upon hers, begging her forgiveness and outpouring mine, for whatever it was worth. What a model you have been, after all, I told her. What force and shrewdness and power of survival you passed on to me, despite your cowardice. Thank you, my love, I'll never cease to thank you. What pride I took, following her death, in doing all that my stepfather's own illness disabled him from doing — funeral home, newspapers, church and flowers, hosting a wake for hundreds of guests. I had gone through every stage of filial struggle with her — wrath, rebellion, reconciliation, acceptance — and now at last I knew the luxury of properly mourning a parent. As my family and I passed by her open coffin at the Russian Orthodox church service, I felt — beyond my immense sorrow, that brutal sense of physical severance most deeply suffered by daughters — something that resembled a kind of triumph: dear God, I've survived her. And now that her grave is totally under my control, she is my docile little girl, sandstone-soft, every memory of her to be sculpted and honed according to my whims. I can erase the sites of darkness and retain only the very best of her — the scathing intelligence, the rage to live, the acts of extravagant kindness. There's nothing like a grave, particularly if your life was almost botched for lack of one. Now the guardians are all gone, I reflect as I drastically prune the rhododendrons back in hopes that they'll regrow, they're all gone, and I'm the sole custodian, the weight of memory and information is all on me, to share or to withhold, I'm finally in charge.

JEFFREY HEIMAN

Vin Laforge

FROM THE MASSACHUSETTS REVIEW

VIN LAFORGE ran the dump. In town they called him the master garbologist because of the tight hold he kept on the green and red levers that controlled the main compactor and also because he liked to talk. He sat in the shack beside the compactor and saw people come and go on Wednesdays, Saturdays, and Sundays, and he knew everyone from Southfield to Mill River. Even my father, loading trash cans into the car on a weekend morning, would call out, "See you tomorrow," and spend a while with a few locals standing by Vin's shack listening to stories of whoever was building or tearing down or in the hospital. But Vin was careful about what he said; he never badmouthed anyone except the doctors who ordered him to keep an inhaler in his shirt pocket instead of a pack of cigarettes, and he never betrayed a confidence except when it came to how much someone had overpaid for a power tool. He wouldn't tell you any more than you already knew about Mike Johns, one of the town kids in jail for his second DWI, and he would not talk about the path that used to run up through the woods from his house in town to my father's house on East Hill when the house belonged to its former owners, Jim and Bea Riordan. The house that became my father's was about a half-mile walk from the Laforge place, around the duck pond in back of the old whip factory, through birches and maples and across a few old stone walls left over from the days when that forest had been clearcut. Aside from a short stretch that led from the bottom of our lawn to the town well, which was under a tiny, shingled A-frame that looked like an elf house, nothing was left of the path. And my father never walked farther than that well, though he knew all the trees in the woods around the house and would cut and split the dead ones for next winter's fires. It's possible that very few people knew about the path, since Vin alone had cut and maintained it so as not to have to explain why he visited Bea Riordan two or three times a week when they were young and married to other people. Maybe her husband Jim did know, but it would have seemed a fair trade for the afternoons he spent with Vin's wife, Katherine, in the shade of an overhanging rock off the Norfolk Road.

That was forty or fifty years ago, when Jim was fire chief for the town of New Marlboro and Vin was building houses throughout the southern Berkshires and their wives were stocking shelves at the new Great Barrington Library. On weekends the four of them would get together, always walking to each other's houses on the road — never on the path through the woods — to play cards and drink. When my father bought the house from the Riordans in the spring of 1978, the kitchen cabinets were full of nearly empty bottles of rye and gin and Hiram Walker brandies, which they drank out of highball glasses with golfers and fishermen painted on the sides. At that point I knew as much as any twenty-year-old about drunkenness, though I'd never had more than a beer with my father, and we packed up most of the bottles without letting on to each other what we may have been thinking of the parties in the house that seemed to go on for years. But in the middle of the process he reached around a cabinet door and tapped me on the arm with a full bottle of brandy. "You want this?" he said. "They left a whole bottle." I did want it. I wanted to combine the dregs of all the like-colored liquors to make full bottles and take them back to college. I wanted the empty fish-shaped bottle for a candle holder. But I sensed he might have been baiting me, and so I said no. It's not that he would have given me the bottle and then accused me of drinking it, but I didn't want to admit to a taste I was not sure I had. Also in the kitchen there was a drawer full of playing cards and poker chips and coasters, and in the living room a liquor crate with 78 rpm recordings of old big bands. There were beds and cots in every free space.

The first time I met him, Vin was drinking coffee on a bench outside the Southfield General Store, the only store in town. It was just before eight on a Saturday morning and already a few of the town's 149 residents were on their lawns, pushing mowers, seeding, cutting shingles to replace what had rotted in winter. The weekenders, most of whose homes were hidden up on East Hill (and who were not counted as part of the official population), were still asleep, but my father, also a weekender, was already inside the store running his hands over a side of beef and showing Bob Orman, the new proprietor, how to get the best steaks and chops. Bob was a former high school history teacher from Michigan who had moved east to marry and had very little idea how to set up shop. My father, who spent his first twenty years after college at the butcher block in his father's grocery store, and then in his own, was a valuable resource. He went down every weekend morning for a cup of coffee and the chance to show Bob or his wife, Susan, what size lump of chop meat made up a pound, and he would be right to within half an ounce. You could blindfold him and place his fingers on a slab of meat, and he'd tell you how many days ago it had been cut. And he knew how much marbled fat a steak could have in it and still be called lean. This was early summer in 1978, and that weekend all the milkweed pods along East Hill Road had opened and sent their cotton blowing down the street in Southfield, filling every crevice and creating drifts up the sides of houses. I had to kick through mounds of it to find the two steps up to the store.

"It looks like snow," I said to Vin, whom my father had introduced me to when he went inside a minute earlier.

"That's right." He took another sip and smiled, showing teeth the color of his milky coffee. "We're expecting three to five tonight.

I finally got to know Vin over the spring and summer of 1997 when I was hauling four or five loads a weekend to the dump before selling the house. At seventy-eight Vin had lost some of the bulk around his chest but the skin of his face was still taut and tan from outdoor work and his hair had only in the past few years started to show streaks of silver. He was still interested in everything, and I came to enjoy the odd pulse of our conversation. He didn't seem to feel it was necessary, or maybe even proper, to respond to a comment right away. Even "nice day" would take him a few seconds to think into. "This day" (he said after one such comment from me) "in nineteen and forty-four Eddie Hughes from over in Sheffield got sent off to Mindanao. Never came back."

"Must have been a sad day, that you remember it so well." I was pitching bags of trash from the open gate of our station wagon into the compactor, and Vin was leaning on the door frame of the shack, a few feet away.

"Well, no, not for me, but it was cold that night, about thirty, and Kate and I were up the Riordan place, your place. Eddie Hughes was his cousin."

I tried to imagine my father standing there with Vin, but I could not get far. My father was impatient. He would tip the kitchen clock forward ten minutes so that when we had to go out as a family we were never late. At functions he would say "Is that so?" until hives broke out on his neck, clipping all his replies unless the conversation was about business. And yet he liked Vin, whose own sentences ticked off from all points on the clock, and wanted to spend time with him. There must have been something else. I started to wonder how much of the history of our house my father knew and never spoke about, and I liked the idea that he knew it in a way completely differently from me, as if the house itself were an old machine, the only one of its kind, and my father its only mechanic. I wanted to ask Vin for something more specific, but he lifted his face with a sudden memory.

"That old meat smoker . . . rusted barrel in the corner of your garage. That was his . . . Eddie's. Put it there before he left so Jim could use it. Never seen it here in all these years, so I figure it must still be there."

I knew the device he meant, though I never knew what it was.

"I'll take it if you don't see a use for it in New York."

One day, a week or so later, he came out of the shack as I was about to heave two rusted bicycles into the dumpster for metal objects and asked me to leave them on the side for Enda Connolly to fix up for his kids. A box of washers, screws, and hinges he had me put right into the trunk of his own car for his son-in-law, who had taken over the construction business he had retired from in the mid-eighties. With little else to do then, Vin began keeping his friend John, the former dumpmaster, company. When John died in 1989, it seemed only natural for Vin to paint his own name on the sign and take the job officially. The town voted him in without a hitch. "Doesn't matter what-all sizes they are," he said, fingering through the box as I held it. "James'll use them."

On another Sunday in late May, as I unloaded a stack of rotten shingles and siding, he came up to the car and said, "Look at them clapboards. Would they be from the shed out back of your place?" He had wide thumbs and he pressed one into the porous wood.

"There is no shed out back, but there is one at the side of the house. You know the one, my father built it."

He gently rubbed and stared into the moist, split-open grains of the siding. "Well, there's a trick of memory. You're right, but there was a fine little shed back there up until some time ago, when the house belonged to Bea Riordan's father. You know he gave the house to Bea and Jim? Built the house in nineteen and eight for two thousand dollars."

"I didn't know, but that would have been William Benn, right? He left all the books."

"Right-o. Professor Benn down at Yale College, down in Connecticut. Used to keep his secretary in the shed and his wife in the house. Same weekend, too."

"You've got to be kidding. I thought people were discreet around here."

"Oh, he was careful. Like I said, she was his secretary and he used to spend all night back there writing books with her." He broke one of the strips of siding in two and pointed to tiny insect larvae and white eggs inside. "Ants'll do this when the ground is too wet or cold. Had some books to his name to prove it."

Vin was interesting and his spin on the word *books* made him funny. But I didn't know why he was telling me this unless he wished me to understand that not even the cover of thick forest keeps the secrets of one house concealed. There was a nervous chuckle inside me about our sheltered house up on East Hill. I wasn't sure how he would read my laugh, and so I flipped some of the rotten clapboards into the dumpster. "Lot of activity around here," I said, nodding toward the three or four cars unloading in different parts of the clearing and asking him covertly how much he knew about my father.

It was only a few days before that I'd learned from Allen Welch, a local builder who helped out at the store, about the path through the woods that Vin had cleared fifty years ago to get to Benn's daughter, Bea Riordan. "Oh, they had a thing," Allen had said. "Weren't that many amusements then. My dad told me about it, so it must have been fairly widely known. Vin and Bea."

The approach to the dump was a winding track off the Sandis-field Road. It was so rutted that unless the compactor was in opera-tion anyone sitting in the shack would hear a car bouncing up, es-pecially a car as laden as mine. I had gotten into the habit of stopping in to say hello to Vin before unloading the car, but since we were about three weeks away from turning over the house to its new owners, with only half the attic emptied, I went one Sunday di-rectly to the recyclable-paper bin on the far side of the clearing and threw away two boxes of my essays and notes from college and dozens of letters. This was hard to do, but with everything I'd al-ready brought home, there wasn't enough closet space in my New York apartment to shove in another pair of socks. The night before I sat among the spilled trays of poison and desiccated mouse pelts in the attic and read by flashlight through my notebooks on Re-naissance History, Primitive Christianity, Pre-Socratic Philosophy, and even Small Business Management — a course my father sug-gested I take or risk losing a good part of my monthly allowance — more interested in my handwriting than in the words on the pages. I must have been an earnest student, somehow managing to make every letter legible and still copy down nearly every word my pro-fessors said; I must have intended to learn something in college. Where I was bored there were drawings in the margins of old men with big noses and witticisms — usually at the professor's expense and meant to be seen by the girl in the next seat — vomiting out of their wide-open mouths. In my attic seat against a trunk I looked down and saw a boy's fingers on my hand holding the pen and put-ting song lyrics that I thought would better express my feelings into letters nearly twenty years ago to Sarah, to Joanne; I reread notes my father had sent me, typed with the script ball on his IBM Selectric, and saved them all and remembered what a dope I thought he was for telling me that "there are a lot of fish in the sea" and everything will "work out fine." I tucked into a folder a few notes and syllabi I thought I might be able to use in classes I now teach and put the rest of the notebooks into boxes for trash.

When I rested the first box on the edge of the recycle bin I re-membered how much of the old world inside had been opened to me the night before and I worried that with these notes and letters would go the keys to memory, the connective tissues that hold a body of life together. Simultaneously I felt the kind of strange, pleasurable spite that a dieter must feel in denial. It has to be good for me. If it isn't good for me, it just has to be. It has to be because my father is dead. He killed himself and because of that I have two lives now, a before and an after.

I dragged a broken dresser to the area for building debris, feeling benevolent. In a few weeks this piece of furniture would be hammered together, repainted and holding someone else's clothes. Then I got in the car and backed up to the compactor. I was surprised with all the noise I'd made that Vin hadn't come out of the shack. When I stepped inside — the shack was about a five-by-five-foot square with two ten-gallon drums for seats and strips of shag carpet tacked to the walls for insulation — I saw that he was concentrating on a Victoria's Secret catalogue, flipping pages slowly and angling them up for a better view. He must have scavenged it from the paper bin, which made me wonder if I should retrieve some of the letters I had never sent and just now thrown out.

"Jeffrey." He looked up. Despite the tactful New England evasions I knew Vin was capable of, he neither laughed off the catalogue nor put it away, and I took this to be an invitation into a circle my father may have joined. There were breasts and lace and bare stomachs between us, between the three of us. I felt awkward, but since Vin didn't seem to notice I tried to push the new intimacy.

"Now I see why my dad used to like to come down here."

"Well, that's right, he did." Vin put down the catalogue and spread a stack on the floor with the tip of his boot. He picked up a mailing from Land's End, thumbed through it backward and stopped on a page of outerwear. "Polartec . . . that's all these plastic bottles," he said, raising a finger crimped like half a hexagon toward the dumpster behind me. Maybe I had disturbed him. He didn't seem to want to talk. Anyway, it was about one forty-five, and if you showed up any time after one thirty — the dump closed at two — Vin wouldn't have much to say. But for some reason, perhaps because in three weeks from now I'd say goodbye for good, I kept on.

"He liked to come down here because he liked to talk to you."

This too felt wrong, as if I'd used the familiar form of address with an elder I did not know well, never mind that we had just been gawking at pictures of nearly naked women. He looked beyond me at wind-bending birches on the back side of East Hill, shifted his weight on the paint drum, crossed one leg over the other. It was late spring but the breeze was still a bit too cool.

"Oh, yes, Paul liked to talk, but he was a busy man."

"He was always working, if not in the woods then in the shop downstairs." I stepped up onto the floor of the shack and leaned against the frame, hoping Vin wouldn't feel cornered but not willing to let him get away. "Always had some project going."

"Did a lot of work up there. Say, I think if I remember you have a wood turner up there. Would that still be in the back by the furnace?"

"A lathe?" It was odd that he knew the layout of the basement.

"Lathe, right. You want to get rid of it? I know my son-in-law would be interested."

"Let me see about that. I'm not sure what it's worth."

"Oh, I know how much your dad paid for it," he said, as if these things were always public. "I couldn't give you that, but James and I might get up a couple hundred."

Vin was lisping, drawing out the *s*'s, thickening the *th*'s, not fully closing his mouth after speaking. I looked at his teeth. They were too good, too clean, obviously not fitting comfortably. I remembered I used to be able to tell on the phone which set of dentures my father had in by the sharpness of his sounds. *Yes* seemed to be easier for him to say than *no* when he had the wrong teeth in, and so sometimes I profited from his discomfort.

"How'd you know about the lathe?"

"Oh, Paul used to get so excited about his new tools. Like a kid, he'd talk about them. Never saw someone so busy with tools and his books about tools."

He stood up and looked over me into the compactor. He put his hand on the green lever and then took it off. What he'd said was true, but it still seemed more than a stranger should know.

"He loved his wood. That's what made him happy."

"Is that right?"

"Isn't that what you just said?" I was sure Vin just wanted to close up and go home. "Anyway, he always said he wanted to live here."

"After the fast life in New York City, it would seem kind of slow."

"Yes, he should have slowed down."

Vin looked directly at me, put his hand back on the green lever and pulled it, even though the compactor was only half full. The hydraulic press inched forward loudly. Deep inside trash bags popped. "He should have taken it easier," I said.

"That's exactly what I said to him."

"You talked about this?"

"Well, sure. I thought he was crazy, always running like that. Where's there to run to? I said to him, 'Paul, slow down. Do it tomorrow. You'll get a heart attack.' And you know what he said to me?"

"I bet he said there's nothing to worry about."

"He said, 'There isn't time.'"

"What did that mean?"

"Don't know."

"How long before he died did he say that to you?"

"Don't know."

I hired a trash hauler to clear out the rest of the attic and basement because there was too much outdoor work to do before turning over the house. The real estate agent had warned us the day before that the buyers were entitled to a "walk through" on the morning of the closing and could justly back out of the contract if they saw that I had not removed all the crap blown onto the lawn from winter storms, or even cut the lawn since last fall. We could not take that risk. No one else had been interested in the house and negotiations on price with this couple had taken nearly three months. It would have been more than a thousand dollars to have the lawn work done by a landscaper, and so I filled the wheelbarrow five or six times with fallen branches, new weeds, and last year's leaves and dumped it all in the woods off the mossy, shaded side, next to the mounds my father left each fall and spring. I saw Vin one rainy Saturday morning before eight when I went into the store for coffee. He never asked again about the lathe. He did tell me that the bicycles took a soak the night I left them but Enda Connolly had salvaged them the next week and his kids were already toodling down the Norfolk Road. We sat quietly together watching the rain from the covered veranda outside the store. "It's really coming down," I said. He said he'd never seen it go up.

EDWARD HOAGLAND

Calliope Times

FROM THE NEW YORKER

IN THE SPRING of 1951, when I was eighteen and finishing my freshman year at Harvard, I wrote to Ringling Brothers and Barnum & Bailey Circus to ask for a job, spurred in particular by my fascination with animals. At home in Connecticut I'd kept dogs, cats, turtles, snakes, alligators, pigeons, opossums, and goats, and knew from seeing the circus perform in Madison Square Garden that it would give me access to bigger creatures. The nightly travel, the exotic crafts and dangerous skills, the association with other handicapped people (I stuttered) who had made a go of life under the big top were more nebulous attractions. I believed I had an intuitive understanding of animals and wanted to test it. To my surprise, a brief note from Winter Quarters in Sarasota, Florida, enclosing a schedule of the route, informed me that I could have a job with the Animal Department if I showed up when school let out. Luckily, my parents didn't object; in both of their families young men went out into the world during the summer and worked — my father on a cattle ship from San Francisco to Europe after his sophomore year, my mother's brothers at logging jobs in the north woods.

Hitchhiking to the show's one playing date in Connecticut that year, near Hartford, I caught my last ride with a middle-aged woman who seemed excited to be helping a boy "run away to join the circus." I thanked her and left the road, surveying and then carefully crossing the intricate tumult of the vast lot, clutching my folded note. Canvas trucks and water trucks roared around. Clowns were changing behind a wagon. A tumbler stood on his hands. Two Caterpillar tractors hitched onto the tongues of a series of other wagons and pulled them into the proper positions. The immense oval of the billowing big top, ocean blue and about five hundred feet long and two hundred feet wide, had already been erected, with flags flapping from the five center poles. A man, a tiny figure, was adjusting the air vents way up on the ridgeline. The sideshow and other satellite tops and tents — olive or white or brown — were laid out all around, with personnel exceeding a thousand moving about, and three times that many rubberneckers. The seethe was matter-of-fact and orderly, however. Performers loafing or darting on errands were dressed like ragamuffins but with astute, daredevil faces. Several elephants had returned from pulling the quarter poles of the big top into place and were being washed and watered.

This was not yet a show. This was an itinerant city. I headed for where the elephants were chained to stakes pounded into the ground in a half-circle: twenty-four elephants, swaying forward and sideways and back, swinging their nimble trunks in idiosyncratic private rhythms. The men who were idly supervising them carried wooden clubs with iron hooks attached to one end, which they leaned on as they stood in the sun and swung like baseball bats if they had to be punitive. These were big men, compared with the agile, wiry horse hands who ran beside their charges during the performance and rode them back and forth like a rodeo string between the railroad yards and the circus lot, morning and night. The elephant men rode, too, from the train, in a more august procession, sitting like mahouts on the elephants' necks, and they were slow-fuse types, tall-legged, barrel-bodied. I approached three of them who were guarding the herd to proffer my note from the front office in Sarasota.

"This ain't the Animal Department. This is Number Twelve Wagon," the bulkiest guy told me, pointing at the Elephant Department's wagon nearby, with the number stenciled on it, and a tent alongside. "You're looking for Number Ten Wagon."

I nodded my thanks, following where he had pointed, and soon spotted Number 10, a fourteen-foot, red-painted wagon on rubber wheels about fifty yards away. It had a certain air of éclat, having belonged to the Al G. Barnes and Sells-Floto Combined Circus during the thirties, and the door at the back was open. An old man with white hair, named Blackie Barlow, sat on a folding chair inside, over the four-foot ladder. A tarpaulin had been tied from the roof like a tent fly on one side to cover half a dozen footlockers, or "crumb boxes," as they were called, and a water barrel and buckets stood beside that. A pickup truck was also parked there, and from its bed a cluster of men had just pulled a dead horse. A Mohawk Indian called Chief was beginning to chop at the horse to dismember it.

A stunning sight, if I had paused to figure it out or let it rattle me. But I went instead to the white-haired man, who was watching from just inside the wagon with an ironic, not unkind smile.

He had a quiet voice with a South Florida accent, and he looked at my note, observing cursorily that I was unable to answer a question because I stuttered, and pointed without further comment to a bigger, fortyish gentleman in a flannel shirt and chino slacks, who was supervising the butchering of the horse. This was the menagerie's head, C. R. Montgomery, who, with his wife, traveled ahead of the show buying horses from farmers when food for the big cats was needed, as well as all the other animal food, and dickered with zoo directors in the towns we stopped in, if a trade seemed desirable. He knew what creatures a dealer had coming in on a ship from Siam or Sumatra to New York or Miami, and he could help the circus veterinarian with basic treatments. C.R. was an all-around animal man of the sort that circuses used to have. He paused to read my note, grinned at Blackie with raised eyebrows, and stopped Chief from chopping the horse to hand me the ax.

I wanted this job, and it was a dead horse lying in front of me, not a sufferer, so I swung and swung at the carcass's haunches, my sneakers slipping in the blood, while Chief and my future comrades Ray and Bible gathered around laughing. After I had proved that I was willing to try doing what I was told, C.R. took the ax away before I lost my footing and hurt myself with it.

"I guess we gotta hire him," he said. Blackie gave me a meal ticket and put me under the wing of Bible, a bespectacled ex-con who took care of Buddy, the baby orangutan; Chester, the big "Nile Hippopotamus"; Betty Lou, the pygmy hippo from West Africa; Bobby, the "African One-Horned Black Rhinoceros"; and a chimp, some green and mangabey monkeys, and an Amazonian tapir. He also helped Ray with the giraffes.

Bible was a reader, a soft-spoken man, a peacemaker, reasonable and civil, a sort of oasis of calm, except during the seizures of binge drinking that ripped out the fabric of his life from time to time. He kept his distance from most of the other workhands, perhaps out of fear that the more visible alcoholism and other problems, from epilepsy to schizophrenia, that some of them had would capsize his fragile equilibrium. And it did collapse after a few weeks, whether by this contagion or an internally haywire clock. Then, like so many of the men I worked with, he disappeared — present at teardown but gone by dawn.

Ray, on the other hand, lasted. A cynic, a curser, a dirty-joke teller, Ray reminded me of a bus driver I had had in school who was raffish, irreverent, unkempt, and taught little kids to snigger and smoke, or told them how sex was accomplished if they wanted to know, but who was steadier than he looked — always showed up early, drove safely, and discouraged behavior that was mean or cruel. Ray was so dependable that he didn't travel two-to-a-bunk, tiered three bunks high, in the windowless dormitory railroad cars that the rest of us fourteen-dollar-a-week men were confined to. Instead, Baby Irene, the Fat Lady, took him into her private compartment on a different train, and bought him clothes that (for all of his talk about how Irene complained his cock "couldn't get past the creases") he kept clean and pressed. He took excellent care of the giraffes, and functioned as a number-three man, after C.R. and Blackie, in the Animal Department. He'd only drink in a beer joint on the nights that it was safe because we were playing a big city and weren't going to travel; the train wouldn't pull out without him.

We had seventy railroad cars on three trains, forty-one of them flatcars for carrying the wagons in which everything, from the cookhouse to the fliers' aerial rigging, was then hauled to the lot. Chester the hippopotamus and Bobby the black rhinoceros had special twenty-foot cage-wagons, and the giraffes, Edith and Boston, were in taller, boxy constructions. Twelve performing bears were crowded into a twenty-two-foot barred wagon. The menagerie and cookhouse traveled on the first train, called the Flying Squadron. We would leave town first — before the performance was over if the hop was long and we needed to — to arrive in the next town around four-thirty in the morning. Ringstock (the ninety performing horses) and the elephants and the men who handled them traveled on the second train, along with the sideshow, the candy butchers, the ushers, the propmen, the pole wagons, seat wagons, canvas wagons, and the canvas crew, who tore down the big top and put it up again the next day. They got in several hours after us; the performers, in sleeper beds or compartments on the third train, arrived after eleven.

But the shrimp-pink dawn was *ours*. In every town, hundreds of small kids had been roused and brought to the railroad yard by their conscientious parents to marvel at our arrival. They stood overhead on a bridge or on the nearest roofs, and lined the service road and the vacant lots, waving politely, timidly calling. When we'd been shuttled by bus the few miles to the new circus lot, we would build a bonfire of scrap wood and stand around it or squat on our heels, waiting for the cookhouse tent to go up and smoke from the stoves to rise — coffee, oatmeal, toast, and eggs — and for our animals to come, while many more locals wandered near, wanting to speak, or waited to witness whatever we did: blow a harmonica, walk to the river, whittle a stick. There was often a river at hand, Ohio-sized or a little one, because the circus grounds were waste grounds, sparsely used during the rest of the year except for a carnival, a revival meeting, or a county fair. Most boosters and businessmen turned their backs on the riverbank for development in the fifties, until nearly all the other land was gone. Rivers had seemed disreputable, like highways now — the haunt of bargemen and tugmen, raftsmen, flatboatmen, keelboatmen, freightmen, drifters, prostitutes, and tramps — a place for fly-by-night people in hobo jungles.

Bible liked to sleep out next to the wagons on the flatcars in balmy weather, instead of inside our rattling, claustrophobic crew cars, having no doubt acquired a love for the open sky in prison. And I sometimes joined him when the moon was out. Crossing Indiana and Iowa, you could hear the lions sniff at their ventilation slats for the smells of the veldt and roar to see if a lion out there on the prairie would answer; they thumped the walls when they scented the Mississippi, or the forests of Minnesota, or the Platte River in Nebraska. When the train slowed, I was sometimes tempted to open their cages so they could go find a life for themselves in the wild, however abbreviated. These were glory nights, vivid nights.

*

I don't remember my various bedmates inside the sleeping car, except if they had nightmares or if a man was so husky that he crowded me on the narrow pallet and I had to lie on my side, keeping my arms over my head in order to sleep. Though we lacked windows, the open gratings in the side of the car provided plenty of wind and a loud lullaby of clicketing rails, pistoning wheels, and the occasional wail of the locomotive's long whistle. Our sixteen-hour workdays, too, encouraged everybody to sleep. When I did have bad dreams, they were very sudden, precipitated by another train on the opposite track roaring past at high speed with a shrieking scream. I would imagine not the train but an elephant stampeding, trumpeting, with me in its path — because I did like to lie on the ground at high noon next to one of them, pretending to nap at a placid moment when the big top was up and the elephant boss was maybe at lunch. The beast's feet and trunk inscribed whimsical circles of her own design in the air not far above my head, like finger painting, dainty and quirky.

If not an elephant's trumpet, my mind might transmute the midnight roar of a passing freight train into a tiger, because I was soon also playing with the big cats. Both Blackie and Chief, their keeper, recognized my interest as useful. Chief showed me how to water them three times a day and scrape dung from their cages with an iron rod that the Ringstock blacksmith had fashioned. Later on, when the circus stayed overnight in a large town — Pittsburgh, Toledo, Detroit, Chicago, Milwaukee, Minneapolis — for extra performances, I slept on the ground under the lions' wagon. Many of us preferred to stay on the lot rather than go back to the railroad yards. The ground was no harder than our wooden-slat beds, and there was a grandeur to the big top, night or day. The sea-colored canvas, 1,140 feet in circumference, mounted in hammocky waves from 116 side poles toward the 65 quarter poles, and then higher and higher, with the immensity and serenity of surf, to the baling rings on the center poles, about 70 feet up. Earlier in the summer, Bible and I had locked ourselves inside Buddy the orangutan's cage, or in one of the giraffe wagons, in order to feel protected from the local muggers who in a city like Albany might roam through the lot during the wee hours. But the farther west I got and the more I knew about the cats, the more I trusted their protection. No one was going to brave the lions' wide forepaws hanging out between the bars over my head after I bedded down.

At the train yards, we played cards on the tracks in the twilight before we left, sitting on pieces of cardboard, and heated burgers on a kerosene stove or ate them raw as "cannibal burgers." Bible leafed through magazines on his bunk when other people were drinking beer; and Chief would generally show up at the last minute, because his particular friends, a Sioux in Ringstock who was named Little Chief, and Navajo Chief, who was an elephant man, took the later train along with their animals, after the show. He'd stay on the lot with them as long as he could. He flared into incandescence when he got loaded, like one of those solitary firecrackers that shoot high and fall harmlessly, but he tried to stay sober. Like the Mohawks who dominated high-steel skyscraper work in New York City at this time, Chief (Ralph Leaf was his given name) indicated that he had chosen a risky vocation on purpose, as if to fly the flag of the Indian Nation and thumb his nose at the pathetic alternatives on the reservation. Similarly, he expected the tigers and lions to maintain their dignity and character, although caged — to make a show of rising, bristling, and roaring at him when challenged to do so. He stood straight to give them an example, emitting a cheeky, deep hiss and raising an arm, his smile admiringly mimicking their snarls. They appeared to enjoy it, as a substitute for exercise. Most of our animals were confined in eleven-by-eight-foot Second World War ordnance wagons that had been bought by Ringling Brothers and converted to carry a couple of lions or tigers, or a mother and three younger leopards, or a jaguar, cheetah, and panther, partitioned apart. Since they were so cruelly cramped, what you could do for their creature comfort was minimal, apart from being friendly and gentle.

Liquor reclaimed people from our train every week, if not every night. They vanished into the oubliette of a binge and woke up alone in a suddenly unfriendly community. A circus hand lost his magic when the show scrubbed off its makeup and left town. He was now an object of police suspicion, a dirty, hung-over bum. Or if he did manage to scramble onto a rolling flatcar but then lost his hold and tumbled off the train in fifty miles, and was lucky enough to survive, he would have to hobble up to some stranger's door with a broken shoulder, torn clothes, a face full of gravel, smelling of alcohol, and no pedigree at all. My friends were mostly living on borrowed time, and giving the big boss, C.R., five or ten dollars a week out of their fourteen to hold for them so that they would have something saved by Thanksgiving to survive on during the winter. Blackie eventually died on the shoulder of a highway at Winter Quarters, hit by a car while drunk, I heard. But Chief left Ringling Brothers even before I did. (I stayed with the show for five months, altogether, from 1951 to 1953.) Clawed by a tiger in Madison Square Garden, he married his hospital nurse and settled in Brooklyn.

A stutter was no big deal if you were a nimble eighteen-year-old — jumping on and off the back of the Caterpillar tractors and scrambling up on top of the menagerie wagons when we set up our part of the show and tore it down again — and you genuinely cared for the animals. After all, we had Charles Bavent, whose hands were attached to his shoulders like flippers and who went by the name of Sealo; and Gilbert Reichert, "The Tallest Man in the World"; and Freda Pushnik, "Our Poor Little Armless and Legless Girl." The gorillas' caretaker never spoke at all. Dressed in black, he lived in a compartment of their air-conditioned, glassed-in wagon next to M'Toto, the famous "widow" of the celebrated silverback Gargantua. Tenacity in this milieu was better than muscles. Blackie, a trouper for decades, a loner who peppered nuisances with his dry commentary ("Elmer" was what he called all the towners), bestowed his approval on me, and even his protection on a few occasions when exceptionally tough guys showed up for a spell, straight from the prison yard — though I was seldom aware of needing it.

The castes of the circus were byzantine. The star performers — of exact balance and surpassing daring — were supreme. Then the money bosses and the performance directors. Then other, run-of-the-mill performers; the logistics bosses and department heads; the clowns, in a class of their own; the sideshow freaks and various attractions; and the longtime senior workhands. Then the come-and-go white roustabouts like me (eighty-some animal caretakers, for instance, counting the horse grooms and the "bull," or elephant, department; and sixty-six men to handle the cookhouse). And finally, the black workhands, who were paid only twelve dollars a week and were limited to the one job of unrolling the big-top canvas, which would eventually seat eleven thousand spectators, sledgehammering the countless side-pole stakes into the ground

for an hour or two in synchronized crews of four — chanting slave
songs to keep their swings falling in perfect tandem — then getting it all up, gradually guying it all out, and tearing it all down
again at eleven at night.

My first contact with blunt Southern racism was here; and although Jim Crow–style bigotry had more complexity and sometimes more "give" than the familiar innuendos of Northern preju-
dice, underneath the South's racism, as late as the fifties, lay the
threat of death. You saw cops — or the elephant men with their
clubs — chasing a Negro, and knew from how frantically he ran
that he might be about to die.

As for us white guys, we could have been fired for talking to the
performers, though the animal trainers might chat with us about
animal handling in passing. The veterinarian's wife had raised our
four leopards by hand and came by every week to play with them in
jeans and a lacy white blouse or a glittery costume, probably to
check out the passing parade of cagehands, in case anybody unkind got hired. The white of her blouse set off her wealth of curly
black hair, which bounced as she walked. She was an aerialist, with
the posture and spring in her step of a star, and — joyfully giving
her hands and whole arms to the leopards through the bars, to lick
and toy with — her back arched, as performers' bodies do without
their even thinking about it, when life is at a peak for them. I had a
crush on Josephine, the Mexican snake charmer, as well, whose
hair hung clear to her coccyx, and who hefted gorgeous boas and
pythons, and was a waitress in Florida in the off-season, and would
talk freely to anybody, being billed with the "freaks."

Pat Valdo was the performance director during my stint, and
Harold Ronk the stentorian ringmaster ("Children of all
ages . . ."). Both of them were circus paragons. Valdo had a mime's
face, protean yet self-effacing, a lightness, a quickness, in and out
of scenes like Janus in the tragicomedy of what a circus is really all
about. The pie in the face, the slipping on a banana peel, the
clockwork horses and obedient elephants, and an ovation for the
high-wire man who doesn't fall to his death. Ours was Harold
Alzana, "Whose Disregard of Danger Has Made Millions Gasp."
Emmett Kelly and Otto Griebling were the tramp clowns (Griebling acerbic and Kelly sweet-sad in the humor they projected), and
Felix Adler famously wore whiteface, using a little terrier and a pig-

let to connect with the crowd. Pinito Del Oro, a superb Spanish aerialist who did headstands and cloud swings on the trapeze bar,
shared top billing with Harold Alzana, and was also the sultry cen-
terpiece of a thirty-two-girl aerial ballet of "web-sitters" thrusting
out their pretty calves from a forest of dangling ropes. And the
Flying Concellos, of lengthy renown, somersaulted to the catcher
over a barge-shaped net. We had foot jugglers, slack-wire artists,
foot-ladder acts, trampoline tumblers, chariot riders, and a break-
away sway pole — plus a band of thirty or so, which Merle Evans directed while flourishing his sterling cornet. By the close of his fifty-
year career he may have been second only to John Philip Sousa in
the pleasure he gave in that line of work.

And we had a lot of Europeans performing, needy and pent-up
from the privations of the war. Some of the young ones bore the
pinch of Occupation hunger. Their faces and frames still hadn't
filled out, and they had the exile's air of wistful, agile dexterity —
always in transit, never at home. Sirens in bikinis, gamines in tank
tops, perch-pole acrobats, Roman riders, slender ethereal pinups,
and simple musclemen — more than our hoboes, who at least
were roaming their own continent, they looked uncommitted.
Whether they had spent the early forties in Naples, Marseilles,
or Frankfurt, it had been a hungry, fearful half decade for circus people, with their animals maybe starving, their wives and
children huddled in cellars, the husbands in uniform, if not in
combat.

There were seasoned female stars who had worked in peacetime
arenas in Bucharest, Budapest, or Berlin, and then done mud
shows under canvas through the ravaged countryside for bread
and vegetables when anarchy had set in. Wiry, resilient, androgy-
nous, ambiguous, they could sneak or swagger — haul trunks and
duffelbags outdoors through a five-hour rainstorm, and then display their sponged-off, Dietrich-type legs in the limelight of the
"spec," alongside the delicate, honey-blond Broadway showgirls
from Billy Rose's Diamond Horseshoe Club in New York, who also
appeared with us. They could stand on the riverbank, ogling some
of us boys swimming nude in the currents (when we stripped off
our coveralls at noontime), and then, during a performance, gaze
down enigmatically, vertiginously, from a trapeze at a young man
in dingy coveralls who was constantly moving underneath them,

anticipating on what part of his body he would take the force of
the blow if a lady fell, but never otherwise exchanging two words
with her. This tour — of Zanesville and Portsmouth, Ohio; Park-
ersburg, West Virginia; Battle Creek, Michigan; Mason City, Iowa;
Ogden, Utah; and Pocatello, Idaho — surely seemed rather idyllic,
painted on top of scarring memories, however comic and unso-
phisticated they may have thought Americans were.

We menagerie hands seldom watched the show. We hung around
at Number 10 Wagon or with our animals to see that no towners
hurt them or got hurt trying to fool with them. Meanwhile, the
band's selections kept us exactly informed of what was happening
inside the big top — Merle Evans's clarion cornet the leading
voice in a medley of something like sixty snatches from many composers that accompanied each turn of the program. Tickets cost
from seventy-five cents to four dollars, and, earning two dollars a
day, we didn't feel obliged to answer for the hundredth time a particular question — like what the animals were fed. For Blackie, after a few years, it was almost torture. He probably sat in his wagon
all day to escape the crowds asking where they could take a piss.
For Chief, it was part of the white man's inanity: What do you think
they eat? Where do you *want* to piss?

The lot supervisor and first-train superintendent was a beefy
showman named Lloyd Morgan. To the sheriff, the fire chief, the
sanitation inspector, the police superintendent who might show up
early, he personified the circus. In his oil slicker and rain boots, or
sunny-weather double-breasted brown summer suit and polished
shoes, with an alderman's big pinkie ring, he was unflappably gre-
garious, yet self-contained and toughly shrewd. Without being at
all discourteous, he let everybody know that he had met about
nineteen hundred county sheriffs before, that the circus had a
"patch" whose job was to put in the fix with any necessary bribes —
not him — and that an awful lot of children were going to have a
splendiferous day if nobody got in the way now and spoiled it for
them.

The marginal is often what's valued later: whether circus tents,
elephants, and gorillas, or the composers, painters, and religious
dissenters who shoot off energetically from the mainstream. I
didn't write down the slave chants that the black workhands sang,

didn't realize that the Sumatran and Siberian tigers I fed and watered might become extinct in the wild in my own lifetime, and the big top itself a subject for grainy documentaries. But I did learn about resilience, mobility, dignity, and even panache — from Lloyd Morgan, Merle Evans, Blackie Barlow, and Chief and his lions and tigers — at eighteen and nineteen, when it counts.

ADAM HOCHSCHILD

India's American Imports

FROM THE AMERICAN SCHOLAR

A FEW DAYS after arriving in India for the first time, I went to see a big Hindi-language hit movie called *Dil To Pagal Hai,* or "The Heart Is Crazy." The film was showing in a small, desperately poor town in the northern state of Rajasthan. Outside the theater, people were arriving on foot, on bicycles, in pedicabs, on motor scooters carrying three or four men each, on packed carts drawn by camels or oxen with painted horns, and on wagons towed by farm tractors. In the theater's men's room, patrons far outnumbered urinals, and dozens of men were simply using the floor.

The film's plot was loosely borrowed from *A Chorus Line.* The director of a musical is torn between his old girlfriend and the star of his new show. Various subplots, dance numbers, and heavily laden glances fluff things out to several hours. In the end the director gets the new star, and the old girlfriend pairs up with the new star's old fiancé, so everyone lives happily ever after. But the curious thing about this film was that although it was made in India, and the producer, director, and actors were all Indian, and the audience and theater could not have been more Indian, there was, on the surface, little Indian about what was on the screen. The film showed virtually no Indian clothing, food, signs, furniture, or anything else.

There were no street scenes in India. There were, however, street scenes in the European Disneyland, and in London, where one of the male characters is making his fortune. When he thinks he has won his woman, he makes the victorious downward jerk of the clenched fist that American pro athletes make after scoring a basket or touchdown. Interior shots showed a modern airport, film studios, a Japanese restaurant, and a luxurious hospital with private rooms. The musical numbers were American disco, not Indian. The stars used a conspicuously displayed variety of cell phones, beepers, and new cars. They sipped bottles of mineral water; wore blue jeans, leotards, and miniskirts; and drank lots of Pepsi — the company must have paid heavy "product placement" fees. But the West itself, paying no fee, was the real product placement, from the California-sleek furnishings of the characters' homes to the distinctly un-Indian rolling green pastures of the hero's imagined dream landscape, through which the heroine runs in a gauzy white dress. So: an Indian film without India in it.

Except that India *was* in the story. The jilted woman, Girlfriend #1, curses the gods for setting her suitor on the wrong track. Girlfriend #2, who falls for the director, is escaping an arranged marriage. Plus, although the film was as chaste as could be (no nudity, barely even a kiss), the audience, except for our small, much-stared-at group of Indians and foreigners, was entirely male. Evidently local women don't come to the late show.

I began thinking about this curious blend of India and non-India as we left the theater and made our way through the camels and pedicabs and farm tractors, and the contradictions remained in the back of my mind for the rest of the five months my wife and I spent living in the country. You normally think of travel as a way of getting to know something unfamiliar. But travel anywhere for an American today involves getting to know not something totally unfamiliar but a combination, often an uneasy one, of the unfamiliar and the familiar.

For the Indians who watched this film, and the hundreds of others like it that their country produces each year, glamour lies in a dreamworld where everything is smooth and clean and electronic, where the artifacts that surround you are American or European. Objects of almost any kind are always advertised in ways that emphasize their foreignness. In the ads in India's slick newsweeklies promoting clothes, cars, cigarettes, computers, there are no dark-skinned models. Either by birth or by the retoucher's brush, the features of many Indian models are ethnically ambiguous — hair dark enough to be Indian, skin light enough to be European, eyes that might be either.

To a country like this, what gets imported is seldom America at its best: a commitment to human rights, American informality and skepticism toward authority, equality between men and women, a school system that values individual creativity more than rote learning. Instead, cultural imports are mainly those things that someone can make money selling. Ideas travel slowly. The desire for objects travels at the speed of a TV transmission.

Through India's importation of such yearnings, the West, mostly the United States, has conquered the country far more conclusively than the British ever did. The British left some monuments and street names and, to the business and governing classes, the English language. But then they went home. The signs of earlier conquerors are even more transitory: I saw squatters living inside sepulchers in an old overgrown Dutch graveyard in the port city of Cochin. But the signs of the new conquest are everywhere — on billboards, on movie and TV screens, in the armloads of gadgets that Indians who live or work abroad bring when they come home. No guns or tanks or ships are strong enough to keep this conquest at bay, for it is a conquest not by the sword but by religion: the religion of consumption.

The new religion outdraws the old. The one other movie I saw in India was a James Bond film. The theater was huge, just across the street from a small Hindu shrine that had few visitors. I tried to watch the film through the eyes of the shrine keeper. The religion Bond represents provides tough competition. Bond braves, unscathed, some of the classic elements that impede mortal beings: air (he flies a jet fighter and does free-fall parachuting), water (he wears scuba equipment), and fire (through which he dashes unharmed while the villain's lair goes up in flames). The chariot of this new god is a remote-controlled BMW whose electrically charged door handles and other secret weaponry make it impervious to harm. Additional devices — which look like Western consumer products such as wristwatches or cell phones, but have other powers as well — serve Bond as amulets, with a supernatural destructive force as strong as any thunderbolt hurled by Shiva.

This is the shape of the new conquest. For any object to be certified as desirable to the Indian consumer, it must have a Western aura, even if it is Indian-made. For example, the house we rented came equipped with an electrically powered water purifier called an Aquaguard — something manufactured in India and sold by the millions. When running, the Aquaguard played synthesized electronic music to remind you it was on, so you wouldn't let the bottle it was filling overflow. And what music did it play, in oven-like weather, only six hundred miles from the equator? Two tunes, over and over: "Jingle Bells" and "Santa Claus Is Coming to Town."

For a week, as part of our time as Fulbright lecturers in India, my wife and I are teaching at something called the American Studies Research Center (since then renamed the Indo-American Centre for International Studies), in Hyderabad. The Center gives courses of various sorts, but its heart is a library — a superb one. It contains the largest collection of books and periodicals about the United States to be found anywhere outside the U.S. and one library in Europe. A reader can feast on the complete works of hundreds of American authors and on back issues of more than seven hundred magazines and journals. From poetry to architecture to national parks, you could find enough material here to write a doctoral dissertation on innumerable aspects of American life, and hundreds of Indians have done so. The Center was founded some thirty-five years ago by the U.S. Information Agency; it is now scrambling for money elsewhere, because the end of the Cold War means no more government funds.

There is something unreal about this perfectly reproduced piece of an American university campus, complete with mowed and watered lawn, plunked down like a green, carefully manicured island in the middle of scorched India. Thousands of yards of shelves house such volumes as *The Papers of John Marshall* and *Interior Department Reports,* when, across the road, squatters are living in the bushes, and a few miles away in the heart of the huge city, tens of thousands of people are living under tarpaulins or sheets of plastic or no roof at all — on the sidewalks, in vacant lots, at construction sites, and beneath freeway overpasses.

I have a similar feeling of disjuncture when I lecture to the Indian college teachers at the Center's American civilization course. Few have been to the United States and almost all are eager to go. Many are leftists who believe — correctly, I think — that the way the U.S. is using the new global trade regime to reshape the world to its liking makes life harder for poor countries like India. But at the same time, America beckons: it is the source of travel grants, scholarships, cutting-edge culture. These teachers sit with us at meals and shyly launch conversations, usually on subjects about which I feel abysmally ignorant. "Can I talk with you about symbolism in John Barth and William Faulkner?" asks one. Another, from Nepal, speaks movingly about the burden of illiteracy and the oppression of women there, but as a scholar he is entranced by Thomas Pynchon.

Am I jealous that these people have been able to make more sense of Barth and Pynchon than I have? Probably. But why are they attracted to the most abstruse and difficult of American writers? Is it because these seem the highest peaks to scale in the American cultural landscape? Or is it because the complexity and sophistication of Barth and Pynchon are a substitute for the complex and sophisticated personal computers, video cameras, and other consumer goods that are beyond the financial reach of most Indian college teachers?

I'm left feeling that if there's anything useful being imported from the United States at this particular spot, it is neither our lectures, nor John Barth and Thomas Pynchon, nor the judicial opinions of John Marshall and the other contents of the library. Rather, it is the example of how the library itself is run. Unlike those in most other libraries in India, and, indeed, elsewhere in the world, the stacks are open to visitors. The catalogue is well organized and up-to-date, and it matches the books on the shelves. The shelved books are upright and in their proper places. There are no dusty, moldering piles that have been waiting to be reshelved for months. And, above all, the librarians — who are all Indians, incidentally — smile. They make eye contact. They offer to help you find what you're looking for. They don't treat library users as unwelcome, lower-ranking intruders. Indeed, when we meet Indian scholars who have been to Hyderabad to use this library, it is these things, not the actual books, that they marvel over. With reason: to my mind, the user-friendly, open-stack American university library is one of the great cultural treasures on earth.

Was this the key part of American culture that Congress and the U.S. Information Agency thought would be imported by India when they set up this place during the Cold War? I'm sure not; otherwise they wouldn't now cut off the money. They were doubtless thinking instead about the glories of free enterprise and the evils of Communism. A paradox of the strange business of cultural imports is that what gets imported may be quite different from what people think they are exporting.

One of the most pervasive of all cultural imports — something reinforced unconsciously by every minute spent looking at billboards advertising apartment buildings, at *Baywatch* or *NYPD Blue,* at any newspaper photo that shows the West — is the idea of what constitutes a proper building. It is built of materials that are inflexible and permanent. They are usually costly and often brought long distances. These notions are American and European in origin, not Indian. Two-thirds of India's structures are still made of mud, and in some parts of the country the roofs are likely to be palm thatch. If you own even a small plot of land, both materials may be plentiful and free and close at hand.

In the South Indian state of Kerala, where we spend most of our five months, I visit a small settlement of "tribals," as they are called, members of one of the many indigenous groups that live close to the land throughout India. The people in this settlement are from the Kani tribe, and they live beneath a rocky mountain ridge in a bamboo forest, raising and eating fruits and vegetables. To reach them requires walking a mile and a half from the nearest dirt road, along a forest trail.

I'm being given a tour of this area by the president and several members of the *panchayat,* or city council, of the municipality that includes the bamboo forest. A hard-driving, energetic man, the president wants to show me the primitive conditions in which the tribals live, "so that you can really understand the need for changes." But the visit has the opposite effect on me.

At the settlement of a half-dozen homes, we go to the house of Mallan Kani, the chief. I am given sliced pineapple, and a coconut with a hole to drink from. Mallan Kani wears only a loincloth. The officials say he doesn't know his age, but they believe him to be between eighty and eighty-five. We find him with his two daughters and two daughters-in-law. A son arrives, returning from an expedition into the forest to gather firewood. Everyone is barefoot.

Almost everything that surrounds us is made of the versatile

bamboo, from the thatch of the roof (which lasts three years), to
the walls of split bamboo, to the woven mats that cover the dirt
floor. On three sides, the house is open to the cooling breeze. The
only furniture is a bamboo cot with another woven mat. More
rolled mats are stored in a rack hanging from the ceiling, reached
by a bamboo ladder. In the kitchen, bamboo racks of various
shapes hold tin pots and plates and spoons. One of the chief's
daughters demonstrates a bamboo bow used to shoot not arrows
but small stones — to force away bothersome wild elephants. Even
the settlement's chicken house is made of bamboo, as are a trap
for catching fish from a nearby stream, and a rat trap, whose spring
mechanism utilizes the tension of a bent piece of the wood.

All this bamboo has been cut within a few minutes' walk.
Gathering it cost no money, depleted no limited resource, required no fossil fuel energy, added nothing to global warming. To
look at a house where everything has been so ingeniously made of
one material takes my breath away. It is like looking at a visual
piece of music: bamboo theme with variations. I am awed by the
beauty. One of the local officials with me seems to have an unexpected twinge of the same feeling, and says, "It's a pity we have to
change all this."

Under a new development plan, the *panchayat* president explains to me proudly, they are building houses for these people —
solid, durable houses of concrete, with tin roofs. It begins to dawn
on me that his zeal to modernize these tribals is related to the way
Indians have come to feel tribal in comparison with the West.

Interestingly, however, one of the Kani tells my interpreter that
many of them don't *want* the new houses the *panchayat* is so eager
to build for them. Even in daytime, it will be dark inside, and under the equatorial sun the tin roofs will get broiling hot. If the
panchayat insists on building the concrete houses, the Kani will use
them to store farm tools, he says, and they'll keep on living in the
bamboo houses. But the next generation, will they continue? I
doubt it. By then the imported idea of what a house is supposed to
be made of will be irrevocably in place.

One of the things I am supposed to do in India is give two- and
three-day workshops in nonfiction writing for students and working journalists. I do this in four different cities. What am I import-

ing? It is not anything uniquely American about writing techniques. The best students know what I mean when I talk about narrative strategy. And some of the published examples of good writing that I've picked for us to discuss are Indian. I think what I'm importing most effectively are some strong beliefs about chairs. Each time I arrive at a university for one of these workshops, the chair I'm supposed to sit in is on a platform, behind a table or podium, and everyone else's chairs are lined up in rows facing me. Often the men are sitting on one side of the room, the women on the other. Each time, I enlist the puzzled class in rearranging the chairs in a circle. I have noticed the same kind of thing in classrooms in Africa. The legacy of colonialism lives on in a curiously ossified form. And thus school classrooms in Africa or Asia are not like the British or French classrooms of today, which are sometimes as informal and nonhierarchical as American ones. Rather, they are like the British or French classrooms of sixty years ago, or the British or French classrooms of someone's imagination. Rearranging the chairs helps, but it is still like swimming in molasses to get a discussion going, to get anyone to speak up or to argue with someone else — especially me. In one workshop it is Day Two before a student finally says, "I think I disagree with your point about . . ." I let go an inner sigh of relief. The right to dispute the teacher: one American import I wholeheartedly like.

Something else American visitors import to India is their own expectations. You expect the unfamiliar, and you certainly find it. What strikes me, though, is not the occasional elephant in the street, or the temples and palaces, or the processions of brilliantly costumed people on a Hindu holy day. These I'm prepared for; they are the unfamiliar made familiar by postcards. More startling and intriguing are the many ways in which all kinds of things that in Western society are usually more hidden suddenly become visible.

The vast yard where old cars are carefully taken apart — hubcaps in one pile, steering wheels in another, axles in another, and so on, right next to a big complex of butcher stalls where taken-apart animals are similarly displayed. The gigantic switch with a six-inch handle, such as one imagines the on-off switch in a nuclear power plant to have, that controls the electrical line entering the mural-sized fuse box that takes up at least fifteen square feet of prominent wall space in our home. Our backyard pit for burning garbage. The vacant lot next door where our neighborhood's unburnable garbage ends up. The fact that, yes, our rented house has a gas-burning stove as advertised, but we ourselves have to go to the gas dealer's office (where the manager's desk has an offering to the gods on a banana leaf) and collect the gas — contained in metal tanks that clank and rattle together ominously beneath our seat in a rickety three-wheeler auto-rickshaw on the way home. The way social ranks are laid bare: a person's degrees and the universities they are from, his profession and title are all displayed on the nameplate in front of his house and, in the case of a government official, on a little red sign on his car: VICE CHANCELLOR, KERALA UNIVERSITY.

Living in India also lays bare the material expectations we export. I may think of myself as nonmaterialistic and deplore the Indian attachment to Western consumer goods, but I'm forced to realize that I take all too many of them for granted myself. Our standard of living in India is far higher than that of most people around us. We tell house rental agents that we're just looking for something simple. But simplicity is relative. For we expect what Americans think of as basic requirements: electricity, a telephone, e-mail, flush toilet, hot and cold water.

We are assured that all these things will be available. And after a fashion they are. But it takes five weeks for the telephone to be installed, sometimes it goes dead, and we can't use it to call abroad. There is hot water, but not in the kitchen. The electricity goes out for half an hour every evening, and sometimes for longer stretches during the day. The voltage is high enough to work the e-mail modem only before 9 A.M. The municipal water supply shrinks to a trickle in the dry season, and sometimes the pump to our backup well fails. When there's water, the toilet flushes, but you can hear it gurgling into the backyard septic tank (which is, strangely, uphill from the well). So: all of these basic things exist, but most of them come and go unpredictably.

This is a healthy lesson. For one thing, it connects us with others. If one or another of these services isn't working, we share with neighbors, or do without for a few hours, or for a day or two. They take buckets of our water if they have none; they bring us candles if we have no electricity. At first I am frustrated when something breaks down — and my impatience makes me feel embarrassingly American, since a few houses away there are people who live by kerosene light and get water from a public faucet down the road. What right do I have to complain? Yet complain I do. Eventually, I come to be more relaxed. To learn that we can survive temporarily without phone or water, or whatever, makes us feel a little more hardy and self-reliant. But that's only because we're doing without things to which we secretly feel entitled. And I'm much more American than I'd like to be in that sense of consumer entitlement. I could do without hot water for a long time when it's one hundred degrees in the shade, but without e-mail?

The U.S. ambassador's house in New Delhi must be one of the most palatial embassy residences anywhere in the world. The visitor crosses a large courtyard, passes through a hotel-sized, two-story-high lobby — its side tables dotted with framed photographs of the ambassador with his children, with Bill Clinton, with various other luminaries — and then passes outdoors again, down some steps onto a wide lawn. This pleasantly warm evening the lawn is filled with tables covered by white cloths, at which are sitting more than a hundred guests: high Indian government officials, members of the diplomatic corps (the Swiss ambassador's chauffeur is a red-turbaned Sikh with white Swiss crosses on his red shoulder tabs), visiting Americans, U.S. embassy officials. White-jacketed waiters serve drinks. As we come in, we see on a raised stage at the back of the lawn, his long hair now gray, the folksinger Arlo Guthrie. He is in the middle of his famous eighteen-minute anthem of protest from the 1960s, "Alice's Restaurant":

> You can get anything you want
> at Alice's Restaurant . . .

The slurred words of the song, full of allusions to draft physicals and the like, are hard enough to follow even for someone who has heard them before and who lived in that place and time. As they listen and then applaud politely, what are these Indians in kurtas and saris making of all this? And what piece of America is being imported here?

When the song is over, the guests head for the buffet tables at the side of the lawn. Some of the younger Americans from the embassy, who look as if they weren't even born in the 1960s, climb up onstage to shake Guthrie's hand and get his autograph. The ambassador, former Ohio governor Richard Celeste, who has invited Guthrie to India, watches approvingly. "Look," he says quietly, pointing at the backs of the crew-cut heads of several Americans clustered around the singer. "Some of the security guys from the embassy. The wounds of that time are really healed now."

Perhaps. But I think what was happening was something else. What was really being imported was the example not of how to heal wounds but of how the passage of time can turn the relics of absolutely anything — even the antiwar movement, many of whose members went into exile or to jail — into a mere cultural ornament, a catchy tune to be cheerfully consumed along with good food and drink on a balmy evening. Sadly, this was a lesson, it turned out, that India already knew. For this evening was in April 1998, and less than six weeks later, with the foreknowledge of some of the men who sat on the lawn, listening to Arlo Guthrie, the country that had just spent many months elaborately commemorating the fiftieth anniversary of the death of Mohandas Gandhi, the greatest teacher of nonviolence in modern times, set off five nuclear explosions. Hypocrisy by those in power is too plentiful everywhere to require any American imports.

Among the strongest American expectations imported to a place like India are fears. At the beginning I am afraid of getting sick, of being taken advantage of, of being robbed. We bring lots of medicines and vitamin pills; I examine all food suspiciously for signs of germs or spoilage. I fear being taken for a naïve tourist by shopkeepers. And it seems that people here are also afraid of robbery: windows throughout India are covered with bars, often even on the upper floors of apartment houses. Thieves must be resourceful, I think, climbing up from below or rappelling down from the roof.

However, we don't get sick. The first time I buy food at a neighborhood fruit and vegetable stall, its keeper comes racing after me, from a hundred yards away, with my change — because I had misunderstood him and left 50 rupees (about $1.25) on the counter instead of 15 rupees. And after a month or two, it dawns on me that the window bars everywhere are not against thieves but against

India's vast population of aggressive, hungry crows, whose taste for human food scraps has been honed feasting on the omnipresent roadside garbage. It takes a few weeks more before I realize that virtually nobody in our part of India worries about street crime. The rare policemen I see are unarmed. Why does it take me so long to let go of my fears? What's most foreign, most unknown, is what we're most afraid of, even when we seek it out. Maybe that's why we seek it out.

I can date the moment I let these fears go. It is about eight o'clock one evening and I'm making my way home from a workshop for local government officials in a distant, unfamiliar part of Trivandrum, Kerala's capital. The isolated building is on top of a big hill. There are no taxis outside, no buses. The nearest place I have any chance of finding an auto-rickshaw is a mile or so away, a traffic circle at the bottom of the hill. I head off down the road. There is no moon, and everything is pitch black. There are no streetlights. Either the electricity is having its nightly shutdown or else the houses in this neighborhood don't have any. Occasionally a far-off kerosene lamp flickers faintly. Occasionally a pair of very dim headlights zooms up or down the road, and I step quickly aside, but not too far, for fear of unseen ditches. I'm wearing dark clothes; the drivers of passing vehicles can't see me. I should have brought a flashlight, worn a white shirt. I should have one of those red reflective safety vests. Dumb. In vain, I anxiously try to flag down what may or may not be a passing taxi that looms suddenly out of the darkness and then disappears. The driver can't see the furled black umbrella I'm waving. The only way I can tell I'm on or off the road is by the feel of the asphalt underfoot.

Partway down the hill, I become aware of the rattle of metal wheels ahead of me on the road, accompanied by another rhythmic clinking. Finally I'm close enough to make out, just barely, the outline of a food vendor's cart. The man pushing it, judging from the sound, is continually stirring something — I can't see what — in a frying pan or wok. But on the front of the cart, his protection against being run over, is a candle. That's all it takes. I realize that the candle can be my protection, too. Flooded with a sudden sense of safety, I follow twenty paces behind this mysterious, candlelit stir-frying for the rest of the way down the hill.

BARBARA HURD

Refugium

FROM THE GEORGIA REVIEW

AT FIRST I think I'm seeing a small cat doing a weak imitation of
an inchworm. It undulates in a strange combination of hunch-and-
slink along the edge of Cranesville Swamp. Covered with dark fur,
its chin dabbed with white, it reminds me of what theologians say
about the life of the personality being horizontal, craving community, and that of the soul being vertical, needing solitude.
Crouching behind some shrubs, I finally see that it's a mink, moving from one alder to another. It manages both landscapes, traces
with its lustrous back a pattern of swell and subside, evokes an image of Muslims prostrating and standing, Catholics kneeling and
rising, pale green inchworms arching and stretching along my
forearm. We are gardeners, all of us, our hands broadcasting seeds
in the spring, our arms in autumn clutching the harvested wheat.
We mingle and retreat, seek company and refuge.

I have been thinking a lot about refuge, how what makes the
swamp a safe hideaway also makes it dangerous, a paradox for all
the scoundrels and saints, artists and hermits, victims and perpe-
trators who have fled there. And how, for all of them, the most difficult question in the end might not be about safety but about duration — how long to stay, how to know when a temporary refuge
is about to become a permanent retreat without exit. The mink, a
solitary creature who tolerates other minks only enough to breed
and give birth, lives on the edge of this soggy Nature Conservancy
land on the western border of Maryland. Cranesville Swamp is a
valley between two Appalachian ridges, a high bowl with poor
drainage. Its ground is spongy, its vegetation matted and damp. I

am with a hermit friend who has sold his house and is dismantling his identity as an artist by living at the edge of the swamp. When he sold his studio a nearby gallery took his work, including a drawing in which the hair of a goddess's attendants is replaced by a waterfall. You can study it and try to puzzle out where their heads end and the waterfall begins.

Michael is after an intimacy in his life that has nothing to do with sex. It's a bit disconcerting to sit with a man — his hazel eyes clear, his beard and hair neatly trimmed — who has no concerns about mortgage payments and insurance premiums or how he'd introduce himself at a campground social. Everything I feel about comfort starts to rattle. He tells me, quietly, *I want to live like an animal, close to the earth, self-sufficient, doing as little harm as possible.* Then, ten minutes later: *And I want to live like Christ, close to God, detached, finding refuge in the unknown.*

We talk for hours on the deserted boardwalk at Cranesville. Michael isn't going into hiding; he's retreating from a path that wasn't headed toward what, for him, is being fully human. He's not sure what that means except a quiet letting go, a deliberate choice to go toward some kind of refuge that nourishes his spirit. All the great spiritual leaders have done it, from Buddha to Christ to Mohammed. They've withdrawn to sit in caves and under trees, to wander in deserts, packing as little as possible into their knapsacks. They were after, I think, some moments of trackless quiet; a chance to blur their footprints, the sense of having been someplace, of having some place to get to; a chance to see what happens when the past and the future stop tugging on the leash and the present opens like a well.

Those who are fond of various retreats — writers, ecstatics, parents with young children — often comment on the silence such time away allows. Silence becomes something present, almost palpable. The central task shifts from keeping the world at a safe decibel distance to letting more of the world in. Thomas Aquinas said that beauty arrests motion. He meant, I think, that in the presence of something gorgeous or sublime we stop our natterings, our foot twitchings and restless tongues. Whatever our fretful hunger is, it seems momentarily filled in the presence of beauty. To Aquinas's wisdom I'd add that silence arrests flight, that in its refuge our need to flee the chaos of noise diminishes. We let the world creep closer; we drop to our knees as if to let the heart, like a small animal, get its legs on the ground.

The mink disappears into the underbrush. If I had been blindfolded and plunked down in this pocket of cool air and quaking ground spiked by tamaracks and spruce, home to hermits and minks, and tried to figure out just where I was, I would have guessed a bog in Canada somewhere, far north of the bustle of Quebec and Montreal. And Canada was probably the original home of this bog. We don't think of landscapes being on the run, though we know birds fly south in the fall, mountain goats trek up and down the Rocky Mountain passes from season to season, and eel journey from the Sargasso Sea in the middle of the Atlantic to North America or Europe in search of fresh water. But stand back far enough in geologic time and you can watch ecosystems migrating north and south across the globe as giant glaciers drag and push up and down the Northern Hemisphere. Almost twenty thousand years ago the last intrusion shoved a wide band of boreal forest south to the mid-Atlantic region. When the glacier withdrew, some ten thousand years later, most of those dark forests withdrew also, reestablishing themselves in Canada while southern deciduous forests reclaimed their usual position here in Maryland. But in a few isolated pockets protected in high-altitude bowls surrounded by higher ridges, boreal forests hunkered down, sank their damp feet into poorly draining clay and rock, and stayed.

Now they couldn't migrate north if they wanted to, for around them is a hostile world — too warm, too dry, the water flushing too fast through the underground aquifers. Dug up and replanted just a mile to the south, the tamaracks would wither, cranberry and sphagnum would curl and crisp, cotton grass would scorch and wilt in what would feel like brutally tropical air. This is an area known as a refugium — a particular localized ecosystem that cannot survive in surrounding areas.

Historically, refuges are retreats in human terms — shelters for protection from danger or distress — and a refugee is one who flees to such shelter for safety. Something in the "outside" world threatens, presses too close, cannot accept the refugee's color or ethnicity or religion or eccentricity, his or her need for so much water and cool air. Something in the refuge spells protection. If you can hack, float, stagger, or climb your way into the jungle, swamp, desert, or mountain, the color of your skin and how you worship won't matter. But something else will. Mohammed in his cave knew this, and Jesus in the desert, and the Buddha under the Wisdom Tree. Michael in the swamp does, too.

Refuge means an escape from what frazzles and buzzes, from what sometimes reminds me of the continuous replay of the final minutes of a tied Super Bowl game — bleachers sagging with hoarse spectators whooping and jeering, the players' one-point attention on flattening whatever comes between them and the triumph of a square yard of pigskin flying over the goal line. On an ordinary day, the human ear is bombarded with sound — anything and everything: the neighbor's lawnmower, a ratchety clock movement, sirens, car engines, and the popping roll of tires on hot pavement. Our minds, of course, automatically filter much of this hubbub. But at what cost? What happens to that filtered material?

Cleaning the lint trap in my dryer yields a fuzzy bedding of dog hair, threads, shredded Kleenex, and, once, a striking black and white feather, small and striped, cleaned and surely destined for more than the trash. I run my fingers across the trap, gathering the clean down. Scraped and softened linen like this was once used as dressings for wounds — a buffer between raw flesh and the barrage of bacteria. Too much lint, though, and the wound can't breathe, the dryer will catch fire, your house will burn down. Does the human mind work the same way? Are there long screens we occasionally need to pull from our heads and run our fingers up, gathering into a pleated, linty accordion the excesses of noise and activity we haven't processed? Do we occasionally need the silence of refuge for the way it lets our minds breathe a bit more easily?

The summer I was twelve, I broke both bones in my right leg. Instead of practicing bull's-eyes at archery camp and swimming laps at the local pool, I read for months. I got out of setting the table, folding laundry, and raking grass to sit on the screened-in porch and plow through biographies and mysteries from May until September. When I lifted my head long enough to regain my bearings, it wasn't to wonder what all the other kids were doing but to imagine what kind of summer my splintered leg would be having if it had its own ears. I reckoned that noises from the outside — clinking dinner forks, whoops from neighborhood kids playing kick the can, the spit of gravel under tires on the shoulder of the road — would have been muffled by all that cast, the thick white walls. I sat in a chaise longue trying to visualize my bones, tender and traumatized, swathed in gauze and then locked into a white plaster tunnel nothing could enter. I thought of how those slim bone stilts had for years propelled me down school hallways, across hockey fields, along wooded paths — and now must lie languid and lazy for three months, lounging inside padded walls with nothing to do but knit back together.

Maybe it was this experience that later led me to find refuge behind the attic insulation. When I shared a bedroom with my twin sister in a house in the suburbs outside Philadelphia, I found a way to unstaple the insulation in the attic, slip between the two-by-fours, and crawl into the space under the eaves behind the attic's knee wall. The process was like crawling into a long, cottony, pink tent — quiet and dark, an unlikely hiding place. I felt the way I imagined my healing bones had — hidden in a padded world with nothing pressing to do but heal. So long as I could tolerate the itching that the pink fiberglass fired in my arms, I reveled in the silence, the guaranteed lack of interruption. Sometimes I took a book to read or a notebook to scribble in, but often nothing, sitting for hours in the darkness.

My childhood wasn't full of trauma I needed to escape. My father worked hard and my mother tended to us children; there was always a beloved dog around, sometimes a rabbit, and, for a while, a couple of roosters. We ate dinner together every night — roast beef and mashed potatoes or hamburgers done on the grill. My twin and I fell asleep holding hands across the space between our beds, and my father made sure to close the windows when a storm came up in the night. But something in me craved a getaway. From a very young age, I was hungry for the privilege of not being interrupted, for a sanctuary nobody else could enter, for a place to which I could retreat, yank those lint screens from my mind, toss them, and then wander or sit with fewer and fewer filters.

Part of the appeal of a refuge is surely its isolation. There nobody can see you still weeping over a lover who hunched off with another some thirty years ago. Nobody is there to notice whether you stand straight or slouch, or how you suck your stomach in. Or don't. A refuge is like a locked bathroom door where you can practice the fine art of extending your tongue until you can finally touch the tip of your nose, which you also feel free to pick as thoroughly as you want. Nobody's watching; you can do whatever you want.

Consider, for instance, the hermit found in 1975 in Florida's Green Swamp by a sheriff and his deputies. This solitary Asian man had been so overwhelmed by metropolitan chaos, he'd fled to the cypress and black water a few miles from the roller coasters and virtual reality of Disney World and lived on alligators and armadillos. Hiding with white ibis and leopard frogs among wild orange trees, he was dubbed "Skunk Ape" by the few who had spotted him. I like to think he earned this nickname, that in the relative safety of the Green Swamp he indulged in some childhood fantasies of branch-swinging and chest-beating, that it was his dark silky hair against a pale back that people saw as he scurried away. Nicknames don't always trivialize and they aren't always meant to humiliate. Consciously or not, perhaps the puzzled observers named his most salient characteristics, the ones that needed the tangled and private understory and the mournful cry of night herons in order to surface.

That need for privacy and a less encumbered life might be what Michael's after, too. In addition to his car and his bike, he's sold his kayak, the one he used to launch by the church at the edge of the swamp and paddle around in, gliding eye to eye with skunk cabbage. He wants to be unburdened. For the Buddhists, *taking refuge in the dharma* means cutting the ties, letting go of whatever hand you've been clinging to, whatever boat you've been floating in. It means shedding your armor, letting what's underneath soften, grow squishy, and open. It means, as Pema Chodron, a Buddhist nun, says, *relaxing with the ambiguity and uncertainty of the present moment without reaching for anything to protect ourselves . . . total appreciation of impermanence and change.* Monks must have loved a swamp. Sometimes I think that their ancient texts must have risen like vapors straight out of the middle of places as wobbly as Cranesville. That the monks, lifting their robes up around their knees, might have simply looked at where they were wading, said *Yes, I see,* and written it all down. Surely there is no better place than a swamp or bog to learn about uncertainty, to notice how we feel when the ground under our feet literally moves, what small boats or dogma we cling to, what we must let go of when we look down and learn to trust that which is holding us now. Something in us gives over to the place, the lines relax, the definitions go mushy, the body goes limp with this landscape — itself so limp and ill defined. Such paradox that, in a groundless refuge, what has been tight and willed relaxes until fear begins to dissipate.

Whether we head to a swamp's isolation with spiritual intentions or a predator close behind, most of us fear the first step onto that other ground. And why not? Longfellow, in his famous poem "The Slave in the Dismal Swamp," describes a place "where hardly a human foot could pass / or a human heart would dare," a morass of gloomy fens, strange lights, and gigantic mosses. Many a human foot has stepped into forbidden territory, but harder than that is to make the heart go too. You stand with one foot on firm land, the other in a canoe. Behind you is light, the expected horizon of your life; in front of you the green overhead hunkers down, crouches over its waters, and you're startled that you could even think of putting your body into this lightweight snippet of rolled aluminum and then paddling, heart in mouth, toward what the Irish poet John O'Reilly branded a "tragedy of nature."

All the ingredients that make the swamp a place of refuge are the same ingredients that make it dangerous: cottonmouths, saw grass so razor sharp it can slit a horse's legs, alligators that can devour a human whole, a sense of the plant-sky bearing down, the need to stay crouched and wary. If you add to the poison the sedge swords, and to the carnivores the prospect of being lost for days or decades, it's easy to see why, no matter how determined your pursuer was, he often paced at the edge of the swamp, plucking off leeches and wondering whether plunging into such unmapped, trackless territory was worth it. Of course, the same concerns ought to arise for you. In a canoe, you watch the water close silently behind you. On the ground, you watch your footprint in the mud fill and vanish.

It doesn't matter who's the hero or who's the villain. The swamp will protect and threaten both. In Cold Spring Swamp in New Jersey during the Revolutionary War, a bunch of men who called themselves the Refugees, who thought of themselves as British loyalists but were, in reality, a band of thugs, terrorized housewives and stagecoach travelers and then hightailed it back to the swamp to gloat over their booty. Scoundrels all, they counted on the inaccessibility of their hideout on a small island in the middle of the swamp.

Also during the Revolutionary War, soldier Francis Marion eluded the British in Four Holes Swamp of South Carolina. Known as the Swamp Fox, Marion could disappear into the cypress with his band of men and stay hidden for weeks. Farther north, the Narragansett Indians holed up in the Great Swamp of Rhode Island beyond the reach of white men bent on retaliating for raids — until December of 1675, when the swamp froze over in an early New England cold snap and what had been almost impenetrable to the white men was transformed overnight into a smooth array of patios and sidewalks. The whites simply walked in, and what followed was the greatest massacre in Rhode Island history.

Runaway slaves, hidden for years in the Great Dismal Swamp making shingles, knew about their own swamp fears and those of their pursuers. And so did the Seminoles who fled into the Everglades after the white man booted them from their homes in the Okefenokee of southern Georgia. Unwilling to negotiate, surrender, or flee, the Seminoles took advantage of the white man's horror of the infested waters of the Glades. They established villages on hammocky islands in the midst of quagmires, built small canoes that could glide over shallow water, and used the dense vegetation for cover. In pursuit, the U.S. Navy in the 1830s sent a Lieutenant Powell, whose men tried pushing and poling their boats, their boots and sticks slurping and sucking in the mud, the vast prairie sea of saw grass closing in on them. When a Lieutenant McLaughlin tried to succeed where Powell had failed, he led his men into Big Cypress Swamp on the western side of the state, where dense overhead vegetation blocks sunlight and the still water is thick with spinachy trailings. When the men in their big boots stirred the dark water, they kicked up noxious vapors that made them retch. Even more disconcerting, the circuitous streams destroyed their sense of direction. They wandered, retracing and detouring, unable to use the stars as navigational help because the canopy was so thick. Where water was low, they portaged again and again, stumbling over cypress knees and dead stumps, always on the lookout for snakes. Mist rose, steamy and blinding, from the muck; when it cleared, the men had only the labyrinthine mirrors of black water, the almost impenetrable green walls of Spanish moss and cypress, with no way to distinguish "here" from "there." From the top of a pine one of the men might climb, he'd gaze down on a maze of channels — a nightmare of fractals and mirrors, a kaleidoscope of water and thicket that disorients not because it shifts at the far end of your telescope but because it doesn't — and still you don't know where you are.

Under *disorientation*, my thesaurus lists *insanity* first, followed by *lunacy, bedlam,* and that charming phrase *not all there.* In psychiatric terms, we think of fugue, dissociation, amnesia, confusion, a dream state. But my favorite option is from the dictionary, which defines *disorient* as *to turn from the east, as in the altar of a church. Hence to cause one to lose one's bearings.* To turn from the east. How curious. If I had to label a swamp's aesthetics and philosophy as primarily Eastern or Western, I'd say Eastern without question. A swamp is receptive, ambiguous, paradoxical, unassuming. There's no logic, no duality, no hierarchy. But does immersion in a swamp have anything to do with turning a person from the altar of a church — especially an Eastern church? Try this: Buddhists say that if you meet the Buddha on the road, you mustn't prostrate yourself in front of him, light incense, ring temple bells, count your breaths, or begin chanting. You should kill him — because any naming, any clinging, can too quickly become dogma. The point is to let go of everything. In a spiritual swamp, there's nothing to hold on to. Everything is fluid, mercurial. You're on a small tussock one minute, chanting *Hail Mary* or *Om Mani Padme Hum,* fingering your rosary or mala, offering dollars or marigolds and rupees. As in the first moments of most flights to safe havens, you're basking in some feeling of grace until you notice that everywhere you turn, the altars keep slipping under the surface, and the next minute there's a copperhead at your ankle and you're fleeing through the sedges, leaving a trail of stirred murk and sludge.

Like most refuges, the swamp makes a poor permanent retreat. You can't stay too long without the risk of its becoming a trap with no way out. The dilemma is recognizing the right moment for return. At the exact midpoint of the *I Ching,* the ancient Taoists provide counsel on the wisdom of temporary retreat, which they imagine as the creative heavens balanced on a mountain — an image of stillness. Such provisional retreat demonstrates strength, they say, while perpetual flight signals weakness. Retreat is never meant as escape, a permanent disappearance. In fact, its purpose is restorative: that which retreats is strengthened by a conscious decision to rest. Retreat can be a wise pulling back, a temporary withdrawal until it's time for what the *I Ching* calls the "turning point," the eventual countermovement and return. At some moment, the energy that has been building underground or under the attic eaves, unseen and in private, turns to resurface in the world. This is supposed to be a reversal of the retreat, a bringing back into the larger community the wisdom gained in the quiet of contemplation. The danger, of course, is that the turning point may come and go unrecognized. Those in retreat may miss the signal and go on fortifying the walls, flooding the moat, growing their own food inside the compound.

When scientists in the early 1800s first studied the bronzy-red and lippy leaves of the pitcher plant, they noted the way it collects water in its base and speculated that this wetland plant served as a refuge for insects eluding predators. Because the insect can actually crawl up the flared flap and hide inside, under the shadow of the hood, it could remain out of sight of any marauding bird or bat. This theory, from early scientists who marveled at such cooperative effort, was soon replaced by the realization that although the pitcher plant is designed to look like safe harbor to fleeing insects, it is, instead, a carefully engineered lure and deathtrap. The welcome mat on the flared flap is spiked with hundreds of tiny hairs, all of them aimed downward, like trail markers, and designed to encourage the insect to descend into the pitcher. Once the visitor crawls or slides past these tiny hairs, it slips into the slick, vertical throat of the plant and down into the main body of the pitcher, which is often full of rainwater. The hapless bug then spends the rest of its life, which isn't long, trying to crawl up the sides of the throat, to take off without a solid runway, to keep its exhausted head above water. Eventually, the insect drowns and the plant has its dinner. If the bug was anticipating an eventual return to leafy branches, a summer of night skies and porch lights, it missed the point of return, misjudged the way a trap can disguise itself as retreat. I think of the 450 or so Seminoles still living in the Everglades, generations of hunters and trappers still gliding their canoes through the saw grass as their ancestors did after fleeing from white men in the 1800s. What countermovement? What return?

Years ago I volunteered at a state hospital. My role was to hang around with a kid named Patty, who was maybe thirteen, her face blank and her tongue silent. We did nothing more than walk around the hospital for months. I don't recall that she ever said a word. I used to imagine that inside her mind was a busy port, a large ship unloading its wares with cranes clanking, foghorns out in the harbor moaning, and men on the docks with small carts, hollering and wheeling the cargo to somewhere else — and Patty's job was to not let anyone else know about the existence of this secret port. She was like the screening fog in a special-effects movie, the blank page that harbors invisible ink. I used to imagine that whatever this secret trading was, it needed a sanctuary, needed the fog screen of Patty so it could carry on its business. I didn't care what kind of business this was or whether it was legal. I remember feeling, more than anything, protective of Patty's silence, as if her retreat were more important than whatever handicap it caused for her in her dealings with the rest of the world. I was stupidly romantic: a part of me even envied Patty her ability to use silence to murder every Buddha in the shape of a psychiatrist who rounded the corners of her ward, clipboard in hand. I used to imagine she had befriended the dockworkers and sailors, that everyone in that fog-shrouded port trusted one another to keep the secret until the ship had offloaded whatever its mysterious cargo was, hauled its anchor up, and set out to sea again, lighter, with a lot more air in its holds and engine rooms.

Later, when I studied dissociative reactions in an abnormal-psych class, I thought of Patty and of Eve — the famous case of the multiple personalities who remained, for a while, hidden inside her because they did not feel safe in the noise and crush of the outside world. Therapy eventually helped them emerge and helped Eve live a more normal life, but nothing seemed to help Patty, who, as far as I know, still wanders the hallways behind locked doors. What counterpoint? What return?

The boardwalk at Cranesville wanders for about a half mile out toward a clump of tamaracks where it slips underwater. No gate, no warning sign, no *This is the end! Turn around!* The crossboards simply disappear beneath the mud and water and, as far as I know, keep heading east. It reminds me of the bridge-tunnel spanning the mouth of Chesapeake Bay between Cape Charles and Norfolk. From the air, the bridge looks more like a causeway that abruptly halts partway out in the gray waters of the bay, then reappears a mile or two away. It's as if some engineer's calculations were horrifyingly off, but they went ahead and built the thing anyway. On the road, of course, you simply rise and drop as you climb bridges and descend into tunnels, and so this is what I think when I stand at the point where the boardwalk dips below water: I'll just keep walking and soon I'll enter a tunnel, a tube perhaps, dug out by some kind of shrew and then widened and braced with pressure-treated two-by-fours, and then I'll reemerge into the sunlight and sphagnum a mile or two farther into the bog.

I think of the *I Ching*'s cheerful coaching: *It furthers one to cross the great water.* The ancient Chinese meant, I suppose, that it's important to persevere through danger and uncertainty, that such perseverance allows the eventual possibility of countermovement and return. But who knows if they had this tangled morass in mind? I inch my way along the disappearing boardwalk.

Michael has wandered off. I feel like an old woman alone on an icy ramp; I want handrails and a walker with ice grippers on its legs. I concentrate on keeping the soles of my sneakers in firm contact with the mud-slicked walkway, but when the water curls around my knees, the wood has softened into slime. My foot rummages around, backs up to the last known point of secure contact, inches forward again to find only velvety ooze. I can't tell if the boards simply stop or if they have sunk down under the mud. I can't see anything below my calves. Now what? The *I Ching* urges me on. Joseph Campbell whispers something about the hero's journey and the need to visit the underworld. My mind ratchets from philosophy and metaphor to the not very concrete world oozing around my legs.

Sometimes, Rilke says, a man has to get up from his table and walk. Walk where? And for how long? Moses and Jesus wandered into the desert. Mohammed hiked up the mountain. Michael is considering wandering from one swamp to another. *Solvitur ambulando* — the difficulty will be solved by walking. Rousseau knew this, as did Thoreau, Wordsworth, Nietzsche, and Austen. They walked out into the hills, country paths, and shorelines, philosophical tramps all, seeking some sort of refuge; some of them found it in the walk itself, some in the desert landscapes stripped of the extraneous where they wrestled with the holy, and others in the muck and ooze of swamplands from Florida to Rhode Island where they holed up in the thick entanglements, the mucky waters, the trackless shallows that twist and bend for miles among overhanging cypress.

What countermovement? What return?

I wonder whether Michael worries about his retreat being a one-way street. What if, twenty years from now, he wanders out of the swamp and finds so much of the world has changed that he cannot even buy a book without access to the Internet, which requires a computer, which he sold when he sold his house, his car, his bike, and his kayak. What if he emerges with a passion for hand-knotted Persian carpets and caviar and no way to make a living? Or what if he emerges and nothing, absolutely nothing, has changed?

Out of the desert Jesus emerged, the devil's temptations strewn and parched on the sands behind him. Out of the wilderness, Moses' people wandered into the Promised Land. Under the Wisdom Tree, the Buddha finally stood and stretched his legs. Out of its cocoon in the pitcher plant, the *Exyria rolandiana* moth unfurls its wings. It had found refuge there weeks ago and reinforced the safety of its retreat by spinning a tight girdle around the neck of the plant's hood. The girdling causes the hood to choke and eventually to flop over the throat, sealing off the pitcher from outside intruders, much like closing the hatch on a boat against threatening seas. Inside, the caterpillar spun its cocoon in a dry haven and waited for the right moment, emerging today with wings the color of claret, epaulets of saffron.

Standing at the vanishing end of this boardwalk, I think of the water shrew whose fringed hind toes can actually trap air bubbles that allow him to scamper across the surface of the water. A sort of built-in pontoon system that eliminates for him any need to stand here debating whether this is the turning point, the right moment to head back. The mink is hiding. Around the edges of the bog, the solitary white flower of *Coptis groenlandica* rises from its thready golden stem, which runs underground in a vast, lacy interlocking, its juice a balm for canker sores and irritated eyes. And Michael has reappeared, knee-deep in the earth, to show me sundew plants, those glistening carnivorous circles the size of thumbtacks that look like the childhood drawings of hundreds of suns, cut out and glittered and strewn across the swamp.

On Impact

FROM THE NEW YORKER

WHEN MY WIFE and I are at our summer house in western Maine, I walk four miles every day unless it's pouring down rain. Three miles of this walk are on dirt roads that wind through the woods; a mile of it is on Route 5, a two-lane blacktop highway that runs between Bethel and Fryeburg.

The third week in June of 1999 was an extraordinarily happy one for my wife and for me; our three kids, now grown and scattered across the country, were visiting, and it was the first time in nearly six months that we'd all been under the same roof. As an extra bonus, our first grandchild was in the house, three months old and happily jerking at a helium balloon tied to his foot.

On June 19, I took our younger son to the Portland Jetport, where he caught a flight back to New York. I drove home, had a brief nap, and then set out on my usual walk. We were planning to go *en famille* to see a movie in nearby North Conway that evening, and I had just enough time to go for my walk before packing everybody up for the trip.

I set out around four o'clock in the afternoon, as well as I can remember. Just before reaching the main road (in western Maine, any road with a white line running down the middle of it is a main road), I stepped into the woods and urinated. Two months would pass before I was able to take another leak standing up.

When I reached the highway, I turned north, walking on the gravel shoulder, against traffic. One car passed me, also headed north. About three-quarters of a mile farther along, I was told later, the woman driving that car noticed a light blue Dodge van heading south. The van was looping from one side of the road to the other, barely under the driver's control. When she was safely past the wandering van, the woman turned to her passenger and said, "That was Stephen King walking back there. I sure hope that van doesn't hit him."

Most of the sight lines along the mile-long stretch of Route 5 that I walk are good, but there is one place, a short steep hill, where a pedestrian heading north can see very little of what might be coming his way. I was three-quarters of the way up this hill when the van came over the crest. It wasn't on the road; it was on the shoulder. My shoulder. I had perhaps three-quarters of a second to register this. It was just time enough to think, My God, I'm going to be hit by a school bus, and to start to turn to my left. Then there is a break in my memory. On the other side of it, I'm on the ground, looking at the back of the van, which is now pulled off the road and tilted to one side. This image is clear and sharp, more like a snapshot than like a memory. There is dust around the van's tail-lights. The license plate and the back windows are dirty. I register these things with no thought of myself or of my condition. I'm simply not thinking.

There's another short break in my memory here, and then I am very carefully wiping palmfuls of blood out of my eyes with my left hand. When I can see clearly, I look around and notice a man sitting on a nearby rock. He has a cane resting in his lap. This is Bryan Smith, the forty-two-year-old man who hit me. Smith has got quite the driving record; he has racked up nearly a dozen vehicle-related offenses. He wasn't watching the road at the moment that our lives collided because his Rottweiler had jumped from the very rear of his van onto the back seat, where there was an Igloo cooler with some meat stored in it. The Rottweiler's name was Bullet. (Smith had another Rottweiler at home; that one was named Pistol.) Bullet started to nose at the lid of the cooler. Smith turned around and tried to push him away. He was still looking at Bullet and pushing his head away from the cooler when he came over the top of the knoll, still looking and pushing when he struck me. Smith told friends later that he thought he'd hit "a small deer" until he noticed my bloody spectacles lying on the front seat of his van. They were knocked from my face when I tried to get out of Smith's way. The frames were bent and twisted, but the lenses were unbroken. They are the lenses I'm wearing now, as I write.

*

Smith sees that I'm awake and tells me that help is on the way. He speaks calmly, even cheerily. His look, as he sits on the rock with his cane across his lap, is one of pleasant commiseration: *Ain't the two of us just had the shittiest luck?* it says. He and Bullet had left the campground where they were staying, he later tells an investigator, because he wanted "some of those Marzes bars they have up to the store." When I hear this detail some weeks later, it occurs to me that I have nearly been killed by a character out of one of my own novels. It's almost funny.

Help is on the way, I think, and that's probably good, because I've been in a hell of an accident. I'm lying in the ditch and there's blood all over my face and my right leg hurts. I look down and see something I don't like: my lap appears to be on sideways, as if my whole lower body had been wrenched half a turn to the right. I look back up at the man with the cane and say, "Please tell me it's just dislocated."

"Nah," he says. Like his face, his voice is cheery, only mildly interested. He could be watching all this on TV while he noshes on one of those Marzes bars. "It's broken in five, I'd say, maybe six places."

"I'm sorry," I tell him — God knows why — and then I'm gone again for a little while. It isn't like blacking out; it's more as if the film of memory had been spliced here and there.

When I come back this time, an orange and white van is idling at the side of the road with its flashers going. An emergency medical technician — Paul Fillebrown is his name — is kneeling beside me. He's doing something. Cutting off my jeans, I think, although that might have come later.

I ask him if I can have a cigarette. He laughs and says, "Not hardly." I ask him if I'm going to die. He tells me no, I'm not going to die, but I need to go to the hospital, and fast. Which one would I prefer, the one in Norway–South Paris or the one in Bridgton? I tell him I want to go to Bridgton, to Northern Cumberland Memorial Hospital, because my youngest child — the one I just took to the airport — was born there twenty-two years ago. I ask again if I'm going to die, and he tells me again that I'm not. Then he asks me whether I can wiggle the toes of my right foot. I wiggle them, thinking of an old rhyme my mother used to recite: "This little piggy went to market, this little piggy stayed home." I should have stayed home, I think; going for a walk today was a bad idea. Then I remember that sometimes when people are paralyzed they think they're moving but really aren't.

"My toes, did they move?" I ask Paul Fillebrown. He says that they did, a good, healthy wiggle. "Do you swear to God?" I ask him, and I think he does. I'm starting to pass out again. Fillebrown asks me, very slowly and loudly, leaning down over my face, if my wife is at the big house on the lake. I can't remember. I can't remember where any of my family is, but I'm able to give him the telephone numbers both of our big house and of the cottage on the far side of the lake, where my daughter sometimes stays. Hell, I could give him my Social Security number if he asked. I've got all my numbers. It's everything else that's gone.

Other people are arriving now. Somewhere, a radio is crackling out police calls. I'm lifted onto a stretcher. It hurts, and I scream. Then I'm put into the back of the EMT truck, and the police calls are closer. The doors shut and someone up front says, "You want to really hammer it."

Paul Fillebrown sits down beside me. He has a pair of clippers, and he tells me that he's going to have to cut the ring off the third finger of my right hand — it's a wedding ring my wife gave me in 1983, twelve years after we were actually married. I try to tell Fillebrown that I wear it on my right hand because the real wedding ring is still on the ring finger of my left — the original two-ring set cost me fifteen dollars and ninety-five cents at Day's Jewelers in Bangor, and I bought it a year and a half after I'd first met my wife, in the summer of 1969. I was working at the University of Maine library at the time. I had a great set of muttonchop sideburns, and I was staying just off campus, at Ed Price's Rooms (seven bucks a week, one change of sheets included). Men had landed on the moon, and I had landed on the dean's list. Miracles and wonders abounded. One afternoon, a bunch of us library guys had lunch on the grass behind the university bookstore. Sitting between Paolo Silva and Eddie Marsh was a trim girl with a raucous laugh, red-tinted hair, and the prettiest legs I had ever seen. She was carrying a copy of *Soul on Ice*. I hadn't run across her in the library, and I didn't believe that a college student could produce such a wonderful, unafraid laugh. Also, heavy reading or no heavy reading, she swore like a millworker. Her name was Tabitha

Spruce. We were married in 1971. We're still married, and she has
never let me forget that the first time I met her I thought she was
Eddie Marsh's townie girlfriend. In fact, we came from similar
working-class backgrounds; we both ate meat; we were both political Democrats with typical Yankee suspicions of life outside New
England. And the combination has worked. Our marriage has outlasted all of the world's leaders except Castro.

Some garbled version of the ring story comes out, probably
nothing that Paul Fillebrown can actually understand, but he
keeps nodding and smiling as he cuts that second, more expensive
wedding ring off my swollen right hand. By the time I call Fillebrown to thank him, some two months later, I know that he probably saved my life by administering the correct on-scene medical aid
and then getting me to a hospital, at a speed of roughly ninety
miles an hour, over patched and bumpy back roads.

Fillebrown suggests that perhaps someone else was watching out
for me. "I've been doing this for twenty years," he tells me over the
phone, "and when I saw the way you were lying in the ditch, plus
the extent of the impact injuries, I didn't think you'd make it to
the hospital. You're a lucky camper to still be with the program."

The extent of the impact injuries is such that the doctors at
Northern Cumberland Hospital decide they cannot treat me
there. Someone summons a LifeFlight helicopter to take me to
Central Maine Medical Center in Lewiston. At this point, Tabby,
my older son, and my daughter arrive. The kids are allowed a brief
visit; Tabby is allowed to stay longer. The doctors have assured her
that I'm banged up but I'll make it. The lower half of my body has
been covered. She isn't allowed to see the interesting way that my
lap has shifted around to the right, but she is allowed to wash the
blood off my face and pick some of the glass out of my hair.

There's a long gash in my scalp, the result of my collision with
Bryan Smith's windshield. This impact came at a point less than
two inches from the steel driver's-side support post. Had I struck
that, I would have been killed or rendered permanently comatose.
Instead, I was thrown over the van and fourteen feet into the air. If
I had landed on the rocks jutting out of the ground beyond the
shoulder of Route 5, I would also likely have been killed or permanently paralyzed, but I landed just shy of them. "You must have piv-
oted to the left just a little at the last second," I am told later by the

doctor who takes over my case. "If you hadn't, we wouldn't be having this conversation."

The LifeFlight helicopter arrives in the parking lot, and I am wheeled out to it. The clatter of the helicopter's rotors is loud. Someone shouts into my ear, "Ever been in a helicopter before, Stephen?" The speaker sounds jolly, excited for me. I try to say yes, I've been in a helicopter before — twice, in fact — but I can't. It's suddenly very tough to breathe. They load me into the helicopter. I can see one brilliant wedge of blue sky as we lift off, not a cloud in it. There are more radio voices. This is my afternoon for hearing voices, it seems. Meanwhile, it's getting even harder to breathe. I gesture at someone, or try to, and a face bends upside down into my field of vision.

"Feel like I'm drowning," I whisper.

Somebody checks something, and someone else says, "His lung has collapsed."

There's a rattle of paper as something is unwrapped, and then the second person speaks into my ear, loudly so as to be heard over the rotors: "We're going to put a chest tube in you, Stephen. You'll feel some pain, a little pinch. Hold on."

It's been my experience that if a medical person tells you that you're going to feel a little pinch he's really going to hurt you. This time, it isn't as bad as I expected, perhaps because I'm full of painkillers, perhaps because I'm on the verge of passing out again. It's like being thumped on the right side of my chest by someone holding a short sharp object. Then there's an alarming whistle, as if I'd sprung a leak. In fact, I suppose I have. A moment later, the soft in-out of normal respiration, which I've listened to my whole life (mostly without being aware of it, thank God), has been replaced by an unpleasant *shloop-shloop-shloop* sound. The air I'm taking in is very cold, but it's air, at least, and I keep breathing it. I don't want to die, and, as I lie in the helicopter looking out at the bright summer sky, I realize that I am actually lying in death's doorway. Someone is going to pull me one way or the other pretty soon; it's mostly out of my hands. All I can do is lie there and listen to my thin, leaky breathing: *shloop-shloop-shloop.*

Ten minutes later, we set down on the concrete landing pad of the Central Maine Medical Center. To me, it feels as if we're at the bottom of a concrete well. The blue sky is blotted out, and the *whap-whap-whap* of the helicopter rotors becomes magnified and echoey, like the clapping of giant hands.

Still breathing in great leaky gulps, I am lifted out of the helicopter. Someone bumps the stretcher, and I scream. "Sorry, sorry, you're O.K., Stephen," someone says — when you're badly hurt, everyone calls you by your first name.

"Tell Tabby I love her very much," I say as I am first lifted and then wheeled very fast down some sort of descending walkway. I suddenly feel like crying.

"You can tell her that yourself," the someone says. We go through a door. There is air conditioning, and lights flow past overhead. Doctors are paged over loudspeakers. It occurs to me, in a muddled sort of way, that just an hour ago I was taking a walk and planning to pick some berries in a field that overlooks Lake Kezar. I wasn't going to pick for long, though; I'd have to be home by five-thirty because we were going to see *The General's Daughter,* starring John Travolta. Travolta played the bad guy in the movie version of *Carrie,* my first novel, a long time ago.

"When?" I ask. "When can I tell her?"

"Soon," the voice says, and then I pass out again. This time, it's no splice but a great big whack taken out of the memory film; there are a few flashes, confused glimpses of faces and operating rooms and looming X-ray machinery; there are delusions and hallucinations, fed by the morphine and Dilaudid dripping into me; there are echoing voices and hands that reach down to paint my dry lips with swabs that taste of peppermint. Mostly, though, there is darkness.

Bryan Smith's estimate of my injuries turned out to be conservative. My lower leg was broken in at least nine places. The orthopedic surgeon who put me together again, the formidable David Brown, said that the region below my right knee had been reduced to "so many marbles in a sock." The extent of those lower-leg injuries necessitated two deep incisions — they're called medial and lateral fasciotomies — to release the pressure caused by my exploded tibia and also to allow blood to flow back into my lower leg. If I hadn't had the fasciotomies (or if they had been delayed), it probably would have been necessary to amputate my leg. My right knee was split almost directly down the middle, and I suffered an acetabular fracture of the right hip — a serious derailment, in other words — and an open femoral intertrochanteric fracture in the same area. My spine was chipped in eight places. Four ribs were broken. My right collarbone held, but the flesh above it had been stripped raw. The laceration in my scalp took almost thirty stitches.

Yeah, on the whole I'd say Bryan Smith was a tad conservative.

Mr. Smith's driving behavior in this case was eventually examined by a grand jury, which indicted him on two counts: driving to endanger (pretty serious) and aggravated assault (very serious, the kind of thing that means jail time). After due consideration, the district attorney responsible for prosecuting such cases in my corner of the world allowed Smith to plead out to the lesser charge of driving to endanger. He received six months of county jail time (sentence suspended) and a year's suspension of his right to drive. He was also placed on probation for a year, with restrictions on other motor vehicles, such as snowmobiles and ATVs. Bryan Smith could conceivably be back on the road in the fall or winter of 2001.

David Brown put my leg back together in five marathon surgical procedures that left me thin, weak, and nearly at the end of my endurance. They also left me with at least a fighting chance to walk again. A large steel and carbon-fiber apparatus called an external fixator was clamped to my leg. Eight large steel pegs called Schanz pins ran through the fixator and into the bones above and below my knee. Five smaller steel rods radiated out from the knee. These looked sort of like a child's drawing of sunrays. The knee itself was locked in place. Three times a day, nurses unwrapped the smaller pins and the much larger Schanz pins and swabbed the holes with hydrogen peroxide. I've never had my leg dipped in kerosene and then lit on fire, but if that ever happens I'm sure it will feel quite a bit like daily pin care.

I entered the hospital on June 19. Around the thirtieth, I got up for the first time, staggering three steps to a commode, where I sat with my hospital johnny in my lap and my head down, trying not to weep and failing. I told myself that I had been lucky, incredibly lucky, and usually that worked, because it was true. Sometimes it didn't work, that's all — and then I cried.

A day or two after those initial steps, I started physical therapy.

During my first session, I managed ten steps in a downstairs corridor, lurching along with the help of a walker. One other patient was learning to walk again at the same time as me, a wispy eighty-year-old woman named Alice, who was recovering from a stroke. We cheered each other on when we had enough breath to do so. On our third day in the hall, I told Alice that her slip was showing.

"Your ass is showing, sonny boy," she wheezed, and kept going.

By July 4, I was able to sit up in a wheelchair long enough to go out to the loading dock behind the hospital and watch the fireworks. It was a fiercely hot night, the streets filled with people eating snacks, drinking beer and soda, watching the sky. Tabby stood next to me, holding my hand, as the sky lit up red and green, blue and yellow. She was staying in a condo apartment across the street from the hospital, and each morning she brought me poached eggs and tea. I could use the nourishment, it seemed. In 1997, I weighed 216 pounds. On the day that I was released from Central Maine Medical Center, I weighed 165.

I came home to Bangor on July 9, after a hospital stay of three weeks, and began a daily-rehabilitation program that included stretching, bending, and crutch-walking. I tried to keep my courage and my spirits up. On August 4, I went back to C.M.M.C. for another operation. When I woke up this time, the Schanz pins in my upper thigh were gone. Dr. Brown pronounced my recovery "on course" and sent me home for more rehab and physical therapy. (Those of us undergoing P.T. know that the letters actually stand for Pain and Torture.) And in the midst of all this something else happened.

On July 24, five weeks after Bryan Smith hit me with his Dodge van, I began to write again.

I didn't want to go back to work I was in a lot of pain, unable to bend my right knee. I couldn't imagine sitting behind a desk for long, even in a wheelchair. Because of my cataclysmically smashed hip, sitting was torture after forty minutes or so, impossible after an hour and a quarter. How was I supposed to write when the most pressing thing in my world was how long until the next dose of Percocet?

Yet, at the same time, I felt that I was all out of choices. I had been in terrible situations before, and writing had helped me get over them — had helped me to forget myself, at least for a little while. Perhaps it would help me again. It seemed ridiculous to think it might be so, given the level of my pain and physical incapacitation, but there was that voice in the back of my mind, patient and implacable, telling me that, in the words of the Chambers Brothers, the "time has come today." It was possible for me to disobey that voice but very difficult not to believe it.

In the end, it was Tabby who cast the deciding vote, as she so often has at crucial moments. The former Tabitha Spruce is the person in my life who's most likely to say that I'm working too hard, that it's time to slow down, but she also knows that sometimes it's the work that bails me out. For me, there have been times when the act of writing has been an act of faith, a spit in the eye of despair. Writing is not life, but I think that sometimes it can be a way back to life. When I told Tabby on that July morning that I thought I'd better go back to work, I expected a lecture. Instead, she asked me where I wanted to set up. I told her I didn't know, hadn't even thought about it.

For years after we were married, I had dreamed of having the sort of massive oak-slab desk that would dominate a room — no more child's desk in a trailer closet, no more cramped kneehole in a rented house. In 1981, I had found that desk and placed it in a spacious, skylighted study in a converted stable loft at the rear of our new house. For six years, I had sat behind that desk either drunk or wrecked out of my mind, like a ship's captain in charge of a voyage to nowhere. Then, a year or two after I sobered up, I got rid of it and put in a living-room suite where it had been. In the early nineties, before my kids had moved on to their own lives, they sometimes came up there in the evening to watch a basketball game or a movie and eat a pizza. They usually left a boxful of crusts behind, but I didn't care. I got another desk — handmade, beautiful, and half the size of my original T. rex — and I put it at the far-west end of the office, in a corner under the eave. Now, in my wheelchair, I had no way to get to it.

Tabby thought about it for a moment and then said, "I can rig a table for you in the back hall, outside the pantry. There are plenty of outlets — you can have your Mac, the little printer, and a fan." The fan was a must — it had been a terrifically hot summer, and on the day I went back to work the temperature outside was ninety-five. It wasn't much cooler in the back hall.

Tabby spent a couple of hours putting things together, and that afternoon she rolled me out through the kitchen and down the newly installed wheelchair ramp into the back hall. She had made me a wonderful little nest there: laptop and printer connected side by side, table lamp, manuscript (with my notes from the month before placed neatly on top), pens, and reference materials. On the corner of the desk was a framed picture of our younger son, which she had taken earlier that summer.

"Is it all right?" she asked.

"It's gorgeous," I said.

She got me positioned at the table, kissed me on the temple, and then left me there to find out if I had anything left to say. It turned out I did, a little. That first session lasted an hour and forty minutes, by far the longest period I'd spent upright since being struck by Smith's van. When it was over, I was dripping with sweat and almost too exhausted to sit up straight in my wheelchair. The pain in my hip was just short of apocalyptic. And the first five hundred words were uniquely terrifying — it was as if I'd never written anything before in my life. I stepped from one word to the next like a very old man finding his way across a stream on a zigzag line of wet stones.

Tabby brought me a Pepsi — cold and sweet and good — and as I drank it I looked around and had to laugh despite the pain. I'd written *Carrie* and *Salem's Lot* in the laundry room of a rented trailer. The back hall of our house resembled it enough to make me feel as if I'd come full circle.

There was no miraculous breakthrough that afternoon, unless it was the ordinary miracle that comes with any attempt to create something. All I know is that the words started coming a little faster after a while, then a little faster still. My hip still hurt, my back still hurt, my leg, too, but those hurts began to seem a little farther away. I'd got going; there was that much. After that, things could only get better.

Things have continued to get better. I've had two more operations on my leg since that first sweltering afternoon in the back hall. I've also had a fairly serious bout of infection, and I still take roughly a hundred pills a day, but the external fixator is now gone and I continue to write. On some days, that writing is a pretty grim slog. On others — more and more of them, as my mind reaccustoms itself to its old routine — I feel that buzz of happiness, that sense of having found the right words and put them in a line. It's like lifting off in an airplane: you're on the ground, on the ground, on the ground . . . and then you're up, riding on a cushion of air and the prince of all you survey. I still don't have much strength — I can do a little less than half of what I used to be able to do in a day — but I have enough. Writing did not save my life, but it is doing what it has always done: it makes my life a brighter and more pleasant place.

YUSEF KOMUNYAKAA

Blue Machinery of Summer

FROM THE WASHINGTON POST MAGAZINE

"I FEEL LIKE I'm part of this damn thing," Frank said. He carried himself like a large man even though he was short. A dead cigarette dangled from his half-grin. "I've worked on this machine for twenty-odd years, and now it's almost me."

It was my first day on a summer job at ITT Cannon in Phoenix in 1979. This factory manufactured parts for electronic systems — units that fit into larger, more complex ones. My job was to operate an air-powered punch press. Depending on each item formed, certain dies or templates were used to cut and shape metal plates into designs the engineers wanted.

"I know all the tricks of the trade, big and small, especially when it comes to these punch presses. It seems like I was born riding this hunk of steel."

Frank had a gift for gab, but when the foreman entered, he grew silent and meditative, bent over the machine, lost in his job. The whole day turned into one big, rambunctious dance of raw metal, hiss of steam, and sparks. Foremen strutted about like banty roosters. Women tucked falling curls back into hair nets, glancing at themselves in anything chrome.

This job reminded me of the one I'd had in 1971 at McGraw Edison, also in Phoenix, a year after I returned from Vietnam. Back then, I had said to myself, this is the right setting for a soap opera. Muscle and sex charged the rhythm of this place. We'd call the show "The Line."

I'd move up and down the line, shooting screws into metal cabinets of coolers and air conditioners — one hour for Montgomery

Ward or Sears, and the next two hours for a long line of cabinets stamped McGraw Edison. The designs differed only slightly, but made a difference in the selling price later on. The days seemed endless, and it got to where I could do the job with my eyes closed.

In retrospect, I believe I was hyper from the war. I couldn't lay back; I was driven to do twice the work expected — sometimes taking on both sides of the line, giving other workers a hand. I worked overtime two hours before 7 A.M. and one hour after 4 P.M. I learned everything about coolers and air conditioners, and rectified problem units that didn't pass inspection.

At lunch, rather than sitting among other workers, I chose a secluded spot near the mountain of boxed-up coolers to eat my homemade sandwiches and sip iced tea or lemonade. I always had a paperback book in my back pocket: Richard Wright's *Black Boy*, Albert Camus' *The Fall*, Frantz Fanon's *The Wretched of the Earth*, or C.W.E. Bigsby's *The Black American Writer.* I wrote notes in the margins with a ballpoint. I was falling in love with language and ideas. All my attention went to reading.

When I left the gaze of Arizona's Superstition Mountain and headed for the Colorado Rockies, I wasn't thinking about higher education. Once I was in college, I vowed never to take another job like this, and yet here I was, eight years later, a first-year graduate student at the University of California at Irvine, and working another factory job in Phoenix, hypnotized by the incessant clang of machinery.

Frank schooled me in the tricks of the trade. He took pride in his job and practiced a work ethic similar to the one that had shaped my life early on even though I had wanted to rebel against it. Frank was from Little Rock: in Phoenix, everyone seemed to be from somewhere else except the indigenous Americans and Mexicans.

"If there's one thing I know, it's this damn machine," Frank said. "Sometimes it wants to act like it has a brain of its own, as if it owns me, but I know better."

"Iron can wear any man out," I said.

"Not this hunk of junk. It was new when I came here."

"But it'll still be here when you're long gone."

"Says who?"

"Says iron against flesh."

"They will scrap this big, ugly bastard when I'm gone."

"They'll bring in a new man."

"Are you the new man, whippersnapper? They better hire two of you to replace one of me."

"Men will be men."

"And boys will be boys."

The hard dance held us in its grip.

I spotted Lily Huong the second day in a corner of the wiring department. The women there moved their hands in practiced synchrony, looping and winding color-coded wires with such graceful dexterity and professionalism. Some chewed gum and blew bubbles, others smiled to themselves as if they were reliving the weekend. And a good number talked about the soap operas, naming off the characters as if they were family members or close friends.

Lily was in her own world. Petite, with long black hair grabbed up, stuffed beneath a net and baseball cap, her body was one fluid motion, as if it knew what it was doing and why.

"Yeah, boys will be boys," Frank said.

"What you mean?"

"You're looking at trouble, my friend."

"Maybe trouble is looking for me. And if it is, I'm not running."

"She is nothing but bona fide trouble."

I wondered if she was thinking of Vietnam while she sat bent over the table, or when she glided across the concrete floor as if she were moving through lush grass. Lily? It made me think of waterlily, lotus — how shoots and blooms were eaten in that faraway land. The lotus grows out of decay, in lagoons dark with sediment and rot.

Mornings arrived with the taste of sweet nighttime still in our mouths, when the factory smelled like the deepest ore, and the syncopation of the great heaving presses fascinated me.

The nylon and leather safety straps fit our hands like fingerless gloves and sometimes seemed as if they'd pull us into the thunderous pneumatic vacuum faster than an eye blink. These beasts pulsed hypnotically; they reminded everyone within earshot of terrifying and sobering accidents. The machinery's dance of smooth heft seemed extraordinary, a masterpiece of give-and-take preci-

sion. If a foolhardy novice wrestled with one of these metal contraptions, it would suck up the hapless soul. The trick was to give
and pull back with a timing that meant the difference between life
and death.

"Always use a safety block, one of these chunks of wood. Don't
get careless," Frank said. "Forget the idea you can second-guess
this monster. Two months ago we had a guy in here named Leo on
that hunk of junk over there, the one that Chico is now riding."

"Yeah, and?"

"I don't believe it. It's crazy. I didn't know Leo was a fool. The
machine got stuck, he bent down, looked underneath, and never
knew his last breath. That monster flattened his head like a pan-
cake."

One morning, I stood at the checkout counter signing out my
tools for the day's work and caught a glimpse of Lily out of the corner of my eye. She stopped. Our eyes locked for a moment, and
then she glided on toward her department. Did she know I had
been in 'Nam? Had there been a look in my eyes that had given me
away?

"You can't be interested in her," Paula said. She pushed her hair
away from her face in what seemed like an assured gesture.

"Why not?" I said.

"She's nothing, nothing but trouble."

"Oh?"

"Anyway, you ain't nobody's foreman."

I took my toolbox and walked over to the punch press. The
buzzer sounded. The gears kicked in. The day started.

After three weeks, I discovered certain social mechanisms ran
the place. The grapevine, long, tangled, and thorny, was merciless.
After a month on the job I had been wondering why Frank disappeared at lunchtime but always made it back just minutes before
the buzzer.

"I bet Frank tells you why he comes back here with a smile on his
mug?" Maria coaxed. She worked as a spot-welder, with most of her
day spent behind heavy black goggles as the sparks danced around
her.

"No."

"Why don't you ask Paula one of these mornings when you're
signing out tools?"

"I don't think so," I said.

"She's the one who puts that grin on his face. They've been tearing up that rooming house over on Sycamore for years."

"Good for them," I said.

"Not if that cop husband of hers come to his senses."

It would have been cruel irony for Frank to work more than twenty years on the monster and lose his life at the hands of a mere mortal.

The grapevine also revealed that Lily had gotten on the payroll because of Rico, who was a foreman on the swing shift. They had been lovers and he had put in a good word for her. Rico was built like a lightweight boxer, his eyes bright and alert, always able to look over the whole room in a single glance. The next news said Lily was sleeping with Steve, the shipping foreman, who wore western shirts, a silver and turquoise belt buckle, and cowboy boots. His red Chevy pickup had a steer's horn on the hood. He was tall and lanky and had been in the Marines, stationed at Khe Sanh.

I wondered about Lily. What village or city had she come from — Chu Chi or Danang, Saigon or Hue? What was her story? Did she still hear the war during sleepless nights? Maybe she had had an American boyfriend, maybe she was in love with a Vietnamese once, a student, and they had intimate moments beside the Perfume River as boats with green and red lanterns passed at dusk. Or maybe she met him on the edge of a rice paddy, or in some half-lit place in Danang a few doors down from the Blue Dahlia.

She looked like so many who tried to outrun past lovers, history. "*She's nothing but trouble . . .*" Had she become a scapegoat? Had she tried to play a game that wasn't hers to play? Didn't anyone notice her black eye one week, the corner of her lip split the next?

I told myself I would speak to her. I didn't know when, but I would.

The women were bowed over their piecework.

As a boy I'd make bets with myself, and as a man I was still making bets, and sometimes they left me in some strange situations.

"In New Guinea those Fuzzy Wuzzies saved our asses," Frank said. "They're the smartest people I've ever seen. One moment almost in the Stone Age, and the next they're zooming around in our jeeps and firing automatic weapons like nobody's business. They gave the Japanese hell. They were so outrageously brave it still hurts to think about it."

I wanted to tell him about Vietnam, a few of the things I'd witnessed, but I couldn't. I could've told him about the South Vietnamese soldiers who were opposites of Frank's heroes.

I gazed over toward Lily.

Holding up one of the doodads — we were stamping out hundreds hourly — I said to Frank, "Do you know what this is used for?"

"No. Never crossed my mind."

"You don't know? How many do you think you've made?"

"God only knows."

"And you don't know what they're used for?"

"No."

"How much does each sell for?"

"Your guess is good as mine. I make 'em. I don't sell 'em."

He's right, I thought. Knowing wouldn't change these workers' lives. This great symphony of sweat, oil, steel, rhythm, it all made a strange kind of sense.

"These are used in the firing mechanisms of grenade launchers," I said as I scooped up a handful. "And each costs the government almost eighty-five dollars."

The buzzer sounded.

In the cafeteria, most everybody sat in their usual clusters. A few of the women read magazines — *True Romance, Tan, TV Guide, Reader's Digest* — as they nibbled at sandwiches and sipped Cokes. One woman was reading her Bible. I felt like the odd man out as I took my paperback from my lunch pail: a Great Books Foundation volume, with blue-white-black cover and a circle around *GB*. My coworkers probably thought I was reading the same book all summer long, or that it was a religious text. I read Voltaire, Hegel, and Darwin.

Voltaire spoke to me about Equality:

All the poor are not unhappy. The greater number are born in that state, and constant labor prevents them from too sensibly feeling their situation; but when they do strongly feel it, then follow wars such as these of the popular party against the Senate at Rome, and those of the peasantry in Germany, England and France. All these wars ended sooner or later in the subjection of the people, because the great have money, and money in a state commands everything: I say in a state, for the case is different between nation and nation. That nation makes the best use of iron will always subjugate another that has more gold but less courage.

Maybe I didn't want to deal with those images of 'Nam still in my psyche, ones that Lily had rekindled.

"You catch on real fast, friend," Frank said. "It is hard to teach a man how to make love to a machine. It's almost got to be in your blood. If you don't watch out, you'll be doing twenty in this sweatbox too. Now mark my word."

I wanted to tell him about school. About some of the ideas filling my head. Lily would smile, but she looked as if she were gazing through me.

One morning in early August, a foreman said they needed me to work on a special unit. I was led through the security doors. The room was huge, and the man working on the big, circular-dome object seemed small and insignificant in the voluminous space. Then I was shaking hands with the guy they called Dave the Lathe. Almost everyone had a nickname here, as in the Deep South, where, it turned out, many of the workers were from. The nicknames came from the almost instinctual impulse to make language a game of insinuation.

Dave was from Paradise, California. He showed me how to polish each part, every fixture and pin. The work led to painstaking tedium. Had I posed too many questions? Was that why I was working this job?

Here everything was done by hand, with patience and silence. The room was air-conditioned. Now the clang of machines and whine of metal being cut retreated into memory. Behind this door Dave the Lathe was a master at shaping metals, alloyed with secrets, a metal that could be smoothed but wouldn't shine, take friction and heat out of this world. In fact, it looked like a fine piece of sculpture designed aeronautically, that approached perfection. Dave the Lathe had been working on this nose cone for a spacecraft for more than five months.

Dave and I seldom talked. Lily's face receded from my thoughts. Now I stood across from Dave the Lathe, thinking about two women in my class back at the University of California with the same first name. One was from New York. She had two reproductions of French nudes over her bed and was in love with Colette, the writer. The other woman was part Okinawan from Honolulu. If we found ourselves in a room alone, she always managed to disengage herself. We had never had a discussion, but here she was, undressing in my mind. At that moment, standing a few feet from Dave the Lathe, I felt that she and I were made for each other but she didn't know it yet.

I told Dave that within two weeks I'd return to graduate school. He wished me luck in a tone that suggested he knew what I'd planned to say before I said it.

"Hey, college boy!" Maria shouted across the cafeteria. "Are you in college or did you do time like Frank says?" I wanted the impossible, to disappear.

Lily's eyes caught mine. I still hadn't told her I felt I'd left part of myself in her country. Maria sat down beside me. I fished out the ham sandwich, but left Darwin in the lunch box. She said, "You gonna just soft-shoe in here and then disappear, right?"

"No. Not really."

"*Not really,* he says," she mocked.

"Well."

"Like a lousy lover who doesn't tell you everything. Doesn't tell the fine print."

"Well."

"Cat got your tongue, college boy?"

"Are you talking to me or somebody else?"

"Yeah, you! Walk into somebody's life and then turn into a ghost. A one-night stand."

"I didn't think anyone needed to know."

"I suppose you're too damn good to tell us the truth."

She stood up, took her lunch over to another table, sat down, and continued to eat. I didn't know what to say. I was still learning.

There's good silence. There's bad silence. Growing up in rural Louisiana, along with four brothers and one sister, I began to cultivate a life of the imagination. I traveled to Mexico, Africa, and the Far East. When I was in elementary school and junior high, sometimes I knew the answers to questions, but I didn't dare raise my hand. Boys and girls danced up and down, waving their arms, with right and wrong answers. It was hard for me to chance being wrong. Also, I found it difficult to share my feelings; but I always broke the silence and stepped in if someone was being mistreated.

Now, as I sat alone, looking out the window of a Greyhound bus at 1 A.M., I felt like an initiate who had gotten cold feet and was hightailing it back to some privileged safety zone. I began to count the figures sprawled on the concrete still warm from the sun's weight on the city. There seemed to be an uneasy equality among destitutes: indigenous Americans, Mexicans, a few blacks and whites. Eleven. Twelve. I thought, a massacre of the spirit.

The sounds of the machines were still inside my head. The clanging punctuated by Frank's voice: "Are you ready to will your body to this damn beast, my friend?"

"No, Frank. I never told you I am going to college," I heard my-self saying. Did education mean moving from one class to the next? My grandmothers told me again and again that one could scale a mountain with a good education. But could I still talk to them, to my parents, my siblings? I would try to live in two worlds — at the very least. That was now my task. I never wanted again to feel that my dreams had betrayed me.

Maybe the reason I hadn't spoken to Lily was I didn't want to talk about the war. I hadn't even acknowledged to my friends that I'd been there.

The bus pulled out, headed for L.A. with its headlights sweeping like slow yellow flares across drunken faces, as if images of the dead had followed Lily and me from a distant land only the heart could bridge.

MARCUS LAFFEY

The Midnight Tour

FROM THE NEW YORKER

WHEN I WENT to work midnights a few months ago, it was discovered that I didn't have a nickname. You need one, to talk casually over the radio: "Stix, you getting coffee?" "Chicky, did you check the roof?" "O.V., T., G.Q., can you swing by?" Nicknames never stuck to me, for some reason, and I always thought that nicknaming yourself was like talking to yourself, something that made you look foolish if you were overheard. So Hawkeye, the Hat, Hollywood, Gee Whiz, Big E., the Count, Roller Coaster, and Fierce pitched a few:

"'Hemingway' — nah, they'd know it was you."

"'Ernest' is better."

"Or 'Clancy' — he'd be a good one to have."

"What about 'Edgar'?"

"What from?"

"Edgar Allan Poe."

"What about 'Poe'?"

As I thought about it, the fit was neat: Poe, too, in his most famous poem, had worked, weak and weary, upon a midnight dreary. He moved to New York City in 1844, the same year that legislation created the New York City Police Department. And he wrote the first detective story ever, "The Murders in the Rue Morgue," in which the killer turns out to be a demented orangutan with a straight razor. There is also a brilliant detective, an earnest sidekick, and a mood of languor and gloom — all now hallmarks of a genre that has endured for a century and a half. Poe spent his last years in the Bronx, living and working in a cottage that is midway between where I live and where I work. I am a police

officer in the Bronx, where kids sometimes call the cops "po-po."
And so "Poe" it was.

Midnights for Edgar Allan Poe seemed less a time than a territory, a place of woefully distant vistas, as if he were stargazing from
the bottom of a well. A lot of that has to do with needing sleep,
I think. Everyone on the late tour lacks sleep, and this state of
worn-out wakefulness while the rest of the world is dreaming tends
to stimulate thoughts that meander. Each precinct has a list of
"cooping-prone locations," which are out-of-the-way places, under
bridges and by rail yards and the like, where bosses are supposed to
check to make sure patrol cars haven't stopped in for a nap. The
list is posted in the station house, and when you're tired it reads
like a recommendation, a Zagat guide for secret sleep, as if it might
be saying, "St. Mary's Park, with its rolling hills and abundant trees,
offers superb concealment in a pastoral setting — we give it four
pillows!" On midnights, we talk about sleep the way frat boys talk
about sex. Did you get any last night? How was it? Nah, nah, but
this weekend, believe me, I'm gonna go all night long! Although
I've asked practically everyone on the tour how long it takes for
your body to adjust to an upside-down life, only three people have
given precise answers, which were "Two months," "Four years,"
and "Never." Nevermore.

I went to midnights after my old narcotics team split up. It
seemed like a good interim assignment, a way station until something better came along, and I thought I could use the free time
during the day. Mostly, you drive around and check things out until a job comes over the radio. There are fewer jobs than during the
other tours of duty — although the jobs tend to be more substantial — and even on weekend nights they tend to taper off after two
or three in the morning. You usually have to check a few buildings,
and you'd probably get into trouble if you never wrote a ticket, but
you have more time to yourself than on any other tour. My uncle
finished his thirty-three years as a cop working midnights in the
Bronx; he would have said that he liked it because the bosses leave
you alone. Still, to be back on patrol feels odd sometimes, and
when I think about my past and the past of this place I wonder
where I'm going. It can bring on a terminal feeling.

One night, I drove with my partner to the corner of 132nd
Street and Lincoln Avenue — a cooping-prone location, though

that wasn't the reason for the visit — which is a dead end at the very bottom of the Bronx, with a warehouse on one side and a parking lot on the other. Across the black shimmer of the river you can see Harlem and the salt piles along the FDR. The Bronx begins here physically, and it began here historically as well; this was the site of Jonas Bronck's farmhouse. Not much is known about him: he was a Swedish sea captain who was induced to settle the area by the Dutch West India Company. A peace treaty signed at Bronck's house ended years of sporadic but bloody skirmishes between the Dutch and the Weckquasgeeks. Bronck didn't have much to do with it, but his house was the only one around. "When did he move?" my partner asked. It was a funny question, because it made me think of the Bronx as a place where people come from but not where they stay, if luck is on their side.

The Bronx was a place of slow beginnings: Bronck came here in 1639 to homestead, and at the beginning of the twentieth century there was still farmland in the South Bronx; it became citified only as the subway was built. A person alive today could have witnessed the borough's entire metropolitan career: two generations as a vibrant, blue-collar boomtown, and one as a ravaged and riotous slum. When Jimmy Carter visited Charlotte Street in September 1977, he saw vacant and collapsing buildings inhabited by junkies and packs of wild dogs. A week later, during a broadcast of the World Series at Yankee Stadium, there was a fire at a school a few blocks from the game. Millions watched it as Howard Cosell intoned, "The Bronx is burning." One of my uncles was a fireman here at the time, and he told me that they were busier than the London fire department during the Blitz.

My partner and I cruised up to 142nd Street between Willis and Brook Avenues, a block with a row of little houses on one side and a school on the other. I used to chase a lot of junkies down that street when they were buying heroin with the brand name President from the projects on the corner. A hundred years ago, the Piccirilli brothers, sculptors from Pisa, had a studio here, where they carved the statue for the Lincoln Memorial, but I don't suppose the dope was named in any commemorative spirit. Four blocks up and two over, Mother Teresa's order runs a soup kitchen and a shelter next to the Church of St. Rita, a boxy old building painted robin's-egg blue. The work the order does is holy and noble, but for us there is something embarrassing about it: nuns reassigned from leper duty in Calcutta to lend us a hand. There was a picture in the *News* a few years back of Mother Teresa and Princess Diana visiting the mission together, and one of my old partners was there, standing guard, just out of the frame. A little farther out of the frame is the building where Rayvon Evans died: a little boy whose parents kept his corpse in a closet until the fluids seeped through to the floor below and the neighbors complained. No one was ever charged with the murder, because there wasn't enough left of him to determine how he died. There is a garden dedicated to Rayvon, but no sign of the Princess or the sculptors. Memory is short here, but the past is visible all around you — at least, until the present calls you back. It can take time for your eyes to adjust.

Midnights tend to magnify things, to set them in sharp relief against the empty night, like gems on a black velvet cloth. You meet lonely people who seem more solitary and sorrowful at night, such as the chubby little woman who reclined in her armchair like a pasha after attempting suicide by taking three Tylenol PMs. Or the woman with dye-drowned blond hair going green, who denied trying to hurt herself, though her boyfriend confided that she had: "She slapped herself, hard." Domestic disputes are all the more squalid and small-hearted when they take place at five in the morning — like the one between two middle-aged brothers who were at each other's throats hours before their mother's funeral. The place stank and the walls seethed with roaches. One brother had a weary and beaten dignity; he was sitting on the couch with his overcoat and an attaché case when we arrived, like a salesman who'd just lost a commission. The other brother shouted drunkenly, jerking and flailing like a dervish afflicted with some unknown neurological misfiring. They had argued because he had started drinking again.

I took the jerky one aside, to let him vent a little. His room was littered with cans of Night Train; military papers and alcohol-rehab certificates were taped to the wall. As he punched the honorable discharge to emphasize that his had been a life of accomplishment, a burst of roaches shot out from underneath. I wanted to punch his rehab diploma, to show that he still had some work to do, but I thought better of it.

My partner and I knew that we would be back if both brothers remained there, and we dreaded the idea of having to lock one of them up before the funeral, so we asked the sane brother if he wouldn't mind leaving for a while. He agreed that it was the best thing to do; we agreed that it was deeply unfair. He used to work as a security guard, and he offered us his business card. "If there's anything I can do for you gentlemen," he said, and he went out to walk until daybreak.

If some people call because they need someone — anyone — to talk to, there are others for whom we're the last people they want to see. For them, we arrive the way the Bible says Judgment will: like a thief in the night. It felt like that when we showed up to take a woman's children away. We were escorting two caseworkers from the Administration of Children's Services who had a court order to remove the one-, two-, and three-year-old kids of a crackhead I'll call Pamela. The midnight visit was a sneak attack, as she had dodged the caseworkers the day before. We were there — not to put too fine a point on it — as hired muscle.

When we knocked, a woman answered ("Who?") and then delayed ten minutes, muttering excuses ("Hold on," and "Let me get something on," and "Who is it, again?"), before surrendering to threats to kick the door down. She was just a friend, she said, helping to clean up — probably in anticipation of such a visit. Pamela was out. Yes, there were kids in the back, but they were Pamela's sister's kids, and the sister was out, too. As we looked in on the sleeping children, another woman emerged from a back bedroom, and she was equally adamant: "But those are my kids, and I'm not Pamela, I'm her sister, Lorraine! I can show you you're making a mistake!"

We grilled both women, but they never deviated from their story, and we could find no baby pictures or prescription bottles or anything else that would tie these children to the case. So when "Lorraine" said she could prove that they were hers if we'd let her call her mother to get her ID we agreed, as it would clearly demonstrate whether we were professional public servants doing a difficult job or dimwitted repo men hauling off the wrong crack babies.

But she didn't call for her ID, she called for reinforcements, and the apartment was soon flooded with angry women. We held the baby boy while Pamela managed to grab the two girls; then a neighbor took one of the girls as Pamela tried to get out with the other, making it all the way into the hall. More cops came, and one started after her, telling her to stop, but a neighbor blocked his way, howling, "Call the cops! Call the cops and have him arrested! He ain't leaving till the cops come and arrest him!"

The sergeant called for backup, and even more cops arrived, two of them running up twelve flights of stairs — but then one had to lie down in the stairwell, and the other was rushed to the hospital with chest pains. The press of angry bodies made the apartment hot, and some women yelled for everyone to calm down, and some women yelled the opposite, and as we tried to dress the crying kids some women tried to help in earnest, finding their jackets and socks, while others were still plainly angling to spirit them away.

When Pamela's last child had been taken, she swung at a cop, but then another cop grabbed her wrists, and her friends took her aside, and after a few more eruptions of screaming we got the kids out. One woman yelled, "This is why people hate the cops!" Although I thought very little of her and the rest of them — Mothers United for Narcotics and Neglect — she had a point: no one likes people who steal babies in the middle of the night. And we had just started our tour.

The midnight tour is also called the first platoon, the second being the day tour and the third being the four-to-twelve. You begin at 2315 hours and end at 0750. If you have Tuesday and Wednesday off one week, say, you have Tuesday, Wednesday, and Thursday off the next, and then Wednesday and Thursday the week after that. It takes some getting used to, because if you're working a Friday you don't come in Friday — you come in Thursday night. Another depressing thing about midnights is that when you finish work in the morning, at ten minutes to eight, you don't say, "See you tomorrow," which would seem soon enough; you say, "See you tonight." Tonight began yesterday, and tomorrow begins tonight, and the days become one rolling night.

When I first went on the job, I started out on steady four-to-twelves, Sunday to Thursday, working in a project called Morris Houses, which, with Morrisania, Butler, and Webster Houses, make up a huge complex of thirty apartment buildings called Claremont

Village, in the heart of the South Bronx. On that beat, I was generally busier than I am now, when I might cover an entire precinct. I knew less local lore then, and the landmarks I navigated by were of recent relevance: the pawnshop to check after a chain snatch; the crack house where a baby overdosed; the rooftop where they fought pit bulls, sometimes throwing the loser to the street below. I still occasionally drive through this area with my partner, but even with my grasp of the neighborhood's history I'm not sure why things turned out as they did, and still less what led me here.

Morris Houses was named after Gouverneur Morris, a Revolutionary War hero, who was with Washington at Valley Forge and later established the decimal system of United States currency, proposing the words "dollar" and "cent." His half-brother Lewis was a signer of the Declaration of Independence, and tried to get the Founding Fathers to establish the nation's capital on the family estate, but the idea was more or less a nonstarter. The Morrises owned most of the South Bronx for nearly two centuries, and their name is everywhere: Morrisania, the neighborhood in the Forty-second Precinct, where my beat was; Morris Heights; Port Morris; Morris High School, which the industrialist Armand Hammer and General Colin Powell graduated from. Yet I couldn't say it means much to anyone here. The kids that Bernhard Goetz shot in 1984 — four thugs who failed to recognize a subway-riding vigilante — came from Morrisania. One of them remains confined to a wheelchair, and I'd sometimes see him around; I locked up another one's sister for robbery, after a nasty girl-gang fight. I can't imagine that her mother said, upon her return from jail, "Gouverneur Morris and his half-brother Lewis must be rolling in their graves!" The Morrises made this place and helped make this nation, but they might as well have knocked up some local girls and split after the shotgun wedding, leaving nothing behind but their name.

On midnights, there is a risk of drifting within yourself, trailing off on your own weird train of thought, so that when the even weirder world intrudes it is hard not to laugh. One night not long ago, it was so slow that three patrol cars showed up for a dispute between two crackheads over a lost shopping cart. To pass the time, we conducted an investigation, asking pointed questions: What color was the cart? Do you have a receipt? It was cold, and after a while one of the cops said we should leave. But I was bored enough to want to talk to the crackheads, who relished the attention. I said to the cop, "They have issues, we can help them work through them, the relationship can come out even stronger than it was before." He looked at me and said, "Hey, I'm no Dr. Zhivago — let's get out of here."

On another job, we received a call for help from an old man and his sick wife. They seemed like good people: he had an upright, military bearing, and she was a stick figure, with plum-colored bruises all over, gasping through a nebulizer, "*Ayúdame, ayúdame, ayúdame.*" We made small talk, in broken English and Spanish, while waiting for EMS. On a shelf, there was a photograph of a young man in a police uniform, who the old man said was his son, a cop in San Juan who died at the age of thirty-four from cancer. The entire apartment was a Santería shrine: cigars laid across the tops of glasses of colorless liquid; open scissors on dishes of blue liquid; dried black bananas hanging over the threshold; Tarot cards, coins, and dice before a dozen statues of saints, including a huge Virgin Mary with a triple-headed angel at her feet. Suddenly, I thought, They keep the place up, but it's more *House Voodooful* than *House Beautiful*. The line wouldn't leave my head, so I had to pretend to cough, and walk outside.

You get in the habit of reading these scenes for signs, whether forensic or sacramental, of sin and struggle in the fallen world. Santería shrines and offerings are often placed in the corner of a room near the entrance, and in just that corner of one apartment we found a black-handled butcher knife next to blood that had not just pooled but piled, it lay so thick on the floor: dark, sedimentary layers with a clear overlay, like varnish, which I was told came from the lungs. The woman responsible for this handiwork explained why she had tried to sacrifice her brother at the household altar: "Two years ago, he broke my leg in five places. I came in tonight, he sold my couch. He killed my mother. Well, she died from him and all his nonsense." She stopped talking for a moment and tried to shift her hands in her cuffs as EMS took her brother out in a wheelchair, pale and still. "I didn't stab him," she went on. "He stabbed himself by accident, in the back, during the tussle."

Some objects tell simple stories of fierce violence, like the two-by-four, so bloody it looked as if it had been dipped in the stuff, that a woman had used to collect a fifty-dollar debt, or the rape victim's panties in the stairwell, covered with flies. Others are more subtle and tentative, like the open Bible in the apartment of a woman whose brother, just home from prison, had suffered some sort of psychotic break. "He sat there reading the Bible for a while, and then he just looked up and said he was going to kill me," she said. The Bible was open to Proverbs 1:18, which states, "These men lie in wait for their own blood, they set a trap for their own lives." Maybe he'd read only the first part of the sentence. The woman's husband had just died, and next to the Bible there was a sympathy card from someone named Vendetta.

As a cop, you look for patterns — for context and connections that tell a fuller truth than a complainant may be willing to tell. Sometimes, though, the parts belong to no whole. So it was with a pair of attempted robberies, only twenty minutes and four blocks apart. Each perp was a male Hispanic, tall, slim, and young, in dark clothes, with a razor blade, though in the second robbery the perp wore a mask and a wig. And so when we came upon a tall, slim, young male Hispanic in dark clothes with a wig, mask, and razor in his pocket, in a desolate park between the two crime scenes, I reasonably expected to have solved at least one crime. Both complainants were sure, however, that he wasn't the man responsible, and we let him go.

In such cases, the solution seems out of sight but within reach, like the winning card in three-card monte. But there are other, older mysteries, and if there is a hint of a game in what unfolds you feel more like a piece than like a player. One night, we went to a routine "aided case," an old woman with a history of heart trouble, whose breath was rapid and shallow. She moaned, "Mami!" as she sat on a red velvet couch, flanked by two teenage girls. As the old lady left with EMS, my partner told me that she was raising her two granddaughters. An hour or so later, we had another aided case, a "heavy bleeder." When we went inside, a woman said, "She's in bed," and then, "It's in the tub." We checked on a teenage girl in the bedroom, who said she was fine, and then looked in the bathtub; there, nestled in the drain, was a fetus the size and color of a sprained thumb. The head was turned upward and the eyes were open and dark.

When the EMTs came — the same guys we'd met on the previous job — they asked for some plastic wrap or tinfoil, and were provided with a sandwich bag to pick it up. As we helped them put the teenage girl in the ambulance, they told us that the old lady had gone into cardiac arrest and wouldn't make it. Nothing else happened that night, and as we drove around I kept thinking that for everyone who dies another isn't necessarily born. It was late but also too early, not yet time to go home.

From the sixties through the eighties, the landscape of the Bronx was a record of public failure, high and low — from Robert Moses, who moved through the Bronx like Sherman through Georgia, evicting thousands in order to build highways, to the scavengers and predators who made ordinary life impossible for ordinary people. I've often wondered what Poe would have thought of the South Bronx at its worst — what his ghost would make of our ghost town. He wrote about loves lost to death at an early age, and set his tales in ancestral houses gone to ruin, but he might have taken to the abandoned factories and the tenements whose graffiti-covered walls had collapsed, leaving them open like doll houses. He might have said, "Don't change a thing!" Then again, such a landscape might have left little room for the imagination, or offered too much.

Since then, the landscape has changed for the better, and the record has been rewritten, often quickly and well. Of course, when something returned from the dead in Poe's world no good came of it, like the hideous beating of that telltale heart. On the other hand, the phrase "with a vengeance" does come to mind when I look at Suburban Place, one block from Charlotte Street, which is now the center of several blocks of well-tended ranch houses. There is something surreal about this development, with its fences and lawns, given both the area's past and its surroundings, which are still rough. You could look at it as a plot twist as unexpected as anything in Poe. You have to wait for it, and be accepting of surprise.

One night, we raced to the scene of "shots fired" from an elevated subway platform — a call that EMS workers had put over as they were driving past. A number of passersby confirmed it, but the shooter was long gone. Four hours later, with little to do in the interim except drive around in the dark, we received another job of shots fired, from an apartment right next to the El. Inside, a lovely old couple pointed out a hole in the window, and the neat chute that the bullet had cut through a hanging basket of African violets, littering stems and leaves on the floor. "I love my plants, they're my babies," the woman said, more concerned about what had happened than about what might have happened. The woman was a kind of grandmother to the neighborhood, and had been for more than a generation. There was a picture on the wall of her with Mayor Lindsay, who she said had let her have a house for a dollar a year to take care of local children. "Give your plants a big drink of water," I said. "And I'll play them some nice soothing music, too," she added. We saw where the bullet had hit the back wall — not far from Mayor Lindsay — but then had to dig around in the kitchen for a while before we found it, under the refrigerator. The heat and speed and impact had transformed the sleek missile into an odd-shaped glob, like a scoop of mashed potato, harmless and pointless. It was a big slug, probably from a .45, and had she been watering her plants it would have taken her head off. It frightened her, to be sure, but she had slept through its arrival and she would sleep again now that it was gone.

The bullet had taken less than a second to travel from the barrel into the couple's home, but in my mind the journey had taken four hours — from when the bullet was heard to when it was found — and I could picture it in slow motion, floating like a soap bubble on a windless night. Both perspectives seemed equally real, the explosive instant and the glacial glide, and I was glad to be able to see each of them, in the luxury of time. The old couple, I'm sure, were glad of it as well. My partner and I took the bullet with us, and morning arrived as we left.

LENORE LOOK

Facing the Village

FROM MĀNOA

> Very young, I left my native place, now very old, I return,
> Village accent unchanged, but sideburns grown thin,
> The children see me but know me not,
> Laughing, they ask, "Stranger, from what place do you come?"
> — He Zhi-zhang (T'ang poet, 659?–744?)

ON THE MORNING of Tuesday, February 3, 1998, during the first hours of the Year of the Tiger, my father abruptly stopped our chauffeur-driven minivan just short of his childhood village in China. It was the end of an anxiety-ridden journey for him, one that he felt he had been dragged into by my mother and me: I was on a search for my roots, and Mother was fulfilling a lifelong dream of returning home. In the stubborn, juvenile way that he resorts to whenever the women in his life get their way and he is all but flailing helplessly, my father was making one last desperate attempt to abort our trip, thwart our schemes, and show us that he was in charge. We had come halfway around the world — my husband and I from New Jersey, and they from Seattle — to the threshold of reunion and discovery, and my father was still determined to turn us back.

"See," Father said in his what-did-I-tell-you tone, "nobody's home."

Father was impatient. He had been irritated by a mob of drivers at Guanghai, the Taishan port on the South China Sea, where we arrived after a four-hour hydrofoil ride from Hong Kong. Each desperate for our fare, the dozen or so drivers had singled out my father as the tribal chief of our party, swarmed him in the dusty parking lot after we had gone through customs, and fallen into an angry shouting match and tug-of-war over the day's catch of overseas Chinese.

"I'll take you for one hundred renminbi!" one man screamed upon seeing us. His shirt, shiny from wear and moist with perspiration, opened between the buttons as he pushed himself against my father.

"No, ninety here!" another man yelled, spitting white foam from between his brown teeth. A million droplets landed on my father's face. He grabbed the suitcase my father was holding and started to pull. Already, our journey to the village was worse than Father had predicted. He had feared that our presence as overseas Chinese in this area of deep poverty and lawlessness might tempt even an otherwise honest driver to take us into a remote field and rob us, but his darkest scenarios did not include stepping into an ambush at the start. It was a terrible omen.

"Don't listen to him!" seethed another, pulling my father's other arm in the opposite direction. "Eighty will do."

"Eighty!" Four or five others joined in, waving arms and fists at my father, who looked like a condemned man facing his executioners.

"Seventy!" another spat, anger pulsing through a blue, hose-sized vein in his neck. A round of "Seventy!" rose up, quick and vengeful.

Crushed on all sides, Father looked frantically for help from the two armed guards standing on the edge of the parking lot. Catching my father's eye, the guards, who had been watching with unguarded amusement, turned as though they were being summoned from their favorite TV program and retreated into the customs building. Left to divide their spoils, the drivers began to tear at the suitcases in our hands and to pull each of us in a different direction.

Then my father spoke. He demanded to see their cars. The man tugging at my bag let go. Suddenly game-show hosts, the men made exaggerated sweeping gestures toward their prizes. To no one's surprise, these were of the booby variety: heaps of rusting scrap metal that might be mistaken for cars in working condition if one were heavily drugged or intoxicated. But there was one exception: a white, late-model Toyota minivan. The driver, with his combed hair and tweed sports jacket, emerged like a shining redeemer. He quickly settled for sixty renminbi (about $7.50) for the hour-long ride to Tai Cheng, the provincial capital of Taishan County, where we expected to find hotel accommodations.

We rode nervously to Tai Cheng. My mother kept trying to make small talk with the driver, a thin, laconic man who had large, bloodshot eyes and protruding cheekbones and who seemed uncomfortable with her prying questions. She extracted from him his surname, Moy, and told him that her mother was a Moy. They must be from the same village, she said, meaning, You wouldn't rob your relations, would you? It turned out they were from the same place. The driver then speculated on our *ho sai gai* (good fortune) at being North American Chinese, by which he meant, I hit the jackpot! My father quickly responded with a tale of hardship, indicating to the driver that we were not worth robbing. Father explained that he had toiled most of his life in the hot kitchens of Chinese restaurants, where there was no money to be made. We are *ho kuung* (very poor), he added. It was true. My mother had recently confided to me that she earned no more than ten thousand dollars last year, sewing at the same garment factory she joined nearly thirty years ago. My father, still a cook at age sixty-eight, has reduced his hours to three days a week, undoubtedly earning much less. For all of my parents' working lives, their income has hovered around the U.S. poverty line, tethered there by their lack of education and language skills and perhaps their self-imposed isolation in a foreign, and often racist, environment. But how do you explain this to someone whose income is even lower than theirs?

While watching the driver's eyes in the rearview mirror, I discreetly removed my jewelry and lipstick, both signs of affluence, and prayed he did not know the cost of airfare. What I thought was Father's paranoia was now a sickening possibility. We were driving through nothing but remote fields on a two-lane highway that held no other traffic. In an area where a family earning the equivalent of fifty dollars a month is considered affluent, we were probably the only ones with cash in our pockets, coveted American passports, and who knows what other items that might enable a poor family to cover medical costs and other basic needs. If the driver were to rob us, there was no better place than right there. Thick and thicker cataracts of suspicion clouded our eyes, and I began to see us as a truckload of fat chickens about to be plucked. We drove on and on into nowhere.

To our inestimable relief, we finally arrived at the Taishan Garden Hotel. Our driver promptly asked if we were intending to *fan heang haa* (return to the village). He was practiced in this. Only overseas Chinese directed him to the town's fanciest hotel, which cost the equivalent of thirty dollars a night. My parents, unnerved by this stranger's foreknowledge of our itinerary, began to say that we had other plans. Sightseeing, they said. The driver was not convinced. Tai Cheng has no tourist attractions, no shopping — nothing. The only visitors are pilgrims. Miserly with conversation earlier, Mr. Moy was now mouthy, even aggressive. He pressed further, offering to drive us to the villages of our choice for another pittance: three hundred renminbi — nearly forty dollars — for the entire day. There were no other cars to hire unless we were to return to the knot of drivers at Guanghai. Reluctantly, my father negotiated again with the man all of us now suspected would eventually rob us.

The Taishan countryside, birthplace of Chinese immigration and the ancestral home of most North American Chinese, is flat as a frying pan. Meaning "elevated mountain" and known locally as "Hoisan," Taishan refers to a small mountain range that appears in the distance. Located just south of the Tropic of Cancer, in southern China's Guangdong Province, it is covered with a patchwork of rice paddies and taro fields, which benefit from the sun's high elevation, even in winter. Elevated dirt roads flanked by ditches four feet deep run between the paddies. These roads are wide enough for one car and one water buffalo. Lone houses, some large and ornately decorated with Victorian gingerbread or Greek Revival motifs, such as Corinthian columns, stand in an area uncharacterized by excess of any sort. Located in the western part of the Pearl River delta region, Taishan is on the margin of the highly commercialized zone centering around Hong Kong and Guangzhou. Too remote to have benefited from the trade with European merchants that began in the early nineteenth century, Taishan continues to sleep on the fringe of commerce, subsisting on a farming economy. But unlike any other part of China, it receives remittances from its native sons and daughters who have left and, with these, has built homes, schools, and roads.

My father's village was not what I had expected. Children's book illustrations, movie scenes of walled Chinese courtyards decorated with swinging red lanterns, fish ponds, and filigree balustrades were what had filled my mind. Perhaps I was also expecting to hear the airy notes of a bamboo flute and the cries of children clad in silk pajamas and playing in leafy bamboo groves. Instead, in front of us was a cluster of low, two-story concrete buildings, gray and darkened by age. Looking like tree branches, cracks ran merciless fingers all over the walls. Windows were boarded. Not a stalk of bamboo anywhere.

The last of Father's immediate family and close relatives had immigrated to the United States in the 1960s, leaving Gnin On, the Look family village, mostly uninhabited. My great-grandfather, Look Ah Lung (Ah Lung, meaning "Big Dragon," was a name he took for himself), was the first of the Look clan to leave his centuries-old village for America. In 1889, seven years after the first Chinese Exclusion Act was passed in the States, thirteen-year-old Ah Lung, fearing starvation, became a stowaway on a ship leaving Hong Kong Harbor for Port Townsend, Washington. A waif-like youth who had a queue when he landed on American soil, he grew into a handsome and affable man who displayed a Western panache in subsequent passport photographs. He made friends quickly in the Seattle laundry where he worked and by 1903 had obtained sworn testimony from white friends that he was a native-born United States citizen, thus assuring himself and those he claimed as children a place in the Land of the Flowery Flag. His remittances and those of kinsmen whom he subsequently brought to the States were what built the concrete-block homes that stood before us. A wealthy man by village standards, Ah Lung died in the village in 1951, two years after he helped his first grandson, my father, make his way to Seattle. His widow, my great-grandmother, was the last to emigrate, doing so in 1968, at the tender age of ninety.

Father expected no reception at the village. He'd sent no advance word of our visit, certain that those who had had no means of leaving several decades ago surely would have found their way by now to Guangzhou, about two hundred miles east. There they would have found work. This remote village was quiet except for our idling car and the song of thrushes in early spring.

Father directed us to stay in the car. He opened his door and stepped out, his shoes crunching the gravel and dirt that he had not touched in fifty years. The last time he had walked that path he was nineteen. It was a hot, tropical day in monsoon season, and he was leaving his village with an older cousin to seek his fortune in America. He had one hundred Hong Kong dollars hidden in small sums throughout the pockets of his thin cotton shirt and pants and tucked into his socks. A short time later, gun-brandishing thugs would hold up their bus, and Father would lose one-tenth of his wealth — having been told by his cousin, who had traveled before, to have the sum ready in a convenient pocket. Father wore cotton shoes on his feet, and on one shoulder had a drawstring bag that contained the rest of his wardrobe and worldly possessions: two extra shirts. His mother had not even packed him a lunch because, as he remembered it, "there was nothing left to eat."

It was 1949. There were rumors that Mao Tse-tung and his army were coming their way. Father's village was familiar with armies, having dodged Japanese soldiers for years: they hid in caves in the nearby mountains during the day and went back to their homes at night, when the enemy would return to camp. Then there was the advancement of Chiang Kai-shek's Nationalist troops, who forced out the Japanese but demanded rice, pigs, and chickens from the villagers. Another army would mean further trouble, so it was arranged for Father, the eldest son, to join his father in America. From this tiny dirt path, the two young men walked out to the larger road, where they hitched a ride on an ox cart that took them into Tai Cheng. Father had attended boarding school there, a privilege reserved for boys from families who received foreign remittances. From Tai Cheng, they took a bus to the seaport of Guanghai, where they squeezed into a jam-packed boat to begin a sixteen-hour tow by dinghy to Hong Kong. In Hong Kong, my father and his cousin boarded a plane for Seattle, where my grandfather resided and where they would resume their lives of toil and hardship, but in a new place.

Father ground his right foot in the dirt as though putting out a cigarette, a habit he had picked up in the village but long since given up. Then I saw him stop, as though caught by something long forgotten. There was an almost imperceptible change in his breathing. Perhaps his toes curled around the shape of a stone, or something about the road felt familiar, or his feet found something he didn't know he was looking for.

"I'll see if anyone's home," he continued in Taishanese, the rural area's patois that I grew up speaking. His tone softened slightly as his curiosity increased.

My father had good reason for resisting a return to his birthplace. As meaningful as such a visit might be, he felt the health risks were too great. As he entered his sixties, he was diagnosed with hepatitis B, a common and sometimes deadly malady among Southeast Asians born under unclean village conditions. For two years, he fought back with the aid of experimental drugs, but these left his body wasted and his spirit despondent. Finally he regained normal liver functions and had enough energy to do more than sleep away his golden years. He was afraid that any contact with the village would trigger a relapse. He fussed about this incessantly. And I bought into it, failing to see until now that it concealed a deeper resistance that he had no words for. He spoke of this only once, many years ago, almost unwittingly, letting it slip out in a conversation about something that has long since run out of memory's sieve. A few years after Father's departure, the Communist Red Guards marched into his village and paraded his mother and grandmother into the grassy area near the common well. The crazed teenagers accused them of being bourgeois pigs, for having built three houses with foreign remittances and sending husbands and sons abroad, and then they whipped them until the women fainted. No one in the village dared come forward in their defense. My grandmother, to her dying day, vowed never to return to the village and admonished each of her children and grandchildren against ever stepping foot in China. She hated her native country with a rancorous vehemence that left no room for further betrayal. But my mother would not return to China without my father; as for myself, I had every confidence that I would have found their ancestral homes on my own, though I now know I was wrong. Without my parents' childhood memory of where things were in the landscape and of the shape of their village rooftops against the sky, it would have been a futile search through a countryside of unmarked dirt roads and people so provincial that no one was certain of the names of neighboring villages.

In my mind, I have written several dozen essays, a book of

poems, a jaunty travel narrative, and a voluminous family biography — all based on what happened next: the moment my father turned to walk toward his village, and the few steps that followed. But in reality, I have created these large things only in my head. None of the many pieces that I've begun have I been able to finish, and each abandoned project has taken me further from the place I need to be in order to begin. As the Year of the Rabbit commenced, marking the first anniversary of our trip, most of my other writing projects stalled or failed as well. Now — strangely and to my chagrin — my inability to tell the tale has become part of the tale.

How hard could it be to write about a simple trip to a poor village? How long should it take to describe the house where my father was born — its wooden door secured with a twist of dried grass for more than thirty years? How is it that I have not been able to describe a place so spare that it did not have electricity or running water?

Setting my own foot in the place that has been my source of myth was supposed to give me a sense of reality and purpose with which to better understand myself and my life. This enlightenment would, of course, cause me to write marvelous things. But, instead, this place has extracted from me more than I could take from it. I've come away with what I could not even dare admit I feared: an overwhelmingly unproductive year and a terrible knowledge of my limitations as a writer. The task, I've taken this long to realize, is not an accounting of details, but the cherishing of events; not the rendering of exactitudes that I have so long mistaken for truth, but a need for remembering the striking and poetic side of things — and accepting that I will never be able to fit the contents of my heart onto a page.

"*Ai yaaaaahhh!*" a man's voice cried deeply across the stubbled fields. The cry startled those of us in the minivan. Birds scattered into the chalky sky. I was transfixed by what happened next. A man had emerged from the village and was striding quickly toward my father, who froze in his tracks as if he were an actor who had stepped into the wrong play. From a distance, the man looked as old as tree bark, his skin tanned and leathery. He wore Western clothes: a striped knit shirt under a thin polyester jacket, belted trousers, and black cotton shoes. His shoulders were slightly stooped, sloping gently like melted snow toward the earth, but his

thick, dark hair was windswept in a youthful way. I needed to get
out of the car, and fast. I knew with an insect's certainty that something big was about to pour out of the sky — the signs were
everywhere — and this was what I'd come for. Yet I could not anticipate it, did not know I was looking for it. With one hand I struggled to unfasten my seat belt and with the other to hold on to my
camera.

"*Hoiiii Lauuuuu!*" the man cried, unfurling my father's milk
name like a banner across the sky and calling the birds back from
their flight. His voice filled the earth, coating every brown blade of
grass and stubble, every stone and pebble between us and the distant blue mountains. It was a name, as ancient and powerful as the
newborn, that I had heard only my grandparents use for him.

Now it was the sound of remembering.

The thunder of resurrection.

The sound of the earth rearranging herself for his steps.

My father stumbled forward as though pushed abruptly from a
long dream and immediately extended his arms in a way I'd never
seen him do, like a child who wants to be picked up, held, and
loved. The long decades of Father's life merged into a few brief
hours, and I knew he had not really been gone from there for fifty
years but only a short afternoon. Hadn't he simply gone up the
path to investigate a rumor of frogs, or into the fields to tie praying
mantises onto his fingers as pets, and wasn't he just now returning
home after a euphoric afternoon? And wasn't his mother about to
put *chaai* (kindling sticks) into the oven and begin preparing the
evening rice?

I felt it: joy filling my father all at once, complete and overflowing. In a slow, peaceful moment, like the one preceding a car
crash, Father floated above his difficult world, looking unfamiliar,
like a stranger. Then I realized I'd never before seen him happy.
He was proud, maybe, when I graduated from Princeton and ap-
proving, perhaps, when I got married, but even on those occasions, the realities of his difficult life were still reflected in his tired
eyes. But here in this village, he was happy — so happy I cannot describe it. *Resplendent* perhaps comes closest. My father was *resplendent.* I had never in my life seen anything more wonderful.

Suddenly, I felt this place was familiar to me, as familiar as my
own house. I was the baby being pushed into the world, I was the

bride being carried down the path, I was the dead entering the earth. I was the departing emigrant seeking a future and the foreign-born daughter searching for her history. This is heritage, and the many layers of mine unfolded and embraced me in a single cry.

By the time I finally escaped from the car, the men had pulled away from their embrace. However, Father's fingertips kept touching — no, kept bouncing lightly on — the back of the man's hand, and up and down the sleeve of the man's thin jacket, as though he could not trust his eyes to believe what was before him.

The man was Father's fourth cousin, Yik Fu, who was either two years older or two years younger — neither man able to remember which. They had been constant companions in their boyhood, but had not seen or heard from each other in the half century since Father's departure.

"How did you know it was me?" Father finally stuttered when he found his voice, looking dazed yet seeming more wide awake than he'd ever been. His eyes darted wildly. In the photographs that I took of him, Father's lips are folded in at this moment, as though he is making a Herculean effort not to cry. In fact, he is wearing the same expression in each photograph I took of him on this visit.

"What do you mean how did I know?" Yik Fu replied, sounding insulted. "How can I remember? Tell me, how can I forget?"

Father folded in his lips even more, looking like a dried-apple granny. Standing next to his cousin, who was lean from a lifetime of farm work and eating only the fruit of his labor, Father looked well fed, even overfed. Father's hair was much grayer than his cousin's, but due to a life lived indoors, his face was as pale and smooth and oiled as a wealthy man's. By then, an old woman and a few children were standing nearby, watching us with curiosity. Father held on to his cousin's hand; they were again boys about to go out to play.

"Is my house still here?" Father asked tentatively, his face lit with wonder.

"Of course," his cousin said, surprised at the question.

The old woman came close to me and slipped her arm in mine. Gaunt and sun-browned, she resembled a mummy. I patted her leathery hand and smiled uneasily.

"You his daughter?" she asked through her toothless grin.

"*Haaile.*" I nodded.

"You come from far?" she asked.

"The Beautiful Country," I said, using a vernacular I thought she'd understand. But she didn't at first. Her eyes drew a blank. *"Aiyaah,"* she said and then exclaimed, "you speak our language!" Her eyes flashed with knowledge. She understood that my father had been gone an afternoon and that I'd come back with him, a daughter he'd found among the grasses, among the frogs, among the happy times clinging to the cool underside of leaves in the nearby fields. Someone from any farther away would not speak her dialect.

Taishanese closely resembles Cantonese, but suggests that the speaker is so ill bred that whenever I used it in Hong Kong and Guangzhou, I would always get the same reaction: laughter. Then feigned horror. Using the dialect made me an instant outcast, a vagrant baring a mouth of diseased teeth. Even in the United States, the dialect's associations with peasantry have not disappeared. Although Chinese dialects vary only in spoken form, not in the written, Chinese-language programs are almost always in Mandarin, the dialect of the northern scholars and now the PRC's official language. While I was growing up in Seattle, where nearly every Chinese family was of Taishan origin and spoke Taishanese at home, Chinese school offered only Cantonese, the urban and urbane dialect. But here, on the soil of my parents' home, my uneducated southern accent, deep from the muddy river delta, gushed pearls. The old woman clutched my arm tighter and looked so earnestly into my eyes that I knew she saw clearly to the bottom of them.

"Come inside for tea," she said as though we had strolled arm in arm every day for centuries. The children, barefoot or in plastic slippers and dressed in varying vintages of sweatshirts and sweatpants and sagging sweaters, shuffled a little closer. A woman about my age who had been gnawing on a sugar cane the size of a broom handle suddenly appeared at my side and offered me a similar treat. Instantly, I felt ashamed. I was ashamed of possessing so many sugar canes in a world so far from hers and not bringing a single one. I had come without gifts and had even talked my mother out of bringing hers.

"They'll laugh you out of the village," I had replied when Mother told me she had packed three sixty-pound bags of her old clothing to take to the villages. She had secretly squirreled away nearly every piece of clothing she had worn since her arrival in the

States in 1960, hoping someday to distribute them in her village. For weeks prior to our departure, we argued about her intended offering. Once, I pointed to a *National Geographic* article on the fashion-conscious in Shanghai and then recounted numerous newspaper reports on China's new middle class. She insisted that her carefully curated collection was an appropriate gift. In the end, I triumphed. She left her used clothing at home. It sounded plausible to her, too, that there had been some changes in China in the forty years that had elapsed since she left.

But how naïve could I be? Where there are no jobs, there is no money, no modernization, not even toilets. Except for the many boarded-up houses, Father's village, which now consists of only four or five families, was the same as when he left it a half century before. The Looks eat what they grow. Without refrigeration, they line up their cauliflower heads and the other *tyoi* that they've harvested from their fields along their cool kitchen floors. Their homes are swept and neat. Each house has the same floor plan, the central area being an atrium that holds the family altar, the main piece of furniture. Every day they wear the same clothes. The youngest children go around barefoot and bottomless. The oldest children were fourteen-year-old girls, who had completed middle school two years before and come to the end of their education. When asked what they'd do next, they shyly replied that they didn't know about "next."

Growing up, I knew my parents sent money to their villages. It was another one of those terrible arguments my parents had over how little money they had. But always the check would be cut, the envelope sealed and mailed. And still we ate, never missing a meal, and heated our home, though not too warmly, and marked the beginning of the school year with new clothes that Mother had sewn from inexpensive remnants. My parents never spoke to me or my brothers about the remittances, so it never occurred to me that there were beneficiaries like myself, whom they helped feed and clothe despite their own meager means. Now those children had grown, and we were meeting their children.

Speaking to me now are the faces and voices of these young women, who share my name, and others whom I met later in my mother's village. The young women are mirrors of who I could have been, and I am a mirror of who they could become and yet should not hope to be. I am a grown woman, the mother of two daughters, a wife, the owner of two automobiles and a house filled with as much comfort as my heart desires. I have never known hunger or cold. I collect things I do not need; I discard things that are still good. I have to exercise to stay slender. I am college educated. I read for pleasure, I attend the opera, I visit museums, I vacation in Europe. I enjoy the benefits of modern medicine. I have all my teeth. I belong to the first generation of my parents' families born outside the village. Growing up, I erased as much of my Chineseness as I could. When my parents spoke to me in Taishanese, I'd reply in English. I refused to attend Chinese school, eat with chopsticks, wear red for luck, refrain from washing my hair on holidays and birthdays. Although I made a concession to my parents to study Chinese (Mandarin) in college and found myself loving the language, I was in complete denial of any deeper links to China. In a society where remaking oneself is nearly a national religion, I was well on my way to being what I wanted to be: white. China was a disembodied foreign entity somewhere far away — interesting to study and analyze and form opinions about, as white people do, but not to be taken too seriously. I belong to the first generation to not send remittances.

Father quietly pressed two hundred renminbi into his cousin's hand before we left. "Spread it around," he instructed. His cousin nodded, teary and quiet, closing his fist around a poor substitute for my father. The next day, Father repeated the gesture, pressing a fold of bills into our driver's hand, who, instead of robbing us as we had suspected he would, insisted on taking us, without charge, to where we could catch the bus to Guangzhou. The giving of money is very Chinese, and for the first time I saw the usefulness of it — and the uselessness of what I had become.

Ironically, it was my arrogance that had brought me to the village: I came looking for what I could take from it. Details for a novel in progress. But somewhere between my desire and the fulfillment of it, I fell into an abyss. Like my father, I heard my name called in that place — audible only to my ears perhaps, but maybe not — and I tumbled headlong after him into that strong morning light, undeserving. In that place full of beginnings and endings and everything in between, I knew that I, too, had come home. Here was the home that I sought. I cannot turn from it — it is more than I deserve, and it is enough.

REBECCA McCLANAHAN

Book Marks

FROM THE SOUTHERN REVIEW

I AM WORRIED about the woman. I am afraid she might hurt herself, perhaps has already hurt herself — there's no way to know which of the return dates stamped on the book of poetry was hers. The book, Denise Levertov's *Evening Train,* belongs to the New York City Public Library. I checked it out yesterday and can keep it for three weeks. Ever since my husband and I moved to the city several months ago, I've been homesick for my books, the hundreds of volumes stored in my brother's basement. I miss having them near me, running my hands over their spines, recalling when and where I acquired each one, and out of what need.

There's no way to know for certain that the phantom library patron is a woman, but all signs point in that direction. On one page is a red smear that looks like lipstick, and between two other pages, lying like a bookmark, is a long, graying hair. The underlinings, which may or may not have been made by the woman, are in pencil — pale, tentative marks I study carefully, reverently, the way an archaeologist traces a fossil's delicate imprint. The rest is dream, conjecture, the making of *my* story. It's a weird obsession, I know, studying other readers' leavings and guessing the lives lived beneath. Even as my reasonable mind is having its say (*This makes no sense. How can you assume? The marks could have been made by anyone, for any reason, over any period of time . . .*), my other self is leaving on its own journey. I've always been a hungry reader, what one friend calls a "selfish reader." But is there any other kind? Don't we all read to answer our own needs, to complete the lives we've begun, to point us toward some light?

Some of the underlinings in *Evening Train* have been partially
erased (eraser crumbles have gathered in the center seams), as if
the woman reconsidered her first responses or tried to cover her
tracks. The markings do not strike me as those of a defiant woman
but rather of one who has not only taken her blows but feels she
might deserve them. She has underlined "serviceable heart" in
one poem; in another, "Grey-haired, I have not grown wiser." If she
exists, I would like to sit down with this woman. We seem to have a
lot in common. We chose the same book, we both wear red lipstick,
and though I am not so honest (the gray in my hair is hidden beneath an auburn rinse), I am probably her age or thereabouts.

And from what she has left behind on the pages of Levertov's poems, it appears that our hearts have worn down in the same places.
This is the part that worries me. Though my heart has mended, for
the time being at least, hers seems to be in the very act of breaking.
A present-tense pain pulses through each marked-up poem, and
the further I read, the clearer it becomes what she is considering. I
want to reach through the pages and lead her out.

My interest in marginalia, reading between the lines, began when I
was an evening student at a college in California, still living with
my parents but working days to help pay my expenses. It was a
lonely time. Untethered from the rock-hard rituals of high school,
I'd been set adrift, floating between adolescence and Real Life, a
place I'd heard about that both terrified and seduced me. As a tod-
dler, I'd been one of those milkily content clingers who must be
pulled away from the nipple; eighteen years later I was still reluctant to leave my mother's side.

My siblings had no such trouble. An older sister had married
and left home, a brother was away at college, and my younger siblings, in various stages of adolescent rebellion, had struck out on
their own. As for my friends, most had left to study at faraway colleges; the few who stayed, taking jobs at the local bank or training
to be dental assistants, seemed even more remote than those who
had left. Whatever had held us together in high school — intramu-
ral sports, glee club, the senior-class play — was light-years away. As
was the boy who'd promised to marry me someday. He'd found
someone else, and though part of me had always known that's how
that book would end (we'd never progressed beyond kissing), nev-

ertheless his leaving was the first hairline crack in my serviceable heart.

My only strike at independence was the paycheck I earned typing invoices at a printing shop. Though I reluctantly accepted my father's offer to pay tuition costs, I insisted on buying my own textbooks. I could afford only used ones, and the more *used* the book, the cheaper it was. Some had passed through several hands; the multiple marked-through names and phone numbers on the flyleaves bore witness to this fact. At first I was put off by the previous owners' underlinings, marginal comments, bright yellow highlighted sections, sophomoric doodlings and obscenities. Worse still were the unintentional markings — coffee stains, dried pizza sauce, cigarette burns.

After a while, however, I became accustomed to the markings. I even began to welcome them. Since I didn't live on campus or have college buddies — I worked all day, then went straight home after class — I appreciated the company the used books offered. I imagined the boy who had splattered pizza sauce across the map of South America. Was he lonely too? Had he eaten the pizza alone, in his tiny dorm room, while memorizing Bolivia's chief exports? What about the girl who had misspelled *orgasm* (using two *s*'s) in the margins of John Donne's "The Canonization"? Had she ever said the word aloud? Was she a virgin like me?

The used texts served practical purposes as well. In the case of difficult subject matter (which, for me, meant political science, chemistry, and botany), it was as though I had engaged a private tutor, someone to sit at my elbow and guide me through each lesson, pointing out important concepts, underlining the principles that would show up on next week's exam. The marked-up textbook was my portable roommate, someone to sit up nights with me, to quiz me with questions I didn't know enough to ask.

Not since I was a child sharing a room with Great-Aunt Bessie, an inveterate reader, had I had a reading partner. Bessie and I would sit up late in our double bed and read mysteries and westerns aloud. We'd take turns, each reading a chapter a night, and at the end, right before Bessie removed her dentures and switched off the light (she was a disciplined reader, always stopping at the end of a chapter), right before she slipped her embroidered handkerchief into the book to mark our place, we would discuss our reactions to what we had read and make predictions about how the story would turn. Because of Aunt Bessie, I never saw books as dead, finished texts. They were living, breathing entities, unexplored territories into which we would venture the next night, and the next. Anything could happen, and we would be present when it did.

Years later, carrying this lesson into my first college class, I was amazed at what I encountered: rows of bleary-eyed students slumped around me, their limp hands spread across Norton anthologies. Most never ventured into the territory Bessie and I had explored. This stymied me, that people could read a poem by Shelley or Keats or Sylvia Plath and not want to live inside it, not want to add their words to the ones on the page. Looking back on my college literature texts, I can trace the journey of those years. In the margins of Wordsworth's sonnets, beside the lines "The world is too much with us; late and soon, / Getting and spending, we lay waste our powers," I can chart my decision to quit my day job and pursue my studies full-time, even if it meant borrowing from the savings account I'd been feeding each payday. "I am done with this," I wrote in blue ink, meaning the commerce of getting and spending, the laying waste of powers I'd yet to discover.

And in the underlined sections of Gerard Manley Hopkins's poems, I can trace the ecstasy of my first spiritual awakening ("I caught this morning morning's minion"), made all the more ecstatic since, because I was unable to understand his elliptical syntax with my *mind,* I was forced to take it in through the rhythms of my body. This was a new music for me. My heart was no longer metaphorical. It beat rapidly in my chest, my temples, in my pale, veined wrists. Suddenly, within Hopkins's lines, I was breaking in new places: "here / Buckle! And the fire that breaks from thee then, a billion / Times told lovelier, more dangerous."

At the time I encountered those lines, I had no knowledge of the fire that awaited me in the eyes of a young man I'd yet to meet. I saw myself vaguely, like a character in one of the books I fell asleep with each night. In dreams I drank black coffee at street cafés, lay beneath the branches of the campus oaks, or wandered late at night, as Whitman's narrator had wandered, looking up "in perfect silence at the stars." In daylight, I pulled another used book from the shelf and fell into its pages. Could it be that Rilke's injunction, "You must change your life," was aimed at me? I high-lighted it in yellow, then wrote in the margin, in bright blue indeli-ble ink, "THIS MEANS *YOU!*"

Had I chosen to resell these books to the campus bookstore (I didn't; they had become part of me), their new owners might one day have read my underlinings, my marginal scribblings, and won-dered at the person who left such a trail. "She needs to get more sun," they might have thought, if they could deduce I was a *she.* Maybe they would have worried about me the way I now worry about the gray-haired woman. They might even have responded, as I sometimes do, with an answering note. It might have gone on and on like that, a serial installment of marginalia, each new reader adding his own twist to Hopkins or Wordsworth — or to me, the phantom whose pages they were turning.

When life interrupts, you close the book. Or perhaps you leave it open, facedown on the bed or table, to mark your place. Aunt Bessie taught me never to do this. "You'll break its spine," she said, running her age-spotted hands across the book's cover, and the tenderness in her gesture made me ashamed that I'd ever consid-ered such violence. After that I took to dog-earing pages, but after a while even that seemed too violent. Now, whenever I encounter a dog-eared page, I smooth its wounded edge.

Aunt Bessie used embroidered handkerchiefs to mark her place, though to me they seemed unnecessary since she always stopped at the end of a chapter. Some readers are like that. They regulate their reading, fitting books neatly into their lives the way some peo-ple schedule exercise or sex: five poems, twenty laps. One of my friends always stops after twenty-five pages so she can easily remem-ber where she left off. Though I admire such discipline, I've never been able to accomplish it. I fall into books the way I fall into lust — wholly, hungrily. Often the book disappoints, or I disappoint. The first flush cools and the words grow tired and dull, or I grow tired and dull and slam the book shut. Occasionally, though, I keep reading, and lust ripens slowly into love, and I want to stay right there, at the lamplit table or in the soft, worn chair, until the last page is turned.

Then suddenly, always unexpectedly, life interferes; it is what life does best. It usually happens in mid-paragraph, sometimes even mid-sentence — a kind of biblio-interruptus — and I grab something to mark my place. Though I own many beautiful bookmarks, they are never there when I need them. So I reach for whatever is close at hand. A newspaper clipping, the phone bill, my bourbon-fossiled cocktail napkin, a note from a friend, the grocery list. Once I plucked a protruding feather from the sofa cushion where I rested my head, once I used a maple leaf that had blown in through the patio door, once I even pulled a hair from my head.

Looking back on my nineteenth year, I am amazed at how easily I closed the books I'd been living inside. What replaced them were the poems the young man handed me across a restaurant table. "Pretty Brown-Haired Girl" was the title of one; "Monday Rain" another. Some were written in German, and I used my secondhand Cassell's dictionary to translate them. The poems were not good — I remember thinking this even then — but they were the first love poems anyone had ever written for me. I ran my fingers across the words. I folded the papers, put them into my pocket, and later that night unfolded them on my bedside table. Already the poems were in my head, every ragged line break and rhyme.

At twenty-one he had one of those faces that might have looked old all along. His hair was retreating prematurely, exposing a forehead with furrows already deeply plowed. But his eyes were bright blue, center-of-a-flame blue, simultaneously cool and hot. He wore faded jeans and a rugged woolen jacket and drove a motorcycle; his mouth tasted of cigarettes. Plus he could quote Wordsworth, which weakened me even more. He was independently brilliant, a part-time student with no declared major, taking classes in subjects like German and astronomy and horticulture — nothing that fit together to form anything like a formal degree. "Come into the light of things," he teased. "Let nature be your teacher."

Nature taught me so much over the next year that it was all I could do to attend classes, let alone sit up nights with pencil in hand, scribbling notes in the margins of textbooks. He'd moved into his own apartment, and his marks were all over me — his mouth on my forehead, his tongue on my neck, my belly, the smell of his cigarettes in my hair. All else fell away. When an occasional misgiving surfaced I pushed it down. I had reason to doubt that I was his only brown-haired girl, the only one to whom he wrote poems. But I hushed the voice of reason, even when it spoke directly into my ear.

My parents disapproved of him, and though Aunt Bessie had moved back to her Midwest childhood home, I was certain she would have disapproved too. I *knew* Carolyn did. She'd told me so, in the same loving yet blatantly forthright tone she'd used on me since I was small. Carolyn was my mother's best friend, and had served as a kind of alternate mother for me as long as I could remember. Perhaps *mother* is the wrong word; *mentor* may come closer. She was a librarian who not only loved books but believed in them, even more so than Aunt Bessie. Carolyn believed that books could change our lives, could save us from ourselves.

My mother also loved books, but while she was raising her six children — sometimes single-handedly, when my pilot father was overseas — she put reading aside. I cannot recall, during those years, ever seeing my mother sit down, except to play a game of Monopoly or Old Maid, or to sew our Halloween costumes or Easter dresses. Certainly not to read. Late at night, when my father was away and she couldn't sleep, perhaps she switched on the light beside their double bed and opened a book, probably her Bible, a beautiful burgundy-leather King James my father had given her early in their marriage and that she kept close at hand. I loved to feel the cover and the onionskin pages that were tipped in gold and totally free of marginalia. The only mark I could find was a handwritten notation on the flyleaf. "Deuteronomy 29:29. The secret things belong unto the Lord our God: but those things which are revealed belong unto us and to our children for ever."

Over the years Carolyn gave me many books that she felt I needed to read at particular stages of my life. Some she'd bought on her travels; some had belonged to her mother; some had been gifts. She shared my passion for hand-me-downs, and never apologized for giving me used books. "Words don't go bad," she'd say, "like cheese. Read everything you can get your hands on. Live inside them." On the subject of my newfound love, she was adamant: "You're too young to give it all up for a man." Carolyn had married an older, stable, kind man who adored her yet allowed the space her inquiring mind demanded. "I'm afraid you're going to lose yourself," she told me. "Besides," she added, almost as an afterthought, "I don't trust him."

"You won't be able to put it down," booksellers claim as they ring up your purchase. But of course you do, you must. The oven timer goes off, the children come in from school, your plane lands, the nurse calls your name, your lover kisses the back of your neck, your heavy eyes close in sleep. By the time you return to the book — if you return — you will be changed, will not be the same person you were ten days, or ten years, before. Life is a river, and you can't step into the same book twice.

One night after we'd made love, he lit a cigarette and leaned back onto the pillows. "I'm in trouble," he said. "There's this girl." Smoke floated around his eyes; he blinked, fanned the air. "*Was* this girl. It's over, but she's been calling. She says she's pregnant." Something hot flashed through my head, then was gone. All I could think was *He will marry her, and I will lose him.*

"There's this place in Mexico City," he continued. "It's nine hundred dollars for everything, to fly her there and back. I have two hundred."

I had seen the word *abortion* in biology textbooks, but I had never uttered it. In 1969, even at the crest of the free-love movement, it was not a legal option. I had fourteen hundred dollars in my savings account, all that was left of nearly two years of typing invoices at the print shop. Each Friday I had taken the little vinyl passbook to the bank window, where the cashier recorded the deposit, half of my paycheck.

"I'll get the rest," I said, surprising even myself.

"I can't ask you to do that."

My next line was from a movie. Something out of the forties. I should have been wearing a hat with a feather. We should have been in a French café: "You're not asking. I'm offering."

"I'll make it up to you," he said.

To this day I can't recall if he repaid me. The passbook shows no record of the money being replaced. Within a year we were married, and what was left of my savings was pooled into a joint account. There was little money and much to buy — a dinette table, a TV stand, a couch. One night he suddenly sat straight up on that couch. "I'll bet she was lying all along," he said, as though continuing a conversation started just seconds before. "Maybe she just wanted a trip to Mexico. She probably spent the whole time on the beach." I wanted to believe him. I hoped the girl *had* spent the weekend on the sand. I hoped she'd gotten a tan. But I knew she hadn't lied. I knew because of what had been set into motion since

I'd handed over the money. The shadow over our marriage had first approached in the bank's parking lot, had lengthened and darkened with each month, and has never completely lifted.

The girl's name was Barbara. She had blue eyes and long brown hair, and she lived in Garden Grove with her parents. She had a lisp. That's all he ever told me. The rest has been written in daylight imaginings and in dreams: Barbara and I are sitting beneath a beach umbrella reading books and sipping tall, cool drinks. The ocean is crashing in the distance, and the child crawling the space between our knees is a girl. She is a harlequin, seamed down the center. Not one eyelash, one fingernail, one cell of the child is his. She is the two best halves of Barbara and me, sewn with perfectly spaced stitches: this is the story I write.

Studying the markings in *Evening Train*, I surmise that the gray-haired woman is an honest reader, unashamed to admit her ignorance. She has drawn boxes around difficult words — *epiphanies, antiphonal, tessellations, serrations* — and placed a question mark above each box. Maybe she's merely an eager learner, the kind who sets small tasks for herself; she will go directly to the dictionary and find these words. Or maybe someone — her husband, her lover, whoever broke her serviceable heart — also criticized her vocabulary. It was too small or too large. She asked too many questions.

In the poem about the breaking heart, she has underlined "in surface fissures" and "a web / of hairline fractures." She probably didn't even notice the fissures at first. Maybe, she guessed, this webbing is the necessary landscape of every marriage, each act of love. But reading on, I sense that more has been broken than a metaphorical heart. She has circled the entire poem "The Batterers," about a man who, after beating a woman, dresses her wounds and, in so doing, begins to love her again. "Why had he never / seen, before, what she was? / What if she stops breathing?" I tell myself *I* wouldn't have stayed in that kind of situation. As it is, I'll never know. He never hit me, though one night, desperate for attention, I begged him to. (How do we live with the knowledge of our past selves?) He'd come home late, at two or three o'clock, with no explanation. Earlier in the evening, returning from a night class and looking for clues to his absence, I'd found a woman's jacket behind a chair. It smelled foreign yet familiar — her musky perfume mingled with the memory of his cigarettes. They had been here together, in our apartment. He had not touched me in weeks.

When his fist finally flew, it landed on the door of the filing cabinet where I kept my class notes, term papers, and poetry drafts. This should not have surprised me. For months he'd been angry that I'd returned to school. "What are you trying to prove?" he'd ask. "Where do you think this is going to get you? Just listen to yourself, can't you just hear yourself?" Though I still worked part-time at the print shop, he spent whole days on the assembly line, drilling holes into bowling balls. Anything to make ends meet. He was hoping, beyond logic, that as a married man with a full-time job, he would be saved from Vietnam. He was terrified; his draft number was low.

The force of the blow was audible: a thud, a crack. Loose sheets flew from the top of the cabinet. He cried out, then brought the fist to his mouth. Surely it was broken, I thought. I rushed toward him, but he held up his other hand to block me. Time slowed. White paper fluttered around me like birds. I stared at his hand, and something went out of me, I could feel it, a sucking force, tidal, pulling me out of myself. Then the moment was over. He turned and walked away, his wounded fist still pressed to his mouth, his blue eyes filling. I knelt on the floor and began to gather the papers. My eyes were dry, my vision clear. This is what hurt the most: the clarity of the moment, its sharp focus. Each black word, on each scattered page, distinct and singular.

Two years ago, when Carolyn was dying, when she could count the remaining months on her fingers, she wrote from her home in Virginia, asking me to come as soon as possible to help her sort through her books. "You can have whatever you want," she said. "The only thing I ask is that you don't cry. Just pretend it's a book sale. Come early, stay late. And go home with your arms full."

It took two full afternoons. Too weak to stand, Carolyn sat on a little stool, pointing and nodding, directing me shelf by shelf. Each row called forth a memory. Her life's story unfolded book by book. She told me she was glad she'd lived long enough to see a grandchild safely into the world. She was glad I had found a husband who was good to me, this time, and she wished me all the happiness she had known. When my car could hold no more books, she handed me a large envelope and explained that one of her jobs as assistant librarian had been to check the returned books before reshelving them. The envelope was labeled in Carolyn's scrawl: *Woodrow Wilson Public Library, Things Found in Books.* "You'd be surprised at what people use as bookmarks," she said.

When I got home, I emptied the envelope onto the floor, amazed at what spilled out. Bits and pieces of strangers' lives, hundreds of markers of personal histories. Love letters, folded placemats, envelopes, sympathy cards, valentines, handwritten recipes, train tickets, report cards, newspaper clippings, certificates of achievement, bills, receipts, religious tracts, swimming-pool passes, scratch-and-sniff perfume ads, canceled tickets for the bullfight, bar coasters, rice paper, happy money. Studying the bookmarks, I slid into each stranger's life, wondering which book he had checked out and whether he had finished it. What calls us away from books, then back to them?

When I am in pain, I *devour* books, often stripping the words of conceptual and metaphorical context and digging straight for the meat. The gray-haired woman seems to be doing the same thing, taking each word personally, *too* personally, as if Levertov had written them just for her, to guide her toward some terrible action. Certainly this wasn't the poet's intention, yet the more I study the markings, the more I fear what the woman is considering. In "Dream Instruction" she has underlined, twice, "gradual stillness," but appears to have missed entirely the "blessing" in the line that follows. The marks in "Contraband" are even more alarming. I want to take the woman by the hand and remind her of the poem's symbolic level, a level that's nearly impossible to see when you are in pain. Contraband, I would tell her, represents the Tree of Knowledge, the tree of reason, and the fruit is the words we stuff into our mouths, and yes, that fruit might indeed be "toxic in large quantities; fumes / swirled in our heads and around us," but those lines are not a prescription for suicide. There are other ways to live with knowledge.

For instance, you can leave, gather up what remains of yourself and set off on a journey much like the journey of faith Levertov writes of. Or, if that proves too difficult, you can send your self off on its own, wave goodbye, step back into childhood's shoes and re-

fuse to go one step further. You can cut off your hair, take the pills
the doctors prescribe and beg for more, then lose yourself daily in
a gauzy sleep, surrounded by the books that have become your
only food. His deferment dream did not materialize, so you have
followed him to a military base where you know no one. Vietnam is
still a possibility. Your heart is divided: you dread the orders yet
pray for them. If they come, you will be able to retreat honorably to
your parents' home. In the meantime, you have the pills and the
books and the bed grown huge by his nightly absence — he is
sleeping elsewhere now, with someone else, and he no longer even
tries to hide it.

If you're lucky, one night your hand will find the phone, and if
you are doubly lucky and have a mother like mine, she will arrive
early the next day, having driven hundreds of miles alone in a car
large enough to hold several children. Though she is a quiet
woman who rarely interferes, in this case she will make an exception. She will locate your husband, demand that he come home,
now, and when he does (this is where the details get fuzzy, you have
sent yourself off somewhere), together they will lift you into the
backseat of her big car and rush you to the emergency room,
where the attending physician will immediately direct you to the
psychiatric wing.

I would remember none of this part, which is a blessing. Had I
recalled the details of the breakdown, I might have felt compelled
to tell the story too soon, to anyone who would listen: strangers on
buses, prospective employers, longtime family friends, men I met
in bars or churches (for months I would search both places,
equally, for comfort). "There's no need to tell," my mother said after my release, and she would repeat this many times, long after I
was out of danger. Though I've finally decided, after nearly thirty
years, to tell, I still hear her words in my head: "You don't need any
more hurt. It's no one's business but yours."

This is my mother's way. Though she freely gives to anyone in
need — food, comfort, time, love — there is a part of herself, the
heart's most enclosed, tender core, that she guards like a secret. In
this way, and others, I would like to be more like her. Less needy,
more protective of private fears and desires. Less prone to look
back, more single-minded in forward resolve. Though I had re-
hearsed his leaving for months, when he finally went, for good this

time (isn't it strange how we use *good* to mean *final*?), I was devastated, terrified to imagine my future. "What should I do," I begged my mother. "What would you do?" I don't know what I expected her to say. My mother has never been one to give advice. Experience, in her view, is not transferable. It is not an inheritance you pass on to your children, no matter how much you wish you could.

If her words held no answer, I decided, then I would read her life. Certainly there were worlds it could teach me. She had left her parents and the family farm to follow her husband from one military base to the next; waited out his long absences; buried one child and raised six others; watched as loved ones suffered divorces, financial ruin, alcoholism, depression, life-threatening illnesses and accidents; nursed them through their last years. "Take me with you," I begged, meaning back home, to *her* home, to the nest she and my father had made.

My mother remembers this as one of the painful moments of her life. "I wanted more than anything to say yes," she recalls. "But I knew if I did, you'd never find your way. It was time you found your own way." So she took my face in her hands and said *no*. No, I could not follow her, I could not come back home. Then she helped me pack my suitcase, and, so I would not be alone, so I would be safe if worse once again came to worst, she made me a plane reservation to my brother's town in South Carolina. Half a world away, or so it seemed to me.

The narrator of Levertov's *Evening Train* sets off on a journey too, and though I suspect that the luggage and racks of the book's title poem are intended to be metaphorical, I cannot help but feel the heft of the bags, the steel slickness of the racks. And as I study the phantom woman's markings, it seems clear that, like mine, her journey required a real ticket on a real train or plane, and that by the time she arrived at the poem called "Arrived," she had already sat alone in a room with "Chairs, / sofa, table, a cup —" and begun the inventory of her life. Was she, like the poem's narrator, unable to call forth the face of the one she had left, who had left her? Why else mark these lines: "the shape / of his head, or / color of his eyes appear / at moments, but I can't / assemble feature with feature"?

In my pain, I prayed for such moments of forgetfulness. How

pleasant it would be not to recall his hands, his tanned, furrowed forehead, the flame-cool blue of his eyes. My only release was to stuff my brain with cotton. That's how it felt when I took the pills. Though they no longer had the power to put me to sleep, they lifted me to a place of soundlessness and ether. I thought of T. S. Eliot's hollow men, their heads filled with straw. The image of scarecrows was comforting, as were thoughts of helium balloons, slow-floating dirigibles, and anything submerged in water. I was an aquarium, enclosed. Amniotic silence surrounded me hour after hour, and then suddenly — *What's that noise?*, I'd think, startled, amazed to discover it was my own breath in my lungs, my heart thumping, the blood thrumming in my ears.

When this happened, when I was brought back to myself, I'd think, *No, please not that.* I had forgotten for a while that I was alive, that there were hands at the ends of my arms, fingers that could burn themselves on the gas stove, the iron, the teakettle's steam. The world was too much with me. Why bother? (*This is the way the world ends . . .*) I fell back into bed, finding comfort in Eliot, and later in Job. The New Testament was stuffed too full of promise and light, but Old Testament sufferings were redemptive, though not in the traditional sense of the word. I was long past questioning why a loving God would destroy Job's house and cattle, afflict him with boils all over his body, and kill his children. The worst is yet to come, I thought — and almost said, aloud, to Job. Happiness is what you should be fearing. Why waste your breath talking back to God, calling out for salvation? The cure might be worse than the disease. If God answers, out of the whirlwind and the chaos of destruction, beware of what will be given: healing, forgiveness, six thousand camels, a thousand she-asses, seven sons and three daughters, each fairer than the next, your life overflowing, another high place from which to fall.

I didn't want to live, but I couldn't imagine dying. How to gather the energy? I didn't own a gun and could see no way to get one. I had no courage for knives. Pills seemed an easy way out; I tried, but my stomach refused to accept them. Over the next weeks I started taking long drives on country roads, staring at the yellow lines and thinking how easy it would be to pull the wheel to the left, into the oncoming truck, which was heavy enough, I was sure, to bear the impact without killing its driver. (I didn't want to kill anyone, not even myself. I just wanted not to live. There's a difference.) Or better yet, pull the wheel to the right, into that stand of pine trees.

What terrified me was not the thought of the mangled metal, the row of wounded trunks, or even of the sheet pulled over me — a gesture that seemed almost a kindness, something a loved one would do. What terrified me that late summer day was the sudden greenness of the trees, the way their beauty insinuated itself into my vision — peripherally at first, vaguely, and without my consent. I blinked to stop what felt like tears, which I hadn't tasted for so long I'd forgotten that they were made of salt, that they were something my body was producing on its own, long after I thought I had shut down. O.K., I said to the steering wheel, the padded dashboard, the pines. If I can think of five reasons not to die, I won't.

When I got back to my room, I pulled from the pages of Eliot a blank prescription refill form I'd been using as a bookmark. I found a pencil in the nightstand, one without an eraser, I recall. I remember thinking that I couldn't go back on what I'd written, couldn't retrace my steps if I made a mistake. I turned the form over and numbered the blank side — 1, 2, 3, 4, 5 — with a black period after each, as if preparing to take a spelling test. It was the first time I'd put pencil to paper since I'd left California. I thought for a while, then wrote beside number one, "My parents," immediately wishing I'd split them into "Mother" and "Dad" so that I could have filled two lines. Then to my surprise the next four blanks filled quickly, and my hand was adding numbers and more numbers to accommodate the names of my siblings, my nieces and nephews, the handful of friends I still claimed and even the ones who were gone. I filled the back of the form and probably could have filled another, but I didn't want to try, I couldn't bear any more just yet — the stab of joy, the possibility.

As months passed, the world slowly continued to make itself known, appearing in small, merciful gestures, as if not wishing to startle: voices, a pair of hands, golden leaf-shadow, a suggestion of sky. Then one morning, for no reason I can recall, the world lifted her veil and showed her whole self. She looked strangely familiar — yes, I thought, it's all coming back. Put on shoes, brush teeth, smile into the mirror, pour orange juice into a glass. *This is the way the world begins. This is the way the world begins. This is the way.*

I smooth the center seam of *Evening Train* and run my hands over the marked-up lines. Poems can be dangerous places in which to venture, alone, and I'm not sure the woman is ready for "After *Mindwalk*." She has underlined "panic's black cloth falling / over our faces, over our breath." Please don't, I want to say. Don't do it, don't drink it, don't eat that apple. I want to tell her about the pine trees, the list, Mother and Bessie and Carolyn and Wordsworth and Hopkins and Job. Look, I'd say, pointing to the footnote. See, *Mindwalk* was a film by Bernt Capra, it's not a real place; don't worry. It's about Pascal and the Void. It doesn't have to be about you. But it is, of course. That's why she is not only reading the book but writing one of her own as well, with each scratch of the pencil. The printed words are Levertov's, but the other poem is the woman's — written in the margins, in the small boxes that cage the words she cannot pronounce, in the crumbled erasures, in the question marks floating above the lines. Wait up, I want to say — a crazy thought, but I can't help myself. Wait up; I want to tell you something.

DAPHNE MERKIN

Trouble in the Tribe

FROM THE NEW YORKER

I'VE BEEN TRYING to lose my religion for years now, but it refuses to go away. Just when I think I've shaken it — put it firmly behind me, a piece of my obscurantist past no longer suited to the faithless life I now lead — it turns up again, dogging me. You'd think it would be easy, particularly in a city like New York, where no one cares whether or not you believe in God; even my friends who do would be hard put to explain why, other than by alluding knowingly to Pascal's wager, in which the odds favor the believer. But as the world becomes a more bewildering place almost by the week, I find myself longing for what I thought I'd never long for again: a sense of community in the midst of the impersonal vastness, a tribe to call my own.

To add to my confusion, Joseph Isadore Lieberman, the first Jewish vice presidential candidate of a major party, and Abraham Foxman, the national director of the Anti-Defamation League, are noisily airing questions that I've been debating internally for decades: How Jewish is too Jewish? Does a public declaration of religious allegiance always come across as self-serving — a sales technique custom-made for the age of identity politics? Whether Lieberman calls himself a Jewish American or an American Jew is a matter of hairsplitting, a preoccupation of the leery. (Will he look out for the country's welfare, or only for the interests of his own kind?) What *is* of significance — to Jews and gentiles alike — is the fact that Lieberman is observant, a man of religious conviction: he keeps kosher, doesn't turn on lights or travel in a car on Shabbos, and regularly attends synagogue services. In doing so, he has given

the beleaguered Modern Orthodox Jewish establishment something to be truly proud about, a reason to kvell. At the Nashville
announcement rally, the Connecticut senator exuberantly (or pre-
sumptuously, depending on your tolerance for direct appeals to
the divine) invoked God, "maker of all miracles," and praised
Gore's "chutzpah" in naming him. Suddenly, the press was brim-
ming with folksy Yiddishisms worthy of Leo Rosten, references to
abstruse Jewish concepts, and discussions about whether Lieberman would be able to attend his inauguration, which falls on a Saturday.

As if I didn't have enough conflicts already about having strayed
from my Modern Orthodox upbringing, there now looms the
temptation to reclaim it and avail myself of ready-made cultural ca-
chet. I can already picture those "revolving-door" Jews, staunch sec-
ularists who disdain visible signs of affiliation, suddenly lining up
to take a closer look at the quaint religious customs long ago left in
the care of tottering relatives in Miami Beach. A few days after
Gore announced his choice of a running mate, for instance, I was
meeting my mother for dinner at nine. She hadn't eaten for the
past twenty-four hours, in observance of the Jewish fast day known
as Tisha b'Av. (All Jewish holidays begin and end after sundown.)
While she was waiting on Park Avenue for me to pick her up in a
cab, a well-coiffed neighbor — whose ethnic origins had been ob-
scured by years of Upper East Side polish — asked her why she was
going out to eat so late. My mother explained that she had just finished fasting in commemoration of the destruction of the first and
second Temple, thousands of years ago. The woman looked startled and then commented, with no small degree of chagrin, "I
guess we'll all have to learn about these things now, won't we?"

It's difficult to imagine a sustained resurgence of serious interest
in either the sober letter or the confining spirit of the law, but for
the moment things are looking up for the "frummies" — which is
one of the terms that Modern Orthodox Jews use for their less
modern compatriots. (Other shorthand designations include "ye-
shiva-ish," "*charedi,*" and "black hats.") The minute gradations between one subset of observant Judaism and another are suddenly
the object of intense national scrutiny, even if they are frequently
misunderstood. More irritating to me are the know-it-all remarks
of my sedulously lapsed acquaintances to the effect that Lieber-

man doesn't wear a yarmulke in the workplace, and that his wife doesn't cover her hair, as though these practices would in any way disqualify him from being a member in good standing of his synagogue.

In the earliest days of Modern — or, as it is sometimes called, centrist — Orthodox Judaism, the public and private demonstrations of one's religious beliefs were kept separate, like the dishes for meat and dairy food. As it happens, the Modern Orthodox movement was founded, in the 1850s in Frankfurt, Germany, by my great-great-grandfather Rabbi Samson Raphael Hirsch, as a response to the increasingly dominant Reform movement. (The fact that I am a direct descendant of Hirsch gives me sterling *yichus* — the Jewish version of lineage, like having a blood relation on the *Mayflower*.) Hirsch, an influential theologian and community leader who admired Schiller almost as much as he did Maimonides, cautiously embraced modernity while insisting on the obligation to observe Jewish law. His credo, *Torah im Derech Eretz* — Torah Judaism in harmony with secular culture — was a bow in the direction of both God and Germany. Hirsch founded the first modern Jewish day school, which was based on an innovative curriculum of secular and sacred studies. My mother, who attended the school in the thirties, remembers that the boys took off their yarmulkes for secular classes. Although such a radical distinction between church and state is no longer made, Hirsch's educational model remains the inspiration for Jewish day schools in cities across America.

By the mid-fifties, when I was born, Modern Orthodoxy was booming. My five siblings and I went to Ramaz, a Jewish day school on the Upper East Side, where we learned to read and write Hebrew. We were also trained in the advanced decoding skills — a pointillist method of inquiry — that were needed to comprehend the voluminous interpretative texts that had swelled, century by century, around the Old Testament: expansive commentaries, colorful Talmudic parables, and competing Midrashic riffs. Why, for instance, when the Torah ascribes righteousness to Noah, does the narrative qualify the description by specifying that he was a righteous man *for his generation*? Everything, it appeared, had a meaning if one only understood how to tease it out.

At home, we recited the Sh'ma before going to sleep, and said the blessings over everything from breakfast cereal to our evening snack of Educator's Smokey Bear cookies (the kosher version of Oreos). But although my brothers wore the ritual fringes known as *tzitzis* beneath their shirts seven days a week, and went to synagogue on Friday night as well as on Saturday, homogeneity and camouflage were the prevailing themes of the Zeitgeist. Ethnic pride, coming in on the wave of the late sixties, had not yet asserted itself. (The manifestations of specifically Jewish pride — like the wearing of *kippot s'rugot*, crocheted yarmulkes — followed the euphoric Israeli victory in the Six Day War.) My brothers wouldn't have been caught dead wearing a yarmulke on the crosstown bus, or to a Mets game at Shea Stadium. Even so, my family's uneasy concessions to the wider American world led to inevitable tensions. After my older brother graduated from high school, he was deemed insufficiently pious — mostly on the basis of my mother's claim that she had overheard him listening to the radio in his room late one Friday night — and was shipped off to Israel, for a corrective program of yeshiva study.

A great deal of the complicated story of modern American Jewry, wherein the lure of assimilation vies with an ingrained tradition of separatism, is recounted by Samuel Freedman in his ambitious new book, *Jew vs. Jew: The Struggle for the Soul of American Jewry* (blurbed, serendipitously, by Senator Lieberman). Freedman, a professor of journalism at Columbia, appears undaunted by the welter of irreconcilable impulses and conflicting reports which awaits anyone who hopes to clarify the recent history of this disputatious bunch. In the author's view, the "ancient bond" that united Jews of every stripe through six thousand years of precarious existence in a hostile world has ceased to do so in a more tolerant one; as the American Jewish community has become increasingly affluent, educated, and successful, its internal divisions have become increasingly rancorous. (Indeed, just contemplating the number of people Freedman must have interviewed — one voluble and tendentious Jew after another, arguing the world — is enough to make a sympathetic reader shudder.)

Freedman has organized his book into six thematically linked sections, centered on specific Jewish neighborhoods across the

United States where the "crisis of legitimacy" has been escalating over the past four decades. He touches down first in the Catskills of the postwar era, where he evokes the last gasp of a Jewish identity forged in purely ethnic terms: the working-class Farband movement. He captures the essence of the movement's kibbutznik style, with its twin allegiances to Palestine and to socialism, in a quickly sketched portrait of the Labor Zionist summer camp Kinderwelt. The camp, founded in 1925, flourished for almost half a century, on a combination of Yiddishist sentiment and Israeli folk dancing (with a few classic Americanisms such as color wars and panty raids thrown into the mix), before it was razed to make way for a housing development. But, when a small group of Kinderwelt loyalists get together for a reunion in a Manhattan apartment in 1998, Freedman finds that, with one exception (a woman whose son became Orthodox and moved to a settlement on the West Bank), they have only the vaguest notion of Jewishness, and it is predicated mainly on trips to Israel and a lingering collective spirit.

With these scenes, Freedman establishes a context for the often repeated thesis of his book. Ethnic Judaism ("'Seinfeld' and a schmear") has decisively failed, as evidenced by the "whopping statistics on intermarriage; at the same time, the Orthodox experience — dismissed in 1955 by one eminent sociologist as "a case study of institutional decay" — is enjoying a wholly unanticipated revival. This shift toward the fundamentalist, God-fearing sort of Judaism is reflected both in the actual demographics (the high birth rate among the Orthodox and ultra-Orthodox, especially compared with the stagnant rate among nonobservant Jews) and in the reconfiguration of American Jewish identity.

Freedman's milling throng of interviewees includes doom-pronouncing traditionalists, entrenched assimilationists, Conservative and progressive Orthodox leaders committed to the notion of a Jewish life "with wiggle room," an impassioned wacko or two, and a feminist activist who scandalized her ostensibly enlightened Conservative congregration by including the neglected biblical matriarchs — Sarah, Rebecca, Rachel, and Leah — in her invocation of Jewish ancestors. All these disparate figures have felt the effects of the Jewish drift to the right.

Perhaps the most admirably principled — and, for me, guilt-inducing — character in Freedman's book is Daniel Greer, an Ivy

League–educated white-shoe lawyer turned religious-school dean. Greer's trajectory is an example of an intracommunity phenomenon known as "flipping" — converting from a more liberal form of Orthodoxy to a more stringent one. Reared in a typical Modern Orthodox Upper West Side home in the forties and fifties, Greer was the first graduate of the Manhattan Talmudic Academy to enter Princeton. He went on to Yale Law School (where he bunked with Jerry Brown), held several high-ranking positions under Mayor Lindsay, ran for local Democratic office, and campaigned for McGovern — all the while wearing a hat rather than a yarmulke in public. But although his career might appear to be a shining testament to the Modern Orthodox ideal of synthesis, Greer became increasingly uncomfortable with the compromises it required. He stopped practicing law, grew his beard, began wearing *tzitzis* outside his clothing, and devoted himself full-time to religious leadership and community service. "So many American Jews were first-generation and so concerned with fitting in," Greer says. "We want to restore a more demonstrative, open, all-encompassing experience." In 1997, one of his daughters became a litigant in the controversial Yale Five case, in which a small group of Orthodox students brought a lawsuit against the university on the ground of religious discrimination.

At the other end of the spectrum is Harry Shapiro, one of the lost souls who latch on to the ultra-Orthodox movement because they have little else to anchor them. The son of a supermarket-chain executive, Shapiro was a gifted mechanic but an academic failure. While still in his teens, he bought a one-way ticket to Israel, but, even after two attempts, he couldn't carve out a tenable existence there. Back in New York, he enrolled in a remedial program at Yeshiva University, only to flunk out; he opened a butcher shop in Florida called Kosher Kuts, but the business went under in less than two years. The only bright spot in Harry's life was his commitment to a fanatically hawkish brand of Zionism, which culminated in a radical but ineffectual gesture of protest. In 1997, he was arrested for placing a homemade bomb in the Jacksonville Jewish Center on the eve of an appearance by the former Israeli prime minister and renowned peacemaker Shimon Peres. Shapiro's bizarre religious journey landed him in federal prison with a ten-year sentence.

Jew vs. Jew is an assiduously researched, up-to-the-minute report, and if it finally fails to cohere in the reader's mind that may be because it is too faithful a reflection of the dilemma it describes. The author is so intent on gluing together the splintered pieces of a once intact community, so determined to transcribe its babble of voices and views, that his book is at times overrun by its own informational anxiety. After I finished it, I felt relieved to be back on my familiar lonely turf — spiritually bereft, perhaps, but safely beyond the din of battle.

Is it ever too late to reclaim your roots? It seems that everyone with even a smidgen of Jewishness in his or her background is doing just that these days, writing a memoir of salvaged ancestral kinship, with the word *Exile* or *Chosen* or *Journey* somewhere in the title. Among such bittersweet reckonings are Mary Gordon's *The Shadow Man*, in which the writer learns that her beloved father was a virulently anti-Semitic Jew; Stephen Dubner's *Turbulent Souls*, wherein the author, having been reared as one of a large Catholic brood by parents who left the synagogue for the Church, reinvents himself as a committed Jew; and Susan Jacoby's *Half-Jew*, in which a secret family history of religious denial is gradually uncovered.

I have been more moved, however, by memoirs that explore a different transformation, in which the narrator questions the presumptions underlying the enterprise of Jewish assimilation. These include Joshua Hammer's *Chosen by God* and David Klinghoffer's *The Lord Will Gather Me In*. Both books offer fascinating glimpses into the growing *ba'al tshuva* movement, in which young men and women from devoutly secularist backgrounds decide to become practicing Jews. In *Chosen by God*, which is narrated with bewildered and occasionally self-incriminating candor, Hammer attempts to come to terms with this phenomenon as it is exemplified by his younger brother, Tony. The siblings grew up in a cosmopolitan, nonreligious Manhattan household, but Tony eventually rejected their background and was reborn as Tuvia, an ultra-Orthodox Jew. Hammer, a *Newsweek* correspondent, is scrupulously fair, conveying both his initial sense of horror at his brother's religious makeover — in which Tony, "the most resolute atheist I had known," comes to resemble "a Hasidic Willy Loman" — and his qualified, begrudging comprehension of his brother's motives in seeking out an insulated life of study and prayer.

Klinghoffer's memoir, on the other hand, charts his growing disenchantment with the flabby values and ostentatious lifestyle of the southern California–style Reform Judaism in which he was reared by his adoptive parents. Klinghoffer was five years old when he was told that neither of his birth parents was Jewish; while still in high school, he decided — in an act worthy of inclusion in Ripley's "Believe It or Not" — to perform a ritual conversion on himself. He soaped up a razor blade and gingerly cut at his penis until "a very small bead of red" convinced him that his circumcision was a success, and then immersed himself in a bathtub, allowing the water to cover his face. (He later underwent a real circumcision at the hands of a *mohel*.) The author is a junior-division neoconservative (he is a contributing editor at *National Review*), and his book is marked by a trenchant wit and an astringent refusal to buy into the liberal nostrums on which he was brought up. Although he announces that he is "the only person I know of who came to Orthodox Judaism via Friedrich Nietzsche," his argument is essentially a fideist one — that the apprehension of a divine presence at work in the world can be explained only on the basis of faith.

I do think that Klinghoffer's newfound zeal leads him to romanticize certain aspects of his chosen creed; for example, he holds up Orthodox bar mitzvah celebrations as exemplary occasions of piety and modesty. His own Jewish coming of age, by contrast, is derided as part of an emotionally bankrupt "circuit" involving a "mass expenditure of cash and credit," a hammy and insipid speech (often written by the bar mitzvah boy's mother or father), and a knock-'em-dead theme party, pandering to the pop-cultural obsession of the moment. Having attended mostly Orthodox bar mitzvahs growing up, I can attest that I never had the good fortune to witness the sort he describes, where, after a solemn ceremony, the celebrants "adjourn to the synagogue social hall for pickled herring and shots of whiskey." This astonishingly humble repast sounds to me like a story out of I. L. Peretz or Sholem Aleichem, but then isn't it the disillusioned who are most in need of someone or something to idealize?

While reading Hammer's and Klinghoffer's memoirs, I tried to envision myself as a kind of double-jointed female returnee, a *ba'alat tshuva* whose odyssey is a curvy variation on the usual linear pattern — a journey from A to B and then back again to A. It's precisely the doubling back on myself that I have trouble with, however, the undoing of accommodations that, for better or worse, I have made. I try to imagine myself bidding goodbye to worldly friends and wanton pleasures, voluntarily tethering myself to out-moded rituals and circumscribed possibilities. But it feels, even at this hypothetical distance, too much like playacting, as though I were an understudy in *Fiddler on the Roof,* tying a kerchief under my chin and taking care of the younger children while waiting for the matchmaker to make me the perfect match.

I suppose some part of me has always thought of my twenty-odd years of religious uncertainty as a passing phase, something I had to wade through in order to get to the other side — which would prove to be, like the most elegant of Zen constructs, my beginning in another guise. But how long can a phase last before it calcifies into a permanent condition?

I've been at play in the fields of heresy ever since the end of my third year in high school, when I walked into Zum Zum, part of a German chain famous for its nitrate-heavy delicacies. It was a fine June day, shortly before I was to go off to work as a junior coun-selor at Morasha, a strictly Orthodox summer camp, where the boys and girls weren't permitted to swim together. I had always liked everything about Zum Zum, from its faux-pewter plates to its hearty Heidi-influenced aesthetic, complete with waitresses dressed in dirndl skirts and aprons. Now I sat down at the counter with its little clay pots of mustard, "Das Hot" and "Das Sweet," and ordered myself a hot dog — an unkosher hot dog — on a caraway-seed bun, accompanied by nicely seasoned potato salad, pepper-flecked sauerkraut, and a tart pickle. It was a revolutionary mo-ment, and by rights I should have been jumping out of my skin. But I wasn't; my hands were steady and my heart was beating at its usual pace. I took my time, savoring every bite.

After this momentous transgression, I quickly reverted to a Morasha girl-camper persona. We *davened* the *shachris* service first thing every morning, clumped together on hard benches in the camp's makeshift *shul,* having been yanked awake by the Hebrew imprecation to "*Kumu, kumu*" (arise, arise) coming over the loud-speaker, followed by blaring Israeli dance music. Given that we were all normal sex-driven teenagers, as well as good Jews in the making, the hot topic of *negiyah* — the prohibition on physical contact between unmarried men and women — dominated the late night conversations. That summer, I myself indulged in my first, highly publicized French kiss, which led to a private talk with my agitated counselor about the ethics of desire.

I felt least ambivalent about my religion when I listened to the merry band of counselors turned musicians who regaled us daily, and who were, indeed, one of the camp's main attractions. The band, made up of Yeshiva University students with names like La-bel, Eli, and Yitzi, performed what I thought of as inspired music, consisting of melancholy but punchy tunes based on a few minor chords and lyrics from the Hebrew liturgy. To the extent that I believed in something called a soul — I waffled on this, just as I waffled on the idea of God — I felt my soul being wrenched as I listened. I floated upward — away from my resistance to a system that seemed more concerned with tiresome strictures and sexist rabbin-ical rulings than with virtues like kindness and empathy — and found myself on a cloud of benign camaraderie. This, then, was the real thing, the gratification that awaited you if you bought into the whole kit and caboodle, from keeping kosher to sitting shivah. These were my people, after all, and for a brief while I wanted to be one of them.

Such havens in the wilderness of my disaffection became in-creasingly rare as I veered between an escalating strategy of reli-gious defiance and passing myself off as an uncorrupted product of an Orthodox upbringing. My real break came while I was at Barnard; since it was my parents' conviction that an out-of-town college would end their control over my religious life, I effected my rebellion while remaining close to home, practically under their very noses. I moved on from Zum Zum hot dogs to Szechuan dumplings and Indian curries, swooning over the sheer abandon of being able to order anything on a menu that caught my fancy. In the middle of all this, I opted to live in one of Barnard's kosher suites, with four other girls. My suitemates hailed from Queens or Brooklyn, homey boroughs that I chauvinistically supposed to pre-sent less of a temptation to stray than Manhattan. Instead of taking part in the bacchanalias of sex and drugs that the rest of the cam-pus was presumably enjoying, they made Friday-night dinners to which they invited Orthodox Columbia boys. If I didn't go home for Shabbos, I joined them.

I felt like an impostor, but I would have felt like an impostor among the non-Orthodox. My frame of reference, beginning with something as basic as the calendar, was marked not by Thanksgiving turkeys or Christmas trees but by the mostly solemn round of Jewish holidays, characterized by endless services, heavy meals, and long quiescent afternoons. Rosh Hashanah was followed by Yom Kippur, which was followed by Succos, Chanukah, and then by Purim, Pesach, and Shavuos (which no one had heard of outside the tight circle of the initiated). Truth be told, the flight into freedom seemed as threatening as it was alluring. I feared being overcome by vertigo — falling off the end of the earth, with no one to catch me. What if it turned out that my early training had left me fundamentally unequipped for a world of wide-open spaces? What if I was so imprinted by dogma that I needed the very narrowness against which I strained?

It went on like this for years, daring violation followed by guilty compliance. In retrospect, I wonder that my flimsy on-again, off-again self didn't simply rip in two, like a piece of paper. It wasn't that I believed in an angry God, looking down at me with a face like Abraham Lincoln's and plotting his revenge. It wasn't that I feared parental rejection, either, although I'm not sure my father ever knew the extent of my sacrilege. (He surely didn't know that I had begun to make it a habit to eat on Yom Kippur and once, in an especially angry period, felt an urgent need for a manicure.) What haunted me was an insistent and morbid sense that I was an outcast — albeit by choice, which only made it worse. I had willed myself into a cold and dark hallway, inches away from a closed door. I could see the light spilling out from underneath it, and if I could just bring myself to open the door and step inside I would come upon some semblance of earthly grace, an imposed order that would feel natural if only I surrendered myself to it.

I've been nonpracticing for more years than I've been Orthodox, but, come Friday evening, wherever I am and whatever I'm doing, I'm always aware that Shabbos is starting. This awareness goes beyond simple nostalgia, yet I have been unable to find an adult definition of Jewishness which I can reconcile with the rigorous standards of my childhood. I have gone once or twice to services at a Reform temple that is affiliated with my daughter's school, and I can't get used to any of it: the mixed seating, the music, the recitation of prayers in English, even the word *temple* instead of *shul*.

Recently, I have begun thinking about making the kitchen in my next apartment kosher. My daughter, who is ten, has wanted us to become more religious for a while now; this summer, she asked me to arrange extra Hebrew lessons for her. I'm sure that some of her interest has been spurred by her desire to *daven* and *bench* along with her first cousins (all nineteen of them), who are being brought up in observant households. But I also think some of it has to do with her own proclivities, just as my discomfort with Orthodoxy had to do with mine. Although part of me balks at the idea of having a child who hankers after a tradition I have spent half a lifetime throwing away, another part feels something resembling pride. When I mentioned these developments to an older friend of mine, an avowedly atheistic Jew from a Camp Kinderwelt sort of background, she reacted with undisguised horror, as though I had declared my intention to join a deranged militant sect in Nebraska. "You're not serious," she said. I shrugged the subject off, slightly embarrassed.

I still have time to scrap my plan to keep kosher — to review the situation in all its unappealing aspects — but I'm not waiting for one of those transcendent, "Aha!" moments to strike, bringing with it a vision of the eternal. I'm not that kind of person, nor is my religion that kind of religion. Judaism is nothing if not down to earth in its approach, and sets more store by behavior than by belief. It's either a weakness in me or a strength — I haven't decided — that I still haven't figured out where I stand on so consequential a matter as the quality of my Jewish life. But if I should happen to die before I've made up my mind, I'm counting on my family to give me an Orthodox burial.

DAVID MICHAELIS

Provincetown

FROM THE AMERICAN SCHOLAR

TWO WEEKS AGO, I heard my phone twittering in the dusk. It was Alec Wilkinson, calling from Truro to ask if I would introduce him at his reading at the Provincetown Art Association on August 8. I told him I wanted a night to think it over, but I could already feel the gritty sand-scored floorboards of the Art Association under my feet. This is what I thought: It's time I went back to P-town.

In Boston, 5:30 A.M. The gulls shrieking over Boston Harbor. Before leaving A Street, I read my grandfather Ordway Tead's essay about Provincetown, "Remembrance of Things Past." His father, the Reverend Edward Sampson Tead, a Congregational minister from Somerville, Massachusetts, had taken the family each July to Provincetown, where my great-grandfather served as the summer preacher in the local parish. Each year on July 1, my grandfather and his brother Phillips would be up at 5:30 in the morning, shivering with excitement about taking the steamer from Boston to the Cape.

Big blue dome over Boston, sun rising behind the steeples of Southie. Down the Southeast Expressway. At the bottom of Quincy comes the big fork: go right for Route 95, Providence, and New York City; go left for Pilgrim's Highway, Cape Cod, and the Islands. The road to New York brings back the whole sense of exile I've lived with ever since we sold the house in Provincetown to pay Mom's estate taxes — that whole epoch in the eighties when it seemed as if we had been banished. But now, for a moment, the old pattern of life seems once more vouchsafed for me: I turn with a great rush of feeling onto Pilgrim's Highway. I'm going home. I'm driving down to the Cape.

I don't know why I feel so guilty about having lost the house in P-town. I never seem able to forgive myself because I always know that, in fact, Choate, Hall & Stewart's distress sale was avoidable. We had a choice. My mother's house in Cambridge could have been sold, though in cash value the loss would have been greater had we sold 19 Berkeley Street in the pits of the real estate market of 1982. I remember it every time I drive through Boston: the way my brother and I sat up there in the cool, collected conference room at the law firm, agreeing with everyone that it was a luxury for a couple of guys in their early twenties to own beachfront property on Cape Cod. And so we sold the thing we loved more deeply than any other.

Now here I am sailing across the Sagamore Bridge to Cape Cod and Provincetown. The word by itself, the length of it on the green roadside sign, the many jumbled letters, gives me a sudden glimpse of the whole town. It's the first glimpse I've really allowed myself. I really see it: Provincetown, lying flat on the harbor, surrounded by the vast plains of the Atlantic, the Pilgrim monument silhouetted against the equally vast sky. "The long, slender, dearly beloved town," as my grandfather called it in his memoir.

I stop for coffee and a bran muffin at a new Friendly's beside the bridge rotary. Even before getting out of the car, I can smell the salty air, the whiff of bayberry. I wipe my eyes. It's 8:30 in the morning, and I am already welling up. It is going to be a long day.

At Orleans, I swing around the rotary and head north on Route 6. This is the last leg. After the Wellfleet Drive-In, the road is dense with the sites and sights of my childhood. There's the Wellfleet A&P, the parking lot where, one rainy day, at age seven, I got hit by a car and cut by its silver hood ornament at the corner of my (right) eye. The A&P is now the IGA, and I have to check the car mirror to see which eye it was. There's the turnoff for Wellfleet Center and for Gull Pond Road — the Sluiceway! And here is Truro, already. My God, it's all here, it's all the same, but it's not. The Package Store is still the Package Store, but Schoonie's isn't Schoonie's and Gilbert Seldes isn't lying abed in a small white clapboard house and I am not being taken in to say hello to the great man at his smelly bedside. And yet here is the sign for Corn Hill, which therefore must still exist, and for Highland Light, whose flashing sequence I used to count from my bunk window in Provincetown.

I start feeling queasy. Not exactly carsick, but somehow ill, not quite myself. The road is hilly in this part of North Truro, but it's not the rolling motion of the car that's making me uneasy. It's not so much what's here as what is *not* here. I keep expecting to see certain vistas open up across the tops of the scrub pine. They are not places you'd find on the map. They are those scenes that, because of annual pilgrimage, become even more affirming of place than the shrines marked by big green reflective signs. I am looking for The Land That Grandma and Grandpa Owned. I am looking for The Bluff Over the Bay with the Edward Hopper House. And for The Field Where We Stopped When the Dog Had to Upchuck. It all seems to have vanished. But then, when I come to a certain point in the road, which we thought of as The Place Where Mom Always Says Whee!, I realize what's happened. Mom always said Whee! because that was the point in the road where we could first see P-town after a year's absence. The reason I can't see P-town from this point in the road is that the trees have grown; they're no longer scrubby.

At the crest of Pilgrim Heights, I come apart a little. I begin sobbing the minute I see it — Provincetown, low and long and clear, a world afloat between sky and sea. To my right is Pilgrim Lake and behind it the dunes, stretching out across the narrow spine of land. To my left, dotting the shore road and the bay, strands of matching cottages, tiny clapboard necklaces looping from North Truro around to P-town. This is the very last piece of northbound road before you turn west. I'm driving and blubbering and blubbering and driving. I'm making sounds I haven't heard me make since the time of Mom's death, ten years ago in December. My skull hurts. I can't find the ENTERING PROVINCETOWN sign — the one that always got my brother and me into a fight (like Ordway and Phillips before us), a contest to see who could get his foot deepest into the car's heating duct and claim to have been first into P-town.

Now I know why my grandfather stopped his lovely memoir at the point of arrival. It's just too much. I feel as if I'm dying, or dead already. I pass the water tower, then the roadside dunes — the shrunken Sahara of my childhood. I slow down to make the left-hand turn onto Snail Road, which goes south two- or three-tenths of a mile before it rejoins Route 6A at the water's edge. I turn, cross the highway, and start down Snail Road. I wish I were a snail, so I could duck back into my shell — back into the life I've improvised since my mother's death. None of my life since 1982 has been real — I feel that suddenly now on Snail Road. I feel completely naked. About halfway down the road, I think: Maybe I really should just turn back, forget it, go back to Wellfleet. But in another second I see the water. This was always the moment when Mom took her hands off the steering wheel and clapped them together. Often she wept.

Provincetown forms a bowl around the sea. The East End, where I'm making landfall, and town center and the West End and all the sandy way around to Long Point form a slender rim. The seaward horizon and the bayside of Wellfleet and Truro complete the rim. If you go out on the water here, or, when the tide is out, if you walk out onto the flats, you feel as if you are in the exact center of creation, suspended in a sphere of light between the dome of sky and the bowl of sea. The land is a line on the horizon, not much more. You can feel the roundness of the planet and the continuousness of the cosmos. The light is the light of miracles. The water is clear and blue and green, so full of salt and shellfish that when you smell its smell you don't think so much of the seaside as of life itself. When, after ten years away, I drive back up to the edge of this bowl of light and water, I instantly dissolve back into it, like powdered remains, white bone fragments, tossed onto water.

I park the car at HoJo's, which is now called Basil's. A can of root beer takes some of the dread out of my stomach. I walk over to the waterside, back at the beginning of the East End, before the tightly spaced houses begin their long march down Commercial Street. It is a glorious day, cloudless, high summer. The water has a sparkle on it. I stand on a sandy spot above the shorefront, and the sea comes up to meet me. The sound of it, the smell of it — it fills me up instantly. I don't know why, but the sea here is so much more completely the sea than almost anywhere else I have ever been. P-town, I keep thinking, this is P-town. I feel myself coming to life, as if a dead limb had been sewn back onto my body and pumped full of fresh salty blood.

I take a deep breath and start down Commercial. I walk in the street, as always, and I pass by the Zinbergs', which has a big FOR SALE sign out front: Dorothy selling after Norman's death? I pass by the Florsheims', also dead. I pass by the Romanos', where I first kissed a girl, Jill Kearney, in a spin-the-bottle game. At the Kearneys', a flock of bumper-sculpture animals materializes in my memory, like extinct creatures in a child's pop-up book. At the Motherwells', the name of the house — a name I have neither heard nor thought of for ten years — offers itself as if it were still part of my everyday mental furniture: Sea Barn. It's all shut up now, following Robert Motherwell's death last month and the memorial service on the flats, which I read about in the *Times*. After Sea Barn comes Harmony, Lily Harmon's house. And then the Friedmans' unnamed house, now the Mailers', with a big black BMW parked out front. Then comes Bissell's and Huber's Hut, and the Packards', and across on the back side of Commercial, facing the water across its parking lot and beach, the White Dory Inn, which is now condominiums. Beside the White Dory stands the Atkins Cottage, where my grandparents spent their honeymoon seventy-six years ago this July.

I can't bring myself to look at the next house on the water. It's crazy, but I feel that if I see this most unimaginable sight — my house, our house, inhabited by us in another time — then I will know what it is like to be dead, or never to have lived at all. And the strangest part is that here, under this sun, and with the wind blowing the sea into my brains, I have always felt completely alive, a fully sentient being restored to my original (which may also be my final) state.

After Mom died, I had recurring dreams for the first time in my life. There were several. The fish dreams. Also the dream of amputation. And the dream where Mom would turn to stone when I kissed her. About once a year for ten years I have had a dream that takes place in our house in Provincetown. There are variations, but the dream always starts the same way. Mom and I are at the window next to the bathroom, and Mom is agitated because she looks out and sees cars parked on our lawn. Then, when she sees that in fact the lawn has been turned into a parking lot, covered in gray spalls, she gets furious and demands to know what has happened. Sometimes she asks what those people think they are doing or why there is a car out there with a Pittsburgh license plate, black with white letters. In any event, she's mad, and I'm the one who's got to tell her that we don't own the house anymore.

Sometimes she receives this news philosophically. When I first had these dreams, right after we sold the house in '82, Mom got very angry. She was baffled, outraged, shaking with fury: "What do you mean, WE DON'T OWN THE HOUSE? Of course we do, Dave! It's our house, Grandma and Grandpa's house, and now it's your house. Don't be silly." She would get so carried away, there was only one thing to do to defuse her: tell her she was dead. In real life, when Mom was in the hospital, dying of cancer, no one broke this news to her. No one ever said: Diana, you're dying. You are going to be dead soon. Is your will in order (it was not), have you taken all the necessary steps? We all acted as if strong-willed Mom would survive. In my recurring dream, when I told her the news that she was dead, Mom would always take it with a smile and a wave, just as she had taken her disease in life. Then she would turn from me, turn away from the window, and start up the stairs. And I always knew that she was going back to the dead because her feet weren't touching the stairs and I could see her heels floating upward.

The side of the house looks exactly the same. The shingles are gray and weathered. Not a single window on the east end of the house looks altered. The seaside deck has the same railing and the same bulkhead. This sounds like a pretty sober description — as if I'm standing there on Commercial Street looking at my old house with a cool, dry eye. In fact, all I really give the house is a glance — before suddenly noticing that the lawn and privet hedges facing the street are gone, replaced by a parking lot with gravel spalls. Several cars are parked in this mini-lot, although none with Pittsburgh license plates. The house has also been christened by its new owners. To us it had always been simply "619." But now it has a name, and there it is in purple letters: LEVITATION. Just as I am turning away, a woman walks out the front door onto the porch. I turn fast.

Completely undone, I float on down Commercial. David Mayo has built a big house beside ours, filling in what was always a vacant seaside lot. Someone else has squeezed an awful house — big and boxy, with a flat-topped roof — between Mayo's and the old Mervyn Jules place: *two* houses where before there was none. Up the street, a fancy hotel with pink umbrellas and white tables has replaced Rosy, the raffish seventies hangout where we met for nightcaps. I pass the small white gate that led through the rosehip-fragrant path to the Tennis Club. And Howie Schneider's house, and Susan Sinaiko's. And the Ship's Bell sign, and the glass telephone booth that used to be in front of the sign. And here is Number One Conway Street — Anna Lewis's house.

I walk up to the gate and stand there without deciding to do anything. The lawn chairs under the trees in the front yard look cool and welcoming. There's some laundry hanging on the line. Flowers border the white picket fence. Inside the small shingled house, the TV chatters. I can hear Anna eating lunch alone in front of the television. I'm not sure what to do, whether to continue on into town or whether to seek refuge here. I've actually never set foot inside Anna's house. All our conversations took place at 619 Commercial or at the gate where I am standing now.

The front door is open, the screen door secure. I call out Anna's name in a small, choked voice. "Yes?" she replies, and I would know that rough, mannish voice anywhere. But when she comes to the door, she does not know me. Her flashing gaze looks right through me. "Anna," I say, "it's David." In a low, nearly inaudible voice, she says, "Oh my gawd." Then, without hesitation, "Come in, come in, dear."

There are four chairs in Anna Lewis's living room, and they tell the story of her Life. Her mother, Wilhelmina Enos, sat in one. Her husband, Manuel J. "Mannie" Lewis, sat in another. Anna sat in a third. The fourth was her father's. He died when Anna was twelve, and now that chair is for company. We cover a lot of ground quickly, starting with the changes at 619 Commercial. As Anna talks her eyes seem always to stray to the horizon, sweeping back and forth. But in fact you can't see the sea from Anna's living room. I guess if you've lived in P-town all your life, as Anna has, that line of sea and sky is probably imprinted on your brain. Anna remembers what the East End was like when Eugene O'Neill and John Dos Passos were her neighbors. When she worked on the old Hilliard's Wharf. When she used to open the house for the Sternes and the Teads. And when she closed it up for Mom, for the last time, that last October. After she spoke with Mom on the phone and heard the sound in her voice, she went home and cried and said, "Oh, Diana, this is it." After a while, we come back to the present. "Well," she says, "if you're going to see town, you'd better go now, or you may never get there."

Back on Commercial Street. It's like having some hallucinogen reactivated in my brain. This again — Provincetown, ten years later.

Oh my God, there's the Cape Codder sign. And the Silvas', which is for sale. Tillie's is all boarded up. The icehouse has become ICE HOUSE CONDOMINIUMS. But Long Point Gallery still looks the same, as does the Patrician Shop, and the playground outside it, where, once, as a six- or seven-year-old boy, I thought I'd lost Mom, and so, quite solemnly, lay down in the sand to die, and cried and cried in deepest despair, until Mom returned from wherever she'd gone and picked me up in disbelief.

Involuntarily, I keep looking for the town that was here when I first knew P-town — the tough, tolerant, blue-collar P-town. It seems finally to have sold out to the tourist trade. Arnold of Arnold's TV and appliance store gets a better return on his property by renting it out to a T-shirt merchant; same for Duarte's Motors and a dozen other old businesses in town center. The Fo'c'sle, the joint I always thought of as the darkest, meanest bar in the world — hangout for local toughs, burnouts, fishermen, and visiting Hell's Angels — has become a tame tourist bar, all watered down. Then again, there was always a layering of P-towns — the P-town of the day-trippers and tourists, of the gays and cross-dressers, of the artists and writers, of the summering shrinks, of the hippies and conservationists, of the year-round off-Cape transplants and drifters, and of the dancing policeman, who still leaps and pirouettes, choreographing traffic at the heart of town. The P-town I'm looking for, the dark, smiling P-town of the Portuguese, was always a little hidden by clannishness anyway.

On the front side of the "front street," as my grandfather called Commercial, Lands End Marine, the great nautical and fishing tackle emporium of my boyhood, is still open for business, and I am glad to see it. In the heat of the sidewalk, I pass by the screen doors, inhaling the cool, sweet perfume of vulcanized rubber, hemp, tar, creosote, varnishes. The uncanny sensation comes over me once more: I feel as if I were discontinued, like a car that's still on the road but for which there are no longer parts. I feel as if my soul never left, but my mind and body no longer belong. My brain is telling me that I'm here, I'm back. It's me again — back in P-town! And yet it's not me exactly, neither the prelapsarian me nor the me I've become in exile. In flashes, it's so easy, so seductive, to see myself here again. If I had a son, a boy at my side, I'm sure I would project all my feelings onto him. It would be the natural thing. The boy would become the boy I no longer am. He would ensure the continuity of these seaside summers. I could give up all this guilt I feel about losing the house, breaking the chain. But I don't have children. I am neither son nor father. I am a freak of nature, a pilgrim, a time traveler.

I turn toward MacMillan Wharf, skirting the lines, the swirling midday crowds, and start out onto the pier. Suddenly I'm glad that I've made my pilgrimage on a dazzling day in high summer. My head is spinning in the bright clean air, the salty smell of the sea, and the mingling aromas of frankfurters, deep-fried clams, warmed-up asphalt, and fudge. The tide is high. The deep green water fills in under the tall barnacled pilings. The Boston boat has just tied up and the day-trippers are streaming landward off the pier. I continue seaward, insanely relieved to find that there are still boys diving for money — the immemorial racket of challenging tourists to "chuck a nickel ov-ah!" They are not the boys (including the harbormaster's son) who swamped Jackson's dinghy and flung it off the end of the wharf the summer we tried to poach coins in these Portuguese diving waters. But the tide is high, the harbor is deep, the Boston boat is in, and it's the same racket and they are the same boys. Huddling in their wet cutoff trunks on the pier's wooden lip, shivering, hair slicked back, brown bodies glistening, they peer through the sun-sparkle, studying the green water for the silvery lie of coins in the sandy bottom. The debate is still the same: whether that's a quarter down there in the sand or just a dime. And they still complain when someone tosses pennies; and they still stand authoritatively, like little pirates, on the cleats and fastened lines of the boats; and they still answer the eternal tourist's question — "How deep is it down there?" — with the eternal boy's deep-voiced answer: "Deep."

The fish-packing warehouse is gone from the end of the pier, and what was once a world of shadows and ice-filled wooden crates and wet, cool, fish-smelling passageways is now ablaze with sunshine. I stand there, astounded. For ten years I have been walking past fish markets in New York, Halifax, Vineyard Haven, County Cork, Porto Ercole, Sag Harbor. Once, outside the Rosedale Fish Market on Lexington Avenue, as I ran to catch the crosstown bus on 79th Street, I stopped dead in my tracks. From the open door came the cold, clean market smell, and I solemnly told myself: Yes, that's P-town. That's what the wharf smelled like, back behind the harbormaster's office, back where my brother and I, no more than seven or eight years old, with Mom standing by, fished for tinker mackerel with hand lines and silver jigs. For ten years I have comforted myself with the lie that other places are this place. But now I smell it, the real thing, and there is nothing like it. There is no place like this in the world, and I don't know what to do. I don't know where to go next.

I get as far as the post office, then turn back toward the East End. I feel as if I'm dying again. I'm either going crazy or just exciting my overexcitable appetite for loss. No wonder I was so moved by visiting the Etruscan tombs in Tarquinia. Maybe next summer I should visit Sioux burial grounds.

I'm dumb with hunger. I haven't eaten since the bran muffin at the bridge, hours ago. But when I come upon the Penny Patch, the candy store of my childhood, I think I'm ready to be gratified. Electric fans are blowing a warm, fudgy aroma out onto Commercial Street. I enter the shop and take a basket. It feels wonderfully inviting and familiar in my ungainly hand, this little wicker basket for penny candies. And I have money — boy, do I have a lot of pocket money. What an allowance. I move forward into the velvety warm Wonka world of candy. The floor-to-ceiling shelves are a riot of fireballs, root beer barrels, jawbreakers, licorice twists, jelly beans, Boston Baked Beans, chocolate babies, anise drops, Tootsie Rolls, Bit-O-Honeys, Mary Janes, white rock candy. Everything looks excitingly the same. Everything *is* the same: the same squares of fudge, the same dumb boxes of saltwater taffy, the same trompe l'oeil "beach pebbles" Grandma sent me in camp. Suddenly I don't want to eat any of it. I'm ragingly, foamingly hungry. I haven't a clue what I'm doing in here. I can't eat fudge for lunch. I'm thirty-three years old. What am I thinking? Atomic Fire Balls? Rainbow Jaw Breakers? I've got to get back to 1991. Nauseous, sick of myself, I put down my empty basket and walk out of the Penny Patch.

The craziest thing is that I'm all memoried out and I have not yet even set foot on the beach or in the bay. On my way back from town, I cut across the Episcopal church's parking lot opposite vanished Tillie's. I sit down on the break wall, take off my sneakers and socks, and leap to the sand. I take a step. My God, I say aloud, it's the sand. The sand. What I mean is: I never knew before that even the sand here has a particular texture, a springiness, which, for me, is sand. All these years away on other beaches I've been misled. I bend over and peer at the smooth, coarse, yellow, orange, brown, blond, and black particles under my toes. So much of memory is invention, but this I know: this is sand.

The tide is going out. I walk in the shallow, receding water, floored by the sense of recognition. The water is so clear and lovely. Every crab seems known to me, every waving shank of sea grass, even the rufous color of certain spots on the beach, such as the stretch outside Gary Silva's old house and over by the Rossmores'. I keep thinking I must be going out of my mind.

The closer I get to the beach side of 619, the weirder I feel. All along this home stretch, people are sitting on their decks, sunning, reading. I can hear the rattle of a spray-paint can; someone is stenciling a chest of drawers. The decks and houses are as familiar as my toenails, but the sunbathers are strangers. This is the summer community I grew up in, and this is a summer day, and the only person I recognize is Norman Mailer, whom anyone would recognize. I've never felt more alien anywhere in all my life. The tide is sloughing out under my knees, so I walk farther out, past the jetties, farther and farther away from shore. I notice that the Big Rock, the tall chunky slab of granite at the end of our jetty, about which I have literally dozens of memories, all keyed to the different heights of the tides, has fallen onto its side. The Big Rock is where we scattered our old dog's ashes in 1980, my mother and brother and I. Each of us took some peppery white dust from the strange small container. Pooey's death was the practice death; his ashes, practice throws. Grandma went next. Then Mom.

Ironically, after gorging myself on every fish hook and sinker in town, I now can't bring myself to look directly at any of the details around 619. The overall shapes — rock, jetty, beach, house — are all I can manage. It's like being at a party when an old lover walks in the room. The more intimate you've been with the object of your desire, the greater its power, ultimately, to alienate. Now that I am here, all I know is I need to get into the water. I don't even need to swim. I just want to lie in the outgoing water. I've worn my bathing suit under my shorts, so changing isn't a problem. Even so, I've got to find somewhere to leave my shorts and shirt and sneakers. And just as I'm puzzling this over, wondering if I have the guts to leave my stuff up on the beach (Mom's voice in my ear: "Can't those day-trippers read the sign: PRIVATE BEACH/NO TRES-PASSING?"), I see Susan Packard. She's directly ahead, in the same stretch of thigh-deep water where I'm sloshing around. It's Susan, all right. She looks exactly the same. The girl next door. She's wearing a two-piece bathing suit, and she's running out into the receding water. Her whole body is pitched forward, her hair in flight, and I have an urge to rush up, throw my arms around her, and thank her. As with the sand, the water, the jetties, the crabs, I'm astonished to the point of gratitude to rediscover my knowledge of this particular girl's particular way of running out of her house and into the water. It locates me.

I approach Susan, both of us knee-deep in the water, and I can see that she remembers me but does not quite know who I am. To identify myself, I point to my house. I don't know why I don't speak first or say my name — I just point like a six-year-old at my house. Susan shrieks a little when she understands. She jumps up in the water. Her gleaming brown hair tosses around her shoulders, her eyes burst with light. Then something intrudes a little on her openness. Maybe I'm not what I seem to be. Maybe I'm — who knows, an apparition, a monster? Anyway, there is this moment of suspense. It's hard to describe, but for a moment we are held on a point of time that seems to contain the possibility of all other points of time. Suspended there together, our feet in the blue water, our heads in the blue sky, there seems an infinity of potential. Love, pity, sorrow — anything might happen now between Susan Packard and me.

Susan, it turns out, is a schoolteacher in California. She's back visiting her mother, and she seems as struck all over again by P-town as I am. Her memories, which she discusses freely, are all sensuous memories. She invites me up onto the Packard deck, back into the life beside the sea. Her mother, Anne, weathered, warm, smiling, welcomes me instantly. Anne is a painter whose work my mother used to collect. Susan's older sister, Cynthia, a painter as well, introduces me to her husband and their older child, a small, naked boy about the age I was when my brother and I made a fort in the pilings under this house in the summer of '62. Also: the same age and color as my mother in the many sepia-toned pictures showing little nude Diana sitting on the pilings below this deck in the summers of '32 and '33.

We sit on the raw-wood deck, and it's a little awkward at first because my enthusiasm is drawn and sustained by things the Packards hardly notice. I exclaim over the Big Rock at the end of the jetty, and they look at this landmark, whose fallen state they now take wholly for granted, and Susan says, "Oh, yeah, that must have happened gradually." From Anne I learn that the two men to whom Choate, Hall & Stewart sold our house in 1982 were an S&M couple who kept the shades at 619 drawn all day, emerging only at night to display the hardware of domination: heavy leather, whips, and, once, even a leash and studded collar. The newest owners of 619, according to Anne, are friendly, neighborly people, the Leavitts — hence LEVITATION.

It's hard not to let my eye stray over to the house. Unwillingly, I suspend disbelief, allow myself to look. I'm fascinated by the changes. The outdoor shower, moved from the front to the side of the house; the voluminous new bay windows; the new kitchen. Mainly, I can't get over the studio: originally Maurice Sterne's paint-daubed studio, later my brother's and my bedroom, which my grandfather, in coat and tie, used as his daytime study, and in which I later wrote my first two books. When I finally allow myself a good look at the boxy studio, cantilevered out over the deck, I'm aghast to find it exactly the same. Even the window frames appear untouched. Through the large asymmetrical bay window on the side, I can see into my room. My God, there is the wall above my bed, the matchboard wall, the tongue-and-groove boards. It's like coming out of surgery and seeing your own skin. No matter what they've done to it, you must now live with it. For the first time, this indispensable thing, this vital substance, which is you, is no longer in your custody.

The more I look, the more accustomed I get to this unaccustomed state of being outside, looking in. The trick, of course, is to be willing to see things as they are — to recognize this house for what it is — not to picture it as I would have it be. At any moment I could take a breath and feel my way back inside the old dead skin. I could be in there, looking out. I could be sleeping in that room tonight, breathing in the sea and the salt on the damp night air. I could hear high water lapping on the sand. I could get up to take a leak and see the moon path on the incoming tide. I can tell you everything about night in that room.

While I am sitting with the Packards, Mrs. Leavitt of 619 Commercial walks from her beach, climbs the stairs to her deck, and steps into a basin of water, removing the sand from her feet before entering the house. Mrs. Leavitt does not resemble my mother, yet she looks so much like Diana doing this — this small orthodox ablution, so characteristic of summer and of the religion my mother and her parents made of summers in that house — that it sets me spiraling again. Even the basin of water is set on the holy altar at the head of the stairs.

I watch Mrs. Leavitt walk into the house in her bathing suit, and I think, How did I lose Diana Tead Michaelis? I mean, really, how? At the end of life there is the mystery of death. This keeps the undertakers in business and the survivors occupied for a couple of months or a couple of years or even a lifetime. Professional mourner is not a bad job when you consider some of the alternatives. But then comes a day, like this one, when you ask the question: Why isn't she here? And the answer, for a change, is not just: death. For once you don't just settle for the mystery of it, or the appalling pain of it, or even the fact of it, expressed in the sad and simple statement "She died." On a day like this it feels as though some other force must be at work — not cancer, not stupidity, not evil — some other power, but my vision is not yet developed enough to see it. How else, on this eye-watering day in high summer, can I account for my dead mother, the lost house by the sea, the lost summers? How can I account for my grief, which ten years later is the only thing in my life that could be called permanent? You hear widows and widowers say: I thought about him/her every day for the rest of my life. But wait a minute: I'm a son, not a widower.

I leave my things at the Packards' and walk out onto the flats, looped on light. I walk out to where the tide has disappeared into green-black grasses and sandy pools with washboard bottoms. The farther out I go, the more I feel that I am approaching the center of things. Under my feet, the small cradling world of the tide pools. Above my head, a wide world, a sphere of light, that seems to give back knowledge of ourselves. My eye fixes on a lone sail, suspended out near the horizon. The sail hardly seems to move. It seems trimmed to the great serenity outside of things, skirting space and time, these dimensions I am stuck in to the end of my life. This has haunted me for ten years, this spot in the center of things, this loss of center. Now that I am here, I am not so much restored to sight as given new eyes. My childhood was presided over by ailing, alcoholic grandparents, obsolete careerists who, before it slipped from their grasp, opened for my brother and me their useful world, their trustworthy heaven. Ordway and Clara's Emersonian message, bequeathed to us through Mom, was "The world is yours. . . . Every spirit builds itself a house; and beyond its house a world; and beyond its world a heaven. Know then, that the world exists for you. For you is the phenomenon perfect. What we are, that only can we see. All that Adam had, all that Caesar could, you have and can do."

The world was mine. Now I stand in the shallow pools, under the deep sky. I lie down in the water. Immediately I cry, I howl, I rage. I think I see. It's no good asking God why this was taken away from us, this paradise. Or scheming to get it back. It's no good living in banishment, in the small exilic world of bitterness and resentment and self-hatred. This is the unhealable place. No house, no home, no Boston law firm can repair this one. This is the place of no flesh, of white dust dissolving in the green water. This is the place where I at last go free.

SPENCER NADLER

Brain-Cell Memories

FROM HARPER'S MAGAZINE

THE BRAIN, unlike the rhythmically contracting heart, sits motionless in its cranium, no more animated than a liver or a spleen. Roughly the size and weight of a cantaloupe, it has the uniform consistency of cream cheese. The gray matter undulates like a bust by Giacometti, and the homogeneous white interior conceals its daedal scope.

Under the microscope, however, the brain comes alive. Stained with a gold or silver impregnation, its blackened neurons dazzle with their inimitable forms. As a surgical pathologist, I've seen them sprout wispy tendrils so long as to seem boundless, coursing the brain like so many fault lines. Neurons can simulate crabs and spiders, brambles, even ornate chandeliers. The smaller companion glial cells, though less conspicuous, are also branched; these groundskeepers outnumber the neurons by ten to one and fill in the spaces between them. Envision your brain, its billions of impulsive neurons, tendrils entwined, connected up in electrical circuits, elaborate glial scaffolds shoring up these circuits like electrical tape. In the synapses, fluid-filled clefts that separate neurons from one another, electrical impulses convert to chemical ones. Brain chemicals seep through the cleft fluid, bridging it with a flow of molecules. Thus do we smile or weep, plumb the ocean or fiddle a tune.

I anticipate a brain biopsy cautiously. Microscope in hand, I peer in at the musters of neurons and glial cells, taken alive, caught unaware in the course of biopsies. These microcosms never appear morbid, for the cells, frozen in the midst of life, have lucid immediacy. Although technically they are dead, their images challenge me to think about their lives: I am familiar with neuronal changes wrought by disease but know little of the responsibilities each neuron bears for thought, emotion, action. On my desk this morning are biopsy slides from a large tumor, born in the brain of M.K., a sixty-three-year-old Caucasian male. To me, this man is a name-with-tumor-attached, not a frightened human in the throes of his harrowing diagnosis. His tumor is derived from his glial cells, a glioblastoma multiforme. The euphony of the name belies its malevolence; it is the most common and malignant of glial tumors. He presents with disorientation, incontinence, and progressive left-sided weakness. The tumor, viewed on brain scans, fills a large portion of the right brain and extends through the body of the corpus callosum (the conduit of nerve tendrils between hemispheres) into the left brain. This image of a central body of tumor unfurling laterally into both hemispheres is a common advanced glioblastoma growth pattern likened to the *Lepidoptera,* or butterfly. The pterosaur — the dragon-like *Dsungaripterus,* a flying reptile far less alluring than the butterfly — seems more appropriate.

M.K.'s tumor, examined in the operating room, is too large and entangled with normal brain tissue for the neurosurgeon to remove; he submits a biopsy wrapped in gauze to the surgical pathology suite. The tissue I receive is variegated — the reds and browns of hemorrhage, the yellows of necrosis. Under the microscope, the tumor cells vary from unobtrusively small to grotesquely large. Hallmarks that enable me to diagnose glioblastoma multiforme are the exuberant "grape bunch" proliferations of small vessels and the jumbled palisade of tumor nuclei that gird necrotic tumor patches. I've seen these cellular glyphs time and time again in glioblastomas. Although the presence of this tumor saddens me, mine is a dispassionate sadness, a certitude that the microscopic events I see will soon culminate in M.K.'s demise. If he is to fight, against all odds, for his survival, I will not be privy to his gallantry. Although I may learn from his diligent neurosurgeon how long he survived, the tumor itself, the maleficent pterosaur, is my only understanding of this man, my lone connection to him.

To fathom the formidable malignancy of glioblastoma multiforme, one must go beyond the two-dimensional pictures of microscope slides and conceptualize the disease in four dimensions: the three spatial vectors and time. Think of a glioblastomatous pterosaur, its malignant cells spreading outward in all directions into the surrounding normal brain, creeping, in the bungling way such cells do, along neuron tracts, arbitrarily coursing through circuits until they short them. The complexity of such a geometry, the numbers and locations and functions of shorted and soon-to-be-shorted circuits, is incalculable, the malignant glial progression all but unstoppable, the patient's behavior and loss of function largely unpredictable. Think of a shot put propelled through the consecutive strings of a million tennis rackets; this conjures the enormity of the glioblastoma's destructiveness.

In his essay "On Probability and Possibility," Lewis Thomas concludes that "we pass thoughts around, from mind to mind, so compulsively and with such speed that the brains of mankind often appear, functionally, to be undergoing fusion." I am aware of this fusion when captivated by meditations, poems, or trenchant discourses. My microscopic vision of a brain biopsy creates a different fusion: when I see the precarious state of M.K.'s neurons in the wake of his spreading tumor, they seem to call out to my own, an urgent message to the living from the cellular dying and the dead.

In his eloquent memoir *Death Be Not Proud*, John Gunther recounts the life and death of his son Johnny from glioblastoma multiforme. The tumor lingered after each therapy as if licking its wounds and, quickly rebuilding its autonomous self, began again to challenge the boy's brain for the fixed space in his skull. Gunther details how his son maintained his faculties — intellect, charm, ambition, courage — despite a fifteen-month deterioration. It is an account that testifies to the glioblastoma's willfulness. Once its blundering cells reach the crawl spaces between neurons, it clings to its brain like a weasel. Although this is ineffective parasitism — the glioblastoma inevitably kills its host — no more can be expected from such cancer cells; their programmed tactlessness and impropriety do them in. The location of a brain tumor partly determines a patient's clinical course. Johnny's tumor flourished in the relatively inactive occipital-parietal areas of his right brain. Apart from some loss of motor function on his left side and restrictions of his visual fields, he remained remarkably functional to the end. The tumor ultimately eroded a blood-vessel wall, and the resulting brain hemorrhage killed him.

How very different was the clinical behavior of George Gershwin's glioblastoma. In February 1937, while playing his Concerto in F at Philharmonic Auditorium in Los Angeles, he suffered a momentary loss of consciousness. He missed a few bars, then continued as if nothing had happened. He later spoke of smelling burnt rubber. When physical examinations found nothing wrong, the incident was attributed to fatigue, the stress of his enormous success. In April of that year, in a barbershop chair, the momentary loss of consciousness and subsequent smelling of burnt rubber recurred. By June, he was suffering agonizing headaches and had become periodically listless, irritable, and confused; there were lapses of coordination; the smell of burnt rubber now haunted him. In this era that preceded neural imaging, his neurologist found no evidence of an organic lesion, and his signs and symptoms were attributed to hysteria. The glioblastoma had avoided clinical detection, living symbiotically with its brain. It had probably been growing in this furtive way long before his first loss of consciousness.

On July 9, 1937, Gershwin had a seizure and fell into a coma. Subsequent surgery disclosed a large cystic mass in the right temporal lobe; it involved too many vital structures to be removed. A biopsy revealed glioblastoma. He died several hours after surgery without ever regaining consciousness.

Despite the perilous ingress of his tumor, Gershwin composed two of his most beautiful songs, "Love Walked In" and "Love Is Here to Stay," in the last few months of life. The processing of music is not as lateralized in adult males as is speech. Notwithstanding the volitant simmerings of Gershwin's right-sided tumor, his left brain could have assumed, over time, essential functions of his musical genius, allowing for his terminal inventiveness. I see Gershwin, his neurons moving like piano keys, playing his concerto; his tumor cells press atop the neurons like so many thumbs, until the music stops.

B.R. is a forty-five-year-old Caucasian woman who presents with a four-month history of headaches. A brain scan reveals a well-circumscribed mass lying beneath the skull and compressing her right frontal lobe. The neurosurgeon is able to scoop out this discrete bulk from the brain tissue it compresses. I receive it in three gray-pink, rubbery fragments that fit together in an oval mass about the size of an egg. I note the gentle protuberances of its surface, the lobulations of its cut edge. These are the overt features of meningioma — a benign tumor arising from the fibrous vestments of the brain. The microscope reveals a whorled growth pattern of meningeal cells that are as furled as a spiral galaxy. The nuclei are agreeably uniform, oval and blue, and the cytoplasm is faded pink, poorly defined. Many of these nuclei are so crammed with their own cytoplasm that they seem eclipsed by it. An occasional amethyst calcification, concentrically laminated, known as a psammoma body, is visible, and clusters of xanthoma cells stuffed with lipid are scattered about.

Each tumor has its own life story — the nature of its cells, the imposition of its growth on surrounding body tissues, the threat it poses as an illness. This type of meningioma has a slow, centrifugal growth that usually yields a globular or oval tumor. Reluctant to invade the brain, it displaces it. When favorably situated, it can grow silently, like a slow bleed, beneath the skull to the size of a large lemon before producing symptoms. It is usually cured by surgical removal.

B.R. can expect a happy ending.

The benign swirls of this meningioma energize me. Although I am not part of a patient's emotional experience, I am not completely extricated from it either. The sight of malignant cellular disarray burdens me with all that it forebodes, gnaws at my own mortality. The vision of a benign tumor's orderly cell growth absolves me, makes me feel as if I myself have been granted a reprieve.

The brain deceives itself and those who would know it. I remember a thirteen-year-old boy who presented with seizures. Scans revealed a space-occupying lesion in his brain that suggested a malignant neoplasm. A needle biopsy was done under radiological guidance. I distinctly remember the tissue I received; it was as white and friable as feta cheese. Under the microscope, a spread of tubercle bacilli, the causative organisms of tuberculosis, appeared as minikin, blood-red leeches. The cells in their wake, as if sucked dry of life-blood, had disintegrated into amorphous fields of debris that stretched to the ends of the cellscape. Against a brilliant green background stain, these organisms resembled red tinsel heralding a high-colored microscopic Christmas. In reality, the causative bacilli of tuberculosis act more like passive bystanders than active bloodsuckers in the wasted tissue of disease. With infection, the body's complex defense mechanisms slowly kick in to destroy these bacilli and the human tissues harboring them. Often it is our powerful defensive arsenals — not the organisms themselves — that ravage infected body organs and create the disease. In an effort to kill off tubercle organisms, the human body is perfectly capable of destroying itself; it has done so for centuries.

I saw very few tubercle bacilli in tissue biopsies in the sixties and seventies. Despite its prevalence in Third World countries, tuberculosis was becoming an affliction of the past in the United States. It was alarming and disheartening, then, to witness a resurgence in the mid-eighties that remains with us today. And deadly new strains — superbugs — have emerged that are unscathed by all known curative drugs, inextricable as a spreading cancer. Tuberculosis that masses in the brain — a tuberculoma — remains uncommon in this country. This biopsy surprised me; I had expected a malignancy. It was one of those humbling experiences that turns out well. The boy was started on antituberculous drug therapy, and within months the brain mass disappeared. The biopsy *was* his microscopic Christmas.

Some time later, I met the boy's father at the local library. He expressed his thanks to me for having been the bearer of such good news. He too had been expecting the worst and spoke of a feeling that God had lent a hand. He likened my diagnosis to a benediction.

Two years ago I read a troubled brain in a whole new way. Although Parkinson's disease is not diagnosed by brain biopsy — the affected neurons are too deep, the structures too vital to warrant entry with a knife or needle — it hovers around me. I stare at the sepia photograph of my paternal grandfather, his facial expression enigmatic, his fingers pressed together in rigid extension like a clue. He and his daughter, Aunt Bess, both died of Parkinson's in their eighties. After her death, I went home to Montreal for my father's eightieth birthday. It was an exuberant celebration for an amiable man whose only concession to age was a rise in his golf handicap from single to double digits. A month later, an orthopedist examining my father's sore back thought he detected the staring visage of Parkinson's. His suspicion was soon confirmed.

The diagnosis of Parkinson's can be made clinically and supported with a PET brain scan. It results from a mysterious degeneration of specific neurons whose pigmented bodies lie in the substantia nigra, which, no bigger than a thumb tip, is the repository for these melanin-laden neurons. The neurotransmitter dopamine, a product of these dying nigral neurons, is also lacking. In this way, the computations of body movements are gradually jeopardized until the body is no more than a casement for the mind and soul. And no two Parkinsonians suffer their motor losses in the same way or at the same rate. Initially, body quirks can be subtle. Eventually, one or more cardinal signs appear to give away the body's morbid secret.

Rigidity is one cardinal sign of Parkinson's; it involves all voluntary muscles. And the poverty of my father's facial movements was an expression of that rigidity. The easy grin I had so often looked to for approval in childhood had permanently vanished as his stare hardened to a mask. It was as though a part of his personality had been stolen from him.

He was treated with Sinemet, which is converted in the brain to dopamine. Stemming his dopamine loss in this way seemed to halt the progression of his stiffness for a few years. At eighty-three, he stopped playing golf with his cronies and expressed a desire to play golf with my mother instead. "I'm making too many bad shots," he told her. "I tell my body to do something and it just won't do it." His hands now seemed too stiff to grip his golf clubs properly, and his postural reflexes were unequal to his task. Over time the Sinemet lost its effectiveness, so his doctor added Deprenyl to inhibit further dopamine breakdown. But drugs could no longer halt my father's increasing stiffness or the slackening of spontaneous movements. He was having trouble walking, even with a cane, and his dawdling gestures lacked dexterity. No longer able to hold cards properly or shuffle a deck, he declined bridge games with his friends.

Two years later, he needed a walker to visit his doctors. Otherwise, he was confined to home. He moved about with slow deliberateness, never laziness, and his daily routine — dressing, eating, using the bathroom, moving about the house, undressing — consumed the greater part of his day. His simplest rituals had become his life. A year later, his debilitation was such that my mother had to cut up his food and turn him in bed. Did he feel dehumanized by his body's dissolution, hopelessly bereft of his dignity? As a former athlete, did he view his rigidity as a bitter paradox? Did his burden dampen his sensuous pleasures, pepper him with despair? He never confided his feelings to me, and, regretfully, I never pursued them. Through it all, he remained mentally acute and uncomplaining. This stoicism seemed to attest to his courage and embody all that he endured.

In his eighty-seventh year, my father was hospitalized for a bladder infection; a Parkinson's sluggishness of his bladder muscles was no doubt to blame. He was joking with the nurses the evening before his discharge, making sure that levity prevailed over illness. Later that night, while sleeping, a massive heart attack killed him.

When I look back, my memories of my father are filtered through my understanding of the changes in his brain. I clearly recall the summer afternoons at his swim club. I was nine or ten years old. His substantia nigra teemed with healthy neurons then; their tapered bodies were so full of gold-brown melanin pigment that they resembled schools of trout. We'd buck the St. Lawrence River currents together, stroke for stroke. I can still feel that cold, choppy water numbing me, smell the scent of riparian elms and maples and oaks, taste the sweet machismo of it.

I remember a day — I couldn't have been more than twelve — when I caddied for my father. The way he drove the golf ball off the tee is what stays with me: there was a confidence in his compact frame, in his bearing, in the way he addressed the ball. His strapping nigral neurons were perfectly attuned, flawlessly promoting his athleticism. His backswing was shortened somewhat, and his stroke seemed easy. It was the hand speed he could muster that was extraordinary. The ball would explode off the tee, splitting the fairway, carrying below the height of the trees. Rising slowly, steadily, borne in its orbit like a distant comet, it seemed to hang endlessly in the clear and piercing sky. And when it finally began its triumphant descent, it faded gloriously in gravity's hold. My father would look away in silence after these towering drives, pondering his iron shot to the green. He was all concentration as he charged down the fairway. I'd slide the strap of his golf bag across my shoulder pridefully and step up my pace alongside him.

Later, when television finally came to Canada, I remember the

Friday night fights. My father had been an amateur boxer in his youth and would perch on the edge of his chair, fists held taut in front of him. In a running commentary, he would instruct both fighters, infuse them with strategy. At first this advice was indiscriminate. As the bout wore on, the winner always seemed to be listening to my father, while the loser seemed to pay him no heed. Although he was usually alone in the room, the house was filled with his heated admonitions. You knew if there was a knockout by the pitch of his fervent cries, and if you sat beside him, as I sometimes did, he'd whip his fists through the winning combinations of lefts and rights. This ritual was my earliest introduction to instant replay and round-by-round fight analysis. Sometimes, if a championship fight went the distance, all that shadowboxing could wear my father down; but I think it was the rejuvenation that he yearned for. He still had his full complement of nigral neurons back then; they were pumping out their dopamine like geysers.

I spent my teenage summers as a stock boy in my father's factory, tallying fabric yardage in storage bins. It was nothing fancy: I would unroll the bolts of cloth and measure their lengths with a yardstick as dust clung to my sweaty skin. But mostly I watched my father's fierce struggle in this highly competitive arena, how it slowly bled the stamina from him. He went to great lengths to fashion dresses that had a certain style and flair, and somehow morally bankrupt infiltrators were always prepared to copy his styles and undercut his prices. I'd watch him try to charm the buyers in his showroom, but quality and style were a hard sell. Although he almost always maintained an outward calm, I know now that the hot wiring of his anger circuits likely set his limbic system aglow. It was almost as if his nigral neurons got singed in the heat of all that stymied him. My father wanted me to succeed him in this business, but I knew early on that I didn't have the gumption for it.

My yearly visits to Montreal during the seven years of my father's illness enabled me to see his slow freeze. Although his body ultimately imprisoned him, it highlighted the quickness of his mind. Often he seemed to use his rigid confines as a springboard, trying to reinvent and reclaim himself. It was this palpable spirit that made his helplessness so heroic to me. I envisioned his nigral neurons, now strangely toxic and fading, pocked with round, pink bodies that looked like dabs of cirrus clouds at sunrise. As these neurons slowly died, incontinent of their melanin, I could see gold-brown granules clustering at neuron death sites, naked and alone as gravestones. And glial cells, ever at hand, blanketing the spaces left by the dead.

These days I think about my own substantia nigra and those of my family. Susceptibility genes for Parkinson's occasionally have been documented in large families, though none so far in Ashkenazi Jewish ones like mine. Since no one in my family is alive with Parkinson's who can be tested for mutations, I have banked a sample of my blood. As new Parkinson's susceptibility genes are discovered, my sample will be checked for each newfound mutation. Do I want to know if Parkinson's lies ahead for me? Do I want to involve other family members, asking them to bank samples of their own blood? I see no harm in facing the threat of this impoverishing illness, and I hope to use the family discourse about it as a means to clarify what binds us to one another.

My family, moreover, tells me how I remind them of my father. Not only the physical similarity, they say, but the voice, the mannerisms. They smile when they tell me these things, and I wonder what memories of my father I trigger in each of them. Is this likeness intensified by my father's absence? Is it my own aging that reminds them more and more of how my father appeared in his healthy old age before Parkinson's became a part of him?

I superimpose my father's decimated substantia nigra on my own and wonder about the similarities. I have no pride, only dread, in any likeness here. In reverie, my face becomes thickset with age, and the grizzled hairs that sprout from my scalp and brows and mustache make me look faded, exposed to time. Then my features freeze, a fixed stare that hardens against emotion. Behind this stony visage perks my lucid brain, its pulsing circuits orchestrating my angst and abject loneliness, my degradation.

If my nigral neurons do falter and Parkinson's entombs me, will other neurons, other circuits, brace me against my own looming rigidity? Will my father's courage and equanimity enable me to move beyond my adversity? For now, my nigral neurons remain loaded with dopamine. Ticking with caution, I feel the silken surge of my body movements, sleek and nimble, flowing free. And my smile affirms all that moves me.

MARY OLIVER

Dust

FROM SHENANDOAH

1

M. WOULD KEEP EVERYTHING. There is not an envelope, with its singular name, address (best if written by hand), postmark, and stamp that she would not keep, though the envelope be empty. To M. its emptiness does not reduce the envelope to irrelevance. Of course she would rather there be something inside — a letter! or, oh lovely chance, a photograph! — but even without these treasures and pleasures the envelope is a part of the mystery to be cherished. What was it the envelope held, to whom was it sent and why, and what did it matter? M. is both a sleuth and a shepherd. She would know all stories that are gone now, dispersed to the wind, to the ages, through layers of uncaring, lost in pigeonholes in the backs of abandoned desks, or the files of defunct institutions, or the sagging brown boxes in yard sales in summer, in distant towns, bought at last for a dollar or a song, and put into someone's car and driven off, or — unsold at the end of a long warm day — carried up the stairs and put back, for another season, under the eaves of the old barn. From none of this can M. back away, or remain indifferent. And, not letters only but things — old clothes, hats, mirrors with a streak of tarnish, books so old and dry they have summoned toward themselves every possible blot of moisture, so that they are swollen and unsuitable now forever, though they have become dry as bone again. Things! Chiffon, and lace, and bruised velvet. Shoes, with tiny black buttons along the sides. And photographs, the unnamable faces gazing out, everything to say and no way, no way ever again, to be heard.

2

It is five o'clock or maybe earlier on a winter morning when I come down the stairs. The sky is black, but not for long. I make coffee and walk from window to window, lifting the shades, watching the pink, tangerine, apricot, lavender light dart and sail along the eastern horizon, then climb like a mist and tremble there, on the inner curve of the darkness. The intimacy of the universe! The colors float down into the water, everything turns blue. Black ducks are dabbling near the rocks. Even now, in winter, many of them remain together in affectionate pairs. Flocks of brant move by, those elegant, small geese. The light grows stronger, whiter, the pinks and rouges fade as the sun hesitates, then leaps from the water. Gulls are already in the air.

In spring these sunrises will continue, beyond the blue iris and pink mallow of the garden. Laughing gulls will fly by the house, with the black faces of spring. Black-bellied plovers feed along the shallows. In April, humpbacked whales sometimes swim into the harbor, tossing as they move their huge bodies forward. Dolphins come, too, leaping through the waves.

Surf-scooters come near the house, and the common eider, and the gentle-eyed old squaw. A red-throated loon appears one morning just in front of the house; like a small torpedo it dashes down through the clear water.

In the summer common terns and least terns gather in the afternoon to feed, dropping, and dropping and dropping again into the waves. The wings of each one are like two white petals on the rise; they give a quick shake to shed water, a break in the rhythm of the bird ascending.

Of course, there are storms, too, when the whole house rocks and the waves upbeat on the underside of the deck boards, and sometimes win, and the wind sizzles, and you had better be on the ocean's side then, or you would be afraid.

In late summer, one or two small dogfish often swam near us. And, once, a pair of swans.

Then the summer would pass, and the long fall, and winter would swell around us again, and we would breathe deep and slow as we did our work in this crooked old seaside house that, for a little while, was ours.

3

For the first time in twenty-five years there is no small footstool next to the bed on which to break one's toes. The little dogs, first Jasper and then Bear, are gone. How neatening is loss, since it only takes away! One less mouth to feed, to walk, to bathe, to hold. One less sentient creature to cherish, to worry over, to feel for, to receive comfort from. And where is he, little Bear, the latest to leave us? We watch the white clouds carefully; sooner or later we will see him, sailing away in careless and beautiful serenity. Of what rich and ornate stuff the powerful and uncontainable gods invented the world, out of the rampant dust! The silky brant, the scarf of chiffon, the letter, the empty envelope, the black ducks, the old shoes, the little white dog fall away, fall away, and all the music of our lives is in them. The gods act as they act for what purpose we do not know, but this we do understand: the world could not be made without the swirl and whirlwind of our deepest attention and our cherishing. And if I mean the god of the sky, I mean also the god of the river — not only the god of the gold-speckled cathedral but the lord of the green field, where people pause casually and snap each other's picture; where thrushes pump out their darkling songs; where little dogs bark and leap, their ears tossing, joyously, as they run toward us.

REYNOLDS PRICE

Dear Harper: A Letter to a Godchild About God

FROM FORBES ASAP

IT'LL BE some years before you read this, if ever. But given the uncertainties of all our futures, I'll set it down here at the time of your baptism and will hope that — should you ever need it — it will be legible still. Since you're under the age of two, chances are slim that you'll feel the need for well more than a decade. By then the twenty-first century will be thoroughly under way. Since it's likely to move as unforeseeably as the twentieth, I'll make no effort to predict how the world will feel then about religious faith.

And I certainly won't guess at what your own relation to faith may be, though your parents and godparents have vowed to guide you toward it. Those adults have old ties to churches, though those ties vary. Above all, none of us who know you in the bright wonder of your laughing, open-armed childhood can begin to imagine who you'll be and where you'll want — or need — to go in your youth or your maturity. So here, by way of a gift, are some thoughts that may interest you in time.

As I write, in the spring of 2000, a large majority of the world's people say that they're religious. This year, for instance, 84 percent of the residents of the United States identified themselves as Christian, associates in the world's largest religion. What did they mean by their claim? The *Oxford English Dictionary* says that religion is:

Belief in, reverence for, and desire to please, a divine ruling power; the exercise or practice of rites or observances implying this.

Most Americans today would agree, and I'd suggest only one

change. Instead of "divine ruling power," I'd substitute "supreme creative power." And I'd wonder if it mightn't be desirable to strip the definition to its bones — "religion is the belief in a supreme creative power." But perhaps those bones define the word *faith* more adequately than the word *religion*.

I hope you'll be interested to know that I — near the start of a new millennium and at the age of sixty-seven — am still able to believe, with no serious effort, that the entire universe was willed into being by an unsurpassed power whom most human beings call God. I believe that God remains conscious of his creation and interested in it. I believe that his interest may be described, intermittently at least, as love (and I say "his" with no strong suspicion that he shares qualities with the earthly male gender).

Whether he's attentive to every moment of every human's life, as some religions claim, I'm by no means sure. But I do believe that he has standards of action that he means us to observe. I believe that he has communicated those standards — and most of whatever else we know about his transcendent nature — through a few human messengers and through the mute spectacles of nature in all its manifestations, around and inside us (the human kidney is as impressive a masterwork as the Grand Canyon).

God created those spectacles many billion years ago and began to send those messengers, to this planet at least, as long ago as four thousand years, maybe earlier. Those messengers are parents and teachers, prophets and poets (sacred and secular), painters and musicians, healers and lovers; the generous saints of Hinduism, Judaism, Buddhism, Christianity, Islam, and a few other faiths — all the deep feeders of our minds and bodies. One of the matchless gifts of our present life lies in the fact that those messengers continue to come, though the task of distinguishing valid messages from the false or merely confused is hard and often dangerous. At least one of those messengers, I believe, was in some mysterious sense an embodiment of God; and it's to him — Jesus of Nazareth — that you were recently dedicated.

Finally, I believe that some essential part of our nature is immortal. The core of each of us is immune to death and will survive forever. Whether we'll experience that eternity as good or bad may depend upon the total record of our obedience to God's standards of action. Most of the long-enduring faiths say that we accumulate the weight of our wrongs — our sins, our karma — and will ultimately be confronted with that weight.

A wide lobe of my brain finds it difficult to believe that the maker of anything so immense as our universe — and of who knows what beyond it — is permanently concerned with how I behave in relation to my diet (so long as I'm not a cannibal), or my genitals (as long as they don't do willful damage to another creature), or my hair (so long as it doesn't propagate disease-bearing vermin), or a good deal else that concerns many religious people.

God likely cares how I treat the planet Earth, its atmosphere, and its nonhuman inhabitants (I think it's possible that he wants us not to kill or eat other conscious creatures, though I'm a restrained carnivore who feels no real guilt). Above all, the Creator intends that I honor my fellow human beings — whoever and from wherever — and that I do everything in my power never to harm them and to alleviate, as unintrusively as possible, any harm they suffer. God likely expects me to extend that honor to other forms of life, though how far down the scale that honor is to run, I don't know — surely I'm not meant to avoid killing, say, an anthrax bacillus.

Though I've mentioned that a preponderance of Americans presently share some version of my beliefs, it's fair to tell you that a possible majority of the social class I've occupied since my mid-twenties — those who've experienced extensive years of academic training — don't share my beliefs nor hold any other beliefs that might be called religious. That characteristic of the intellectual classes of the Western world and China (at a minimum) is more than a century old and is the result largely of a few discoveries of the physical sciences and of the worldwide calamities of war and suffering that have convinced many witnesses that no just God exists.

My own educational credentials include nineteen years of formal schooling. I've likewise read extensively in the literatures of many cultures that are not my own. How then can I explain my defection, in the matter of faith, from the doubts or flat rejection of so many in my social class? And am I suggesting that the reasons for my defection should have any weight with you, if you should face a crossroads of belief and rejection, at whatever point in your life?

In fact, I haven't defected. Put plainly, I have never held all the central dogmas of my caste. I received the rudiments of my faith long before I began to read or attend school. And while that faith has undergone assaults — from myself and others — it's never buckled. To be honest, I've sometimes been suspicious of that apparent strength. Shouldn't anyone who's lived as long as I, on two continents, and who's sustained more than one maiming catastrophe, have felt occasional very dark nights? Well, of course I have; but they've been dark nights of the sort described by the Spanish monk and poet Saint John of the Cross — certain souls may feel God's absence as a form of near desperation, but that pain (which may last a very long while) never tumbles finally into disbelief.

Note that I said just above that I received the rudiments of faith. They came from the usual sources — my parents and other kin, the natural world around me (which tended to be rural or wooded suburban), and from God and his various messengers. To say that much, here and now, runs the severe risk of pomposity, an absurd degree of self-love, and a ludicrous elitism. Yet I know of no more accurate way to describe a situation that's far from uncommon.

My preparation for faith likely began with the gift of two Bible storybooks — one from my Grandmother Price when I was two or three, the second a year or so later from my parents. They proved to be long-range endowments for the only child I then was (my brother was born just as I turned eight). Each of the books contained strikingly realistic illustrations; and with a small amount of guidance from my parents, I launched myself on an early fascination with the prime characters and stories from Hebrew and Christian sacred texts — Abraham, Isaac, and Sarah; Ruth and Naomi; David, Jonathan, and Saul; Samson and Delilah; Joseph, Mary, and Jesus; Jesus and the girl he raises from the dead; Jesus himself rising from the dead.

At about the same time I began occasionally to go to Sunday school with my father; and there I glimpsed the fact that those stories meant something important to other men, women, and children. I must likewise have begun to sense how vital this thing — whatever it was — was to my father. It would be years before I understood that he was, at just that time, withdrawing from years of alcoholism. And in the absence of Alcoholics Anonymous in our part of the world, help for him could only have come from my mother, his minister, and his own tenacious will to quit (he'd reached the age of thirty-three before beginning his battle).

When I was six years old, we lived on the edge of a small town. Within roaming distance for me were thickets of pine with plentiful birds, rabbits, foxes, possums, and raccoons; and there was a small stream filled with crawfish, toads, turtles, minnows, and snakes. I spent countless solitary and silent hours exploring that teeming world. And there I began to store up an invaluable sense of the endless inventiveness of life and the savage conditions of so much animal existence. In those same woods, I even found and saved my first flint arrowheads from long-vanished Indians. The simple endurance of those shaped stones helped me further onward with their intimations of the doggedness, and yet the frailty, of human life.

Then late one afternoon, still alone but blissful in that world, I was given my first visionary experience. I'm still convinced it came from some inhuman force outside my own mind and body. And though it would be years before I knew it, it was a vision of a kind experienced by more than a few lucky children. In brief, in a single full moment, I was allowed to see how intricately the vast contraption of nature all around me — and nature included me, my parents a few yards away in the house, and every other creature alive on Earth — was bound into a single huge ongoing wheel by one immense power that had willed us into being and intended our futures, wherever they led.

We were all, somehow, one vibrant thing; and even the rattlesnakes, the lethal microbes, and the plans of men like Adolf Hitler (whom I'd heard of from my father; it was 1939) were bound with the rest of us toward a final harmony. At the age of six, of course, I couldn't have described it in such words, but memory tells me that the description is honest. And there that day, in the core of a much loved but often unaccompanied childhood, it seemed a benign revelation.

While it didn't result in an immediate certainty that God exists and knows me and tends me, it left me watchful for further intimations. And in some way that I've only just realized six decades later, it became the first private knowledge of my life. I never mentioned what I'd suddenly learned, not to my parents nor to any child I knew and trusted. My life as a largely solitary mystic had begun.

I don't recall other such climactic moments in my childhood. But my interest in Bible stories continued; and because at the age of nine I won a free New Testament for bringing a new member to Sunday school, I eventually began to read the Christian scriptures directly, not in someone else's version. Above all, the four Gospels interested me with their varying but complementary pictures of a man as mysterious and potent, yet credible, as Jesus. For reasons I can't explain, Jesus became one of the figures I often thought about and drew pictures of, along with Tarzan and King Arthur.

Since I was then hoping to become a painter in my adult life, I was also increasingly aware of the towering presence in Western art of Jesus at every stage of his short, and brilliantly depictable, life. In a way that it may be difficult for you to imagine years from now, the world around me — which was most of America from the 1930s onward — was as permeated with reverberations of the life of Jesus as the sea is with salt. For good or ill — and he's still outrageously invoked as the guarantor of hatred, violence, and endless fantasy — he was a constant component (even for those who entirely rejected him) of the air we breathed.

The fact that Jesus was also plainly a man who'd suffered and died for his acts made him more and more interesting to me as I entered adolescence and encountered the usual daunting amount of unhappiness. Mine, like that of so many others, came at the hands of a pair of school bullies. Like many boys who grew up in Christian cultures then, and perhaps even now, I spent a fair amount of secret time in prayer to Jesus. I'd ask for the meanness to stop and for kinder friends to materialize (my demons had once been my friends). It was my first acquaintance with unanswered, or partially answered, prayer. Other friends appeared but the bullies never relented till we moved from the town.

Somehow that partial success with prayer didn't stop me. I thought I'd heard the beginning of a dialogue. And life improved rapidly. Relations with my schoolmates in the new town were free of hostility, and I made a handful of friends who've lasted. But almost anyone's adolescence, as you may know by the time you read this, is subject to frequent attacks of self-doubt and melancholy, even bouts of hopelessness. Life sometimes seems too bleak to continue. Why should young people believe that things change — and often for the better? They've frequently had little experience of such improvements.

I don't recall ever plunging so low; but still I went on investing a fair amount of time in prayers to Jesus and his mother (a beautiful Catholic girl had taught me the rosary, and it became a part of my attempts at reaching and persuading the Creator and — what? — his household). And in the absence of the old tormentors who'd even made churchgoing difficult, I began attending church — my mother's Methodist and my father's Baptist. The Methodist minister took an interest in my developing curiosities about the historical Jesus and the origins of Christianity; and he readily agreed to what must have seemed peculiar requests from a boy — requests for private communion at times when I needed special help, like college scholarship competitions.

By age seventeen I clearly had some sort of vocation for a life with regular attempts at persuading God's attention and cooperation. I don't think my daily behavior looked unusually "holy," and I don't recall that my parents or my minister ever mentioned the possibility. But toward the end of high school, one of my teachers suggested that I think of preparing for life as a pastor. Though by then I'd joined the Methodist church, I felt at once that the idea was wrong. My sexual energies and their direction seemed far too powerful and heretical for such a career. In any case I'd already decided on the parallel careers I've ultimately followed — life as a writer and a teacher — and as I moved on to college, I headed for those choices.

As I worked even more steadily at my undergraduate studies and my writing (especially poetry) — and as I began to express my sexual needs — I slowly began to feel less compelled toward the public worship I'd enjoyed for the past few years. I'd begun to suspect that a yen for display played a part in public worship, especially my own. Yet despite my involvement in a number of academic courses that questioned, and occasionally mocked, the foundations of religious thought, my withdrawal from church represented no loss of the faith that had grown as I grew.

My withdrawal was likewise a response to my increasing awareness of the hostility or indifference of all major American churches to the coming crises in racial justice and sexual tolerance. Most honestly, though, I was returning to a means of worship that was more natural for me: private prayer, reading, and meditation, and the beginnings of a comprehension that the chief aim of any mature religious life is union with the will of God, as opposed to one's own, and the finding of ways to assist other creatures.

My first year of graduate study in England, where study is largely self-monitored, marked also my launching on a near full-time dedication to my writing and on my first real delight in reciprocated love. In the chilly atmosphere of one of the oldest colleges at Oxford and the beautiful thirteenth-century chapel whose emptiness echoed the rapid expiration of Protestant Anglicanism, it was easy enough not to seek out a congenial church, and my sense of the Creator — of the duties I might owe him and the means of communicating with him — continued on the solitary track to which they'd reverted. Yet in normal human fashion, I was now praying mainly when I needed quick help.

I felt mild guilt at my separation from a religious community, especially when my mother or my old minister inquired about my British churchgoing. But I told myself I'd made a necessary choice. I imagined I'd learn to locate — through my teaching and writing — communities where my own questions and whatever useful findings I might make could be best conveyed to others, potentially a wider community than I might have found in a dedicated building and a congregation.

In retrospect, I estimate that my subsequent years of work may have communicated to a few thousand readers and a few thousand students how one relatively lucid and respectably educated man, in the final two-thirds of the twentieth century and somewhat thereafter, has managed to live at least six decades of a life that (while it's committed a heavy share of self-intoxicated incursions on others and has broken at least five of the Ten Commandments) has so far hurled no dead bodies to the roadside, abandoned no sworn partners or children, and has managed to turn up — shaved and sober — in a writing office, a teaching classroom, a kinsman's or lover's or friend's place in time of need on most promised occasions.

I've been especially chary of broaching discussions of my relations with God in the arenas of either of my careers, in books or in classrooms. That's partly because, by nature, I'm among the world's least evangelical souls but also because my own beliefs were acquired so gradually, and in response to such personal tides, as to be almost incommunicable if not incomprehensible. In recent years, however, I've relaxed a little in that reluctance.

I've spoken of my faith in two volumes of memoirs, a number of poems, and a published letter to a dying young man who asked for my views; and I'm writing this new letter to you. After more than thirty years of teaching Milton's *Paradise Lost*, I've begun, very lightly, to confess to my students that I'm a renegade Christian and that they might be at a certain advantage in studying a Christian poet with me. Wouldn't they like to study Homer with, say, an actual Zeusian?

So my life has gone through youth and middle age. It was normally subject, as I've said, to serious wrongdoing. And it was frequently challenged by disappointment and at least one bitter remorse. Throughout — despite several deep dives into self-blame and the sporadic lack of any clear view ahead — my faith has been the prime stabilizer. Like many other navigational aids, it's done most of its work when I had only the dimmest awareness of its service.

Then, when I was fifty-one, I found myself having difficulties walking. After a few weeks of denial, I was discovered to have a large and intricately entangled cancer of the spinal cord. Despite surgery, with the best technology of the early 1980s, the tumor couldn't be removed; and no chemotherapy was available. The only medical hope was five weeks of searing radiation, directly to the fragile cord. I was warned that such a brutal therapy might leave me paraplegic or worse. The alternative, however, was to wait while the tumor paralyzed my legs, then my arms and hands, and finally my lungs. With no other imaginable choice, I agreed to the radiation.

A few mornings before the daily treatments were to start, I was propped wide awake in bed at home, when I experienced the second visionary moment of my life, some forty-six years after my childhood glimpse of the unity of nature. I've written about this second moment in other places. Enough to say here that I was, suddenly and without apparent transport, in a different place — by the Sea of Galilee — and a man whom I knew to be Jesus was washing and healing the long wound from my failed surgery, the site of my coming radiation.

My conviction, since that second vision, is that the experience was in some crucial sense real. In that moment I was healed, and the fact that my legs were subsequently paralyzed by radiation two years before a new ultrasonic device made the removal of the tumor possible, the tumor was merely a complexity in the narrative that God intended. There does seem a possibility that, had I avoided the withering radiation, I might have been healed in any case. My doctors felt that, along with its damage, the radiation had stalled the tumor for a lucky while.

I'm aware that many of my contemporaries will read such a statement as groundless, if not howling crazy, and I can all but share their laughter. Yet sixteen years after my initial diagnosis, I'm an energetic man working when virtually none of my therapists thought I had a serious chance (one of them told my brother that I had eighteen months at best). And since I've mentioned my healing in print, I've had dozens of letters from patently sane strangers who confide similar transcendent experiences in a time of crisis.

They mostly describe an experience in which some entirely real figure, whether Jesus or some matter-of-fact plainclothes angel, comes and consoles or heals them. Such confidences almost always end with their telling me that they'd mentioned their experience to no one else for fear of ridicule. My correspondents also generally say that their experience, like mine, was singular — that is, never repeated, thereby eliminating the possibility that we'd all been merely cheering ourselves with pleasant dreams in the face of calamity.

My moment by the Sea of Galilee occurred sixteen years ago and has not recurred in any form. Those years have brought me an unprecedented amount of work — twenty-one books since the cancer — and an outpouring of affection and meticulous care of a sort I wouldn't have allowed myself to expect from kin, friends, and strangers. In addition to the books, I've continued my regular schedule of teaching. I've traveled for business and for pleasure more than in my able-bodied life. And those changes have only deepened my certainty that my illness — its devastations and its legacies of paralysis and chronic pain — was intended for me at that point in my life and perhaps ever after.

What the ultimate intention of such a blow may be, I barely guess at. Time, or beyond, will presumably uncover as much of that mystery as I'll ever need to know. I can say, however, that the drastic reversal led me to abandon certain choices that I'd always explored with both pleasure and uncertainty of purpose. I've made that simplification because I've slowly come to suspect that a curbing of past choices was intended. And while this new course has left me deprived of a few physical rewards, I've all but ceased to miss them. If nothing else, paraplegia either leads to a rapid refining of human focus and one's expectations from other creatures or it plunges its cripple into querulous, or wailing, neurosis or worse.

Yet now I've outlived both my parents; and though I'm nearly seventy, I'm hopeful of as much more time as I have work to do, the resources with which to do it, and the help I need in my straitened circumstances. My relations with God run a fairly normal course. They intensify when I'm in trouble; and when things go smoothly, they tend to resemble the domestic relations of family members — a good deal of taking-for-granted on my part, with a dozen or so snatches of prayer per day (mostly requests to understand God's intent, if any; to learn patience, to bear what I can't change and then to incorporate it). I'm aware of no substantial fears of age or death, though I won't say I welcome either prospect. And I have no doubt that the usual calm I live in — and here I tap on the nearest wood — comes as a form of mercy from whatever force created the world and knows of me in it.

Can I expect that spotty run through sixty-some years of faith to be of any weight for you, years from now, or for anyone else to whom religious belief is either a baffling phenomenon, an inviting curiosity, or an intellectually impossible position? From a friend, I might hope for the patience required to read these pages — something less than an hour. But I can hardly expect it to be convincing or even comprehensible for unbelieving strangers. One of the characteristics of faith that can seem so repellent is the apparent necessity that faith be given help from God. The most sophisticated theologies of the Western past — millennia of rabbinical debate, the treatises of Augustine, Aquinas, Calvin, and Barth — deduce a similar necessity.

The leap of faith that believers so often recommend is preceded by a serious hitch. It almost invariably requires God's presence, on the far side of the abyss, saying, "Jump!" In Christianity, anyhow, Calvinists agree. God calls certain creatures to believe in him and thus win salvation; others he simply permits to live and die in preordained damnation. It's another idea that looks absurd to anyone who has not been inclined to faith by a propitious early atmosphere and training. For me, as for more than a few writers of the early Christian documents comprised in the New Testament, that terrible prior choosing by God seems at times the baldest deduction from attentive witness of the world.

How can anyone reared in the desert air of contemporary science — physics seems the most relevant science — even begin to move in the murky direction of faith, especially when so many manifestations of religious faith lead to violence, disdain, if not outright hatred, and dithering or murderous nonsense? In any day's news, half the world's human wrongs are done in God's name. That one obstacle to faith, if no other, is all but impassably high. (Yet, again, the majority of human beings claim some form of faith.)

It's my seasoned instinct, then, that any slow scrutiny of contemporary science will demonstrate at many points its intellectual inadequacy as an ample chain of theories to explain the face and the actions of the world. Thus Isaac Newton, who in many ways invented modern science, was a fervently convinced believer; and physics, here at the beginning of the third millennium, is uncovering at a breathtaking rate subatomic phenomena that surpass the imaginings of the wildest hierophant scraping his sores with a cast-off potsherd.

That's not to claim that anyone should fling posthaste into the arms of an invisible God or any religious cult simply because science has proven so prissily bankrupt as a guide to what's here and what's there (here and there seem increasingly to be the same thing). Helium-filled New Age unfortunates are steadily chattering away on television to warn us about that. Yet if nothing else, an honest, well-informed creature must now acknowledge that the world — the universe of physical objects, forces, and actions above, within, or below the range of human or instrumental vision — far surpasses in extent and wonder what we can see and absorb.

But if anyone with a persistent curiosity about faith, anyone who has lacked a sane early grounding in one of the central faiths of his or her culture, were to ask me where to go to begin to understand the inevitability of belief and its mixed rewards (faith is more difficult than unbelief), I'd suggest two initial courses, each to be pursued with quiet steadiness. First, begin to read the sacred texts of your native culture. For the majority of Americans, those texts would include the Christian Bible (which includes the Hebrew scriptures).

Simultaneously, begin to read the thoughts of the great believing minds. For you, friend, those would include a concentration on the actual words of Jesus as preserved in the four Gospels of Matthew, Mark, Luke, and John and then an awareness of the lives and works of figures (among hundreds) such as Francis of Assisi, Søren Kierkegaard, Albert Schweitzer, Simone Weil, W. H. Auden, Dorothy Day, and Flannery O'Connor.

Second, considering that your family will have reared you in a world deep in the knowledge and the resonance of the arts, I'd urge you (and others) to immerse yourself in the lives and works of the great believing musicians and painters — such witnesses as the preservers of Gregorian chant, Giotto and Michelangelo, Palestrina, Rembrandt, Bach and Handel, Mozart and Beethoven, Van Gogh and Rouault, Messiaen and Pärt. None of those believers was a fool nor a mere hired hand of the pope nor some prince with an idle and unadorned chapel.

On the contrary, the inspiration of their work, the craft it employs, the makers' surviving personal statements, show them to be intellectually and emotionally tough-minded and trustworthy — and I've omitted the whole world of poetry, which is, if anything, even more bountiful than music and painting. The same advice can be given for virtually all the world's religions, freighted as they are with glorifications of the mystery and presence and the dreaded absence of God, though the artists of Judaism and Islam (because of their prohibitions against the portrayal of living things) have brilliantly concentrated their findings in such non-visual forms as prophecy, poetry, and music.

While you're reading and listening, you might want to try — if you never have — speaking short sentences to the air around you (be sure no one is watching; people have been carted off for less). Call the air God if you can, though it's not a god; and state as honestly as possible some immediate need, some hope for guidance. With luck and further effort, your sentences will grow less self-obsessed. They may even begin to express occasional thanks. For long months you may get no trace of notice or reply. In time, however,

you may hear answers on the same scale as that on which we measure the masters I've just named. And if an answer comes, you can
be almost sure it wasn't simply the air that answered.

There are numerous possible next steps. You might want to begin frequenting spaces that have a natural benignity for you —
whether it's the lobby of Grand Central Station or a quiet corner
church or a one-man fire-watch tower high above some primal forest. You might begin to talk about your findings with some friend
whom you suspect of having similar curiosities. You might commit
some part of your time to working with the wretched of your neighborhood or town — the homeless, hungry, abused, the unloved
whom most religions insist that we comfort. You might want to try
attending some regular religious ceremonies. If they fail you, go
back to yourself and the ambient air.

Soon or late, you'll likely get some response from that space to
which you first spoke. It may say what it's said to many good people: "There's nothing here but atoms of air. Get a life." It may also
say what it's said persuasively to even more of the earth's human
beings: "Keep talking. Learn how. You're listened to. One day you
may hear me, should I need or want you."

You may, in short — and finally, my valued young friend — have
begun to speak with and to hear from the truth, some form of the
truth that wears many masks for its likely sole face.

Yours in hope,
Reynolds

TIM ROBINSON

The Fineness of Things

FROM THE RECORDER

ONCE, looking out into the poplar tree that tapped with hundreds of triangular leaves at a window of our first-floor flat in London, I saw a small furry caterpillar. I have always been fond of such creatures, so I opened the window and collected it into a jam jar. It had a creamy stripe down the back from which four tufts of brownish hairs stood up like a liner's funnels, and longer sheaves of hairs stuck out in front of it and to the rear. I still possess my 1946 reprint of Richard South's *Moths of the British Isles,* probably the most intensively read book of my childhood, and from it I was able to identify this curiosity as the larva of a vapourer moth — "quite a Cockney insect, and found in almost every part of the Metropolis where there are a few trees." A few days later it retired among the leaves I had given it to feed on, spun up its cocoon, and pupated. I left the jam jar, open, on a windowledge, and a month or so afterward noticed that the moth had emerged and crawled out of the jar and was clinging to the inside of the windowpane. It — she — was a poor-looking, grayish spider-like object; the female of this species is wingless. She was motionless, apparently inert. I raised the sash window a few inches to see if fresh air might invigorate her.

By a marvelous chance later in the day I was passing through the room and happened to glance out just as a small moth came flying toward the window from across the lawn. Its course was slightly irregular and sideslipping, but as purposeful as a saw biting through wood. It shot in through the narrow slit under the sash, went across the room and down to the floor, where it fumbled and tumbled, gradually backtracking to the window and eventually finding its goal after many dartings and near misses. It — he — was a bright-winged little creature, red-ochre with a whitish spot on the trailing edge of each forewing. They clung together immediately, and she began to lay her eggs as they mated, egg after egg after egg, her body slackening and thinning, until after a few hours and about two hundred eggs, she was empty, spent, dead.

One of the hundred threads of implication one could tease out from this passionately observed event — like all such, a knot of parables — is that the transparent space above our lawn that day was seething with messages. The male moth had been able to lock onto the plume of eroticism emanating from the female, which if it had been visible would have looked like a wavering magic carpet unrolled through the air from the narrow slit under the window sash. Simultaneously countless other insects, indifferent to the vapourer's aphrodisiac effluvium, had followed the scent of their own destinies across the garden. But these pheromones — externalized hormones that coordinate, and sometimes destabilize, social and sexual behavior — are not peculiar to insects; from the single-celled protozoan partaking in a slime-slow conglomeration with indefinite numbers of its like, to the rational human being flustered by a *je ne sais quoi* wafted into the margins of consciousness by another's passing-by, we all are subject to their persuasions. The substance secreted by the female vapourer's sex glands is known to the specialist as (z)-6-Heneicosene-11-one (there is a Web site where one can find such recondite information). Its molecules are built of twenty-one atoms of carbon, thirty-eight of hydrogen, and one of oxygen, combined in a specific shape; they go twirling through the jostling throng of lesser molecules constituting air until, perhaps a mile away, some of them happen to fall into the right position to fit the equally specific shape of receptor molecules in cells of the male vapourer moth's antennae. Pheromones are clouds of keys, drifting at random but in such billions they will find their locks.

The Cockneys' mating took place in high summer; Earth was rounding that part of its orbit where its northern regions are favorably inclined toward the sun by day, splendid energies were being lavished on the Metropolis, and sequences of influences we hardly know about had primed the moths to multiply while food for the next generation was green and juicy. What are the proportions between these realms, of the solar system and the moths' sexual chemistry? When I was a child my fond parents wrote a rhyme in which they boasted: "Tim will discover stars / forty times as big as Mars!," and although I may have disappointed them in that respect, I have learned something of the relative scales of things. The diameters of the smaller planets such as Mars and Earth stand to my height in roughly the same ratio as I do to a single cell of my body, while stars, like molecules, figure in ranges much remoter from the human scale. It is only in a very narrow range that we have a natural sense of size. The degree of smallness that most impresses us is, by a perspective effect, the closest to us; not the microbic or atomic but that of objects a tiny but appreciable fraction of our own size, down as far as dust motes, the vanishing points of the domestic. In folktales a sprinkling of "fernseed" renders one invisible, and indeed the size of fern spores marks one of the two exits from the world of naturally visible objects. The further reaches of smallness, like the figures astronomy offers for galactic distances, fade into the abstract, the inconceivable, the incomprehensible. Contemplation of these two vistas led Pascal to his magnificent meditation on the abysses between which the human being is suspended:

> Let man then contemplate the whole of nature in its lofty majesty; let him look at the blazing light hung like an eternal lamp to illuminate the universe; let the earth appear to him as a point in proportion to the vast circuit this star describes, and let him be astonished that this circuit itself is only a very fine point compared to that traced out by the stars that revolve in the firmament. But if sight stops there, let imagination go beyond. . . . All this visible world is no more than a fleck in the bosom of nature. No idea approaches . . . the reality of things. It is an infinite sphere, its centre everywhere, its circumference nowhere. . . .
>
> But to present man with an equally astonishing prodigy, let him search out the most delicate things he knows; let a mite show him how its tiny body has legs with joints, veins in these legs, blood in these veins, humours in this blood, drops in these humours, vapours in these drops. Subdividing these last, he will perhaps think he has arrived at nature's least diminutive. . . . I will make him see in it a new abyss. I will paint him all conceivable immensity of nature in this atom's shrunken bounds. Let him see in it an infinity of universes each with its firmament, planets, earth, in the same proportions as in the visible world, with animals

in this earth, and finally, mites, in which he will find all that he found in the others. . . . Let him lose himself in these marvels, as astonishing in their minuteness as the others in their extent. For who will not wonder that our body, imperceptible in the universe, is now a colossus, or rather a world, compared to the nothing one can never reach? Whoever thinks of himself in this way will be terrified at himself; and seeing himself sustained in the substance nature has given him between these two abysses of infinity and nothingness, he will tremble.

Awe-inspiring as this is, and profound in its anticipation of so much that has been established or hypothesized since his day, I feel that it runs off to infinity too readily, too tendentiously; Pascal is frightening us into the arms of God. Believing that for good or ill our life is totally of this universe, I will look down these perspectives again.

Powers of ten are a useful way of keeping one's head in plumbing these dizzy gulfs. Let multiplication by ten and division by ten be taken as steps up and down, respectively, in the scale of lengths; then one step up from me is the height of a big house, two steps, representing a factor of a hundred, is a hill, three a mountain, four the distance across a town, five a great city, six a country, seven the diameter of Earth. Downward, one step brings me to the rat, two to the moth, three to its egg, four to a single iridescent scale of its wing, five to the single-celled forms of life. Already I need instruments to extend my senses. In exploring my landscapes in the west of Ireland I have often called on scientists to show me how much I'm missing, and what they let me glimpse through their microscopes is astounding in its variety and complexity. A drop of pondwater from the limestone hills of the Burren is a toy chest of darting, wriggling, lumbering, colliding, shunting contraptions so ingenious in their modes of locomotion one is struck by the absence of the wheel; some of the busiest of these untiring searchers are single-celled algae, photosynthesists, therefore members of the plant kingdom. In Connemara, Dog's Bay has a white beach mainly composed of the shells of Foraminifera, single-celled animals that draw calcium carbonate out of seawater and use it to make themselves external skeletons. Each sort — and about two hundred species have been recorded here to date — builds to its own design, and these tend to the fantastic, the obsessional, and the absurd, at least to our eyes accustomed to reading human purposes into artifacts: I see among them cakes from confectionery competitions, fretted globes of Chinese ivorywork, spiky hot-water bottles. Praeger, in whose books I first read about this beach and saw Foraminifera shells illustrated, wondered how each of these minute blobs of jelly knows what sort of shell it is supposed to produce. Nowadays at least parts of the answer are known in outline, in terms of instructions encoded in DNA, interference patterns of chemicals flowing across cell surfaces, and so on. I will also mention the fossil pollen grains preserved at various levels in bogs and lake sediments, from which paleoecologists can reconstruct the plant life of landscapes long gone under the ground. Pollen, that aerial silk, epitome of what is dispersed as irrecoverably as breath, is one of nature's toughest products; long after root and bark have rotted, pollen remains and keeps every detail of its species characteristics. Hazel pollen is a plump triangular cushion with a pore like a porthole at each corner; pine has two reticulated airbags to help it drift far and wide, which give it the appearance of a fly's head; elm is almost spherical, with five pores evenly spaced around a circumference, and a brain-like surface pattern. So we know that in about 3800 B.C., when Neolithic settlers first cleared the forest around Lough Sheeauns in northwest Connemara, the ribwort plantain sprang up, a wildflower reinventing itself as a weed of cultivation. It is not the specifics of such knowledge that astound me, but its quality of specificity, the fineness of detail with which the world records itself and in which its records can be read, through the optics and insights of the various sciences.

Looking outward, perhaps the order of planetary movements, insofar as we see them inscribed upon the sphere of night, answers to that of fernseed in the inward perspective. And that is why astrology arises here, at the apparent limits of naturally comprehensible space, making our inner selves visible as fernseed makes our outer selves invisible. The theory of the direct influence on our characters and careers of the planets' "aspects" at the moment of our births, the whole creaking medieval apparatus of oppositions, conjunctions, sextiles, squares, and trines, is inconsistent with both the findings of science and its self-critical procedures; however, when I say this to an astrologer friend, she replies, weakly but indefeasibly, "But it works!" If so, that is because astrological lore — the never-quite-repetitious starry cycles and all that has been piled up in writing on them since Sumeria — is a rich enough archive of patterns to suit any interpretation; we project onto it hopes and fears that we cannot face directly, and then can recognize them, like Leonardo's faces of all humanity read into the stains on a wall.

Far beyond this delusive order, and the related one of the constellations, that index to world mythology, is the reality of the solar system. Eight steps up in the scale of powers of ten from the human body bring us only halfway to the moon, the orbits of the inner planets including Earth lie around the eleventh step, and the outer orbits of the giant planets from Saturn to Neptune, the twelfth. But it would be an equal and opposite mistake to that of astrology to imagine that the planets pursue their tremendous courses indifferent to our fates; indifference is a human failing, possible only where there is potentiality for caring, and we indulge ourselves in imputing it to the inanimate. In fact we could come to feel affection for these close-to-home features of the solar system, learn to recognize them after a long journey through the comparative emptiness beyond, because they are composed of the same materials as we are, originating probably in a star that once partnered the sun and that ripened and burst and spread its heavy elements about, to be swept together and molded by gravity and electromagnetism into dust clouds, asteroids, comets, and the planets with their rings, moons, atmospheres, seas, and living things. This is not the infinitude of silence that frightened Pascal; this is a space which, in its slower tempo, could be imagined as garrulous as the air above our lawn on a summer's day, teeming with news, fertile in invention.

Such arenas of fruitful interaction are only now beginning to be understood in their general laws; a hierarchy of sciences — chaos theory, complexity theory, new mathematical flesh on the vague old concept of "emergence" — has recently arisen, itself emerging by the very processes it formalizes out of a chaos and complexity of ideas. The essence of these theories is this: that if a collection of entities is sufficiently numerous and richly interactive, and if it is continually fed with energies that disturb it from sluggish equilibria, eventually parts of it will fall by chance into patterns or cycles that have some capacity for persistence; and if such persistences are continually forthcoming, eventually some will arise that have the property of seeding the development of their like, of replicating themselves; and once there are relatively stable dynamic systems all calling on the same resources of material and energy, they will evolve, be co-opted into systems of higher order. All this is a consequence of the law of large numbers — that if enough things happen, then it is certain that something extremely improbable will happen. Life, intelligence, and love are not aliens marooned in a hostile world of iron determinism, doomed to be chilled to death by the dreadful second law of thermodynamics if left unredeemed by the transcendental, as they must have seemed to thinkers of the last century. The furthest developments of these processes, so far as we know and as of today, occur on Earth. A rich enough mix of chemicals, interreacting and fed with heat to keep it far from equilibrium, may spontaneously produce a substance that catalyses other reactions, and then develop more elaborate networks of mutually catalysing processes; hence arises life, hence breeding populations and evolution, hence networks of neurons, thoughts, and dreams, social systems that can reflect upon themselves, books that are written to find out what they are about. This is the Eden of autopoiesis, of self-creation; some social-systems theorists claim that Spencer-Brown's *Laws of Form* is its Book of Genesis, and at least one can agree that endlessly reiterated discrimination of one form from another is its dynamics *in abstracto*.

The popularizations of these theories — paradoxically, many of them pioneered in an institute in Santa Fe that is historically downwind from Los Alamos — are among the most liberating texts I have read in recent years. But at a much earlier stage of my life, and in connection with orders of existence one or two steps above and below those just considered, I struggled with those two great intellectual constructions that stand like the Pillars of Hercules at the opening into twentieth-century physics: relativity and quantum theory. It must have been in my middle school years that I heard Fred Hoyle's BBC talks on the new cosmology; I remember vividly his explaining that the universe is expanding like the surface of a balloon being inflated, of which "the radius, of course, is Time," and I was particularly struck by that "of course," which made me want to be on such first-name terms with Time. I read and convinced myself that I followed Einstein's popular book on relativity, and at least I could appreciate and be amazed at the fact that the famous equation $E = mc^2$ falls out from some comparatively simple mathematics with heart-stopping suddenness. (It expresses the equivalence between energy and mass, c being the speed of light, which is an enormous number, so that c^2 is, one could say, enormously enormous, implying that a stupendous amount of energy can be derived from a very little mass, as had been demonstrated a few years earlier when two cities and their inhabitants were deleted by a few grams of uranium, and as we can feel every day from the sunshine on our faces, the sun having been pouring out that flux of radiant energy not just toward the tiny distant dot of Earth but into all the vastness of space surrounding it, day in day out for millennia, without appreciable loss of substance.) One or two images from Einstein, in particular that of the observer sitting on a rotating disc as a ray of light passes, which I associate with Tenniel's illustration of the caterpillar smoking his hookah on a mushroom, still lie in a cupboard of my mind and come to light now and again. The curvature of spacetime as the gravitational effect of mass, and the speculation that our universe may be finite and yet have no bounds, became easier on my brain when I studied Riemann's generalized coordinate geometry at Cambridge later on, and it does not distress me that our evolutionarily conditioned powers of visualization are inadequate to them. The more recent postulation and subsequent detection of black holes, formed by an old star collapsing into a little sphere of such density that it draws space closed around itself as if to die in utter seclusion, have for me been one of the finest intellectual adventures of our age.

The other great monument of early-twentieth-century physics, quantum theory, is conceptually much more testing, and those who really understand it claim that those who claim to understand it show by that very claim that they do not. However, I can see that once again a most dangerous little formula hops out of the mathematics of it at a very early stage: the notorious uncertainty principle, $\Delta x \cdot \Delta y \geq h$. To predict the course of an atomic particle, or indeed of any body, one would need accurate information as to its present position and momentum; but the principle states that the uncertainty of position multiplied by the uncertainty of momentum cannot be reduced below a certain amount, called Planck's constant, so that if one of these quantities is known very precisely the other can be measured only imprecisely, and vice versa. Hence the future is inherently unpredictable and causality is replaced by probability — not through shortcomings in our understanding or our experimental means but as a fundamental feature of the nature of things. Since Planck's constant is extremely small, these ineluctable uncertainties only begin to become apparent at the atomic level, which begins about nine steps down the scale of powers of ten from everyday life. Quantum theory undoes the comfortable little picture we used to have of atoms as like solar systems, with their electrons circling a nucleus. Rutherford in the 1900s used to claim that he solved problems in electron scattering by asking where he himself would go were he an electron, but in truth another reality underlies the world of solid, handleable entities our imaginations grew up in, and at our present level of evolution mathematics is the only language that can capture it in detail. A long way further down the scale of powers of ten, far past the nucleus at step fourteen, the uncertainty principle upsets the simple negative ideas we have of what Pascal would have called the Void, the perfect vacuum of empty space. The more accurately the time of a process is specified, the less predictable is the energy involved. For the extremely short interval in which two atomic particles are in collision, a wild fluctuation of energy can manifest itself as mass in accordance with Einstein's little equation, in fact as a pair of "virtual" particles, an electron and its opposite, a positron, which flash in and out of existence and can influence the interactions of more normal particles. Thus the "quantum vacuum" is very different from the utter nothingness of the vacuum as conceived by classical physics; it is a perpetual seethe of being, the source of infinite possibility. Finally, at what is called the Planck length, which is about a millionth of a billionth of a billionth of a billionth of a centimeter and corresponds to the thirty-fifth downward step in my schema, the uncertainty principle may demolish the continuity of space itself. At this scale, say some theorists, huge momentary concentrations of energy whip space into a froth of self-occlusions analogous to the black holes of astronomy, the concept of length loses its coherence, and one cannot approach any nearer to the dimensionless points conceived in pure geometry. What form of reality underlies this "quantum foam" is the subject of theories and mathematizations — superstring theory, Penrose's "twistors" — so recent and advanced, and probably so evanescent, that to summarize my slight understanding of them would be mere name-dropping. But I delight in the knowledge that human thought is already probing this incomprehensible space riddled with riddles.

Strangely, images of foam abound at the other end of the scale of powers of ten. At twenty-one steps above the human measure we have the galaxies, of which our Milky Way, containing a hundred billion stars, is one; at step twenty-four, clusters of thousands of galaxies; at twenty-five, a sheet of clusters of galaxies called the Great Wall, three hundred million light-years across. This last was until recently the largest known structure, but now seems to be just one of many such sheets surrounding and separating regions of the universe in which galaxies are rare, like the films of liquid in a mass of bubbles.

One more step brings us to the limit of all we can ever observe, at a distance of about fifteen billion light-years, or a hundred million billion billion miles — not that there is nothing to observe beyond this limit, which is really one of time, set by the fact that light has not had long enough to reach us from any farther away, since only fifteen billion years have elapsed since the universe was a dot the size of the Planck length. "*Is lú na fríde, máthair an oilc,*" less than a speck is the mother of evil, an old Aran man told me. Everything we see or ever can see is born of that speck, for good or evil. But, according to one of the most audacious speculations of contemporary cosmology, we may call on the existence of indefinite numbers of other universes to explain the properties of this one, including its manifest ability to support intelligent life. For, as Hoyle pointed out a long time ago, physics cannot derive and has to take as given the values of certain constants (I have mentioned two, the speed of light and Planck's constant), and if these were only slightly different from what they are, we would not be here to comment on the fact. A universe with other values of the universal constants might be too small and short-lived, or too vast and dilute, for stars to form; or its stars might not last long enough for nuclear fusion within them to forge the large nuclei of atoms such as carbon, necessary for life; or the whole story might go awry and fade out in some other way. For some, this fine-tuning of the universal constants is proof that we were meant to be, that the universe or its creator had written us or something like us into the plans from the beginning. But there is no need to abandon a thoroughgoing naturalism even at this extremity of the thinkable. A universe that gives rise to stars long-lived enough to form carbon and the other necessaries of life is also going to produce stars that go on to collapse into black holes; and black holes, being portions of space that have closed in on themselves and are no longer in contact with the universe they form in, could be the buds of new universes. Suppose that these offspring universes inherit the constants of their progenitor, with slight variations, rather as living things do; then universes that fail to thrive and do not produce black holes will not be represented in the next generation, and those that bear plentiful buds will preponderate. So the reason we find ourselves in a universe hospitable to life is that the vast majority of universes are so, for such universes themselves are prolific breeders.

This heartshaking vision of the grounds of our possibility in a perhaps eternal and infinite profusion of universes is strangely like that of the foam of being we glimpse at the other end of the length scale. We are not desolate creatures helplessly adrift between two deathly abysses. The perspectives I have sketched span the perilous sea of our universe from shore to shore. They are two wings of not-quite-inconceivable breadth and power that bear us up for a time. Not for long enough, but for a time.

CARLO ROTELLA

Cut Time

FROM THE AMERICAN SCHOLAR

RUSSELL, a pleasant young man who split his time between the
college on the hill (where I taught) and the boxing gym down below, came up at the end of class one day to tell me that a card of
fights would be held in a couple of weeks in nearby Allentown,
Pennsylvania. He knew I was interested in boxing and thought I
might like to go; also, he needed a ride.

I had figured he was not stopping by to continue our discussion
of "Bartleby the Scrivener." Seated front and center, in a posture of
polite interest but not taking many notes, Russell followed the action in class without committing to it. Some students, infighters, sit
up front to get your attention, but others do it for the opposite reason: one way to avoid getting hit is to get in too close, nestled cozily
against your opponent's clavicle, where he cannot apply the leverage to hurt you (unless he fouls by head-butting, ear-biting, or calling on people who do not raise their hands). Russell did the reading and wrote his papers, but he was not swept up by fictions and
make-believe characters. The class met in the afternoon just before
he headed down the hill to the Larry Holmes Training Center, and
I suspected that he daydreamed about the imminent shock of
punching rather than concentrating on the literary matters at
hand.

Every once in a while, though, Russell would say something that
reminded me that he was paying attention. Impressed by Frederick
Douglass's late-round TKO of the overseer Covey, he spoke up to
remind us that this scene dramatized the red-blooded ideal of self-
making with one's own two hands. But he had also been moved to

speak by Melville's Bartleby, who comprehensively rejects one of the fight world's foundational principles: protect yourself at all times. Russell, breaking form, had his hand up first and initiated the discussion of Bartleby with references to Gandhi, Martin Luther King, and the difficult principle of moral inaction. Russell encouraged us to consider whether the pacific Bartleby, by preferring to do nothing, was acting decisively against the grain of his situation, or was simply not much good with his hands and therefore destined to be acted upon by a world that kept the hard knocks coming in a steady stream. At least that is what I took him to mean, and I got busy parlaying it into a general discussion in which Russell, having said his piece, declined to participate further.

Once the other students had risen to the bait and were doing the talking, I had a chance to look Russell over for new damage: this week it was a thick, dark line, resembling lavishly applied lampblack, that ran under his right eye from nose to cheekbone. Another black eye, and this one a prizewinner. One of the quiet dramas of having Russell in class was seeing what kind of punishment he had incurred of late. He was so placid in his manner, so Bartleby-like in his pale decency, that I was always jarred by the various lumps, welts, and bruises that passed over his face like weather fronts. Having seen him spar in the gym, I should not have been surprised. He was strong but not quick; and he came straight at his antagonist, equably accepting blows as the price of getting into range to deliver the one-twos he favored. I knew that Russell's style ensured that he would get hit often, even on his best days; but when I saw the marks of his latest lesson on his face, a little click of alarmed recognition still ran through me — registering somewhere in a roped-off area of my mind devoted to boxing — as I managed the discussion and scrawled on the blackboard, chalk dust all over my hands and on the thighs of my pants where I wiped them.

I gestured at the new black eye when Russell stopped to talk with me after class. He just said, "Sterling," looked at the floor, and shook his head, smiling faintly. Sterling was one of the gym's rising stars, a teenager already poised and smooth in the ring. Russell had several years and a few pounds on Sterling, although neither advantage did him much good. Sterling was so preternaturally fast and clever that he had fallen half in love with the idea of his own

genius; that — and a tendency to switch back and forth too pro-
miscuously between right- and left-handed stances in order to
baffle his opponents — was his only evident weakness. He was the
kind of evasive, willowy counterpuncher that solid hitters long to
pummel. Russell, for one, believed with doctrinaire intensity that
he could hurt Sterling if only he could catch him. I had not seen
the two of them spar together, but I had seen Russell's face after
their sessions and I had seen both of them spar with others, so I
could imagine the encounters: Russell following Sterling doggedly
around the ring, absorbing jabs and the occasional speed-blurred
combination as he sought to fix the skinny body and weaving head
in his sights long enough to throw a meaningful punch. When Russell drifted far away in thought during class, I assumed he was pur-
suing Sterling in his mind's eye in the hope of finally nailing him
with a big right hand.

On our drive down to the fights later that month, Russell described
himself as discouraged about boxing. He had been scheduled to
make his first amateur fight in the Golden Gloves, but he had canceled it. He knew he was not ready. I asked if Sterling was still beating him up in the sparring ring, and he said, "Well, yeah, him, but
also everybody else. A while ago I was walking around with two
black eyes and loose cartilage in my nose and I started to get . . . *discouraged* thinking about it." Russell's stated ambition was to win an
official boxing match, not just to spar or fight creditably, but the
accumulating pain and damage made him worry that he might be
foolish to pursue this goal any further. At the same time, he was
wary of giving up too easily, of mistaking for perpetual futility what
might be only a difficult period in his fistic education. He said,
"When I spar I'm getting really beat up, like, humiliated, in there. I
can't get better until I practice more, but I can't practice without
getting beat up." I asked why he could not stop now, with no sig-
nificant damage done, having learned the basics of boxing, having
done much to inculcate in himself the generally applicable virtue
of disciplined hard work, and having absorbed an instructive dose
of the kind of violent extremity from which college usually shelters
a young man or woman.

Russell had two answers to that. First, the ever-present threat of
pain and humiliation in boxing inspired him to rigor in his train-

ing, and he worried that if he stopped going to the gym he would backslide in other endeavors that also required discipline. "When I first got to college," he said, "I slacked off a lot, just hung out and messed around, and it really affected me — my school work, my life. But once I found boxing, I got disciplined about everything. School, eating, sleeping, everything. This week I was getting really discouraged and I didn't go down to the gym at all, and I already felt myself letting things go. You know, falling back into bad habits." Second, he said, discipline aside, "It could turn out that pain and damage are important just by themselves. That's a kind of life experience you can't get as a middle-class college student. Maybe it's worth getting banged up to learn about yourself and, you know, the rest of the world." There were guys down at the gym who had been in jail, who had been addicted to drugs, who had given and taken beatings in and out of the ring, who had been out on the streets broke and without prospects. That was what Russell meant by "life experience."

He seemed to want an argument, so I gave him one. Boxing was not the only way to sample the world beyond College Hill. Most experience of that world fell somewhere between the extremes of reading about it in books and insisting on getting punched out over and over by experts. Warming to the task, I argued that his fixation on getting hurt as the key to authentic "life experience" took the school out of the school of hard knocks, reducing an education in pugilism to an elaborate form of self-abuse. If ritual humiliation and physical damage became his antidote to slacking off and a sheltered upbringing, wouldn't that formula for gaining "life experience" give him no reason to improve as a boxer? And, anyway, what made boxing necessarily a better path to "life experience" than college? Wasn't college, ideally, supposed to be about exactly the things he saw in boxing: rigorous self-knowledge, encounters with the wider world, the inculcation of discipline? After all, Frederick Douglass presents himself as a student first and a wordsmith last — a reader, writer, and speaker. He disdains boxing, like whiskey drinking, as a waste of a Sabbath day better spent in learning to read, and he fights only twice — when cornered, rather than going in search of beatings — in a definitively unsheltered life.

Russell said "I see that" and "Right, right" in the way a person does when he means that he has stated his position, he is pleased that you agree it is worth discussing, and there is nothing more to discuss.

We were on our way to see Art Baylis, who also worked out at the Larry Holmes Training Center, fight on the evening's card. Art was getting old in fighter-years. Sometimes in the gym, wrapping his hands before he got to work, he would complain, "I'm tired of this bullshit. I'm not making money, I'm getting all beat up for nothing." The other fighters were sympathetic: it's a rough business, they would agree, nobody here is getting rich. (Actually, Larry Holmes, the heavyweight ex-champion who owned the gym, had been rich for some time, but that was different.) Some tried to jolly Art out of his dark moods, but he would say, "Don't tell me I'm not tired," and they let him be, exchanging smiles behind his back. They knew he would return the next day, or the day after that. Art fought for small purses and worked as a sparring partner for more accomplished veteran fighters or younger men on the way up, men with some money behind them. When he sparred he sometimes wore not just the standard headgear but a mask, a simultaneously futuristic- and medieval-looking helmet made of bright red cushiony material mounted on a rigid frame that fit over his whole head. It had two slits at the eyes and projected out, beak-like, over his nose, mouth, and jaw. He had been cut up over the years and there was no reason to open old wounds in the gym.

Art had turned pro relatively late, in his mid-twenties, and there were gaps in his record, periods of a year and three years in which he had not fought at all. There was talk of a stretch in the joint and a drug problem that had undercut his development as a fighter. A small, competent heavyweight who also fought as a cruiserweight, he was still solid in the legs. Shirtless, though, he did not look like God in a painting. His chest drooped, unlike those broad armor-plate pectorals proudly sported by men drawn obsessively to the bench press. People who run and lift weights to get buff, who are "into sports" and speak of "intimidation" and "dominating," might make the mistake of thinking Art was soft and could be overwhelmed by a younger man in better shape. Art knew better. He did best fighting anatomically impressive whippersnappers whose principal investment was in their bodies rather than their craft, men who had the advantage of him *only* in youth and physique. Except when he was chosen as a plausible opponent to lose a fight to a hot property, he was past the point in his career at which he might find himself matched regularly in bouts against genuine talents.

Art was not necessarily quicker or more gifted than the men he beat. Rather, he knew how to fight and had few expectations of glorious success to interfere with his capacity to endure hard times. He had won enough fights to know what it felt like to outlast the other man, but he had been beaten up often enough to know what a well-crafted beating should feel like. He knew the difference between that and a couple of rounds of rough treatment at the hands of an opponent who will soon have overextended himself in the flush of what feels like incipient triumph. Typically, Art lost or split the early rounds, throwing his left jab and hook to the head, holding his right hand in reserve, and weathering the other guy's best shots. After a couple of rounds of this, once both men had spent the first increments of energy and were taking stock of what remained, just about the time when a younger man had begun to realize with some distress that he was tired and there was still a day's work to do, Art settled in to win the fight: he began hammering the body with both hands to slow his opponent down and discourage further offense, then went upstairs to the head. When Art won, it was usually by decision rather than knockout.

Some of the victories came easy, most came hard. On the night Russell and I went to see him fight in the ballroom of the Days Inn in Allentown, Art got cut badly in the second round. The other fighter, Exum Speight, was a professional opponent, considerably younger than Art but with more fights and many more losses on his record. The matchmaker had chosen Speight with the expectation that Art would defeat him, but not without a crowd-pleasing struggle. Although Speight rarely won a bout anymore, he had gone the distance with some of the best in the business and he looked the part of a tough guy. While Art's size and strength resided in his thick legs, Speight's was in his upper body: bulky shoulders, prominent veins branching across biceps and forearms, a strongbox of a chest. Speight came out briskly, circling first one way and then the other, firing punches in a commanding rhythm. Art followed him around the ring, eating jabs and throwing left jabs and hooks of his own, looking for an opening to deliver the right. Perhaps because Speight was acting like a man who expected to win, and seemed unaffected by the older man's punches, Art forgot himself. He became impatient and tried his right hand too early, before the younger man's force had been sufficiently denatured by frustration, fatigue, and punishment. Art loaded up leverage to throw a right at the head through what looked like a gap in his opponent's defense, but Speight sensed Art's balance shifting and beat him to the punch. Speight snapped his low-riding left hand up and around to deliver the best blow of the night, a crisp hook that interrupted Art's own slower-developing punch and landed flush to the right side of Art's face. There was old, soft, much-torn scar tissue around the outside corner of Art's right eye, the kind that parts like wet paper when force is applied to it. Blood came up enthusiastically out of the mess, a rich, awful, seductive red under the ring lights. Within seconds it was running down Art's face, getting all over his chest and Speight's gloves, then Art's own gloves and both fighters' trunks. Art's white trunks began to turn pink.

A serious cut seems to change everything. I think of it as making a sound one can almost hear, a droning, keening note that hangs in the smoke-filled air of fight night. The almost-sound is like music played in a difficult, awkward scale and time signature. When blood from a serious cut finds its way into the lights, it is as if some sinister bandleader, black-suited and Fu Manchu'd behind his horn, has cued a frantic, dissonant foray into cut time. The almost-music of cut time strums the optic nerves, vibrates in the teeth; it encourages fighters to do urgent, sometimes desperate things. Spectators, too, shamed and fascinated, plunge headlong into this alien-familiar moment. What was inside and hidden, implicit in the fight, has come outside and taken form.

Art grabbed Speight as often as he could and held him, hoping to make it through the rest of the second round without further damage. To shield the cut, Art put the uncut left side of his face against the left side of Speight's and kept it there in the clinches, which created the illusion that Art was searching the crowd for someone over Speight's shoulder. Unhinged by cut time, I imagined for one bizarre moment that he was trying to make eye contact with me (at ringside) and Russell (back in the crowd somewhere) in order to call on us. "See? 'Life experience.' Discuss." A great slick of fresh blood covered the right side of Art's face, which was stretched into a desperate-looking grimace. It was hard not to believe that he was silently entreating us, the referee — anybody — to stop the fight. But of course he was doing no such thing. Art had an education, not only in fighting but in being hurt, that made the cut a problem to solve. He had to negotiate the difficulties of cut time while conducting the fight back into more manageable form — a twelve-round blues, say, or the stately largo movement of a concerto that had begun at far too brisk an allegro. He had sprung a leak and he needed to fix it.

Art bled and bled. The ring doctor visited his corner between rounds to inspect the damage. Art's seconds, seasoned practitioners who had worked more illustrious corners in the past, stanched the flow as well as they could, but the cut opened anew as soon as Speight started hitting it in the next round. Art knew he was in danger and picked up the pace, throwing wilder punches with both hands in the hope of hurting his man before the cut would oblige the ring doctor to end the fight. Driven out of his customarily measured boxing style, Art began to make a sobbing, effortful noise as he threw outsized blows. Most of them missed, which caused him to sob more dramatically as he expended even more energy to regain his balance after every staggering miss, but some of his blows hit Speight's guard or landed glancingly on the chin or body. There were so many of them that Speight, instead of counterpunching in earnest to make Art pay for exposing himself so rashly, changed tactics and waited for the older man to run out of steam. Speight made a fort out of his forearms and gloves, risking only an occasional sortie to throw a punch in the lulls between Art's assaults. This went on for another three rounds. Art's blood splattered both fighters, the canvas underfoot, and the judges, functionaries, and reporters at ringside. A slick-haired guy from the boxing commission, seated a few places down from me at the long table abutting the ring apron, pulled up the white tablecloth and tented it over himself to the eyes. Perhaps he was squeamish, or protecting his suit, or worried about AIDS. The referee was awash in the blood, but did not seem to mind; he had been bled on before.

(Later, at the end of the night, the referee used a stopped-up sink in the men's room to soak his shirt. A pale-skinned, beefy fellow with an iron-gray crew cut and copious body hair, he had stripped down to a dark blue sleeveless T-shirt and was kneading his once-light-blue dress shirt in a pool of pink water. He had taken off his black bow tie and once-white surgical gloves and set them at the edge of the sink. One of the gloves, inside out, seemed to be pointing a finger at the mess in the sink. It looked as if he had performed a successful roadside appendectomy with his car tools on the way home from an evening at the Rotary Club. Men from the audience made wide detours around him on their way to the urinals, all but one of which had backed up and were no longer flushing. The referee patiently did his laundry amid the comings and goings of men, the cigarette smoke, the cloying stink of deodorant cakes in the urinals, and the strong, astringent smell of beer drinkers' piss.)

It took a couple of rounds for the spectators, who flinched every time flying blood caught the lights, to realize that Art was winning the fight. The mostly inaccurate punching frenzy he embarked upon after suffering the cut gradually wore Speight down, accomplishing the goal Art usually pursued with several more rounds' worth of studied sharpshooting. Speight was probably in better shape than Art, but having a groaning, bloodied maniac flailing after him for long three-minute stretches seemed to drain Speight's energy and resolve. By the fifth round, Speight was no longer circling, no longer throwing many punches. He snapped occasional jabs at Art, but none of them landed near the cut and they did not bother Art much. Art, realizing he had messily accomplished an important task — breaking Speight's initial energy and confidence — and was now ahead of schedule to win by decision, reined himself in but kept up the pressure. He began to land hard, accurate punches and Speight found himself backing sulkily toward the ropes, well behind on points, as usual. Having taken command of the fight, Art threw rights with renewed authority, confident that Speight would not take advantage of the openings for counterpunching that he created. The younger man's offense slacked off to almost nothing. By midfight, Art was no longer bleeding from the cut next to his right eye, and was bleeding only a little from another cut in the scar tissue on the bridge of his nose; Speight, though, bled in a slow, dark flow from both nostrils.

Cut time was over. The black-suited bandleader played a last atonal screech, took his horn from his mouth, and stepped back as the drummer changed pace and kicked into a straight-ahead 4/4 standard: The Exum Speight Loses Another Fight Blues.

The fight entered its last movement. Both men tired, and both had gone the distance often enough to be familiar with bone-deep exhaustion, but Art was better at fighting to win in that state. He seemed to welcome fatigue as a condition in his favor, in the way that certain racehorses favor a muddy track. For Speight, being tired was part of a familiar process in which resolve gave way to resignation and, almost inevitably, to the referee's raising the other man's taped hand. Experience had formed a rut rather than a reserve in him. One problem with being tough and strong is that the realization of being bested, of feeling the other fighter's hands shaping the bout, comes as a terribly dispiriting shock every time, no matter how often it happens and no matter how familiar it becomes. Speight, having become excited and perhaps even a bit frightened when he saw that Art was badly cut, and having plunged steeply into a depression when Art had not quit because of the cut, now looked as if he had a headache and wanted to go home. But Art — tired as he was and would be, without grandiose prospects but possessed of a thick and instructive past — had found his rhythm. He moved fluidly and with great purpose, cutting off the ring, controlling Speight's movements with jabs and double jabs, snapping Speight's head back with hard rights. Speight roused himself to hit Art on the chin, a hard shot, after the bell at the end of the fifth round; Art, unshaken, grinned at him evilly before going back to his corner. Both of them knew that Speight already regarded the fight as lost and done with: if a professional opponent in good fighting trim has gone deep enough into a bout to be genuinely tired, it means he has already earned his paycheck by putting up a creditable battle.

Storybook logic does not apply to tank-town fights. Once Art had the fight in hand, there was no reason for him to get all crazy in trying to knock Speight out. As Art piled up rounds with the judges, he became more careful. By the end he was doing just enough to win every round, and the two men spent the last couple of rounds leaning on each other, for which Speight had a point deducted by the blood-soaked referee. Art won the decision by a wide margin on every judge's card. It had been a difficult job of work, and he had been obliged to do it the hard way, as usual.

Russell did not talk much on the ride back later that night. We sped along the highway in reflective silence. When I got home, having dropped him off along the curving drive that bisected the darkened campus, my wife was sleeping and the house was still. I was living then in Easton, a Pennsylvania college town so quiet that after midnight one can hear traffic on the highway in the distance. Fight night was in my head, strong against the stillness, as I made my way through the dark house and up the stairs: the red gloves and infinitely redder blood, the moving bodies, the ceaseless oceanic sound made by even a small fight crowd, the clarity of every stain and thread under the ring lights, the smoke, the shock of solid punches, the complicated rhythms of clinches and infighting, the high, wavering almost-note of cut time. Bending in front of the bathroom sink to wash my face, I looked in the mirror and discovered that there were bright spots of blood on my pale green shirt. Three more, crusted and almost black, made a kind of Orion's belt across my forehead. I had already noticed at ringside that there was blood on my notes and my pants. It was almost certainly all Art's, although I suppose some of it could have come from Speight's nose. I washed my face and then I ran water in the sink to soak the shirt.

In the months that followed, Russell found a teacher, a retired fighter who sometimes worked with novices, and eventually declared himself ready to try the Golden Gloves. He was wrong. Russell described his amateur debut as a sort of out-of-body nightmare. He felt himself submerged in a flatfooted torpor in which he moved with desperately inappropriate serenity while the other fighter, unspeakably quick and confident, pounded him at will. Russell was not badly hurt, but he was thoroughly beaten. After the first round, the referee came to Russell's corner to ask if he wished to continue, and he did, but the referee stopped the bout in the second. Feeling himself profoundly out of place in the ring and in his own body, sustained only by courage once his craft had deserted him, seemingly unable to defend himself or fight back, Russell had frozen in the ring, as novices sometimes do. "I never got started," he told me. "It was like I wasn't even there."

I moved away from Easton soon after, but, back to visit a year later, I dropped by the Larry Holmes Training Center one afternoon. The fighters poured sweat in the late September heat.

Stripped to a black tank top and shorts, Art was hitting a heavy bag steadily and well — first the left hand twice, a jab and a hook, then a right cross. Somebody was hitting the other heavy bag very hard; it jumped with each blow, and the thump-crack of sharp punching filled the long, low room. When the second hitter moved around his bag and out from behind Art, I could see it was Russell. There was a new weight and speed in his punching, and he had his legs and shoulders into the making of each punch. His diligence and his teacher's efforts had evidently paid off in an improved command of leverage. He was working on power shots: his left hooks made a perfect L from shoulder to glove, staving in the bag on one side; his straight rights imparted the illusion of animate sensitivity to the bag as it leapt away from the impact. He looked bigger than before, having begun to fill out, but, more than that, he looked looser, more competent, more alert. He had lost the quality of undersea abstraction that had always surrounded him in the gym. There was confident vigor in the way he shoved the bag away so it would swing back at him: he looked forward to its arrival because he was going to hit it just right, with all of himself behind the gloved fist.

I raised an eyebrow at Jeff, a stocky gym regular who worked for the grounds crew up at the college in the mornings and for Larry Holmes in the afternoons. He looked over at Russell, smiled and nodded, and said, "Yeah, Russ has been getting it together. He can *hit,* man. He was in sparring with one of those boys last week and the guy's head was just going like this: bop! bop! bop!" With each *bop!* Jeff threw his head back, chin up, like a fighter getting tagged. One of Holmes's seconds, a round-bodied, characteristically surly fellow named Charlie, chimed in: "Russ can hit. No doubt about it. He had his problems for a while, he got beat up, but he stayed with it and he's getting good. He gets in there this time, he'll surprise some people. Hurt 'em." This was unlooked-for, wildly enthusiastic praise coming from Charlie, who usually ignored the younger fighters in the gym except to shoo them out of the ring when Holmes was ready to work out.

Loyal to one of the gym's most diligent regulars, if not one of its most talented, Jeff and Charlie were talking Russell up to one of his professors, but anyone could see that he had made an important step forward on the way from dabbler to fighter. It looked as if he had arrived at a sense of belonging in the gym, not because he was training next to Art, but because he was doing it right and knew himself to be doing it right. Maybe the Golden Gloves beating had helped to drive home the lesson that just wanting to be in the ring is not a good enough reason to be there; you have to accept responsibility for your part in the mutual laying on of hands. I expected that Russell would not freeze up in his next fight. He was still slow and hittable, and he might well lose; if he did, however, it would not be because he felt out of place in the ring but because he was outboxed or made mistakes or was simply not quick enough. And if the other guy let Russell start throwing punches, Russell might just give him a beating, or at least a stiff punch or two to remember him by.

When I got back home to Boston I sent Russell an e-mail saying I was pleased to see that he had made such progress in the gym. I admitted I had worried in the past that he would get seriously hurt, perhaps even in a life-changing way, because he was in the gym for the wrong reasons — to absorb "life experience" passively rather than to train actively at a craft — but I was less worried now that he had evidently got down to work in earnest. I was initially surprised, then, when Russell wrote back a couple of weeks later to announce a retirement of sorts:

> In earnest, I have become somewhat disenchanted with boxing. There seems to be a level, which I have reached, at which it has lost to some extent its seductive and mesmorizing effect. While I will always retain an interest and awe in the sport, I feel that I can understand the subtleties of the sport and could even execute them given the proper conditioning and practice. While I regard Larry and other successfull boxers with the utmost respect and admiration, there seems to be a lack of transcendence into a higher state of more complete perfection in the human realm. Financial gain does not take the fighter out of the street and its culture, nor does it provide him with any solice or real advancement. I may be sounding somewhat highbrow, however, I now realize that I have bigger fish to fry. With my college education quickly coming to a close I need to focus the resource of my time on things which will propel my advancement after graduation. I will certainly remain active in training and boxing but I realistically can no longer give it my full commitment (and just when I was starting to see the fruit of my labor) . . .
>
> Still in need of an appropriate nickname,
> Russell

Seduction, proper conditioning and practice, a lack of transcendence, bigger fish to fry, a reapportioning of resources: a college man's romance with boxing in brief.

Russell's retirement should not have surprised me. He finished with boxing when he had learned enough — about hitting and about being hit, about other people and himself, about what Douglass and Bartleby had to say about "life experience" — to understand how fighters submit to being molded by one another. The long line of men who had hit Art in the right eye had contributed to making him a man who could handle cut time. If the line continued to get longer, though, Art would inevitably deform his style to protect the weak spot, leaving new openings for opponents to exploit. Too much of that would cause Art to end up like Exum Speight. The already too long line of men who had outpunched Speight had taught him to expect defeat and even collaborate in it. Red-blooded convention treats boxing as a matter of one fighter asserting himself forcefully over another, but boxing is just as much a matter of accepting that what you become rests in the hands of others. Or in the hands of orchestrated circumstance: summoned to Allentown to lose a fight, Speight did not set out to initiate cut time in the second round of his bout with Art; he just counterpunched into a hole in the hometown favorite's defense. Had Russell gone further than he did in boxing — and especially had he turned pro, shedding the amateur's protective headgear — he would have had to accept cut time as a reasonable possibility, a condition likely to be thrust upon a hard hitter who takes too many punches in return. Both Art and Speight, both the man who was cut and the man who cut him, knew themselves to *deserve* cut time. Russell quit before reaching that stage of resignation, but he went far enough that his Golden Gloves opponent, his trainer, and his sparring partners helped him get the feel and the sense of it in his body, where they will persist.

Russell carried six courses in his last semester of college, which left little time for boxing. He said, "I'll spar again, maybe, but I don't think I will fight in the Golden Gloves. I'm too busy, and I'm not as hungry as I was. It's not worth the risk." Art, of course, kept fighting. I have seen him in action twice since then. In the first bout, he suffered a dubious first-round knockout at the hands of an overrated prospect named Baby Joe Mesi. The first time Mesi threw a hard punch, Art went over backward and lay still, like a Hollywood stuntman leveled by an action hero. It was a record-padder for Mesi, a quick if humiliating payday for Art. In the second bout, a difficult victory of the kind in which Art specializes, he outlasted a bruiser from Philadelphia named Byron Jones. The victory evened Art's lifetime record at thirteen wins and thirteen losses. After sixteen years of hard going in and out of the ring, he had fought the business to a bloody draw.

ASHRAF RUSHDY

Exquisite Corpse

FROM TRANSITION

IN AN EARLIER TIME, a lynch mob would display the body of its victim with impunity, often gathering around it for a group photograph. These images, and the bodies they represented, were the icons of white supremacy. Circulated in newspapers, the pictures displayed the power of the white mob and the powerlessness of the black community. After the highly publicized lynching of Claude Neal in 1934, photographers took hundreds of shots of his mutilated body and sold them for fifty cents each. The photograph of Neal's hanging body eventually became a postcard. One group of white people, gathered around a burned black body, was communicating to another group in another county: they had done their part, asserted their place in the world. The image was certain to incite other communities to follow their example: this was the golden age of lynching.

The body of the victim assumed a magical quality for the lynch mob: the corpse was an object to be tortured, mutilated, collected, displayed. To snuff out life was rarely enough: more ritual was required. In 1937, when a Georgia mob was unable to lynch Willie Reid because the police had already killed him, they broke into the funeral home where he lay, carried his body to a baseball diamond, and burned it. Even a mob that had already hanged, maimed, and burned a man might still feel compelled to exhume his body in order to inflict further indignities; so it was with the corpse of George Armwood, in 1933.

As the historian Jacquelyn Dowd Hall has noted, the spectacle of lynching dramatized a social hierarchy where whites and blacks, women and men, knew their place. Blacks were terrorized, white women were vulnerable, and white men were on top, invulnerable and free. Still, whites projected immense sexual power onto blacks; the terror of lynching reflected their own anxieties.

Indeed lynching also seems to be the expression of a peculiar necrophilia, manifest in the desire to possess the bodies of victims, in the passion with which dead bodies were handled and displayed — as if they were talismans of life itself. The East Texas lynch mob that killed David Gregory in 1933 pulled out his heart and cut off his penis before tossing his body onto a pyre: those were the most potent emblems of vitality. Such actions bespeak nothing so much as a perverse fondness for the dead body.

While lynch mobs subjected the corpses of their victims to the most spectacular abuse, victims' families were more concerned with matters of the spirit. Most often they buried their loved ones in silence: for these families, the corpse was less important than the soul.

The same can be said of those families who refused to bury lynch victims. In 1889, after a mob broke into a Barnwell, South Carolina, jail and lynched eight African American men, the local black community displayed its solidarity at the funeral. More than five hundred people lined the street, and several women implored the Lord to "burn Barnwell to the ground." The community refused to bury six of the men, claiming that the whites who killed them should bear that responsibility. In Virginia, Joseph McCoy's aunt refused to bury the body of her nephew, who was lynched in 1897. "As the people killed him, they will have to bury him," she explained. The body, whether buried or left to the elements, had become a symbol of the injustice and barbarism of the white community, the failure of the nation's founding principles: let the dead bury their dead.

When Emmett Till was lynched in 1955, Mamie Till Bradley refused to hide her son's corpse. His mutilated and decomposed body was found in the Tallahatchie River three days after he died. Despite the sheriff's opposition, she insisted that her son be returned to Chicago. Bradley opened the casket as soon as it arrived at Illinois Central Terminal and promptly announced that she wanted an open-casket funeral so everyone could "see what they did to my boy." On the first day the casket was open for viewing, ten thousand people saw it; on the day of the funeral, at least two thousand mourners stood outside the packed church where the services were held. The body of Emmett Till — "his head . . . swollen and bashed in, his mouth twisted and broken" — became a new kind of icon. Emmett Till showed the world exactly what white supremacy looked like.

According to one report, Till's funeral created an "emotional explosion": "thousands of cursing, shrieking, fainting Negroes" responded to the "corpse . . . displayed 'as is.'" The Southern media denounced Bradley's decision as "macabre exhibitionism" and cheap political "exploitation." But African Americans who attended the funeral or saw pictures of Till's body were transformed. One reader congratulated the *Amsterdam News* for "putting the picture of the murdered Till boy on the front page"; a writer for the *Pittsburgh Courier* predicted that Mrs. Bradley's decision might "easily become the opening gun in a war on Dixie which can reverberate around the world." A photo-essay in *Jet* proved electrifying: Representative Charles Diggs remarked that the "picture in *Jet* magazine showing Emmett Till's mutilation . . . stimulated . . . anger on the part of blacks all over the country." A black sociologist later wrote that "the *Jet* magazine photograph of Emmett Till's grotesque body left an indelible impression on young Southern blacks"; they went on to become "the vanguard of the Southern student movement."

The influence of the *Jet* photographs has been well documented. As a girl, civil rights activist Joyce Ladner kept clippings in a scrapbook. She responded to the picture of Till's bloated body in the magazine "with horror that transformed itself into a promise to alter the political and racial terrain where such a crime could happen." Cleveland Sellers, an activist and field director in the Student Nonviolent Coordinating Committee, remembers how pictures of the corpse in black newspapers and magazines — showing "terrible gashes and tears in the flesh . . . [giving] the appearance of a ragged, rotting sponge" — created a stir about civil rights when he was a youth in South Carolina. A thirteen-year-old boy named Cassius Clay stood on a street corner in Louisville, transfixed by pictures of Emmett Till in black newspapers and magazines: in one picture, smiling and happy; in the other, a gruesome mockery of a face. Muhammad Ali says he admired Mrs. Bradley, who had "done a bold thing" in forcing the world to look at her son. Fifteen years later, Ali met Brother Judge Aaron, a man who had survived a Klan lynching attempt in the 1960s. (They had carved the letters *KKK* into his chest and castrated him to send a "message" to "smart-alecky . . . niggers like Martin Luther King and Reverend Shuttleworth.") Ali responded by dedicating all his future fights to "the unprotected people, to the victims."

By the time of Emmett Till's murder, lynching had begun to decline, and pictures of lynching victims were becoming scarce. What had once been viewed with pride now seemed like barbarity: the victim's body became less an icon of white supremacy than a denunciation of it. As popular opinion turned against lynching, the sight of lynched bodies became an embarrassment for white communities squirming under the glare of national and international scrutiny. In fact, these corpses became potent weapons in the political struggle to enact a law against lynching — a struggle that continues today.

The 1959 murder of Mack Charles Parker was representative of this new climate. The lynch mob wore masks to hide the identity of its members; they gave up on their original plan to castrate their victim and hang the body from a bridge: instead, they weighted the body and dumped it into the river. When Parker's body was recovered ten days later, town officials worked furiously to keep it from being entered as evidence before the Senate during deliberations on antilynching legislation. Police officers and state troopers guarded the body in a funeral home, and after *Chicago Defender* reporter Tony Rhoden managed to sneak in and take a picture of the badly mutilated body, there was a frantic search for him and his camera. Two hours after the coroner's inquest, before Parker's mother had even heard that his body had been recovered, he was buried in a hasty ceremony.

It is not clear what happened to Rhoden's photograph of Parker's body. If it was not published, it might have been because of the censorship that has restrained mainstream photojournalism in times of extremity. *Life* magazine had to wait eight months while government censors debated whether it could publish a picture of a dead American soldier on Buna Beach, New Guinea, in 1943.

While pictures of dead bodies were widely published during the Vietnam War, a *Detroit Free Press* photographer had to beg military censors to approve a photograph of an American soldier crying over a body bag during the Persian Gulf War. And even in the absence of official censorship, Americans' delicate sensibilities have prevented the widespread dissemination of gruesome pictures. A *New York Times* reader wrote an angry letter to complain about a photograph of a Kosovo massacre victim in October 1998. His brief comment — "This is not something I wish to see alongside my breakfast" — aptly characterizes a reading public that does not expect graphic violence in the responsible media.

In June 1998 an African American man named James Byrd was murdered in Jasper, Texas, by a white ex-con named John William King and two accomplices. It was determined that Byrd's body had been dragged from a pickup truck and that the body had been dismembered along the route: the head, neck, and right arm were severed from the torso. During King's trial in February 1999, the prosecution presented photographs that documented Byrd's suffering: his knees, heels, buttocks, and elbows were ground to the bone; eight of his left ribs and nine of his right were broken; his ankles were cut to the bone by the chains that attached him to the truck. A pathologist testified that Byrd's "penis and testicles [were] shredded from his body," and we learned, with horror, that "Mr. Byrd was alive up to the point where he hit the culvert and his head separated from his body." For months, the story of James Byrd's brutal slaying transfixed the nation.

No picture of James Byrd's corpse has ever been published. Indeed, when the *New York Times* interviewed several editors for a story on newspaper photography, none had seen the prosecution's photographs. In a strange twist of fate, however, King's own body served as evidence in the state's case against him: it seems he had a passion for racist tattoos. Prosecutors showed thirty-three slides and photographs of the images inscribed on King's body: a cross with a black man hanging from it, a swastika, the insignia of Hitler's SS, a woodpecker peeking out from a Ku Klux Klan hood, the Virgin Mary holding a horned baby Jesus, images of Church of Satan founder Anton La Vey, goat heads, Valentine hearts turned upside down, playing cards showing eights and aces (the dead man's poker hand), a dragon emblazoned with the words *Beto I* (the Texas prison where King was incarcerated from 1995 to 1997), the slogan *Aryan Pride,* and several allusions to "peckerwoods" — rednecks — in prison. (It had been reported earlier that King had a tattoo of Tinkerbell on his penis; the DA declined to mention this.) It was King's body, not Byrd's, that became an advertisement for white supremacy, and judging by the John William King tribute pages that have sprung up on the Internet, the advertisement has been successful.

It is not likely that anyone other than the lawyers, the jury, and the courtroom spectators will ever see the photographs that the court accepted as evidence. In the only well-known image of Byrd, he is wearing a Colorado Rockies baseball cap, looking directly into the camera. The most graphic picture appeared on the cover of the *Boston Globe* on June 12, 1998: it showed the dried blood that stained the Jasper street where Byrd's torso had been dragged.

The Byrd family was singularly gracious in promoting reconciliation and defusing racial hatred in the aftermath of the murder, and it may have been out of respect for their feelings that photographs of James Byrd's body were not published. Indeed, for about six weeks after the murder, the major story in Jasper was the tension between the Byrd family's desire for privacy and activists' eagerness for publicity. Even as reporters set up a media circus around the funeral, they wrote compassionately of the pain that politicians and political advocacy groups created for the Byrds. When the Klan gathered for a rally to distance themselves from John William King and his cohorts, and the Dallas-based New Black Panthers gathered to respond to the Klan, the Byrd family tried to remain above the fray. As the *Houston Chronicle* reported, "Byrd's family was uncomfortable with the idea of turning him into a national symbol, and would have preferred to have had a quieter service without the political rallying cries."

Despite these pleas, this case demanded national attention. In newspaper stories that pit a grieving family wishing for peace and quiet against a flock of politically motivated vultures intent on creating a self-serving spectacle, the true complexity of the Jasper saga is lost. It is despicable, of course, to use Byrd's funeral to promote racism, as the Klan did; and it is wrongheaded to use the event to promote armed self-defense, as the New Black Panthers did. But there are other considerations — considerations that are at least as compelling as a family's grief. Those who attempted to situate the murder in its historical context, while respecting the family's wishes for a degree of privacy, should be praised.

At James Byrd's funeral, Jesse Jackson said that "Brother Byrd's innocent blood alone could very well be the blood that changes the course of our country, because no one has captured the nation's attention like this tragedy." Jackson asked the town of Jasper to erect a monument in Byrd's memory, "as a tangible protest against hate crimes." I applaud Jackson's sense of urgency, but his proposal is in the wrong tenor. Indeed, I would suggest that Jackson went wrong precisely when he departed from his insight: spilled blood is a valuable representation of the search for justice. In his resolve to create a monument, he shifted his focus from blood to image, from body to stone.

The connections between the Till and Byrd lynchings are striking. Part of the evidence against King was an *Esquire* article on the Till lynching that he had kept in his apartment: this suggested that his actions were premeditated. Mamie Till Bradley spoke about the Jasper murder on a New York radio talk show; two weeks later, she held the hand of James Byrd's father at a Harlem memorial service. There were some coincidences, too: after the trial of Till's lynchers, newspapers reported that Till's father had been hanged in 1944, after he was convicted of rape and murder while stationed in Italy with the army; after the trial in the Jasper case, it was revealed that John William King's uncle had been acquitted of killing a gay man in 1939. More than half a century of hate crimes has ensnared these families — the Tills, the Byrds, the Kings — in America's quiet history of guilt and grief.

But there are disparities. In 1955, the American public learned about Emmett Till's life and they saw his death: the contrast between a vibrant youth and a violent end helped ignite the outcry that followed. In 1998, even as contemporary readers learned about James Byrd's life, they were denied the pictures that might have inspired a greater and more productive outrage. On February 24, 1999, the same day the *New York Times* reported the jury's verdict in the Jasper trial, it ran two other stories about hate crimes: in Virginia, a jury convicted a white teenager of burning a

cross on the lawn of an interracial couple; and in Louisiana, a
white man was sentenced to twenty years in prison for trying to set
fire to two cars and their African American occupants. Hatred is
far more pervasive than we would like to admit, and representa-
tions of it are critical to the education of the majority of white
Americans who believe that racism was a phenomenon that ended
sometime in the sixties.

Of course, publishing pictures of James Byrd's corpse might fan
the flames of white supremacy. There were reports of copycat
crimes within a week of Byrd's murder: in Louisiana, where three
white men taunted a black man with racial epithets while trying to
drag him alongside their car; and in Illinois, where three white
boys assaulted a black teenager in almost exactly the same way.
Three months later, New York City police officers and firefighters
parodied Byrd's murder by imitating it in a Labor Day parade float.
And while the trial was under way, a Washington, D.C., radio announcer — the "Greaseman" — responded to a clip from a song
by soul singer Lauryn Hill by commenting, "No wonder people
drag them behind trucks." (He was fired the next day.) In a climate
where people still respond to lynching with jokes and mimicry, pictures of James Byrd's body might have fed this evil appetite.

So why do we need to see the corpse? It is possible that pictures
of graphic violence still have the power to make an impression. At
least one member of the jury found the pictures of Byrd's body almost unbearable; she had to force herself to turn each page. Indeed, one Jasper resident suggested that the lynchers should be
sentenced to life in a cell "with pictures of James Byrd's body parts
pasted all over the walls" — expressing the hope that even the
murderers would find such images sickening. This kind of shock
therapy might work for the public at large. It would have been difficult for policemen and firemen in New York, or a DJ in Washington, to joke about the murder of James Byrd if their jokes summoned images of the horrific crimes they were taking so lightly.

These photographs could also turn the tide of history once
again. African American men have long been portrayed as comic
buffoons or dangerous criminals, and a large segment of this nation remains incapable of imagining black suffering. A study concerning the effects of race on the death penalty found that there is
"neither strong nor consistent" evidence of discrimination against

black defendants in death penalty trials. But the study also concluded that the race of the victim matters greatly in juries' decisions to sentence a murderer to death. Convicted murderers who kill a white victim are more than four times as likely to be condemned to death as those who kill a black victim. Only 8 whites have been executed for murdering black Americans since the death penalty was reinstated in 1977, but 123 blacks have been put to death for murdering whites. Predominantly white juries seem unable to sympathize with black crime victims. It is possible that this crime, fixed in memory, could transform the nation's moral imagination.

To have wounded the Byrd family any more would have been intolerable; and pictures of their relative's body would have wounded them. To have created conditions that satisfied the blood lust of white supremacists would have been criminal; and photographs of the remains of James Byrd would have given them glee. To lower the already low level of public discourse would be shameful; and publishing more photographs of violence is not likely to elevate it. But our primary concern must be to prevent another family from feeling as the Byrd family now feels; we cannot determine how best to combat hatred by focusing on the response of the most incorrigible purveyors of hatred. The past teaches us that images of terror — used responsibly — can foster a climate in which terror is no longer tolerated. I suggest that we aspire to the courageous example of Mamie Till Bradley, not the cautious compromises of newspaper editors who fear to offend their readerships. A citizenry alert to the horror of hate crimes would be compensation enough.

EARL SHORRIS

The Last Word

FROM HARPER'S MAGAZINE

CLAUDE LÉVI-STRAUSS had set me on the wrong path: first through his work, then in a brief correspondence, and finally during a visit to his office at the Collège de France. The anthropologist had written, in *Tristes Tropiques* and then in *The Savage Mind*, of broken cultures, of the inability of a culture ever to recover from a visit by an anthropologist, let alone Aristotle or the Beatles. And almost everything I saw at the end of the 1960s, when I thought I was writing in defense of American Indians, as he would have, had led to the title of my book: *The Death of the Great Spirit*.

I sent the galleys to Lévi-Strauss, who made no reply until he was inducted into the French Academy, where he spoke against this tragic view of American Indians, contending that indigenous people and languages *could* survive the incursion of European culture. His argument seemed flawed to me then, a romantic contradiction, for cultures cannot be both broken and whole.

The worm of my error was hidden by the immense suffering of the Indians. While traveling the country, visiting the vast and the tiny reservations where Indians lived, I had glimpsed resilience only once, in Anita Pfeiffer's Rough Rock Demonstration School on the Navajo Reservation. She taught the children in Diné, their own language, but I did not think it could last. And I may have been correct about the effect of one demonstration school on a nation of 100,000. In those days, most Navajo children entered school speaking Diné; a quarter of a century later, most of the children speak only English. There would seem to have been a death in the family.

The linguist Michael Krauss says that as many as 3,000 languages, comprising half of all the words on earth, are doomed to silence in the next century. According to Krauss, who, as the director of the Alaska Native Language Center, keeps count of dead and dying languages, 210 of the original 300 or more languages once spoken in the United States and Canada remain in use or in memory; 175 are spoken in the United States, including Alaska, and of these all but 20, perhaps fewer, cannot survive much longer. Only 250 languages in the entire world have at least a million speakers, considered the necessary safety level as globalization homogenizes every nation, every village, no matter how remote. Only languages with state sponsorship seem likely to survive: Spanish, French, English, Italian, etc. What of the more than 800 languages of Papua New Guinea? The 410 of Nigeria? The more than 300 in India? The unknown and as yet uncounted languages in the Amazon?

The effort to preserve these and other languages is furious, as linguists and their students across the earth record whatever they can find — songbirds or carrion, it matters not at all. Noam Chomsky made it clear that the study of language itself does not require more than a few examples here and there. Two are sufficient, three a plethora, because the same structure, he says, lies deep in the brain of every *Homo sapiens*. Given the apparent truth of Chomsky's work, only a few of the scholars in his footsteps involve themselves in keeping languages alive. The business of their lives does not encourage it: no university offers academic credit for the survival of the object of one's dissertation. Chomsky himself gives only mild assent to such work.

Increasingly, our own language, English, dominates the world. It is the lingua franca of science, the Internet, the movies, rock and roll, television, and even sports. The word for home run in Spanish is *jonrón*. Weekend in French is *week-end*. While the rest of the world complains that English is taking over its speech, just as the dollar took over the Ecuadorian currency, the forces of English Only grow stronger in the United States. On the other hand, English does not stand still, which frightens the devotees of English Only as well as those who admire diversity but cannot bear to part with a vocabulary that has fallen from general use. I count myself among the latter group. The letters *obs* in the dictionary pain me. Another word is passing; the vocabulary available to the writer is shrinking.

Hard to bear. A book reviewer in the *Boston Globe* once took me to task for using too many Greek words.

English, as it is generally spoken, appears to be losing more words than it gains. You need only look at the thin thesaurus that came with your word-processing program to see how the English language is losing its internal diversity. Nonetheless, ailing languages can be resuscitated; words can be brought back. The advent of another Shakespeare could vastly expand the vocabulary again. Cultures change, and languages survive by metamorphosis and the aesthetics of their creators. Who now speaks in the language of Beowulf?

The death of a language is another matter. When I was a young man, predictions of death came easily to me, but now I am at the age when men wish forevers, and I understand, as did Lévi-Strauss so many years ago, that dying languages may be saved. But how?

There are theoretical answers, of course. Yet had I not traveled to the Yukon and Kuskokwim deltas and the Yucatán-Campeche border to start in both places a Clemente Course in the Humanities,* such theories would have remained to me as elegant and remote as they once seemed. Whether what I saw in the jungle and on the tundra proves that languages should be kept alive, or that those we have all but lost can be brought back to life, will remain open to debate. But for me, the first question left the realm of mere theory in Alaska.

A bush pilot had flown me in a single-engine plane to the landing strip at Akiachak on the Kuskokwim River north of Bethel. I walked through the mud to the library in the tiny village. Our purpose was to hold a town meeting to gain consensus for the beginning of a Clemente Course in the Yup'ik language and culture. The meeting began with a conversation in English and Yup'ik. The chatter quickly gave way to a level of seriousness I had not expected. I know now that this is often the case with Yup'ik intellectuals and elders, but here it grew out of the mention of teaching philosophy in the course.

---

*A one-year university-level course that will be taught to poor young people at twenty-six sites this fall in the United States, Canada, and Mexico, the Clemente Course was described at length in the September 1997 issue of *Harper's Magazine*. The majority of the sites in the United States are supervised by Bard College.

The Yupiit listened first to elder Joe Lomack, the former chairman of the fifty-six Yup'ik villages, who spoke so eloquently and with such an astonishing vocabulary that they murmured *ii-i* in appreciation of the very words themselves. The others around the table were mainly scholars and professors, teachers of Yup'ik, but some of the words he used — the multiple suffixes, each one modifying meaning — were new to them, subtleties they had never heard before. As he spoke, there were pauses while they translated. It was the first time I had heard the problematic phrase "consciousness of the earth." I asked what it meant, and there ensued a conversation that was neither Thomistic nor Talmudic but Yup'ik.*

Peter Andrew, as old as Joe Lomack but not an elder, respected rather than revered, all angles and wrinkles under a red baseball cap, explained his idea of God by holding up a white Styrofoam cup half filled with coffee and with his other hand describing a circle beneath the cup. The professors, Cecilia Martz and Lucy Sparck, who prefer to use their Yup'ik names, Tacuk and Uut, translated his words, but it was not necessary, for Andrew had made a Judeo-Christian tableau of Styrofoam and circles in the air, with God above, separate and presiding over the universe. The Yupiit offered no argument, but neither did they agree. They were all Christians, Moravian or Roman Catholic, but God and God were not the same.

All the while grade school kids kept sticking their heads in through the side door of the library, whispering and giggling at the old people sitting around the table, then running out. More and more people joined the group around the table: nurses, schoolteachers, other members of the community. Everyone had the same silent response to Peter Andrew's words and gestures. Later, I came to understand why.

What he had described was *Agayun*, the Christian notion of God, which had arrived with the white missionaries in the nineteenth century. *Ellam Yua* is the Yup'ik phrase sometimes translated as God, though it has no such meaning. *Ella* means consciousness

---

*There are two dialects spoken in the Yukon and Kuskokwim deltas. Yup'ik is the most common, being spoken in all but two villages near the Bering Sea, where the people speak Cup'ik. The plural noun is Cupiit or Yupiit. I have conflated the dialects into Yup'ik and the plural Yupiit here, which is a common practice, even among the Cupiit/Yupiit, and not considered harmful.

and world or universe; in other contexts it means outdoors, weather, and air. *Yua* is the more complex notion, for it is the possessive form of *yuk*, which means person, and what can a person own in the natural world other than his or her personhood?

The Yupiit have a word for consciousness, another for mind, yet another for the physical brain itself; and then there is this business of *yua*. According to Tacuk, if a person sees a piece of driftwood on the frozen tundra, he or she must turn it over to expose the other side to the air. It is a gift to the *yua* of the wood. If one behaves that way toward the wood, perhaps one day the wood will return the favor. Hunting and gathering follow the same rules: the seal, salmon, herring, duck, moose, caribou, cloudberry, all things living and inanimate — all have this *yua*, and all are deserving of kindness. Was this pantheism, foolishness, a system of morals? What would Kant say? Was this a version of the categorical imperative "Act only on that maxim through which you can at the same time will that it should become a universal law"?

Ellam Yua — in two words ethics is born of metaphysics. Or is it the other way around?

I tried to understand the idea by comparing it to other notions that I knew better: the Mesoamerican Ometeotl, God of Duality, the Mother/Father; Tloque Nahuaque (the Close and the Near), meaning omnipresent.

"Seen and not seen," Uut said, as complete a description as the spoken and unspoken of a writer's world.

So the question was on the table: Of the three thousand languages that will be granted life beyond the middle of the next century, is Yup'ik a worthy candidate? Is there something unique and irreplaceable in other languages? In the words themselves? Is there a reductive and even murderous aspect hidden in Chomsky's view of language? If the survivors were limited to three hundred, would Yup'ik make the cut?

I went north, to Fairbanks, to see the man best prepared to answer such questions. Michael Krauss prowls the file cases of his office there like an Arctic bear. His passion is such that the Yupiit say of him, "Ask Michael one question and he will speak for three hours." Krauss has published an oral history of Anna Nelson Harry, one of the last speakers of Eyak. The last speaker, Marie Smith Jones, is eighty-one years old, and there is no other native speaker of Eyak on earth. What must she think of us? Neither T. S. Eliot nor Claude Lévi-Strauss knew how the world would end, but the last speaker of Eyak knows: it will end in silence.

The Eyak language and others are collected in manila folders on the open shelves of the steel cases in Krauss's office. Since these folders contain the pronunciation, grammar, and vocabulary of Eyak, you might say that the language has been preserved. He has made, in effect, a museum for Eyak. But this is not Alexandria; a museum is not a university now. A museum displays the peoples and works of times past, musty no matter how interactive or holographic. The American idea of manifest destiny was to consign the native peoples to museums, to make them as dead as yesterday.

Anthropologists and, until quite recently, most linguists have been content to embalm the dead, preparing languages for the file cabinet and the museum. This killing of a language happens exactly as one would expect: the weak must speak to the strong in the language of the strong. Eventually, the language of the weak loses its utility, except for secrets and the making of ill-fated rebellions. The Eyak fell into silence in the old way, caught between two larger nations on the south coast of Alaska, crushed to a whisper, until the whites came and reduced the Eyak to a single speaker. The Darwinian way of the world bears some responsibility, globalization does the rest: movies, television, Reeboks, and the Internet. The single most prominent feature of the landscape of a Yup'ik village on the Alaskan tundra is the dish for the cable television system. In the homes of the Yup'ik poor, as in the homes of all the poor of the United States, the television set plays during all waking hours.

Steven A. Jacobson, who operates the Alaska Native Language Center with Krauss, has produced both a Yup'ik Eskimo dictionary and a grammar, good work and useful, but what if the Yupiit had only the dictionary and the grammar without the question raised on the first day of Tacuk's class in Chevak, a little village a few miles from the Bering Sea, where the winter wind chill reaches one hundred degrees below zero and at least 69 percent of the residents collect some kind of federal assistance? Tacuk and her students were speaking in Cup'ik of the *ircinrraq* world. From dictionaries and anthropological works written by outsiders, one may gather little more than that this world is home to tiny creatures, perhaps half human and half animal. Although I was familiar with some of the English-language literature about the Yupiit, which mentions these little people, I had not read anywhere of an entire alternate world.

During the discussion, two elders who were teaching along with Tacuk spoke of directions in the *ircinrraq* world, one of which is known as *qetegkun*, the other as *qelakun*. Then they came upon a problem. The elders knew the meanings of the words in what they refer to as the "tangible" world. The words have to do with going toward or coming from the sea. But even the elders were not sure which meaning went with which word in the other world.

Yup'ik is an agglutinative language, in which base words change and become more subtle through the addition of postbases (or modifying suffixes), generally one or two, though half a dozen is not unusual. Eloquence depends on one's ability to use postbases, and the status of elder is conferred upon only those who speak eloquently. It appears that one's ability to use the language implies knowledge and even wisdom for the Yupiit. Knowing the meaning of words referring to the *ircinrraq* world is vital for an elder, but direction in the *ircinrraq* world does not follow the same rules as in "the tangible world." The elders of Chevak would have to consult with elders from other villages to learn the proper definitions of the words. There was nothing unusual about the quest; the Yupiit are a nation of lexicographers.

How can this be? They are hunters and gatherers, still living largely by subsistence on fish, seal, caribou, moose, and berries. Where are the books? How can one be a lexicographer without a book?

I spent several days with elder Joe Lomack. We ate together, flew in tiny airplanes, sat beside each other in meetings and during an Eskimo dance in Chevak. And all the while we spoke. I told him I was going to write about the question of the survival of languages, and he agreed to help. Joe Lomack's English is sufficient but not good. I know only a few words in Yup'ik, and I usually mispronounce them. I noticed that when I wanted to say *angalkuk*, which means shaman, what emerged caused great laughter among the Yupiit. They finally told me I had been saying "an old piece of shit." Uut tried desperately to help me to pronounce the word correctly, but every time I said it, she and Tacuk and the others could not help but laugh. Now I say "power person," which is a poor translation of *angalkuk,* but not funny.

Joe Lomack and I conversed according to the eccentricities of his English. He seldom made assertions, except to explain that a person who went out on the tundra in winter might "get dead." He told stories, and from the stories I was expected to infer theory. Joe had no interest in the bluntness of mere exposition; he made daily life into a series of fables, history into story, the world into an epic seen and not seen: literature.

As the days went by I learned his English, though he was not much interested in mine. The old man, slightly bent, round as innocence, bald, brown, his ancient eyes gone yellow, his lower lip full and thrust out as if in contemplation or pout, mesmerized Eskimo people with his oratory. *He* was their dictionary and their grammar: words.

If the words are lost, silenced, what of *Ellam Yua?* If no one thinks of the meanings of *Ellam Yua,* what of the words? Joe Lomack answered with long stories of what sounded to me like the uneventful routine of life on the tundra; he never used the abstract language I thought I needed to hear. I asked Uut if she would help me to ask the question in Yup'ik, thinking he had not understood me. "But he just answered it," she said. "Weren't you listening?"

Yup'ik immersion courses now extend through the fourth grade in southwestern Alaska. They will taper off as the children grow older, limiting the study of the language and thought to the primary schools. If the silence of the next generation begins at the entrance to complexity, the vision of those who believed in the manifest destiny of the United States and all it inherited from Europe will have been fulfilled: speakers of Yup'ik will have been reduced to the level of children.

Miguel León-Portilla, the renowned Mexican historian and translator, has said, "In order to survive, a language must have a use." He has worked for many years to keep languages alive in Mexico, which was once home to 240 different living languages. Like all Mexicans, he has had the nearby spur of the great, silenced Olmec and Teotihuacán civilizations.

In the city of Teotihuacán, which was one of the largest cities in the world in A.D. 600, speakers of various languages lived in neighborhoods of foreigners, but the language of the Teotihuacanos, perhaps 125,000 to 150,000 within the city itself and many more in the surrounding area, can no longer be heard. The pyramids and palaces stand in the sun, beautiful and magnificent, but no one speaks their language. For all the wonders of its structures, sculptures, coffers, and painted walls, Teotihuacán has no history other than in your imagination or mine.

Perhaps the death I saw from inside the preposterous garrison of youth must eventually occur, not only the *Death of the Great Spirit* in the Americas but the death of hundreds of languages in France, New Guinea, the British Isles, India: 3,000 within a hundred years, soon 5,750 — a catastrophe. To save languages, to provide some use, might require wars or nationalistic urges, the desperation to exist that drives the people of Wales and Catalonia. The example most often given of the rejuvenation of a language is Hebrew, which had been limited almost entirely to religious and scholarly use until it was made the state language of Israel.

In Guatemala, the K'iche' Maya struggle to stay alive in their own words. Humberto Ak'abal said, in one of a series of many brief poems in K'iche':

> Elaq'an chaqe
> ri ulew, ri che', ri ja'.
>
> Ri man a kowinan taj
> xa are ri', ri Nawal.
>
> Man kekuwinta wa'.

The work cannot be adequately translated. The best one can do is:

> They have robbed us
> of lands, trees, and water.
>
> They have not been able to take
> what belongs to the Nawal.
>
> Nor shall they.

Ak'abal's poem can only be explained, and then with difficulty, because the concept of the Nawal — one's other, not exactly one's alter ego, nor exactly one's spirit, but an other, parallel but of a different order, like and unlike, impossible to summon, found or encountered but never merely dreamed — has no English or Spanish equivalent. It cannot be appropriated by the more powerful, not even by military dictators or death squads. The Nawal has no natural enemy but silence.

To save the sound of the Nawal, the K'iche' are willing to die, and many have been shot, dismembered, burned, buried, or thrown into volcanoes in Guatemala. Perhaps the war itself worked on the Maya in some Nietzschean way, strengthening those it did not destroy. But the history of wars between cultures would argue that the K'iche' Maya were an aberration; the odds favored the Spanish-speakers and their helicopters.

For all that I admire the fortitude of the Guatemalans, their situation did not prove the error of what I had written in that long-ago book. Silence had not yet fallen in Guatemala or in Chevak; these were among the living languages, those that *could be* lost. The demonstration of my mistake began one afternoon in a tiny village in the low jungle of the Yucatán, where I went to do research for a book and found myself starting a Clemente Course in Maya.*

The situation requires a few words of history. The decline had gone on for many centuries. The Maya city-states had ravaged one another in terrible wars of betrayal and fire. Then the Spaniards invaded, burning the painted books, destroying culture for the sake of culture. The Maya resisted the Spaniards, attempted to secede from Mexico, prayed to Yum Chac when the Christian God and his saints failed to bring rain, but they could not stand up before the economic power of the henequen planters. Henequen, the agave fiber used to make rope and sisal matting, had finally been the worst enemy in that part of the peninsula.

The Maya descended into the depths of colonialism. The planters owned everything; they brought overseers to the peninsula to work the Maya like beasts in the fields all day and lock them into cells at night; they devoted themselves to silencing the language as a defense against rebels and other heretics; and all the while the

---

*Maya may be transliterated into roman letters or written in its original form. The key to pre-Hispanic Maya writing appears to have been deciphered by the Russian Yuri Knorosov, though many people since Knorosov have advanced the work. If they are correct, the writing is both phonetic, in the sense that symbols represent sounds, and ideographic, with symbols representing entire words. The technical term is logosyllabic.

henequen fields displaced the corn and beans and squash of the Maya farmers and the forage food and medicinal plants of the low jungle. Then the market for Mexican sisal collapsed in the mid-twentieth century and with it the economy of the henequen area. The people lived on government welfare until in the late 1980s President Carlos Salinas de Gortari ended the welfare, and nothing remained.

The professors and I traveled about two hours from Mérida to the village in a van driven by Raúl Murguía Rosete, who directs more than fifty programs for the United Nations Development Programme in the Yucatán. The faculty was to meet the students for the first time that afternoon. I had prepared the students, working in the comfort of Murguía's genius for organization and the trust he had earned from the villagers. The students and I had discussed the Socratic method, which would be used in the course, though the entire project had come near to ending in laughter after I told them I would be their *partera*, or midwife. Murguía had leapt in to explain that I meant *diálogo maieutico*, but even he could not help but laugh, so far was Socrates from the Yucatán and so inept was my explanation.

After the long trip in the air-conditioned van, the heat and humidity of the village staggered us. We went quickly into the shade of the single room of the building that had become our school. It was hotter inside. With neither glass nor screens in the windows and nothing except a sheet of metal to cover the entrance, the building gave shade but amplified the heat. It offered little protection. If a drop of sweetness spilled, the flies that came from the dilapidated remnant of a henequen-shredding plant covered the spot in no more than a minute. Mosquitoes sped through the windows as darkness fell. Some may have carried dengue fever.

The students sat around a long table, a place made for dialogue, but that evening there would be no midwifery. It was an orientation, a greeting, nothing more. Each member of the faculty would speak for his or her subject. Alejandra García Quintanilla of the Autonomous University of Yucatán, a historian and the head of our faculty, spoke first. She did not hide her hope to win the students over. It fluttered her hands and took her breath. The students watched her, perhaps more than they listened, for they had never seen anyone like her in this village of 1,400 people. They knew how the mestizos and whites of Mérida treated the Maya: the household slaps, the public insults, the ingenuity of exploitation. And here was a woman of Mérida, one with the word *doctor* before her name, who had come to a place without running water or sewerage and yet had dressed so carefully out of respect.

By the end of the afternoon the sun had turned the building into a sweat lodge. The skin of the students shone. In the humid air, perspiration had no cooling effect. The faculty sat in wet clothing, as if they had just come in from a salty rain. All but Miguel Angel May May. He was the last to speak. The students had been waiting for him. They saw him as the true test of these outsiders. They had been told that he would teach them their own language in their own place, as if they did not speak Maya to their own grandmothers every day. He had come to teach them their own secrets in a place not fifty yards from the house where don Romulo, the ancient *h-meen,* or doer, or shaman, kept his hollow cane filled with rattlesnake fangs and stingray spines and sang in the sweetest tones to cure the colic of infants and the madness of men and women as old as the *h-meen* himself. The students, some of them not yet twenty years old, trusted the *h-meen*'s herbs but not his words; a distance had developed in the henequen areas, a silence had grown among the generations.

After he was introduced, May May, a writer, critic, and professor in the Academy of Maya Languages, paused for a moment, as if to acknowledge the silence. Then he stepped out of the shadow of the western wall of the building into the center of the room. His white guayabera reflected the last of the light. He was as cool as old stone; more brown, more Maya, against the white of the guayabera; taller than the other Maya, young yet with flecks of gray in his hair. He greeted the students in their language as their language had been spoken before the henequen planters, before the Caste War. He spoke easily; every accent, every tone of the complex language came clean and clear into the room. He laughed; he made them laugh. He walked the length of the room, words pouring from him as if he meant to hold off the silence forever.

Almost two years have passed since that steamy evening. In the village, where only 120 people have work and those who work earn no more than eighty-five cents a day, the students speak of the literature of their ancestors. They know the poetry and stories and those works the ancient Maya called histories of the future. May May taught them the difficult and subtle sounds of their language again, using the ring of coins on stone and the clack of bricks and the conk of wood. He gave them writing as well as reading, and the other teachers built the culture again in the minds of the students, starting from the corn, as everything among the Maya starts with corn, the one grain that cannot live without the help of man.

At first, the eroticism of the Kay Nicte, the Flower Song, embarrassed them: naked beside a stone pool set them to giggling, but then the gorgeous language of the old Maya poem reached them, and they understood that language also carries meaning in the sound, and at last they knew that they are descendants of singers and also sing.

The students read the *Popol Vuh*, a work with deep pre-Hispanic roots sometimes known as the Maya Bible, and spoke of the suffering that lies behind the making of art. They understood the homologous lives of heroes and corn. They learned the fate of the ancient men of wood, those early technologists who were destroyed when the things they had made to serve them rose up and tore them apart.

Soon, other villages heard of this antidote to silence and asked to be part of it. One evening, I met with a group of old men in a town north of Mérida. They asked for help in putting off the silence, but not with children's words, kitchen Maya, the overseer's vocabulary of force. That was another silence. The old men knew; they remembered. They wished to be philosophers, mathematicians, poets, artists. One old man sang songs he had composed, but they were in Spanish. The others screwed up their faces.

What could they hope for now? Why did the old men want to know? Linguists divide the world of languages into four classes in descending order: those spoken by children, those spoken by people of childbearing age, those spoken only by people beyond childbearing age, and those spoken or remembered only by a few old people. Many of the languages of the world are in the last three categories, apparently moribund.

Then why did the old men, moribund themselves — hobbling, toothless, aged leather valises full of bones — want the words? "Will you come back next week?" they had asked.

"I cannot."

"Then who will tell us our stories?"

"Perhaps . . . ," I had said, offering a common Spanish antidote to despair.

I think now that every language has its *Ellam Yua*. The consolation the old men sought existed only in Maya. Every epithet implied a unique set of attributes, every sound described a unique Being. It is not merely a writer's conceit to think that the human world is made of words and to remember that no two words in all the world's languages are alike. Of all the arts and sciences made by man, none equals a language, for only a language in its living entirety can describe a unique and irreplaceable world. I saw this once, in the forest of southern Mexico, when a butterfly settled beside me. The color of it was a blue unlike any I had ever seen, hue and intensity beyond naming, a test for the possibilities of metaphor. In the distance lay the ruined Maya city of Palenque, where the glyphs that speak of the reign of the great lord Pacal are carved in stone. The glyphs can be deciphered now. Perhaps. Only perhaps, for no one knows what words were spoken, what sounds were made when Pacal the Conqueror reigned. It may seem cryptic or even Socratic to say, but, in truth, only spoken words can be heard.

There are nine different words in Maya for the color blue in the comprehensive *Porrúa Spanish-Maya Dictionary* but just three Spanish translations, leaving six butterflies that can be seen only by the Maya, proving beyond doubt that when a language dies six butterflies disappear from the consciousness of the earth.

BERT O. STATES

On Being Breathless

FROM THE GETTYSBURG REVIEW

MY ONLY NIGHTMARE occurs rarely and almost always at high altitudes. But now and then I have a really convincing variation at sea level, where I live. I am usually in a dimly lighted room; there is a vague presence of people, activity of some sort in progress, but the main event that takes place is what you might call a personification of my attempt to breathe. The dream is divided into two parts: inhaling and exhaling. When I exhale everything is fine until I approach the bottom of the "stroke"; when I try to inhale it seems that the sides of my lungs are stuck together, producing a sensation of extreme vertigo, as if my brain were a centrifuge spinning in a furious upward spiral. And all of my dream characters, if there are any, simply disappear, as if thrown against the wall of my skull. It is hard to describe because the details are mostly sensory rather than visual. The sensation is similar to swimming under water to the point of oxygen exhaustion, at which point one experiences the so-called "rapture" of suffocation. I am always snapped awake immediately and take a deep breath. Presently I fall back asleep, and the same thing occurs within a few minutes. I bottom out; then the vertigo swirls me into a panic. Then again — again — and again; if it is really bad, I simply get up and weather the night sitting upright in a chair.

Apart from the vertigo the most distressing feature of the dream is that I have no awareness of having a body. I have turned, as it were, into a pair of thinking lungs. Now and then I have the impression that someone is trying to reach me — to draw me into a conversation, see how I am, or bring me back to what reality there is. With only that exception, my entire sensory apparatus, my consciousness, consists of an attempt to breathe and the terrifying sense that it is my mind that is inhaling and exhaling, and whirling at immense speed, and that while doing so my thinking (all there is of me) is being scrambled and spun out into a granular, cotton-candy fuzziness. All in all, it is the kind of dream I imagine a blind asthmatic might have on a bad night following a near-drowning experience in an ocean cave.

It has since been determined that this dream is related to a condition called COPD, or Chronic Obstructive Pulmonary Disease, which has since been stabilized following surgery for a badly deviated septum. A happy result of that operation was that, without the slightest exercise of self-discipline or abstinence, I lost all interest in smoking, a lifetime habit that began at the age of fifteen. In any case, my doctor assures me that smoking was the main cause of my COPD, though I find it curious that I was an especially lung- or air-oriented person long before I started to smoke. I imagine that the deviated septum was a contributing factor, though my first real "airless" memory dates back to a playground episode that took place in my boyhood. It occurred (probably) on a Saturday morning at the rec field in my hometown. Seven or eight of us — including several older boys — were wrestling, following a game of touch football. I was the new kid on the block, having just moved into town from the country. As often happened, when we ran out of interesting things to do, our play degenerated into a game of King of the Hill. The objective was to form a human pyramid with our bodies, and to succeed, each player wanted to be able to escape the bottom and remain on top. Being smaller in size, I sank to the bottom of the pile, unable to move — and unable to breathe except in frantic gasps. I could hear the laughter and joy of my friends above me, but I could do nothing: I was submerged in a sea of levity made up of companions oblivious to my panic.

Years later, in college, I read Camus' description of the "Little Ease," a prison cell just slightly larger than a normal-sized human body in a fetal position. Into this space the prisoner was more or less stuffed, unable to sit properly, to stand, or to stretch out — every possible position compromised by the ingenious frugality of the design — and thereafter ignored for the duration of his sentence, except, one would imagine, for feedings and elimination.

This seemed to me the most incomprehensibly evil thing one human being could do to another. When I read about the Little Ease I was taken back to my pyramid on the playground. And when I think of either, it is always with a revulsion that asserts itself in a full body shiver. Over the years the two memories have been a rich source of spin-off dreams, chiefly of falling into a pit of granular, semiliquid sand, as if I were being blended into the earth; or of simply being trapped, sometimes in the rear seat of a Volkswagen, beneath the bodies of high-spirited friends who are trying to see how many people can be crammed in.

On the lighter side of this same history, when I was in junior high, about the same time as the pyramid incident, one of my favorite radio programs was called something like *Jack Westaway, Deep Sea Diver*. It began, if memory serves, with some sort of *Jaws*-y music beneath the sound of bubbles and amplified breathing, clearly coming from the interior of a diver's helmet. Then we hear Jack say on the intercom, "I'm on the bottom," and the theme music bursts into full wind-in-the-rigging flower, soars for a time under billowed sail, then dips under for the announcer's elongated "Jaaaack West-a-wayyyy!" followed by the "brought to you by the fine folks who make whatever-it-was." Every week Jack would be required to combat sea marauders, save a foundering ship, or rescue a fellow diver trapped in the jaws of a giant clam. What was so riveting about the adventures was the thought (which I sketched in scores of drawings) that the divers were connected to the ship by thousands of yards of rubber hose, at once a lifeline and a long, thin, constant invitation to peril. It was breathtaking to sit before our Philco radio, plosively exhaling in rhythm with the bubbles, while imagining all that sea intervening between Jack and his friends and the airy azure world of the surface ship where all usually went well. And always, always, there was the unbearable thought of being confined in the brass-domed cage of a helmet slightly larger than my head with the infinite Deep enviously rubbing its back against the barred window plate, waiting for an error (hence my nomination for the most terrifying movie of the period, *The Man in the Iron Mask*). And of course every week the lines would get snagged, fouled, or pulled taut by a monstrous cuttlefish, or the metal door of a submerged wreck in which Jack was working would threaten to clank shut and sever the line. But the episode I recall most vividly involved a struggle between Jack and a rogue diver at incredible depth, where the pressure was something like a trillion pounds per square inch. The audience had been warned in advance of the unspeakable consequences of making a mistake at this depth, and somehow, in the fight, the rogue's pressurized suit sprang a leak (no fault of Jack's, I am sure) and the air streamed upward in a great vascular swoosh as his suit deflated to an unnatural size. Inside we heard the usual bubbles, desperate breathing, then muffled screams, over furious nothing-can-save-you-now music, as the diver's body — all this reported on the intercom ("Good God! What a way to die!") — was slowly sucked, bones and all, into his own headgear like so much canned tuna, as densely packed as a neutron star.

Maybe this is funny now, but it was not funny to me then. In those days stories of the sea thrilled and horrified me. The sea, an undifferentiated, inexhaustible singularity, was the ultimate lurking place of pulmonary terror.

Since then I have read Sherwin Nuland's book *How We Die,* which maintains that, although we may die of various causes — heart disease, cancer, AIDS, Alzheimer's, murder, suicide, old age — there is but one true killer that finishes us off: the eventual breakdown of the body's oxygen cycle. Death, then, is a complex form of suffocation in which each organ "drowns" at its own individual time in the cycle, depending on the disease; for what destroys life in a drowning (to draw a subtle distinction) is not the intake of fluid but the progressive deoxygenization of the body, each phase of which is reliant on the others. In most slower cases, then, death is not a single event but a chain of little deaths, each one irreversible, leading to the final one physicians call clinical death — which simply means that the great, bountiful twin banks of the heart and the lungs, having suffered the last withdrawal of their investors, have closed shop forever.

I read this book in the light not only of my own pneumatic history, but having just witnessed such a breakdown when my sister died in a hospital in Monterey. Dying, I now understand, is a nightmare from which there is no awakening. If dreaming is a rebirth after the "counterfeit death" of sleep, the nightmare is the threat of death that occurs within dreams. Among the leading characteristics of nightmares is almost always some form of radical incapacitation, danger, or extreme loss of control, freedom, or life. The best term for this state of mind is panic, which the dictionary defines as groundless, pandemic, contagious, or extravagant efforts to secure safety. Whatever the nightmare is about, it is finally its potential for killing the dreamer that causes the panic. And the usual logic of these dreams is that, as with the race between Achilles and the tortoise, death (or the Monster) always catches up. If death is defined as the terminal closure of all the body's "branch" operations — or what Miroslav Holub more colorfully calls a molecular farewell symphony — then the nightmare is its analogue in the dreamworld. The nightmare enacts a descent into what Tolstoy called "the black sack." The difference is that — presumably — in dying one does not get jolted awake en route.

Nuland quotes Tolstoy's *Death of Ivan Ilyich* — the most compelling account I have read (including Sartre's story "The Wall") of what must go through a dying person's mind. The quote occurs in connection with the charade that people play out when someone in a household is in the process of dying ("We knew — she knew — we knew she knew — she knew we knew" is how Nuland phrases it), though probably no one says a thing. Tolstoy sends Ilyich through an excruciating version of this scenario: as cancer chases the air out of his systems, one by one, his family maintains its fiction of ignorance and well-being. But in the end the pain miraculously stops for Ilyich, and there is a light.

> "So that's what it is!" [Ilyich] suddenly exclaimed aloud. "What joy."
> . . . Something rattled in Ilyich's throat, his body twitched, then the gasping and the rattle became less and less frequent.
> "It is finished!" said someone near him.
> He heard these words and repeated them in his soul.
> "Death is finished," he said to himself. "It is no more."
> He drew in a breath, stopped in the midst of a sigh, stretched out, and died.

The physiological part of this description is almost identical to what I have seen in the hospital at first hand. As for the metaphysical part, Nuland is not so sure, and I am afraid Nuland's skepticism is more convincing than Tolstoy's strange faith that there is light on the other side of the black sack, or anything more than a dulling of pain through increasing doses of morphine, together with the gradual slipping of consciousness into an undifferentiated numbness, similar perhaps (if we are lucky) to the consciousness we attribute to healthy vegetables. Certainly there can be nothing left of thinking of the sort that would allow one to say (to oneself), "Death is finished," a pretty sophisticated conception at that point in Ilyich's life, since the brain, by then, has suffered the same loss of oxygen as the rest of the body. But of course, we do not know. We will never know — or more conservatively, we will never be able to report what we may eventually come to know just before the light goes out — or on, as the case may be. It is nice to think that it goes on, and it costs nothing to think that.

The term *nightmare* has very specific meanings. Psychologists differentiate it from night terrors, daymares (daydreams that go berserk), and the incubus attack (in which a beast sits on your chest, as in Henry Fuseli's painting). Psychologists have to make these distinctions, I gather, in order to know what species of terror they are treating. But I think in experiential terms it comes down to something simpler — that the nightmare (and its various subspecies) is linked inevitably to death and dying, whether it be your own death or the death of a loved one, which is really a personal death at one remove. Death is the true source of the nightmare in the sense that any extreme loss of control or insufferable apprehension and anxiety has inevitably to be based on the fear of its leading all the way to the end. At the back of every pain is the possibility that it will not stop (this is why dentists always tell you, "Just a few more seconds"), and even steady pain characteristically seems to increase with duration in psychometric increments.

This general idea is not new with me. In Freud and Norman O. Brown, for example, one commonly reads that there is a deep connection between anxiety and death. Anxiety, Brown says, "is a response to separateness, individuality, and death," the three being, from one point of view, synonyms of each other. What is death, or at least dying, but at once a progressive separation from the world and the achievement of one's complete individuality — as in Sartre's claim that at the moment of our death we are finally ourselves: no more than our past. Most descriptions of anxiety, at the panic stage at least, could scarcely be distinguished from nocturnal nightmares — and I find it hard to separate real physical pain and trauma from the "mental" pain and trauma one experiences in dreams and in all nightmares. If I were to fall off a cliff, or out a high window, my situation could be described as traumatic in the physical sense (something is definitely happening to my body), but I would also (for a brief interval) have awful thoughts about what is happening. I cannot see how these thoughts — based as they are on physical truths — are much different in intensity from thoughts I might have while dreaming of being in the jaws of a Great White. And the bottom line in both cases would be the fear, or certainty, that I was about to die — and of course the panic that goes along with that.

Thus someone who has been held hostage by a maniac is entitled to say, on rescue, "It was a nightmare." Technically, it was not, because nightmares are dreams; but there is a figural truth in the description and it is that the person's survival has had his undivided attention. There may be other kinds of nightmares — about financial ruin or failing exams — that have little to do with death, but the real nightmares are soaked in panic, and panic is not panic until everything is on the table. Nightmares are pinpoints of total-fear concentration, sudden holes in one's pressurized suit in the deep of a dream.

Not long ago, I had an experience that aroused further thoughts about dream, reality, and nightmare. At about four o'clock on a Friday afternoon in early June, my wife and I heard a loud explosion, much like a cherry bomb being thrown into a metal drum. Then we heard a cry for help coming from the vicinity of the power station at the foot of our property. I ran down the easement road and saw a young boy trying to help another boy out of the juniper bushes at the foot of the electrical tower just outside the Edison plant. Immediately, my wife went back to the house to call 911. The boy in the bushes was struggling in a strand of barbed wire, one of seven such strands strung in a flat band around the tower at about seven feet to discourage climbing.

My immediate thought was that he had tried to climb the tower and had fallen because he could not get past the wire, one of the strands of which had slashed the flesh inside his left arm in five or six places. But then I saw that his face was an ashen gray and covered with what I took to be debris from the juniper bushes, which had broken his fall. His clothing was ripped and snagged in various places from his shirt to his trousers, much as if it had been splashed by acid. I managed to get him out of the wire strand and to stop the flow of blood, surprisingly small, by closing his arm at the elbow. His left arm was, like his face, gray in color. At this point I sent the other boy up to my house to tell my wife that a paramedic unit would be necessary.

What I did not know at the time is that the boy had actually reached the top of the tower, which was some forty feet in height, and somehow managed to short out the 66,000-volt lines apparently without touching them directly. Otherwise there could have been no explosion. He had been "radiated" by the discharge rather than been plugged into it, which would probably have electrocuted him immediately. The explosion had blown him backward off the tower and down into the barbed wire which cushioned (some cushion!) his fall. And he landed in the juniper bushes less than a foot from the asphalt walkway.

No one who was on the scene, or at the hospital, can understand how he survived a fall from that height under these conditions. By all estimates he should have been killed at the top of the tower and "again" when he struck earth. I knew nothing of this at the time. I laid him down in my lap on the asphalt, tried to calm him, and only then noticed that the back of his head was singed, and that his face, in addition to being gray, was covered with little epidermal patches, much as if he had been caught in the swoosh of a small gas-stove explosion. The hospital later found that he had electrical burns over 40 percent of his body and sent him on to the Sherman Oaks Burn Center for further treatment and skin graft surgery. More than a month later, he was still in the hospital expecting further surgery.

What holds my interest is what passed between us during my time alone with him. Thinking that he had fallen roughly six feet with minor flesh injuries, I was not surprised that he was so lucid, garrulous, and able to walk. When the paramedics came he gave them his name, age, and street address and answered all of their questions without the least hesitation. But in the ten or fifteen minutes we were alone, before the emergency unit arrived, he kept repeating variations of one sentence over and over: "Is this a dream?" or "This is a dream, isn't it?" or "Tell me this is a dream." I assured him that it was not and tried to calm him by telling him he was very lucky, that he was going to be fine, and would be able to tell his friends about his adventure, and so on. This would satisfy him for a moment at best, and then he would ask again, "This is a dream, isn't it?"

I do not really know how to account for this single-mindedness (the technical name for dream consciousness). On one level the boy's reaction was a common idiomatic response to experiences that are not quite believable (the "pinch me" syndrome). But I think the young boy meant it — he did not know whether he was experiencing a dream or reality. I think his shock and fall had knocked the reality out of him, the sense that he was *there,* and an older stranger was inexplicably, but undeniably, trying to calm him over something that had just happened. He was awake, as one always is in a dream, and everything had the vagueness of dream. Then too, his request, "Tell me this is a dream," suggests that on some level of awareness he knew he had been through something bad but that it was not over; he did not know what it was but wished it could all be erased, as the panic of all dreams is mercifully erased on waking. It was reality, and it was not reality; or to put it another way: it was reality to the tenth power, intensified, electrified, drained of all auxiliary features, with none of the keen sensory discriminations I was feeling, as the full weight of his body in my lap pressed my left ankle into the asphalt.

It seems likely, then, that the only other experience he could identify with his fall was that of a dream, which is always followed by a return to the real world through the decompression chamber of surfacing, or waking up. This is all speculation on my part, and it is drawn mostly from certain personal experiences of the same kind, among them the morning of my near suffocation in the piling-on incident. Somehow I seem to collect these incidents and align them on a certain frequency of memory, like a friend of mine who collects crucifixion jokes. They get processed in my hippocampus, I think, and marked with a black tag. They are not linked together in my mind in the way that Freud was able to trace the images of a particular dream backward to a single determinant, something traumatic that started it all rolling in infancy. Rather, they are clusters of memories that run in parallel; they are like a gradually accumulating flock of birds that have that uncanny ability to perform the most elliptical maneuvers in unison without breaking the rhythm of flight. I have always wondered which bird in the flock is the one that initiates the banking movement or the deep swoop, or the sudden sharp turn in the sky, that all the other birds, even those on the periphery, can follow so simultaneously, like a celestial drill team. So too I wonder which experience in my life began the flock of steadily accumulating memories having to do with small, panic-inducing, airless places. Which part of my temperament opened me to this preoccupation, rather than another? Why is breathlessness, in any form, so chilling a thought to me?

It so happens that there is a first episode in my own case, but I do not know what it has to do with breathlessness. My parents often told me the story that at my birth an inebriated nurse at the community hospital failed to secure a hot water bottle tightly and the water drained out through the towel onto my chest and upper body, scalding me so badly that my survival was doubtful for several days. I am told by my mother that the pain of hearing my screams as she bathed my blisters in salt water was one of the most unbearable experiences of her life. Like the boy on the tower, however, I was not there to appreciate it. But needing some representation of such an event, I have evolved a version of it in my memory's eye: I have, as it were, mythologized it, given it my own hypothetical actuality. I see the room where it took place, and I see the crib. I see this screaming little thing, and I have some notion of what she looked like, this woman (who was fired for negligence, her life thereafter following a different course "because of" me — and where, I wonder, are her children now?). This is the brain's stubborn rule: it has to spell things out, draw a picture, and this is one reason, I suspect, that we have dreams and nightmares to account for feelings caused by our flocks of traumas, fears, and pleasures. And for reasons I do not pretend to understand, this event is there at the center of my ongoing thoughts about breathing, rather as if it were the hook on which everything after it could be hung. Perhaps the connection is obvious (death again); perhaps it is subtler than I think (the infant screaming with first breath).

There was a curious development following the tower incident. The boy's companion began bringing his friends past our house to the scene of the accident. I do not know how often this happened, but we saw him at least twice riding with a friend down the easement road, which is just thirty feet from our back deck. He apparently took them down, one at a time, to the tower to tell them the story, which obviously went through junior high school society like a brushfire. On the last occasion I heard him say (as they passed on bicycles), "Don't tell anyone I told you about it." I would give a great deal to have overheard what unfolded as they stood under the tower, like two boys out of Mark Twain, and he related the event he was the only person to witness. It has idly crossed my mind, not at all maliciously but with some distinct memory of boyhood practice, that he may even have "charged admission" for his story. Or perhaps his reward was just in being envied for having been there on that afternoon when the summer was so explosively interrupted.

More than anything else, though, it would be interesting to know how the boy himself (who is thirteen) will deal with his tower experience in years to come. How often will he tell the story, how will it change in the retelling, and what other experiences will it collect about it in the course of his life? Will his mind eventually convert it — irony of ironies — into what he wanted it so desperately to be on that afternoon? And what form might such a dream or nightmare take, since (in a manner of speaking) he was not really *there* when it happened to him, but off in a dream, feeling dream-pain? Whose version will he use? Will it become, finally, a fixation, the ur-fixation around which other experiences of its kind will cluster? What, for example — for the rest of his life — will he think about electricity or about towers?

Two years ago, my pulmonologist, while making his physical examination, asked me about the scars on my chest and upper arm, and I told him the hapless story of my birth.

"Did your family sue?" he asked.

"No," I said. "My family got poor advice."

"Pity," he said, smiling. "Today you could have bought the hospital."

I asked him if the scalding might have had something to do with my COPD. "No," he said thoughtfully. "The two things aren't related." I am satisfied that he is right, from the physiological point of view. But physiology and mind are two different things, and just as the attributes and powers of water are different from the elements of oxygen and hydrogen that compose it, so there is a sense in which all these things do have something to do with each other, disconnected as they are. They are all there, in mind, in a sort of fraternal order of pain. And the dream, and its fellow traveler the nightmare, is the one mental agency designed to put them all together in an exquisite sensory correlation. So some night, on one of those mercifully rare occasions when my mood and my physiology are running in sync and something fresh from my day residue opens the gate a crack, they will all come roaring like bats out of their caves, flock together in my sky, and perform the breathless flight of my undoing.

WILLIAM T. VOLLMANN

Upside Down and Backward

FROM FORBES ASAP

I

UPON THE shallow curved bowl within the camera obscura, the gray sea began to turn. It had been turning before, but until my pupils dilated I saw nothing but darkness. A circular railing protected me from falling into this living picture of organized daylight projected into that concavity. Came the Cliff House, out of focus because it was too near. I might have seen two lovers wandering hand in hand into the Musée Mecanique.

Then the great lens swiveled severely up and about, the beach now offering itself to my gaze, more lovely in similitude than it actually was: brown and silver, long and lonely, bordered by an unstable line of foam from the streaks of the blue-gray sea, which in their pale and silent motions were streaks of life, streaks of time. Beachwalkers got doubled by their reflections in the wet sand. Now the Seal Rocks went swimming by like hoary, barnacle-encrusted seashell creatures. I saw a blurred bird. Then the lens tilted upward so that the boundary stretched between sea and sky.

The real world's horizon has haunted me, although I've looked at it for forty years.

Shouldn't a walk on San Francisco's Ocean Beach have felt more vivid than any projected image of it? But the focused transcendence of the display, set off by darkness, forced me to see. Every time I paid my dollar to enter the chamber on the ocean's edge, I lost myself in the contemplation of movement and space. Neither pacing nor selection was mine. My imagination had to follow the lens.

The camera obscura focused my attention on a certain scene, at a certain angle of view, at a certain tempo. Like it or not, that was how I had to look. I'd glimpse a seal, and then the picture had left the seal behind, and I found myself thinking more about the animal because I hadn't gotten to gaze at it as long as I wanted. But in compensation for the loss of the seal, here was the most marvelous wave I could ever remember . . . forgetting it immediately, I saw another marvelous wave.

When, at last, I stepped outside, back into the brilliant sea fog, I felt a greater awe for this world into which I could now venture almost as freely as did the great lens in its stately whirling. If I descended to the beach, the crunching of my heels in the wet sand was real enough, but I remained within a splendid dream. Anyone inside the camera obscura could see me. I was a part of that pure, pale music-box world that my baby daughter could still perceive — she still embraced her own shadow; she waved goodbye to dogs and characters on television screens; all was real to her, and all new.

II

Sometimes my daughter grows heavy in my arms, and I'll set her down. Fearing that I might never pick her up again, she weeps in grief and terror. I hope to teach her faith in my constancy. As long as I live, I'll always love her. But her certainty of my solicitude, if I succeed in conveying it to her, will doubtless arrive alongside a certainty of the law of gravity. In time she'll simply think: Yes, that's Ocean Beach. It will be time for the camera obscura.

Freshness wilts. We arrive at a spuriously eternal kind of knowledge: When I open my fingers, the pen will always fall from my hand. I am alive; everything I see is familiar to me; therefore nothing new will disturb my activities. I will never die. These propositions are equally parochial. Knowledge proves them so.

But the strange thing about knowledge is that the more one knows, the more one must qualify perceived certainties, until everything oozes back into unfamiliarity. The poems of Mandelstam,

the body of a lover, an Arctic landscape, these are composed of ingredients as basic as the chemical elements — Mandelstam must
use the same letters of the alphabet as every other Russian! — and
yet the words grow new; the world renews itself.

III

For several years, I made a regular pilgrimage to the camera
obscura (it's closed now). After the first time I knew "how it would
be," of course, and yet I wanted that strangeness. The fact that it
became a familiar unfamiliarity did not detract from it a single jot.
If anything, I was able to enjoy the delights of its world more in-
tensely than ever.

I haven't felt the need to look into the camera obscura now for
two decades. Lately this other world, the one outside the camera
obscura, has come to seem so real and strange to me. Could that
be because I finally believe in my own death? My profession as a
journalist is occasionally dangerous. Many of my assignments require me to interview terrorists, travel to pariah nations and war
zones, and other oddities.

I have seen some very sad things. I have almost died violently. I
am ready to die at any time. My affairs are in order; all I fear is torture, and the secondary torture it would cause those who love me.
Every day, I try to think about what I have seen in the world I perceive. The lens of my vocation has shown me the agony of a Cam-
bodian woman whose entire family was beaten to death with shov-
els by the Khmer Rouge. The survivor, who had to watch, dwells
alone with their screams. I don't want to forget her, or them, for
the same reason that I prefer not to forget the intricate streak patterns of the ocean within the camera obscura. This is what is real.
Those who live as though any part of the world does not exist lose
some of their own existence. What is the dull boom of mortar fire
far away across the border? Or the shit stench of Colombian refugees in a Red Cross compound. The great lens turns and turns. I
see a Tasmanian cloud peak; a Jamaican ghetto boy standing in no
man's land making defiant gang signs, but the other side holds
fire; or the Burmese prostitute combing her hair into something as
rich and dark as some tincture of shadows; she hooks her shim-
mery black tights over her feet. The great world whirls.

IV

How can it be that the first woman I ever loved is now dead of breast cancer, leaving three small children to grieve without comprehending? How can it be that my own dear child, whose birth I witnessed, was born only so that she will someday die? It is all such a mystery to me, and only by studying a lover's body, or an Arctic landscape, or gazing through other focusing lenses of strange knowledge, can I hope to see a little farther within that mystery.

I will never solve the mystery. I know that now. Could it really be explicated, except through the elliptical means of poetry, why we were born or why the camera obscura's ocean is quite literally marvelous? I would follow that rotating horizon in every direction if I could. I would make my own way, take my own time. I would fall into error many times, to be sure, but I would go my own way. For what purpose do we walk this earth? Nobody can tell me truly. I cannot tell myself.

V

Not only does the quest to the mystery require the skills of the hunter, the laborious patience of a hod carrier, and the faith of a saint, but murderers lie in wait along the path. Their names are Necessity, Egotism, Misconception, Distraction, and Censorship. And now they've crept into the camera obscura itself. Within that bowl on which the light of reality was projected, they've over-painted the blankness with their own spurious clouds and seagulls, whose garish falseness occludes the delicacy of the world I came to see. They've murdered my view. When I complain, they promise me that the imitation will soon be better than the real thing, and that I'll thank them in the end. Soon they'll seal off the aperture to the sky, the better to insert their own movies behind the lens. They'll allow me to choose the color of their ocean — "I preferred it when it was gray" — "Next week you'll be able to have a gray ocean, too! And you'll be able to make it stormy. . . ."

VI

In our country, the murder of reality has proceeded not without pleasure to the victims. We have spun the lens to so fast a velocity that only the most fluorescent patterns, and of only the greatest crudity, can register on the gazer's perception. Well, why not? People like bright colors.

After the hydrogen bomb, perhaps the most dangerous American invention is television.

VII

Dostoyevsky tells me that the only way to make meaning out of the suffering of others is to assume responsibility for it. If a man is murdered on the other side of the earth, then I stand guilty of that murder, for I am a human being just as the murderer is. What an insane principle! When I first read it, it terrified me, and I rejected it. I still reject it. But it hoards a strange purity. The soul must enter the camera obscura to read *The Brothers Karamazov*. Slowly, the soul's pupils dilate in that dreary, muddy, provincial nineteenth-century darkness. It takes many pages and characters for Dostoyevsky to say what he needs to say. He is not to be rushed.

VIII

The lens whirls over a map of Afghanistan. We see points of light. These mark the sites where our cruise missiles have struck. Whom did we kill and why? No matter — the lens must move on. What do our new enemies say about us in their capital? Well, we can imagine — or more likely, we can't imagine — and it's time to move on.

Here is Kabul at night: headlights, lanterns within wheeled fruit stands, people in buses packed tightly together like the inmates of mass graves, turbaned Talibs sauntering down the street, lords of all they survey, everything dark and dim, then just dark with snow falling. Women in blue and black *burqas* are walking home. I hear the rattle of handcarts, and now it's darker and darker. My lens moves on. Have I "understood" Afghanistan? Not by a long shot. But at least I saw it. I didn't just watch it on CNN.

IX

"Do you think they're having a good time?" I ask the waitress at the Las Vegas Millennium Café. "Those people on the slot machines, when the payoff comes out, they don't even look . . ."

"Oh, they're always grouchy," she says.

"I feel sorry for them. How about you?"

"How about me what?"

"What do you think about it all?"

"I don't think anymore. I just work."

Are they weary because their experience is inauthentic? I doubt it. More likely, the illusion isn't good enough. The corporate logos that now crowd the camera obscura have changed shape and color too many times. They obscure the obscura.

X

An old lady in a Canadian Arctic town once told me what had happened on the day that television arrived: The children didn't go out to play. People stopped visiting one another. While she exaggerated the case, it did make me sad to come in from the frozen ocean and see the blue glow coming from windows and not see any people. I have seen that same blue glow in California and everywhere else in the world.

If the camera obscura were ever reopened, with the lens set back to its thoughtful speed, and the great image bowl scrubbed blank again, we might well perceive that those who've been robbing and murdering reality have made the world into a very ugly place. *(Editor's note: Since this essay was written, it has reopened.)*

XI

The murderers can't yet murder me. Any place can be a camera obscura, and so I defy them. For you too. Just look around. From the twenty-first floor of the Century Hyatt in Shinjuku I see the moment when twilight has almost given way to full darkness, skeletons of light. Soon the velvety spread and moss-pad treetops will be gone, fading like the intermediate graynesses of the skyscrapers. For the moment, they're both still there, but what increasingly represents the entire world beyond my window is light alone. The red eyes of cars recede from me, and the yellow eyes of cars rush close. The skyscrapers are fast becoming hollow latticeworks of yellow light. Far away, on the very horizon, another city slowly pulses dark and bright, a ball of violet-blue luminescence like some immensely powerful firefly.

Above everything, in the middle of the sky, I see a blinding white object, most vivid and strange because it excludes not only light but also texture. For a moment I cannot tell what it is. Finally I realize that it must be the reflection of my pillow, on which the bedside lamp is shining, projecting its starched whiteness to the edges of divinity.

Biographical Notes

DIANE ACKERMAN is the author of eighteen works of poetry and nonfiction, including, most recently, *Cultivating Delight: A Natural History of My Garden* (prose) and *I Praise My Destroyer* (poetry). She also writes nature books for children. She is the recipient of numerous awards, including the John Burroughs Medal for nature writing and the Lavan Award for poetry. A five-hour PBS television series, inspired by her *Natural History of the Senses,* aired in 1995 with Ms. Ackerman as host. She has the unusual distinction of having a molecule named after her (*dianeackerone*). She's at work on a new collection of poems, *Origami Bridges.*

BEN BIRNBAUM has published short fiction, essays, and poetry in journals that include *TriQuarterly, Midstream,* and *Nimrod.* He is executive director of marketing communications at Boston College, where he also serves as special assistant to the president and editor of *Boston College Magazine.*

CHARLES BOWDEN has written fourteen books, including *Blood Orchid: An Unnatural History of America; Blue Desert; Juarez: The Laboratory of Our Future;* and (with Michael Binstein) *Trust Me: Charles Keating and the Missing Billions.* He is a contributing editor of *Esquire* and *Harper's Magazine* and lives in Tucson, Arizona, with a malevolent tortoise and a witch.

JAMES CAMPBELL is the author of several books, including *Invisible Country: A Journey Through Scotland* (1984); *Talking at the Gates: A Life of James Baldwin* (1991); and *This Is the Beat Generation.* The last has just been published by the University of California Press, which is also reissuing the Baldwin biography with a new afterword. He works for the *Times Literary Supplement.*

ANNE FADIMAN is the editor of *The American Scholar.* She is the author of *The Spirit Catches You and You Fall Down,* which won the National Book Critics Circle Award for general nonfiction, and *Ex Libris,* a collection of essays on reading and language. A winner of the National Magazine Award for reporting, she has contributed articles and essays to *Civilization, The New Yorker, Harper's Magazine,* and the *New York Times,* among other publications. She lives in western Massachusetts and teaches writing at Smith College.

FRANCINE DU PLESSIX GRAY was born in the French embassy in Warsaw, where her father was a member of the diplomatic corps. After receiving a degree in philosophy from Barnard College, she worked as a reporter and book editor, and in the 1960s began publishing fiction and political essays in *The New Yorker.* Her work has appeared in such periodicals as *The New York Review of Books, The New York Times Magazine, The New Republic, Rolling Stone,* and *Vanity Fair.* She is the author of three novels — *Lovers and Tyrants* (1976), *World Without End* (1981), and *October Blood* (1985) — as well as a number of award-winning nonfiction books, including *Divine Disobedience: Profiles in Catholic Radicalism* (1970), *Hawaii: The Sugar-Coated Fortress* (1972), *Soviet Women: Walking the Tightrope* (1990), and a collection of essays on the political, domestic, and literary scene, *Adam and Eve in the City* (1987). She has written three biographies: *Rage and Fire: A Life of Louise Colet* (1994), *At Home with the Marquis de Sade: A Life,* which was a finalist for the 1999 Pulitzer Prize in biography, and, most recently, a brief life of the French philosopher Simone Weil. A member of the American Academy of Arts and Letters, she has taught at the College of the City of New York, Yale, Columbia, Brown, Princeton, and Vassar College. She is currently at work on a family memoir.

JEFFREY HEIMAN teaches English in the City University of New York system. His work has appeared in *The Massachusetts Review* and other journals and has been anthologized in *Travelers' Tales: Nepal.* "Vin Laforge" forms a part of his nonfiction novel *East Hill.*

EDWARD HOAGLAND has published eight collections of essays, most recently *Balancing Acts* and *Tigers & Ice;* five books of fiction, including *Seven Rivers West;* and two travel books, *Notes from the Century Before: A Journal from British Columbia* and *African Calliope: A Journey to the Sudan,* both of which were reissued in 1995. He also writes criticism and is the editor of the Penguin Nature Classics Series. He is a member of the

tary, Mademoiselle, Esquire, and *The New Republic.* She is currently a staff
writer for *The New Yorker,* where she was formerly a movie critic, and is at
work on a new book, *Melancholy Baby,* a personal and cultural history of
depression. She teaches at the 92nd Street Y's Unterberg Poetry Center
and Marymount College.

DAVID MICHAELIS is the author of *N. C. Wyeth: A Biography* and a con-
tributor to *Wondrous Strange: The Wyeth Nation* and *One Nation: Patriots
and Pirates Portrayed by N. C. Wyeth and James Wyeth.* His previous works include a collection of biographical sketches, *The Best of Friends,* a novel,
Boy, Girl, Boy, Girl, and a nonfiction narrative, *Mushroom.* His writing has
appeared in *The American Scholar, American Heritage, The New Republic,*
and *Vanity Fair.* He received the 1999 Ambassador Book Award for biography, given by the English-Speaking Union of the United States, and is
currently at work on the life of Charles M. Schulz.

SPENCER NADLER is a physician whose essays have appeared in *Harper's
Magazine, The American Scholar, The Massachusetts Review,* and *The Missouri
Review.* A collection of his essays, *The Language of Cells,* was published in
August 2001. He lives in Palos Verdes, California.

MARY OLIVER is well known as a poet; her volume *American Primitive* received the Pulitzer Prize in poetry in 1984, and *New and Selected Poems*
won the National Book Award in 1992. Additionally she has written two
books of essays and two handbooks on the writing of poetry. Her latest
book is a single poem: *The Leaf and the Cloud.* She holds the Catharine
Osgood Foster Chair for Distinguished Teaching at Bennington College.

REYNOLDS PRICE was born in Macon, North Carolina, in 1933. Educated at Duke University and Merton College, Oxford, he has taught at
Duke since 1958 and is James B. Duke Professor of English. His first
novel, *A Long and Happy Life,* was published in 1962; since then he has
published thirty-three volumes of fiction, poetry, drama, essays, and
translations. He is a member of the American Academy of Arts and Letters, and his work has been translated into sixteen languages.

TIM ROBINSON was born in England in 1935. He studied mathematics at
Cambridge and worked as a teacher and artist in Istanbul, Vienna, and
London. In 1972 he moved to the west of Ireland and began writing
and making maps. He now lives in Roundstone, Connemara, where he
runs the Folding Landscape Studio with his wife, Máiréad. He is the author of a two-volume survey of the Aran Islands, *Stones of Aran: Pilgrimage*
(1986) and *Stones of Aran: Labyrinth* (1995). *Setting Foot on the Shores of*

Connemara and Other Writing appeared in 1996. *My Time in Space,* a collection of autobiographical essays, was published in 2001.

CARLO ROTELLA'S essays have appeared in *The American Scholar, The Washington Post Magazine, Doubletake, Harper's Magazine, Critical Inquiry,* and other publications. "Cut Time" is drawn from a book in progress, *The Distance: An Education at the Fights.* Another book, *Good with Their Hands: Makers of Culture in Postindustrial America,* will be published in 2002. He teaches in the English department and the American studies program at Boston College.

ASHRAF RUSHDY is professor of African American studies and English literature at Wesleyan University. He is the author of a book on John Milton, *The Empty Garden* (1992), and two books on contemporary African American cultural and literary history, *Neo-Slave Narratives* (1999) and *Remembering Generations* (2001). "Exquisite Corpse" was written while he was a fellow at the National Humanities Center. He is currently at work on a book about racial violence in America.

EARL SHORRIS is the author of fourteen books of fiction and nonfiction and numerous essays and reviews, many of which appeared in *Harper's Magazine,* where he has been a contributing editor since 1972. He received a National Humanities Medal in 2000 and the John Dewey Award for public service earlier this year. Among his books are the novels *In the Yucatán* and *Under the Fifth Sun: A Novel of Pancho Villa.* A new edition of *Latinos: A Biography of the People* and *In the Language of Kings: An Anthology of Meso-American Literature,* which he coedited with Miguel León-Portilla, were published this year.

BERT O. STATES is the author of eight books on literary theory and dreaming, most recently *Seeing in the Dark.* His essays and fiction have appeared in *The Hudson Review, The Georgia Review, The Gettysburg Review, The Kenyon Review, The Yale Review, Salmagundi, The American Scholar, Boulevard,* and elsewhere. His autobiographical essay "My Slight Stoop" was reprinted in *The Anchor Essay Annual* of 1998. He has taught at Skidmore College, University of Pittsburgh, Cornell, and University of California. He is now blissfully retired in Santa Barbara, where he just completed a book on metaphorical vision titled *Seeing Double: Reflections on the Metaphorical Eye.*

WILLIAM T. VOLLMANN is the author of a dozen works of fiction and nonfiction. He lives in California.

Notable Essays of 2000

SELECTED BY ROBERT ATWAN

ANDRÉ ACIMAN
   Arbitrage. *The New Yorker,* July 10.
GARY AMDAHL
   Narrow Road to the Deep North.
   The Gettysburg Review, Summer.

ERIK S. BARMACK
   Lo Spirito Femminile. *Northwest
   Review,* vol. 38, no. 3.
RICK BASS
   A Winter's Tale. *The Atlantic
   Monthly,* January.
ANN M. BAUER
   The Oil Man. *River Teeth,* Spring.
J. BILL BERRY
   The Southern Autobiographical
   Impulse. *Southern Cultures,* Spring.
WENDELL BERRY
   Life Is a Miracle. *Orion,* Spring.
CHARLES BOWDEN
   Blue Mist. *Aperture,* Summer.
THERESA BOYAR
   Peaches. *Florida Review,* Summer.
LAUREL BRETT
   Where Were You? *Nassau Review,* vol.
   8, no. 1.
CATHARINE SAVAGE BROSMAN
   A House Apart. *The Sewanee Review,*
   Summer.

FRANKLIN BURROUGHS
   Returning Home to Rivertown.
   Preservation, September/October.

KELLY CALDWELL
   Garret Girl. *House Beautiful,*
   February.
BONNIE JO CAMPBELL
   New Windows. *Meridian,* Fall.
PHILIP CAPUTO
   Goodnight, Saigon. *War, Literature,
   and the Arts,* Spring/Summer.
DAVID CARKEET
   The Linguist Goes to the Movies.
   New York Stories, Summer.
VIKRAM CHANDRA
   The Cult of Authenticity. *Boston
   Review,* February/March.
NORMA COLE
   The Poetics of Vertigo. *Denver
   Quarterly,* Winter.
TREVOR CORSON
   The Telltale Heart. *Transition,* no.
   84.

JOHN D'AGATA
   And There Was Evening and There
   Was Morning. *The North American
   Review,* November/December.

MIMI SCHWARTZ
Improvisation on "I Do." *Puerto del
Sol,* Spring/Summer.
AMARTYA SEN
Other People. *The New Republic,*
December 18.
BOB SHACOCHIS
Learning to Be at Peace with War.
Oxford American, May/June.
AURELIE SHEEHAN
A Little Tooth. *Shenandoah,* Winter.
DAVID SHIELDS
Rebecca's Journal. *Quarterly West,*
Autumn/Winter.
CHARLES SIMIC
What Dreams May Come. *Harper's
Magazine,* November.
FLOYD SKLOOT
The Watery Labyrinth. *Boulevard,*
vol. 15, no. 3.
LAUREN SLATER
The Devil Inside. *Nerve,* November.
MARK SLOUKA
Blood on the Tracks. *Harper's
Magazine,* June.
JANE SMILEY
Why Marriage? *Harper's Magazine,*
June.
BERT O. STATES
Death as a Fictitious Event. *The
Hudson Review,* Autumn.
ILAN STAVANS
On My Brother's Trail. *The Literary
Review,* Summer.
On Packing My Library. *Transition,*
no. 81/82.
M. G. STEPHENS
Thoughts on Monk's Dream and
Other Things. *Speak,* Fall.

KERRY TEMPLE
The Geography of Grace. *Notre
Dame Magazine,* Autumn.
SALLIE TISDALE
Mean Cuisine. *The Sun,* October.

GORE VIDAL
Washington, We Have a Problem.
Vanity Fair, December.
ROBERT VIVIAN
The Dark Hangnails of God. *Creative
Nonfiction,* no. 14.

PAUL WEST
The Fool of Light. *The Yale Review,*
April.
DAVID WHITFORD
A Breadwinner's Tale. *Fortune,*
January 24.
ALEC WILKINSON
Sam and Other Reflections on
Being a Father. *Esquire,* June.
NANCY WILLARD
From the Ancestors. *The Gettysburg
Review,* Spring.
JASON WILSON
Dining Out in Iceland. *North
American Review,* January/
February.
SIMON WINCHESTER
A True Daltonic Dandy. *Doubletake,*
Fall.
S. L. WISENBERG
The Language of *Heimatlos. New
England Review,* Summer.
TOM WOLFE
In the Land of the Rococo Marxists.
Harper's Magazine, June.
SIMON WORRALL
Emily Dickinson Goes to Las Vegas.
The Paris Review, no. 154.

STEPHEN ZANICHKOWSKY
Fourteen. *The Atlantic Monthly,*
September.
PAUL ZIMMER
The Condition of My Faith. *The
Georgia Review,* Winter.

Note: The following periodicals arrived too late for consideration:

Fourth Genre (Fall), *Meridian* (Fall), *CrossConnect* (vol. 4).

Interested readers will also find many essays in the following periodicals and special issues that appeared in 2000:

Alaska Quarterly Review ("One Blood: The Narrative Impulse"), ed. Ronald Spatz.

Creative Nonfiction ("The Line Between Fact and Fiction"), ed. Lee Gutkind.

Fourth Genre (Spring issue), ed. Michael Steinberg.

North Dakota Quarterly (American Indian issue, Summer/Fall), ed. Robert W. Lewis and Peter Nabokov.

River Teeth (Fall issue), ed. Joe Mackall and Dan Lehman.

Ruminator Review ("Generations"), ed. Bart Schneider.

Under the Sun, ed. Michael O'Rourke.

THE B·E·S·T AMERICAN SERIES ™

THE BEST AMERICAN SHORT STORIES 2001
Barbara Kingsolver, guest editor · Katrina Kenison, series editor

0-395-92689-0 CL $27.50 / 0-395-92688-2 PA $13.00
0-618-07404-X CASS $25.00 / 0-618-15564-3 CD $35.00

THE BEST AMERICAN TRAVEL WRITING 2001
Paul Theroux, guest editor · Jason Wilson, series editor

0-618-11877-2 CL $27.50 / 0-618-11878-0 PA $13.00
0-618-15567-8 CASS $25.00 / 0-618-15568-6 CD $35.00

THE BEST AMERICAN MYSTERY STORIES 2001
Lawrence Block, guest editor · Otto Penzler, series editor

0-618-12492-6 CL $27.50 / 0-618-12491-8 PA $13.00
0-618-15565-1 CASS $25.00 / 0-618-15566-X CD $35.00

THE BEST AMERICAN ESSAYS 2001
Kathleen Norris, guest editor · Robert Atwan, series editor

0-618-15358-6 CL $27.50 / 0-618-04931-2 PA $13.00

THE BEST AMERICAN SPORTS WRITING 2001
Bud Collins, guest editor · Glenn Stout, series editor

0-618-08625-0 CL $27.50 / 0-618-08626-9 PA $13.00

THE BEST AMERICAN SCIENCE AND NATURE WRITING 2001
Edward O. Wilson, guest editor · Burkhard Bilger, series editor

0-618-08296-4 CL $27.50 / 0-618-15359-4 PA $13.00

THE BEST AMERICAN RECIPES 2001–2002
Fran McCullough, series editor · Foreword by Marcus Samuelsson

0-618-12810-7 CL $26.00

HOUGHTON MIFFLIN COMPANY / www.houghtonmifflinbooks.com